FIT FOR
THE GODS

FIT FOR THE GODS

GREEK MYTHOLOGY REIMAGINED

Edited by
Jenn Northington &
S. Zainab Williams

VINTAGE BOOKS
A DIVISION OF PENGUIN RANDOM HOUSE LLC
NEW YORK

A VINTAGE BOOKS ORIGINAL 2023

Introduction and compilation copyright © 2023 by Jenn Northington and S. Zainab Williams

Grateful acknowledgment is made for permission to publish the following: "A Resume" by Fran Wilde, originally appeared in *Clock Star Rose Spine* (Lanternfish Press, 2021).

Pages 381–2 constitute an extension of this copyright page.

Library of Congress Cataloging-in-Publication Data
Names: Northington, Jenn, editor. | Williams, S. Zainab, editor.
Title: Fit for the gods : Greek mythology reimagined /
    edited by Jenn Northington & S. Zainab Williams.
Description: First edition. | New York : Vintage Books, 2023.
Identifiers: LCCN 2022057283 (print) | LCCN 2022057284 (ebook)
Subjects: LCSH: Mythology, Greek—Fiction. | Short stories,
    American—21st century. | LCGFT: Mythological fiction. | Short stories.
Classification: LCC PS648.M98 F58 2023 (print) |
    LCC PS648.M98 (ebook) | DDC 813/.6080378—dc23
LC record available at https://lccn.loc.gov/2022057283
LC ebook record available at https://lccn.loc.gov/2022057284

Vintage Books Trade Paperback ISBN: 978-0-593-46924-8
eBook ISBN: 978-0-593-46925-5

Series design by Nicholas Alguire
Book design by Steven Walker

vintagebooks.com

Printed in the United States of America
1st Printing

This is for everyone who read under the desk, under the covers, and in the back of the auditorium when they were supposed to be doing anything else and imagined themselves on the page.

—Jenn Northington

To my big sis, Ustadza White, the Artemis to my Persephone

—S. Zainab Williams

CONTENTS

Goals include: meaningful work, using my skillset,
        preferably by the sea.
Experienced in shipwrecks, sea chanteys, hospitality.
Career Highlights: You've heard of Odysseus? A rare near miss.
        Also search party experience,
        though Demeter wasn't thrilled with the outcome.
Close call at a singing competition, but Hera rigged that.
        Orpheus too.
Languages spoken: Greek and Latin.
References: Achelos at RiverGods, Inc., several Muses,
        and my equally talented sisters.
Willing to relocate.

—Fran Wilde, "A Resume"

INTRODUCTION

Jenn Northington & S. Zainab Williams

It feels as if we're in a golden age of retellings. So many authors are diving into the Western canon and beyond, paying homage to their favorites while bringing readers their own takes on those favorites. We're getting the perspectives of characters long relegated to the margins from the Arthurian legends (see *Sword Stone Table*), from Shakespeare, from fairy tales and fables. It's a feast for the imagination, and as readers, we are at the table, digging in.

It continues to be true, however, that the vast majority of writers who are given a platform to retell these stories are from a narrow group. Publishing continues to work toward uplifting the voices of creators from marginalized communities, but progress is slower in some places than others. While there is no shortage of diverse voices telling stories both old and new, we've struggled to find a range in one of our favorite fandoms: Greco-Roman mythology.

As with many of our peers who became devotees of this mythology, we found our way to these stories through the classics: Thomas Bulfinch's *Mythology* and Ingri and Edgar Parin d'Aulaire's *Book of Greek Myths*. Jenn got in trouble for reading Bulfinch at the back of the auditorium during her brother's high school concert recital, and while she still doesn't know how to pronounce *d'Aulaire*, she has bought their book for every child in her life. Likewise, young Sharifah made countless repeat visits to the library at Carthay Center Elementary School to thumb through the brightly illustrated pages of the d'Aulaires' volume (she may have had to pay some late fees for "forgetting" to return it). Returning to the stories as adults through another classic, Edith Hamilton's *Mythology*, brought home the urgency to usher inclusive, feminist, progressive, and less Eurocentric perspectives to some of our favorites—to respond to the discordant note these stories struck in us. Despite haters' unfounded assertions, the ancient world was incredibly international and diverse, just like today's world. (Ask Jenn about her bachelor's thesis on premodern globalization sometime if you really want an earful about this.)

There's no doubt that readers are hungry for new takes on the Pantheon, that delightfully messy family of immortal weirdos; on the characters who still leap off the pages of *The Iliad* and *The Odyssey* the same way they must have once leaped off Homer's lips. And there's no doubt that writers are thoughtfully and joyfully remixing the gods, the heroes, and the villains so many of us know and love. As is always the case with something we love, we wanted more!

We set out to find a broad range of writers who share in our love of this particular corner of mythology and wanted to dig in and get their hands on these stories, to make them their own. We could not have been more overwhelmed or gratified by the response. Between targeted asks and an open call, we received enough submissions to make several anthologies! Narrowing it down to the stories you hold in your hands was a special kind of torment. When you have such riches to choose from, the criteria shift; now you're trying to find the relationships between the stories. Which speak to each other? Which go to places the reader hasn't been before? Which were the most surprising, the most unexpected? Even then, we had to let go of some pieces we wish we had room for; we devoutly hope that those stories will be in your hands thanks to other editors and publications, because there's a gloriously monstrous amount of talent out there.

These fifteen stories take our beloved favorites and reimagine them in new, fun, strange, and/or terrifying ways. After several rounds of debating story order, we present you with what we like to think of as a five-course meal:

First, whet your appetite as Zoraida Córdova resurrects the players in Medusa's story in the modern era with hilarious results, and editor and contributor S. Zainab Williams imagines a millennial Dionysus plotting the overthrow of the Pantheon.

Then we dig in a little more. Zeyn Joukhadar's Tiresias contemplates fate, choice, and transformation. Sarah Gailey finds Thetis fighting for her freedom from the chains of others' expectations, as does Juliana Spink Mills's Penelope. Susan Purr situates her Aphrodite in a small community where Love can influence as many people as she likes (wink, wink). Suleikha Snyder turns Theseus's story into a meditation on how far someone might go to bring their love back home, while Mia P. Manansala reimagines the Furies as a small family detective agency.

Then we range further afield as Valerie Valdes takes us into space with Atalanta, and Jude Reali asks how far Odysseus would go to get home to their loved ones.

The world may crumble, but there will always be stories.

Marika Bailey's transformed Daphne plots her revenge, while Alyssa Cole gives us a far-future take on Hades and Persephone that will melt your heart. Taylor Rae's gender-bent Aeneas asks what it means to carry the weight of the lost on your shoulders.

And sometimes, you just need to burn it down. Wen Wen Yang's nameless narrator considers the price of power; Maya Deane's unapologetic and rage-filled Amazons don't care—they're ready to pay the price.

As we worked on assembling this collection, we couldn't imagine a finer epigram than Fran Wilde's "A Resume"—all these gods and goddesses, heroes and villains, monsters both creature and human, are more than willing to move, and to move readers in turn. We hope you find much to enjoy in these pages, and maybe even a little bit of yourself.

FIT FOR
THE GODS

THE GORGON CONFESSIONALS

Zoraida Córdova

A year ago, the ancients regenerated into new corporeal forms, their powers and influence a whisper of what they once were. The age of heroes they knew is long gone, and now they must make a go of this strange, new world.

This is their story.

❧

NARRATOR: The daughter of Keto and Phorkys, Medusa was the most beautiful girl of her age. Suitors came from all over the known world to ensnare her in marriage, but her heart was dedicated to Athena, virgin goddess of war and wisdom.

STHENO, *Medusa's eldest sister*: Between us, Medusa was always quite squeamish. She wouldn't even eat oysters.

EURYALE, *Medusa's middle sister and author of* Such a Pretty Face: My Life in Medusa's Shadow: I think it reminded her of her own mortality. It wasn't our fault that Stheno and I were born immortal. Though our father always suspected she might have been the . . . What do you call it now?

STHENO: The milkman's daughter. Don't mind Euryale. It's been millennia, and she only recently had her first therapy session. In our day the only way to process my rage was to devour the hearts of humans. But enough about me. This is the Medusa Show.

EURYALE: *Who's* the jealous one now?

STHENO: As I was saying, Medusa was squeamish. She ate nothing but honey and anemone petals, and even then she apologized to the flowers when she plucked them. She talked to birds and butterflies and tended to Athena's temple.

EURYALE: A lot of good that did her.

STHENO: What did Dr. Tsamis *just* tell you, Euri?

EURYALE: I told Medusa she should have gotten that internship with the Hesperides. Athena always preferred her *heroes*. But Medusa loved Athena and there she went . . . We tried to avenge her. We did. That's how I lost my pinkie finger. But I've got it back this time around, don't I?

STHENO: Glory to Zeus. Who else can say they get a second chance?

⚱

ATHENA, *goddess of war and wisdom, CEO of Aegis Private Security*: Stheno said that? I suppose I can't be too bothered. Of *course* I loved my heroes. They were *my* heroes. Those who were worthy of my grace received it. Those who called my wrath also received that. I should pay Stheno a visit . . .

MELPOMENE, *Muse of tragedies, host of* The Gorgon Confessionals: Is that a threat? Have your powers returned? I heard it can take a few months or even years, if they return at all.

ATHENA: Look, I have a very busy schedule now, as I did then, and I'm going to tell you the same thing I told Odysseus—honor me and I will honor you.

MELPOMENE: Is that what you said to him? I suppose Homer left that part out.

ATHENA: You always were a shit stirrer, Mellie.

MELPOMENE: I simply eked out the truth from my favorite writers. You didn't seem to mind as long as you came out virtuous. But this segment is about Medusa. We'll get to your Trojan War bros next season.

ATHENA: What do you want me to say?

MELPOMENE: I want to go back there. Back to your temple, with the world at your feet. I want to know what you were thinking when you punished her. This girl who loved you.

ATHENA: Fine, I loved her, too. I loved her, and that's why it hurt me more than it hurt her.

NARRATOR: When Medusa was raped by Poseidon, Athena cursed her so all who looked upon her turned to stone.

MELPOMENE: Is that how you see it?

ATHENA: It's literally what I just said.

Melpomene patiently waits.
Athena stares unblinking.
Melpomene checks her watch.
Athena sighs, exasperated.

MELPOMENE: Do you have any regrets?

ATHENA: Have you asked Poseidon that question?

MELPOMENE: I'm getting the sense that you're a little bit defensive right now. Perhaps let's shift to a different topic: Perseus. He was one of your heroes. What made him special?

ATHENA: Oh, Perseus. He truly was special, wasn't he? People always say that our heroes never have happy endings, but then there was Perseus. He slayed the Gorgon, gave Atlas his rest, saved Princess Andromeda and took her as his queen. He didn't break the mold. He *was* the mold. And the thing about him was that he had no fear. Not for a moment. Do you know why?

MELPOMENE: Tell me why.

ATHENA: Because he had faith in the gods. He'll tell you.

MELPOMENE: I spoke to Perseus.

ATHENA: So you know.

MELPOMENE: He tells the story a little differently.

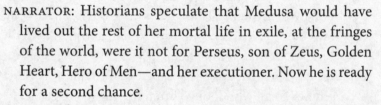

NARRATOR: Historians speculate that Medusa would have lived out the rest of her mortal life in exile, at the fringes of the world, were it not for Perseus, son of Zeus, Golden Heart, Hero of Men—and her executioner. Now he is ready for a second chance.

PERSEUS, *former king of Argos, currently unemployed*: I don't like to be called that anymore. Gorgon Slayer just sounds so *ahhh*, you know what I mean? I feel like this time around I just want to see this world. When I was king of Argos, I thought I knew where the edge of the world was. But there is so much of it. Sometimes I think about it and I feel like I'm *this* small.

That's why I'm backpacking. When I regenerated, I woke up in Greece. It was good to be home, you know? But then I caught up on everything that's happened since. It was overwhelming, to say the least. So I hit the road. We call ourselves "hiker trash" now. Although, if I still had Hermes's sandals it would make travel a whole lot easier. Instead, he's producing this series. I wouldn't change a thing, though.

Is it hot in here? Can we open a window? I've been a little claustrophobic, since, you know. What was your question again?

MELPOMENE: Perseus.

PERSEUS: Hm?

MELPOMENE: I haven't asked a question. All I said was that you were once called Gorgon Slayer.

PERSEUS: Yeah. I don't like that anymore.

MELPOMENE: Take us back, before that fateful day. Did you know your calling?

PERSEUS: No, I didn't.

MELPOMENE: What did you know?

PERSEUS: I don't like to dwell on the past. It was literally ages ago. I can say that.

MELPOMENE: Perseus.

PERSEUS: I actually like to be called Percy now. My name's famous, did you know? There's a whole series.

MELPOMENE: Clash of the Titans?

PERSEUS: Gods no. Percy Jackson and the Olympians. The books, though.

MELPOMENE: Well, I don't want you to dwell on the past. I want you to heal from it. Most of us regenerated in the place we died. Me, I woke up fully formed in the middle of the Gershwin Theatre during a matinee.

PERSEUS: The crowd must have gone wild.

MELPOMENE: Oh, they were professionals. The show must go on, darling. But I know it's been jarring for all of us. I still haven't found all my sisters.

PERSEUS: Is that why you're hosting this documentary?

MELPOMENE: My agent said it could help. But I think you're avoiding, Percy.

PERSEUS: All right, I'll tell you what you want to know. When

I got my calling, back then, I didn't know anything. Not a thing. I mean, I knew we had a rough life. I was born in a tower, and then my grandfather sent us out into the sea in that golden tomb. When I was in there, my mother told me that my father would protect us, and I was so little, so little, but I remember thinking, *Then how come he didn't protect you?*

Zeus never even spoke to me.

MELPOMENE: How did that make you feel?

PERSEUS: I don't know. It was a long time ago. He helped me twice in my life, which I suppose is what matters, right? I always thought of Dictys as my father. He was a good man. He taught me how to fish. He taught me how to survive when there's a drought. That actually helped when I hiked the PCT. That's the Pacific—

MELPOMENE: I know what it is. What else did he teach you?

PERSEUS: He taught me how to sail. For a boy from Serifos, that's what mattered, really. He was a good man. Do you know who wasn't a good man? His brother, the king.

MELPOMENE: Polydectes. He hasn't regenerated, I hear.

PERSEUS: Good. I mean, not good. I'm working on that. For-giveness. Anyway. How it all happened: Polydectes is this king, and he wants to marry my mother, but I'm in the way, so he gives me this impossible quest: bring him the head of the Gorgon. Then Athena shows up and hands me a shield. Hermes lends me his winged sandals. I lost one, did he tell you?

MELPOMENE: He mentioned it. But tell me about your other gifts. What else did you receive to help you on your quest?

PERSEUS: Zeus helped.

MELPOMENE: Your father.

PERSEUS: My birth father. Dictys is my father. Was my father.

MELPOMENE: What did Zeus give you?

PERSEUS: A harpe sword. He didn't say it was the same one he used on Cronus, but I felt its power. Oh, I can't forget my kibisis. I do prefer the backpacks of this age to that one, though. Far more sturdy.

MELPOMENE: After you were outfitted to fight the Gorgon, Medusa, did Athena tell you why she was helping you?

PERSEUS: I didn't ask. I just knew my mother was waiting for me, and if I didn't return with the head of the Gorgon, then my mother would have been forced to marry Polydectes. I wasn't thinking of myself or the gods, though I was grateful for their help. To be completely honest, I'd never been more afraid in my life. No one tells you how to use winged sandals. I think that's why I like long-distance hiking now even though it's rough out there. But then I get to Medusa's island, and the first thing I do is throw up the bread and honey I'd eaten that morning. The second thing I do is get tangled in a thornbush. I know she can't see me because I have my uncle's helm of invisibility, but I know she can hear me and smell me. I knew she was waiting for me.

MELPOMENE: How did you know that?

PERSEUS: She told me.

MELPOMENE: You talked?

PERSEUS: Well, yes.

MELPOMENE: What about?

PERSEUS: Nothing. Everything. She laughed at me at first. Thousands of years later and I still remember her first words to me. She said, "Show me your face." And I said, "You first." Obviously, that would have been very bad for me, but I was nervous. At the time, the worst thing I'd ever fought was a sea monster. Now I know it was something called a basking shark.

MELPOMENE: What happened after you talked? You and Medusa.

PERSEUS: It went on for three nights. She'd built a temple for herself. Brick by brick. Statues lined the path, and you could tell how old they were because some of them had their noses and ears and arms eroded. She could have killed me right away, but she didn't. I was a boy from nowhere, and she spared me.

MELPOMENE: But you're not just a boy from nowhere. You're the son of Zeus.

PERSEUS: So was Heracles. So were scores of my brothers. Whatever I became, I was still raised as the son of a fisherman. That's why I needed so many trinkets, I suppose. I had no preternatural strength or gifts. I bleed gold, which is . . . expected. It didn't save me, in the end.

MELPOMENE: You are the greatest of all heroes, Percy. And yet when you speak you almost sound like you're mourning something. What do you regret?

PERSEUS: I don't know if I have any regrets. How can I regret something that was fated, right?

MELPOMENE: Do you wish things had been different?

PERSEUS: That's not a fair question, is it? Because I had a good life. Better than most. I was king. I was Perseus. I gave mercy to Atlas, and I saved Andromeda. That's what everyone focuses on. But sometimes—

Sometimes . . .

I don't know.

Sometimes, long ago, I used to lie beside Andromeda, and she'd be asleep. She'd stopped having nightmares, but I still did. And for the briefest of moments, for a heartbeat, I'd stare at the ceiling and wonder if I'd have been happier if I'd never left home and lived out a quiet life by the sea.

MEDUSA, *youngest of the Gorgon sisters, president and founder of Inner You Cosmetics*: Thank you, it's great to be back. You look well, too.

MELPOMENE: I'm a huge fan of your Va-Va-Venom Peel.

MEDUSA: But you're not here to talk to me about skin care, are you?

MELPOMENE: You know me so well.

MEDUSA: I've been expecting this since the regeneration.

MELPOMENE: Let's start with where you were when it happened.

MEDUSA: I was underground. I think because my body had been severed into pieces, my regeneration was like crawling out of my grave. The first thing I did was touch my throat. I breathed in dirt and realized I was whole again.

MELPOMENE: Did you know what was happening?

MEDUSA: In the early days, I'd heard about the regeneration of the gods, like a prophecy security blanket to assure us of our immortality. But even my parents thought it was a myth, because they never expected to die out in the first place.

Though I suppose I was born to die, being the mortal of the Gorgons. That and the mark Athena placed on my head.

MELPOMENE: Following your resurrection, your eyes no longer turn people to stone. Thank—well, not Zeus. Don't tell him I said that.

MEDUSA: Whatever the reason, I am glad I still have my snakes. They're a part of me. One thing Perseus and I have in common is that I don't want to dwell on the past. I created Inner You Cosmetics to show humans that they are already beautiful. You just have to care for the person you are.

MELPOMENE: Does that mean you're ready to see him again?

MEDUSA: Who?

MELPOMENE: Perseus. He wants to be called Percy now.

MEDUSA: Do you know what I want, Mellie?

MELPOMENE: What do you want, Medusa?

MEDUSA: I want to be able to make three million in revenue without having to be defined by Percy or Athena or Fucky Fish Man.

MELPOMENE: Tell us about how you built your empire.

MEDUSA: Well, I found a good lawyer. The number of brands that already use my likeness simply needed to give me credit for it. A little Versace seed money, and boom. Here we are.

The future looks bright, doesn't it?

HERMES, *herald of the gods, founder and CEO of Air Hermes, executive producer of* The Gorgon Confessionals: I have a big meeting today, so I'll make this quick. Like I told you eons ago, I did give Perseus those sandals. Athena told me to, and you do what Athena says, you know? It was a wild time. I was just reading about New York in the eighties. That's what our age of heroes was like. But no, I just gave Perseus some shoes. Tell that motherfucker I still haven't found the one he lost.

POSEIDON, *god of the sea, lifeguard at Coney Island*: I told you to get that fucking camera out of my face.

NARRATOR: Poseidon could not be reached for comment.

DANAË, *princess of Argos, currently a freelance jeweler and dominatrix*: Percy was such a good boy. A good boy. Do you know that when we were alone in that tower, he'd spend hours looking at the moon? He thought it was a silver apple and wanted to take a bite out of it. Sure, he always wondered about his father and why we were in that terrible room. But I didn't know how to tell him. What was there to say? Your father is the lord of the gods? Your father looks like golden rain? Percy was too curious, and he kept asking. Once we got to Serifos, he stopped asking. Dictys was the only man in my life who mattered. I think that's why Zeus chose to help Percy in his quest to kill Medusa. The king of Olympus, outdone by a fisherman.

Everyone says Zeus saved us from drowning, but now that I've had some distance, I don't know what's real. I don't *know* what he sounded like. I don't even know what he looks like. Well, that's not true. I do now that he's regenerated and running for office.

I have to say, I think I prefer him in his transmutable form.

MELPOMENE: I think all of us have wondered what that was like.

DANAË: Warm. One minute I was wishing for the sun, and then the next it was pouring through the skylight. There was a moment when I thought I was going to burst from within. Part of me has always been chasing that high. I do think that's why I regenerated, even though I was human. Part of Zeus was always within me.

    Maybe he did save us.

    I have a lot of feelings.

    That's why my work is so important for me.

MELPOMENE: Your sex work or craftwork?

DANAË: Both. Though sex work is craftwork. I've changed quite a bit.

MELPOMENE: How so?

DANAË: Well, now I'm the only one giving the golden showers.

From the office of Republican presidential candidate Zeus:

I was there at the beginning, and I will be there at the world's end. Who is to say that I am not the God you were told about? Who else can protect you from the cycle of destruction that arrives every age? Vote for Zeus and make Earth the most powerful place in the cosmos.

ATHENA: I honestly feel like you've done nothing but attack me.

MELPOMENE: All I asked was whether you regret cursing Medusa now that you know how Perseus feels.

ATHENA: I don't care how Perseus feels. I thought he was stronger. I thought he had what it took. You know, it's not true what they say about me.

MELPOMENE: Can you be more specific?

ATHENA: That I only punished women.

MELPOMENE: Let's go through the list, shall we?

ATHENA: Oh, I don't think that's necessary.

MELPOMENE: Arachne?

ATHENA: I don't like pride.

MELPOMENE: Agraulos?

ATHENA: I don't need to listen to this.

MELPOMENE: Auge? Iodama? The Kekropses? Harmonia?

ATHENA: I cursed Ajax for violating Cassandra during the Trojan War. The last great war.

MELPOMENE: Mmm. I don't think that's true, about it being the last. But, um, you punished Ajax. Why not punish Poseidon for the same crime?

Athena shakes her head.
Melpomene checks her watch.
Athena yanks off her mic.

ATHENA: I think we're done here.

APOLLO, *god of many splendored things, patron of Delphi, currently finishing his residency at Mount Sinai*: I don't really know why I'm here. I had nothing to do with Perseus and Medusa. But you've always been one of my favorites, Mellie, so you've got me for five minutes before my evening rotation starts.

MELPOMENE: Thanks, Sun Daddy.

APOLLO: Stop it, you.

MELPOMENE: Very well. I find it curious that you think you have nothing to do with Perseus and Medusa when it was your oracle's prophecy that set the hero on his journey.

APOLLO: I don't see it that way.

MELPOMENE: You don't?

APOLLO: Think of it like this. I had a patient come in the other day. He had to get his stomach pumped. He still seemed a little off. Mind you, it's been a while and I'm not at my full strength, but I've always been an excellent student. So I order all the tests, and boom. I discover a jellyfish tumor in his stomach. I give him the diagnosis. He decides he doesn't want any treatment. Six months later he's back, but it's too late. There's a cluster of them now. Why am I telling you this? Because I'm giving a prognosis. I'm reading a chart. I've uncovered something within, and sometimes that thing is good and at other times that thing is fatal. I didn't implant those jellyfish tumors there. Neither I nor my oracle told Acrisius to lock his daughter in a tower, and I didn't tell Zeus (Vote Hades!) to fall in love, and I didn't tell Acrisius to send his daughter and divine grandchild to the bottom of the ocean in a tomb.

MELPOMENE: Do you say "Vote Hades" because you know the outcome of the next presidential election?

APOLLO: You little devil. The thing about divination is that everyone thinks they want to know, but they don't. So when something terrible and out of your control happens, there's someone to blame.

Perseus was going to be born with or without my oracle's prophecy.

It's a little thing called fate.

MELPOMENE: But isn't medicine different?

APOLLO: Medicine. The things humans have created are wondrous. I love these tender, breakable beings. Truly. Medicine gives us a way to treat problems. No matter what I did for Patient Jellyfish, I could only advise.

MELPOMENE: So there's no way to treat fate?

APOLLO: You've seen it time and time again. Everyone who tries gets fucked. But what do I know? I'm only the most gifted of my brethren.

MELPOMENE: What happened to your patient? Patient Jellyfish?

APOLLO: I took him out on the town and showed him there was something worth living for.

MELPOMENE: Would you say it was his fate to meet you?

APOLLO: That's why you're my favorite. You know, I can't say. It's a whole new world and I'm still learning the rules, but even though I don't have my powers back yet, I have this. It's a beautiful thing.

***

PERSEUS: Sure, I can walk you through my journey. Like I said, I had to find Medusa's lair. I went to the Graeae and snatched their eye. It was a lot drier than I thought it would be. I expected it to be wet. Anyway, they wouldn't tell me where she was because Medusa was still their sister. Instead, they sent me to the Stygian nymphs. I heard they've started a rock band. Not my taste, but good for them. Anyway, they were the ones who gave me Uncle Hades's helm of invisibility, and they told me it was the only way to get a jump on Medusa. They told me of all the other so-called heroes who tried to slay the Gorgon and failed.

MELPOMENE: Who were they?

PERSEUS: Treasure hunters. Pirates. Opportunists. Glory seekers. The worst of humanity. The righteous. The curious. The foolish. The ones with death wishes.

MELPOMENE: Where do you think you fall among them?

PERSEUS: Foolish. Righteous. A mix of both, perhaps? Anyway, I ventured so far from home I came upon Atlas on the way. I'd never seen anything like that. More than a god. A *Titan*. He was this hulking giant, and he kept his eyes shut. When he opened one to look at me, it was like looking into the night sky. He was so tired. So tired. I kept thinking of him on the way to Medusa.

ATLAS, *Titan, heavyweight champion*: Yeah, I remember Perseus. Good kid. Good kid. Put me out of my misery. That's all I have to say. Oh, yeah. Vote for Hades. *Fuck* Zeus.

MEDUSA: Nearly a week, I think?

MELPOMENE: A week?!

MEDUSA: I know the stories say that Percy just showed up and hacked my head off, but it took longer than that. We were in a game of chicken. I couldn't see him. But I could smell him the minute he landed. Sweat and salt and honey, plus something else. You know that bitter scent all the heroes had?

MELPOMENE: Yeah, it's almost like char.

MEDUSA: Exactly. And he was so loud. I could tell I was his first.

MELPOMENE: First what?

MEDUSA: Quest, Mellie. Don't read too much into it.

MELPOMENE: Medusa said she was your first. What do you have to say to that?

PERSEUS: Um.

MELPOMENE: . . .

PERSEUS: Wait, hold up, what did she say?

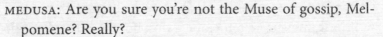

MEDUSA: Are you sure you're not the Muse of gossip, Melpomene? Really?

MELPOMENE: Look, I think everyone wants to understand what things were like back then. We've been gone from the world for ages. Our stories have been told and retold and changed. What is the truth? If we want to clear our names and set the record straight, this is the chance. Plus, I don't think I asked anything that was gossip, per se.

MEDUSA: Percy—Perseus—he was different from the others.

MELPOMENE: The others who tried to kill you?

MEDUSA: And failed. Perseus had real motivation.

MELPOMENE: What did you speak of for those seven days? Don't look at me like that. I bet you're really wishing you could still turn people to stone.

MEDUSA: I never said I couldn't. *You* assumed that.

MELPOMENE: What does that mean?

MEDUSA: It means that contact lenses in this age are very advanced. And no, that's not a threat. I never wanted to hurt anyone, remember that. I was a girl who made the mistake of putting my faith in the wrong goddess.

MELPOMENE: We can all empathize with that. Back to those seven days. When did you first *see* Perseus?

MEDUSA: It's fuzzy. But it was three days in, I think. He took off the helm. Undressed. Washed in the sea. I never used to venture to the shore. That's why, this time, I built my compound as far away from the ocean as possible.

MELPOMENE: What did you think when you first saw the man who was there to execute you?

MEDUSA: Unlike some goddesses, I'm going to be candid. I thought he was beautiful. He didn't have the same arrogance as the others. Maybe it was because I could smell his fear, and after we spoke, I knew he wasn't afraid for himself. I don't know if he remembers this, but he didn't think he was going to walk out alive.

PERSEUS: I thought she was going to kill me right away. Of course, I was outfitted by the Olympians themselves, but there was this fear in the back of my head: *You're just the son of a fisherman.* She's—well, she's not who you think she is.

MELPOMENE: What does that mean, Percy?

PERSEUS: Well, around the third night, I had run out of food and was using Zeus's harpe sword to skewer *fish*. I went into her temple. I had to get home. My mother was waiting for me. Athena was in my ear reminding me that Medusa was a Gorgon, a monster.

    I'd been prepared for her sisters to be there, but they weren't.

STHENO: Where was I? You know, I can't say, really. I had my own heroes to slay.

EURYALE: Besides, Medusa liked to be alone too much. She was depressed. Back then we prayed to the gods and went on killing sprees. Now we have Zoloft. I tell you what, I've never felt more myself.

MEDUSA: Wouldn't *you* be depressed? If you'd been betrayed by your mother? I became a priestess of Athena because I knew I'd never be alone. I'd have her divinity with me. But then it was gone, and she punished me, and I was more alone than ever. There were times when I tried—I tried so hard to hide from my hunters, to avoid them completely. Or I closed my eyes. I tried not to look.

But it always ended the same.

MELPOMENE: What made Perseus different?

MEDUSA: He talked to me. His voice—do you know what it's like to be alone for so long that you don't even recognize voices? Perseus did have a beautiful voice.

PERSEUS: I sat on the ground. There was a statue of someone who looked like a king, and I sat at his feet. She—Medusa— was in her garden courtyard only feet away. I remember there was a beam of moonlight that fell on her. I'd started using the reflection off my shield to see then. The smell of petrichor and wilted flowers was thick in the warm rain. She asked me why I was there, and I told her. I told her everything. I also hadn't spoken to anyone for days, except to get directions.

MELPOMENE: What about Athena?

PERSEUS: You've spoken to her. That's more of a one-sided conversation.

MELPOMENE: Don't I know it. But tell me about the moment you saw Medusa through the shield. What did you think?

PERSEUS: I thought that King Polydectes was more monstrous.

MELPOMENE: What about the snakes? Weren't they disconcerting?

PERSEUS: Not really. They were ethereal. They were always moving, shimmering against the moonglow, sunbeams. Just catching the light. Their strange susurration kept me up.

MELPOMENE: Did you sleep in the temple, then?

PERSEUS: I did.

MELPOMENE: Weren't you afraid she'd turn you to stone? Devour you in your sleep?

PERSEUS: No. I knew she wouldn't hurt me. That's not who she was. That's what makes what I did so much worse, doesn't it?

MELPOMENE: Have you asked her?

PERSEUS: I haven't.

MELPOMENE: Do you want to?

PERSEUS: I've thought about it. I've written letters. Emails still confuse me. I don't think I've acclimated to this time as well as some of the others, which is why I suppose I'm going to hike the Andes in South America next. I need to clear my head.

MELPOMENE: What if I told you Medusa was here in the studio?

MEDUSA: I've always imagined my death. Ever since I was a little girl. I was the mortal sister, remember? I knew I would end. I knew that there was no way to escape my curse during our age of gods and heroes. But I knew something the gods didn't.

THE ORACLE OF DELPHI, *oracle of Apollo, influencer*: I was the one who told Medusa what to do. There was no getting away from the gods during our time. Immortals have nothing to fear. But gods wane when humanity stops believing in them. Perseus had to be born. He had to be the greatest hero of man, but he also had to be the hubris of the gods.

MELPOMENE: You're saying you knew we'd regenerate? Did Apollo know it was more than a myth?

THE ORACLE OF DELPHI: Some things aren't even for the gods to know.

APOLLO: Look, my darling. That's the cycle of it all, isn't it? I've seen the breath of the galaxy, the end of the world, the dark heart of gods and humans and monsters and everything in between. There are thousands of prophecies that never came true. A prophecy that would have put the gods to sleep for *centuries*? Zeus would have pulverized me irreparably into stardust if I'd uttered it in the halls of Olympus. I buried that prophecy so deeply it became myth.

MELPOMENE: Until it wasn't. Oh, my gods . . .

APOLLO: That's the funny thing about fate, isn't it?

MEDUSA: Do you think a boy with a few trinkets was enough to destroy me?

MELPOMENE: I never believed it.

MEDUSA: Perseus was a pawn. But so were we all. Do you know that when I prayed, when I turned my adversaries to stone, when I offered their souls to the underworld, I was speaking to kindred spirits?

MELPOMENE: The Oracle of Delphi.

MEDUSA: And Hades himself.

MELPOMENE: Are you saying that you allowed Perseus to kill you?

MEDUSA: Oh, no. I fought back. That's why it hurt so much. I'd started to like him. The gold freckles on his shoulders. The rumble of his voice when he first woke up. The furrow of doubt on his brow. That secret smile when he thought I wasn't looking. That's why it hurt so much to know I would fail.

PERSEUS: Where is she?

MELPOMENE: Percy, calm down. If you could just stay seated—

PERSEUS: *Where* is she?

MEDUSA: The oracle told me there was a time and a place when I wouldn't have to fear my curse. When I could be myself, exactly as I was, and have everything I'd ever wanted. I wouldn't be alone. That time is now.

MELPOMENE: Are you ready to see him? I asked him to wait after his interview. He's just next door. Do you know what you'll say?

MEDUSA: It's been so long. I often— [*Turns toward the sound of banging on the door.*] That's—

PERSEUS, *voice muffled behind the door*: Medusa!

MEDUSA: Oh, my . . .

MELPOMENE: Do you want me to let him in?

MEDUSA, *smirking*: Yes. It's our time.

MELPOMENE: Security, let him in!

Percy *walks across the studio. Kneels at her side. Averting his gaze at first, he lets her take his chin and slowly tilt it up.*

PERSEUS: Medusa.

MEDUSA: Hello, love. Show me your face.

DION AND THE MAENADS

S. Zainab Williams

Dion blinked thick tears out of her eyes and scanned the wreckage of beer cans, red cups, oily paper plates, and sweaty bodies. It had been exactly twenty-four hours since the gods suspended her and the Maenads from entering the halls of Olympus.

In a nearish bathroom somewhere down the main hallway of the sorority house, Mai was making a Pizza Bros. sacrifice to the porcelain god. Dion recognized her telltale gurgle. If the pantheon could see them now.

Zeus! That undying monster. That absolute predator. Boy, would he be furious. Or maybe he'd be proud. There was only one thing you could predict about him, gods save the girls.

Damn Zeus, thought Dion. *And damn his complicit entourage that chooses silence over doing the right thing. As usual.*

Only the Maenads had come through and backed her up in that hallowed wasteland. Just because her predecessors, countless incarnations of Dionysus the First, had played respectability politics didn't mean she had to. Wasn't she the best of the demigods so far? Didn't they want a fresh perspective? Hadn't they invited her to Olympus to contribute this very thing?

Dion had spent too much of her youth feeling guilty for slinking back to the mortal world to avoid acknowledging the harm done to the god-king's victims. But it was the bravery of mortal women that had forced her back to face the truth and all the gods at last.

Sinking into the cracks of someone's musty couch, Dion hugged her boxed wine close, ready to wallow in red fantasies, when her best friend stumbled into the living room and kicked up the settling gloom. Mai wiped her stained lips with the sleeve of her cardigan. She looked like a baby chick in yellow cashmere, and the memory of their first thrift store haul when they were teenagers (some twenty years ago, by Geras!) brought Dion some rueful cheer.

"Don't know how many times I have to tell you not to mix your wine and your spirits," said Dion.

"May is panting under the kitchen table, and Mei can hardly lift her head," Mai croaked. "Make us better already."

Dion wagged a finger at her bestie. "We have to eat what we serve. It's important, Mai."

"I ate it and I threw it up. Make with the health."

Dion sighed change into the air—a bit of blessing almost as good as a steaming bowl of phở—and she and Mai were soon joined by May and Mei. The three of them looked ruffled but alert.

When the Maenads stood side by side, you couldn't help but assume they were related, although they looked nothing alike. Mai, short and sturdy with bleached white hair, was Japanese and Korean and spoke with the singsong lilt of a Valley girl. May was a tall Afro-Latina—Puerto Rican, but best not ask her to speak Spanish—and a retired rivethead whose reverence for Trent Reznor only occasionally inspired jealousy in Dion. Chinese Malay Mei, with their carefully formed curls and dimples, never failed to remind Dion of *Wizard of Oz*–era Judy Garland. Mei looked like they only ever listened to music their parents would approve of. Everyone trusted them, and that's what made Mei especially dangerous. They were, all three of them, dangerous.

The Maenads draped over one another. Not physically—not always—but empathetically, their moods and sentiments overlapping and braiding. They had a persistent read on one another, and they could call upon this gift to navigate and harangue and support one another. Dion had once longed to be a member of the Maenads. While she was similar in many ways, including, but not limited to, being completely incapable of fitting neatly into a box, and while she'd quickly claimed her place as know-it-all older sister (by mere months), her godhood always held her slightly apart. In fact, because she still hadn't found her groove as a god, separate was her current and, as far as she could tell, eternal status.

Zeus had swooped into her life to tell her she was Dionysus incarnate twenty-two whole years ago, and it still felt new. While Dion rarely thought about her forebearer, she often pined for Ariadne, abandoned on the abrasive shore of Naxos. Call it what you will—Dionysus's phantom heart still beating for his lost love, perhaps—but Dion empathized with her, the Cretan princess lifted to a place among the stars, imprisoned in the heights of cold, dark space.

The Maenads had saved her from an existential crisis. They'd met and become fast friends in a Gothic Lolita Live-Journal community. She had been drawn to their loyalty, and they, to her chaos. She had offered them eternal shelter in her temple as her BFFs, and they had accepted.

Now here they were, loitering in a sorority house after their traditional break-out-of-a-bad-mood bender (a warm-up, really), freshly and forever thirty-six. Thirty-six was the agreed-upon Goldilocks age when you got serious, but not too serious; when you could still be a hot mess. Hot mess was their speed—but the time for serious business had arrived. Dion heaved herself off the couch and stood before her fellow elder millennials, gripping the handle of her boxed wine like the shaft of a scepter.

"If the Olds of Olympus think they can send us to our rooms and give *Father* a pass, they're wrong," Dion announced. "We're going on the bender of all benders. We're going to expose this whole charade, and we're going to make them show up."

The Maenads each grabbed a red cup from the ruins of the coffee table. Dion filled them to the brim with merlot, and the Maenads raised their cups to the sky.

"This one's for the gods," said Dion. She threw back her head, positioned the spout, and let the wine flow.

Paper crinkled and slapped the air as tourists fanned themselves with glossy winery maps highlighting the Willamette Valley's finest. Summer had decided to peak unreasonably early, and the bus's air-conditioning had died, along with everyone's sense of humor. Only the driver laughed at his jokes about tree stumps and filberts.

Dion registered muttered complaints. This was Portland's cheapest wine tasting tour—what had these people expected? She had not only expected the busted bus but its passengers as well: broods of junior-level professionals in their late twenties and early thirties, and one thrifty family visiting their drinking-age daughter. Dion eyed the dad's lime-green fanny pack.

"Fuck is that stink?" May's gravelly voiced rumbled from the neighboring seat.

Dion felt passing pity for May, who severely lacked an appreciation for fake nacho cheese dust. She stuck her head around the tall seat back in front of her.

"Pass the bag," said Dion.

Mei sucked gold dust off their fingertips before handing over the chips. May sneered as Dion crunched.

"There's beef jerky," said Dion.

"Not interested."

"Two drinks in and you'll be hunting down stale oyster crackers—you know it, I know it, we all know it," said Dion.

Back when they were teens, May used to tell the rest of them she was hypoglycemic when she got irritable, but over time Dion came to understand that her friend didn't enjoy the offerings of mall food courts or any fast food and thought *hypoglycemia* and *hanger* were synonymous.

"I'd kill for a big, fat, bloody steak," May said to no one in particular. "Marbled and buttery and dripping."

Mai popped up in the seat next to Mei's to stare down at Dion and May.

"Who's our target?" She didn't even attempt to keep her voice down. Didn't matter, absorbed as everyone was in their own suffering and thirst.

"Everyone is our target," Dion said through a mouthful of chips. "Everyone on this bus and every boozehound we meet along the way. No stuffy types and"—Dion graced May with an archly malevolent smile—"no insufferable cynics, please. We need wonder, belief, and, above all, inebriation. Skip anyone using the wine spittoon."

"Or anyone drinking dessert wine," Mai said with a gag.

Mei crossed their arms. "Don't be a jerk, Mai," they said.

"Oh shit, I totally forgot you like that stuff," said Mai. Mai absolutely knew they liked that stuff.

"There's nothing wrong with a good port," Dion said in hopes her expertise would nip the argument in the bud, rare as it was for expertise to win a battle against personal opinion.

"Sure, sure, a good port, a good pineapple wine—what's the diff anyway?" asked Mai.

Mei threw their arms above their head. "I was drunk, and it tasted good in the moment!"

"Oh my god, you two have zero chill," said May, fingers splayed at attention on both sides of her head, looking not *entirely* unlike a horse with funky blinders when she stretched her neck and rolled her eyes.

"Who needs chill when you've got dance moves like these?" With an open-mouthed smile, Mai proceeded to perform a tragic cross between the sprinkler and the Carlton.

"Stop antagonizing, Mai," Dion chastised, but the Maenad was rewarded with applause from the less wilted passengers.

May practically disappeared into her seat, while Dion shook her head and stuffed the bag of chips into a tote bag with *Wine Aunt* printed in a looping red font across cream canvas. The bus couldn't have pulled up to their first stop sooner.

"Everyone ready?" Dion asked the Maenads. They looked excited. Maybe too excited? Oh well. By Dion's estimation they were overdue for some mischief.

They'd all thought they were in for a new adventure when they were promoted and allowed to cross Olympus's threshold years ago, the old guard having need of new blood—younger, more diverse iterations who might sit at the table and help them solve the impossible problem of how to reach a modern, less familiar generation. Dion and the Maenads hadn't been the only recruits. There were Pan and the Nymphs, for instance. But that Gen Z cohort eternally dithered between self-righteousness and abstractedness. Dion had tried to hang with them, but she was sure they fashioned new lingo out of thin air for the sole purpose of confusing her. *Kids excited about decoder rings.* Dion snorted. And. And! Pan and the Nymphs were practically teetotalers. They'd rejected a glug of Dion's best (in a customized corked bottle, no less) in favor of CBD gummies purchased down the road. Circus had long ago perished on the doorstep of Olympus.

Unfortunately for Dion and her circus-thirsty friends, they would have to continue to wait for debauchery, which was taking forever to meet them at their first winery of the day. They'd arrived around eleven thirty, and yet everyone insisted on swirling their wine for eons, practicing pranayama with their wineglasses in between noncommittal sips as if the delay might deliver them to a more conservative drinking hour. Dion wanted to slap them. What was the point of brunch if not to give morning drinking the thumbs-up all around?

These tourists forced Dion and the Maenads to waste time with the sobering banality of a visit to the gift shop. They had to do *something* to maintain their charade as civilized people. They needed their prospective disciples to like them, or at least be curious, and sloppiness would make them a hard sell.

Things didn't pick up until their second stop, when the lightweights showed early signs of ditziness. The first bubble to pop was the drinking-age daughter of the thrifty family. Dion clocked the symptoms of the young woman's escalating buzz right away, and was calculating the expense of bringing a dubiously attached neophyte into the fold, when the lamb's searching eyes locked on hers. Everyone else had a satisfactory party or had found one to join, while this tipsy saint looked ready to flee Christian summer camp.

"What're the chances she's never talked to Black and brown folks?" Mai said, picking up what the tasting room was putting down.

The young woman took her first uneasy steps toward Dion and the Maenads with one strategic glance over her shoulder to make sure her parents were still preoccupied at the counter. Dion overheard the couple squabbling over which of the cheaper wines to buy for someone—a boss, or an in-law, or someone else they felt obligated to consider but didn't particularly like.

The young woman stood before them, lagging a beat behind an introduction to stare down into her glass in puzzlement. She could've sworn she'd had only a drop left. Dion's hand reached over the pinot noir.

"Hi, I'm Dion," she said. "And this is Mai, May, and Mei."

"Are those nicknames?" The young woman giggled. She caught herself and cleared the air with a hand. "Those are very pretty names. I'm Nicole." Dion forgave her for the moment and shook on it.

Dion and the Maenads watched Nicole's brow furrow. She'd come to the meeting unprepared, and she tripped over her words as she pushed them out on the fly.

"Have you ever done anything like this before? I mean wine tasting. Here or somewhere else maybe?"

Dion softened her eyes and turned up the brightness of her smile. "A few times. What brings you and your parents here today?"

"Oh." Nicole barely spared her parents another glance. "I just graduated from college—PSU. They wanted to do something for me while they were out here visiting from Florida. I kind of wanted to go with my friends, but Mom and Dad

wanted to check out the Willamette Valley, and my room-
mates were busy with their own stuff anyway."

"Their loss," Mei said, cocking their head and shrugging
their shoulders ever so cutely.

Nicole lit up, and Dion could practically hear her carefully
coifed good-girl waves relating to Mei's shiny, suddenly near-
perfect-match hair.

"You'll find good company in us, if you want it," Dion said
seductively.

"Hey, princess, making friends?" Nicole's dad appeared out
of the crowd and clapped a hand on his daughter's shoulder. Nicole's mom stood just behind him like Her Lady of
Perpetual Concern. She managed to produce a grimace of
encouragement.

While Nicole again searched for her words, her dad regaled
them with the story of his daughter's graduation and a full
breakdown of the ceremony, including what they'd eaten for
dinner that night. May looked pained throughout the recita-
tion, while Dion recalculated the cost of recruiting Nicole.

"Now let me ask you something," said Nicole's dad.

Dion blinked a few times as she surfaced from deep
slumber.

"What's all this?" Nicole's dad waved a hand in front of
Dion's face.

The Maenads bristled. Nicole stared wide-eyed into
the space just beyond Dion's right ear, while her mom
squeak-laughed like someone startled by a loud fart at the
museum.

Dion tried to give the man a moment of silence so he
could think about his words, but Nicole's mom was at the
ready.

"Tom is Irish, German, and French," she blurted out. "He's taken a real interest in learning more about his background, and he's naturally curious about other multiethnic peoples."

Tom pushed on, not bothering to acknowledge his wife's attempt to mitigate.

"I'm sure people have told you you've got a real different look," he said. "What are you?"

Dion nodded knowingly. People sure had told her that. And a follow-up demand to identify herself was the gold standard among such people.

"I am the product of South Asian diaspora and the Atlantic slave trade," she said. And then she grinned at the man's pink nose. "But, to you, I am a god."

Tom snorted. "Is this another identity thing? Jaysus. Nicole here tried to explain that pronoun stuff to us, and I couldn't make heads or tails of the sci-fi she-shim universe y'all are living in. What're these kids going to come up with next, Alice?" he asked his wife.

"Oh my god, Dad." Nicole covered her face with her free hand.

Dion's nose flared as the thick iron tang of bloodlust radiated from the Maenads. A whisper like chiffon ribbon wound itself around the group as Mei exchanged a thought with Dion, who gave Tom a hard look and recalculated once more. Her smile flicked back on.

"Bet it's been a minute since anyone invited you to a party, Tom—we're hosting a little soiree after this wine tasting tour. Free drinks, free hors d'oeuvres. Everything top shelf. We booked a tricked-out barn on a lush winery with beautiful views and an amphitheater. You and your wife—Alice, is it?"

"Alice," Alice agreed dreamily. Dion knew the woman

wasn't looking at her but at the specter of a gorgeous evening out.

"You and Alice and New Friend Nicole should come on down and continue the celebration," said Dion.

"Isn't that nice? You see, Nicole," Tom said as he rapped his daughter on the shoulder. "You worry too much about saying the wrong thing. Say what you want, and the good eggs will float to the top."

The arched brow May produced would've put Maila Nurmi to shame.

To Dion, Tom added, "But as nice as that all sounds, I'm sure the three of us'll want to get back to the hotel for a good night's sleep. Hell, I'm already too tipsy."

"Mm, the spirit moves in mysterious ways," Dion drawled.

"Speaking of moving, looks like our group's about to leave without us. Let's get to going, girls."

Dion and the Maenads watched the family leave, Alice pleading "beautiful views," Nicole crying "just for an hour," Tom shaking his head. Fumes rolled off his gyrating skull in thick, dark tendrils. They reeked of chardonnay and entitlement. Dion clenched her teeth, Zeus's holier-than-thou voice echoing in her head. *Leave it alone*, he'd often warned.

The god of wine took a deep, clearing breath, turning Tom's fumes into a tempest that whipped around the room. Outside, the wind howled through the vines, and the tipsy tasters squealed and shouted as they fled into the bus, shawls and caps and skirts flying. At the tail end of Dion's inhale, Tom's fumes funneled up her nose and disappeared. Dion experienced a second of inebriation with a dangerous chaser of deep insecurity before the sensation blessedly fizzled away. Mei would get theirs tonight. They all would.

The sound of a wineglass shattering on polished wood was music to Dion's ears. Nobody else paid any mind to the shout of "Party foul!" in the distance. Her audience was rapt.

"And that's how I fucked with Pentheus," Dion concluded. She put an arm behind her as she bowed to applause.

"That's cute and all, but Dionysus you are not," said some dude dressed like a hopeful applicant to the school of dark academia. "I still have my copy of *d'Aulaires'*, and you look nothing like him. No offense, but firstly, Dionysus was a guy. Secondly, he was Greek, not Black."

"Okay, firstly," said Dion, "that's not how you pronounce *d'Aulaires*, and secondly, Greek is not a race. But I can appreciate a fact-finding mission. If it's proof you want, it's proof you'll get."

A woman swaddled like a boho-chic baby in layers of colorful silk clapped her hands and cried, "I'm game."

The woman wasn't part of their group but had shown up at the vineyard where their party bus had stopped for its final tasting with only the desire to treat herself, Dion had learned during her recruitment tour of the room. She was some kind of playwright, she was celebrating the completion of a new play, and she was in search of good times and inspiration.

"Bring on the show," called the playwright.

Dion had to resist the urge to rub her hands together like a cartoon villain.

"You'll have to find your way to the after-party for that," said Mai.

"To the hills, to the hills," Mei chanted eerily.

"Call your friends and tell them to meet up with you," May

commanded the crowd. "Invite whoever you want as long as they're not assholes."

Nicole raised her hand. "Even if we wanted to go, some of us are on tours," she said as she scanned the room. She needn't have worried. Tom was too busy staring at a glass of water, unable to hear his own trickling thoughts past the roar of Cyndi Lauper's "Girls Just Want to Have Fun" on permanent loop in his head, while the task of reminding her husband of the last time they went out on the town (in the late nineties) kept Alice preoccupied. "We don't have any way to get to the after-party or back home," Nicole continued.

"Not a problem," Dion said authoritatively, like the grown woman she was pretending to be. "Tell your drivers you'll be staying here and leave the rest of your unforgettable night to me and my friends. We'll pick up you and your crew at dusk."

"Uh, what?" Dark Academia guffawed. "We can't tell our drivers to abandon us and hope some random person who thinks she's a god doesn't leave us stranded."

Dion wasn't taken aback by the young man's resistance. She'd encountered one or two of him at each of their wine stops. While the Maenads had used their stockpiles of charisma and Dion had wielded her godly power of persuasion to charm so many individuals under the influence, some people were beyond help.

"You'll just have to take that leap of faith." Dion shrugged, and as she turned around, she added, "This round's on me."

May their cups be full, thought Dion. She practically floated away on the gasps and sighs of her audience.

"Time to bounce," Dion told the Maenads. They strutted across the tasting room, mission almost accomplished.

"You think we have enough?" asked May.

"Half of the last tasting room were on their phones calling friends," said Dion. "Same with all the others. We're good."

The four of them slid a glance at Tom, who wobbled at the tasting table beside his wife. He looked one part baffled and one part trashed.

"You mean it, Tom? We can go to the party?" Alice asked.

Tom nodded, the wrinkle between his eyebrows deepening as Cyndi spread the gospel between his ears.

"See ya later, Tomcat," said Dion. The Maenads bared their teeth as they walked out the door.

The gilded sun was preparing to tuck its day-drunk head under a blanket of deep green vines when Dion and the Maenads arrived at the farmhouse. They'd found the place on one of those glamping apps and paid a pretty, fabricated penny for the chance to stay at a working winery and vineyard. In exchange, the owners got a distant but comforting view of four quiet women having a cozy evening on the property and in their empty amphitheater (available at additional cost), no matter what actually happened on that side of the vineyard.

Mai ran off without warning the minute the immortals' feet touched the sweet, dusty lane. That's just how Mai was. Dion shook her head at her friend. Then she gathered old vines from a pile ready to be burned and twisted bits of the stuff into crude, boxy shapes. She set them on the ground.

"Go on," she said, pointing at them. Mei and May took a step back, their ears popping as the crude shapes ballooned into two school bus–size woodie wagons.

"This is some serious Cinderella shit," May said with a nod of approval.

"Right?" said Dion. "On, O joyful, be fleet," she said to the wagons. She was waving the vehicles down the lane when Mai reappeared, presenting the hide of a cartoon deer.

"Absolutely not," said May.

"What in Persy's underworld is that?" asked Dion.

"I can't decide if it's cute or ghastly, but I think I like it," Mei declared.

"It's a costume," Mai exclaimed. "May or Mei can be the ass, and I brought these as a consolation prize for our third." She brandished a pair of plastic light-up deer antlers glued to a headband.

May snatched the antlers out of her hand. "Sorry, Mei."

Mei shrugged on the deer's ass. "It's kinda cozy in here," they said. "Come on in."

Mai hurried to join her half to Mei's. As the severed halves became one ugly deer, the animal folded in two with an explosive "Oof!" The fuzzy antlers smacked the floor as the back end caved in and re-formed anew. A sweatier, dustier Mai now took up the rear, while Mei helmed the monstrosity.

Dion pinched her chin as she considered the result. "Okay, well, we've all been very productive here. But how about we start prepping for our guests?"

Mai's furious face dropped like intestines from the deer's midsection. "What do you think I'm doing?"

"Serving wildness and revelry and everything else I like about you, I suppose, Mai." Dion sighed. "But also, we can't have an outdoor fête without a bonfire."

Dion and the Maenads threw armloads of pine cones and old, dead vines from a big mound into the bonfire pit beside the amphitheater. They listened to the satisfying crackle until it was interrupted by a distant hum and the crunch of rubber against packed earth.

"Friends," Dion said, her face alight with fire. "Our guests have arrived."

Dion spun around and examined the purple silk jumpsuit that had replaced her skinny jeans and blouse.

"So extra," said Mai. "I like it."

The four of them strutted down the lane until they reached the woodie wagons, now brimming with drunk wine tourists and more sober friends.

"Welcome to the after-party," Dion shouted at them as the doors sighed open.

Every person stepping out of the buses looked amazed and grateful to have arrived in one piece. Dion pursed her lips. Her kind of magic and vehicles didn't mix well. She made a mental note to set up a ride share next time.

Dion needed to loosen things up. "Drinks, anyone?" she asked. One hundred hands shot up.

Dion and the Maenads dipped behind a copse of trees, reappearing with armfuls of red cups. As the crowd handed them around, the friends filled the cups out of plastic wine sacks that never seemed to empty. Once every person had been treated, the godly cohort led the charge up the sloping vineyard to the farmhouse near the amphitheater.

"Everyone's so quiet," Mei whispered.

"Make them shotgun their wine," said May.

"Hmm, I don't think barking orders to glug is going to be helpful here," said Dion. She took one look over her shoulder at the motley crew and knew exactly what they needed. She started humming a tune and waving her hands.

"Yay!" Mei the deer head squealed, front legs prancing.

"Heyyyy, I know that one," Mai the rear deer said, and set her back legs stomping.

May turned her kohl-inked eyes to the sky, antlers beaming bright as Vegas, and groaned, "Thanatos, claim me."

Dion belted out the first line of "Dancing Queen."

In no time, everyone had joined in, dancing and singing like they'd tapped into a shared premonition. *Almost* everyone.

May clamped her lips shut as she turned her pained face to Dion. "Dion. You are so tragic."

"Girl, I know," Dion shouted above the din of Swedish pop. "But one finds joy where one must when living in the darkest timeline."

And this merry band was wild with joy. Dion tasted it on her tongue, more rich and more supple than any vintage she'd sampled that day.

"We've got dolmas, we've got grape sorbet, we've got wine— red and white—we've got everything you need and more," Dion announced as she poured chardonnay for Alice. Tom stood beside his wife, scrubbing his ruddy face with his hands. He blinked at the crowd cavorting around the bonfire.

The revelers had grabbed bits of old vine, and they'd begun to light the frayed tips. Dion tried to recall whether she'd seen any fine print about arson in their booking agreement. Meanwhile, Alice moved on, towing her husband behind, oblivious to her daughter skipping around the fire in her bra and knee-length skirt.

"Ah, youth," said Dion.

May strode up, followed closely by two halves of a drunk deer.

"The time has come," they said as one.

Dion looked around. "I suppose you're right. Maenads, to the stage."

Dion and the Maenads leaped onto the amphitheater stage.

"Hey, party people," Dion spoke into the mic. "I said hey, party people, it's time for a show!"

The playwright whooped and made for the steps, gathering the crowd in her wake.

"I knew I liked her," said Dion. "Come ooooooon over!" she sang into the mic. "I told you all I was a god, and now I aim to prove it."

Near the front of the crowd, Dark Academia frowned—a poor attempt to disguise his curiosity. Tom, on the other hand, made no attempt to hide his feelings. The haze and the '80s pop had cleared, and his waking mind lasered in on Dion and the Maenads. Tom broke free of Alice's grip and bulldozed his way through the crowd.

Mei wandered up to the mic. The deer head dragged on the floor in front of them. "I think we have a volunteer from the crowd," they said into the mic.

Dion swept an arm in Tom's direction as he scrambled onto the stage. "A round of applause for our volunteer, Tom."

Their audience cheered and whooped and clapped. They whipped their flaming wands above their heads as they hollered and hooted. Tom froze onstage. He stared at the revelers, his face getting redder and redder. He charged at Dion and snatched the microphone from her hand.

"Has everyone gone mad?" Tom's screech echoed in the mic's feedback. "This isn't a god y'all are looking at! These aren't nymphs or whatever the hell they've been blabbing about being all day. These are little girls with big mouths." Tom swayed and clutched his mottled sweating face. "Now I don't know what these mongrels did to my drinks to get me here, but I'm getting out, and the rest of you should get out too before they steal your information, or brainwash you, or microchip you or whatever it is they're up to."

"Would you like the honors?" Dion asked Mei.

Mei opened their arms wide and received Dion's gift. Dion had brewed the curse, but it had been blessed by the whole crew. Mei hugged the hissing, spitting, bristling spell to themself and then hugged Tom. They held him tight until it sank into his bones. Tom recoiled, falling backward as if Mei had sunk their sharp teeth into his peach flesh.

Mei giggled as thick vines bursting with glossy fruit slapped across the stage, gyring and shushing as they reached for Tom. A pool of dark red pinot oozed from the stone. A large looming shadow with a long snout scratched its clawed paws against the floor as it let loose a bellow.

Tom scrambled up. "Is that a bear?" he panted. "Did you bring a bear here?"

Dion and the Maenads watched him. He stared back at each one of them, beetling his brow at last at Dion. Her curly black hair glinted blue in the unnatural moonlight. Tom studied her face and seemed to realize she was bored. Bored! He swung around, loose-jointed, to glower at the people to the left of the stage. "Look around! Look at what they're doing to this place. Look at what they're doing to *you*." He pointed a shaking finger at Dion. "She's a monster. They all are. So what're ya doin' just standing there?" he whined at them. "Do you *want* to be MEOW MEOW MEOW? Are you MEOW?"

Tom's marble-green eyes widened. His whiskers twitched. Something was very wrong.

Dion cupped a hand around her ear and crouched way down to Tom's height. "What's that, Tomcat?"

Alice and shirtless Nicole approached the stage, blinking

intently at their feline husband and father, who, tail twitching, continued to mouth off to the crowd.

"He's all yours if you want him," said Dion.

"Is he . . ." Alice faltered.

Dion shook her head mournfully. "Unfortunately, he'll be back to normal by tomorrow."

As Alice and Nicole gathered their hissing, spitting bundle of fuzz, Dion and the Maenads reclaimed the stage.

"I am Dion, daughter of Zeus!" Dion punched the air with a fist, and the crowd cheered.

"And, together, we are Dion and the Maenads, scourge of Zeus!" She pumped her fist, and the crowd cheered louder. "You all know the stories, and even if you don't know them all, you know Zeus. Zeus the rapist. Zeus the manipulator. Zeus the cheater. Zeus the terror of women and all humankind."

"Zeus sucks," shouted Dark Academia.

"That's right," Dion said wryly. "You won't find half the stuff I know about Zeus in *d'Aulaires'*. History has pardoned and turned a blind eye to his bullshit behavior, but we're not going to let him get away with abuse, are we?"

"Hell no," shouted the playwright. "Tell it like it is."

"We're not going to let him hurt and oppress and exploit. We're not going to let him sit comfy in his high seat enjoying that rarified air, empowered to make messes of other people's lives."

"Cancel Zeus," Mai shouted through teeth bared in a brutal grin. The Maenads' eyes dilated as the crowd took up the chant.

"Cancel Zeus! Cancel Zeus!" Backlit by the roaring pine cone fire, they whipped the air with their grapevine wands.

Dion and the Maenads raised their drinking cups as one. "Cancel Zeus," they proclaimed.

One hundred drinking cups miraculously filled to brimming joined theirs in a toast. "Cancel Zeus!" The crowd roared and drank every last drop.

"Bring the mayhem, bring the magic," recited Dion and the Maenads.

A blinding bolt of lightning cracked the night sky, and its accompanying thunder shook the earth. The deed was done; the warm-up was over. If the crowd screamed, no one could hear.

Like the coiled vipers the gods ascribed to them, Dion and the Maenads crouched low as they faced the epicenter of the storm—that absolute beast, that undying monster, that party pooper. The four of them balled their fists, chaos, danger, and vengeance swarming out of them like a fury of yellowjackets. They gathered the strength of their believers and held it for one last beat as that being came into focus.

"Time to take it home?" May rasped.

Dion widened her ferocious grin. "Time to tear it down, friends." She hurled a bottle of wine at the figure.

Dion and the Maenads sprang, vivid as neon, screaming a battle cry into black velvet before they cannonballed into the searing light.

TIRESIAS

Zeyn Joukhadar

Watch for snakes when we get out, Giulia said with a tap to the spot where our knees touched. Ormai non è più tenuto il giardino, who knows what could jump out of that grass.

I hated snakes, and I hated parties where I didn't know anyone. Giulia's yellow Fiat Panda had been nearly out of gas, and she didn't want to get stuck on the winding road up to the mountain, where the mansion lay. Out here, she said, you could go tens of kilometers without seeing a gas station or—porca miseria!—an Autogrill.

Niccolò was already two beers into the evening, and Lucio refused to drive at night. Saoirse was determined to see the mansion, though, had told us about the wild parties that happened there and the fantastical and famous people who frequented them. I had my suspicions about how Fede knew Saoirse, since from what I could glean in the days we'd been here, she was only a tangential member of their friend group, and this was the first time Fede had been back in years. We'd met in Berlin, had shared an apartment there for two years, and I'd always associated Fede with the city. This was my first time meeting any of his friends back home. I was trying to play the part of the accommodating boyfriend, so when Fede offered to take all seven of us in Lucio's Cinquecento, I shut my mouth and stuffed myself into the middle seat. The others piled onto one another's laps.

Sprawled across Giulia's legs, Saoirse draped her arms around the back of Fede's headrest and launched into a convoluted story, mostly in dialect, of which I promptly lost the thread. She'd supposedly lived here for years, long enough to speak like a local. Her Italian was so fluent that I wondered, in a flash of jealousy, if she weren't a good deal older than she claimed to be. Un montone tutto nero, she said at one point, something like that, and made a sweeping gesture with her hand that set her cascade of red-blond hair swinging. I figured she'd said something about the mountain but couldn't be sure. Vincenzo and Niccolò were too busy bickering over a dropped cigarette to translate, half crushing me in the middle seat. As for Fede, we hadn't talked since our fight that morning, when Lucio had overheard our angry whispers in his bathroom. He'd knocked so politely my face burned, as though one of our housemates in our flat in Berlin had walked in on us fucking.

Let me open the window, Lucio said in Italian, the child lock is on.

Niccolò kneed the back of Lucio's seat. If I catch your puke in my face back here, I'll throttle you. Why do you think we put you up front?

I was used to only Fede's Italian; I kept getting lost in other people's accents. I wondered how many people would be at the party and wished I'd worn my contact lenses. The mansion, Saoirse had said, had once been owned by the eccentric parents of the Milan art world's darling du jour. Now, since their passing, it was a squat occupied by said darling's sustainable art collective, a group of thirty- and forty-somethings in the throes of second youth. After Saoirse said this, Giulia had coughed *Fricchettoni!* into her fist. I was prepared for blond dreadlocks, linen pants, and pubic hair in the bidet.

Without Fede in the mood to introduce me, I would spend most of the night being misgendered; even in dialect, I had a wretched gift for telling when people read me as a woman. The whole operation: the waiting, the cataloging of every motion of my wrist, controlling the pitch of my voice—I was exhausted already. Before our fight, I'd woken up that morning from a dream in which I was waiting for a car, a feeling of dread I'd tried to dispel by applying black winged eyeliner, a kind of faggy playfulness I never would have allowed myself if I'd known Fede would give me the cold shoulder all night.

Giulia tugged her hair from her lipstick. Federico told me you see things, she said in English, and then they happen. She was a little buzzed. Her breath smelled like beer and fruit.

Ma va', Niccolò said, then followed Giulia into English. Seriously?

Still nothing to gender me. Fede probably meant my bird-reading app, I said. You see a flock of birds, you take a little video of how they move. It tells you the likelihood of hurricanes or the risk of earthquakes, things like that. Giulia blinked at me, and I stammered on. It's called Augr. I made it back when all the app names ended just with *r*.

You are like a psychic, Vincenzo said. Like Divino Otelma.

Not exactly, I said.

Vincenzo waved an open hand in a little windmill of dismissal. Dai, he said. With less tax evasion.

Giulia tsked. No, no. Fede said you see the *future*. He said you once saw his great-aunt in a coffin, and the next day she was *dead*.

I glanced at Fede in the rearview mirror, but he was

watching the road. In reality, I'd had a dream where I'd washed her hair and plaited it, the way one does for burial. I was shocked and annoyed that he'd shared something so intimate with someone I'd only just met. I didn't like other people to know, didn't want to carry their disappointment and their hope. Well, she was pushing ninety, I said, and the way my voice squeaked out I could've booted myself out the window.

Ma che figata, Saoirse gushed. I want to know what else you see!

No, really, I said, I just made a stupid weather app that earned, like, fifty bucks. It's not even for sale anymore.

Niccolò, who had already started to check the app store, wilted and let his screen go dark. Fede turned up the radio. Vincenzo shifted Niccolò's weight to check his phone, then put it away, too. There's no field anyway, he muttered. None of us had any bars.

Giulia touched my knee again. It seems cool, she said, addressing me by name. I was surprised she'd remembered and that she'd touched me twice now. She hadn't yet misgendered me, and against my better judgment, I'd taken this as a sign we might hang out, that maybe the party wouldn't be so bad.

My eye stung, like I'd been poked. Through the window Lucio had opened, a crumb of pollen had swept in and lodged itself under my glasses. I rubbed furiously, then remembered my eyeliner. I was sure I'd smudged it, but it was too dark to see in the rearview, and I didn't want to ask the others.

We arrived at the entrance to the mansion and pulled off into a long, winding drive through a grove of pomegranates bearing yellow fruit. Everyone slid out, dazzled by the headlights of a car pulling in behind us, and moved off in the direction of the mansion. I clomped through the beds of the old garden, now overgrown with cheatgrass like the lot of an abandoned factory, conscious of my exposed ankles. We meandered toward the lit windows of the mansion, the silhouettes of bodies moving across the rooms. Italian synth-pop floated out to us. Giulia had disappeared, along with Saoirse, Vincenzo, and Niccolò.

Ducking under clusters of summer grapes, we came into a courtyard. A jet-black ram stood dour-faced in a little pen, fenced in beside a makeshift coop whose chickens strutted among the party guests' feet. I polli sacri, someone said, laughing as they threw down fistfuls of feed. The sacred chickens of Apollo! Brown hens scrabbled after yellow crumbs, leaving nothing behind.

What an inevitable disaster this night is turning out to be, I thought.

Tanti auguri a te, someone was singing as we entered the mansion, tanti auguri a te—

At the back of the foyer, someone had brought out a birthday cake and candles. Though the celebration was happening in a private corner, they'd set up their little crew in front of a mirror, in which the guest of honor and his friends all seemed to be doubled. In spite of the size of the foyer, which was so bare it was like the place had been robbed, watching the birthday guest taking selfies in the gilded mirror felt shameful and intimate, like I'd stumbled into the wrong apartment.

In the middle of the hall was a white card table topped with an assortment of liquors and surrounded by folding chairs, all but one occupied. Clumps of people collected near the walls and by the French doors that led out onto the patio, where the music floated in. Nearly everyone was dressed better than me, in sleek jeans and thick-soled boots, or else sporting the kind of artfully oversize jackets and fresh undercuts I'd never managed to pull off.

Our group turned inward to form a little bubble. Lucio announced that he was thirsty. He wore dark brown work boots and black skinny jeans rolled up at the ankle. He wasn't much taller than me, with a short dark beard. I'd never seen pictures of him and Fede when they'd met at university—it would have been the late nineties—but he must have been attractive. Lucio looked at me strangely. Did I have eyeliner smeared across my face?

You know, I blurted out, I didn't know until today that *auguri* comes from *augury*. You say I wish, but what you really mean is that you want to read the signs—

The group had begun to drift apart, and no one answered me. They've got a case of Ichnusa, Fede said in Italian, jerking his head toward the patio. I gave him a blank stare, mortified at myself. I go with Lucio, he explained in English, thinking I hadn't understood, I'll bring you a drink. They turned and set off across the room hip to hip, a hum in the air between them. Fede bent under Lucio's arm and laughed at something he'd said. Then they ducked out through the clot of bodies and were gone.

Vincenzo and Niccolò had disappeared, and Giulia had slipped away upstairs. I found myself next to a group of musicians who had drifted over in black trousers and white shirts, as though fresh from a concert. You can't be serious, one of them was saying. He turned to me, reiterating in slurred Italian, But, sorry, can someone explain to me what cocked-up thing he's got in mind, that one? He was referring to someone, something I'd missed.

He went on, not waiting for a response. He was entertaining

when he talked and beautiful to watch. He was slender, and the top three buttons of his white shirt were undone as though he'd loosed a button with the movement of his bow. A drop of caramel-colored liquor had dried on his lapel, an endearing imperfection, as though he were too carried away by the conversation to notice. I'd always wanted to be that kind of person but had never managed it. Yes, he could be a violinist. I pictured him practicing alone in his room for hours, his delicate fingers on the neck of his instrument, stroking the bow like the quivering thigh of a future lover. The amaretto stain was not a point in favor of his being queer, though, and neither was the black plastic of his hideous sneakers. But then, he might have just come from a performance, maybe that was forgivable; and if butches could revive the mullet, after all, who could say? He was a good head taller than me, the shadow of a black beard coming in above his lips and around his chin. His nose was attractively too large for his face, his eyes downturned with long dark lashes. He declared to the group that a certain concerto had never been written for violin. Then he turned to me without warning: You went to the concert too, right?

A kernel of ice formed between my ribs. I'd hoped he would avoid gendering me. Sei andata, you went: unmistakably female.

I turned away, and the conversation continued at my back. I wished Giulia were here and, for a moment, was embarrassed for having thought she'd noticed me in the car. I remembered my smudged eyeliner. I brushed past someone at the folding table, where a bottle of Vermentino di Luni had appeared.

We've gone all out this time, someone said with a whistle. Who wants a glass?

I'd been hearing about this wine all week and about the

ruins of the city whose hills bore the grapes. It had once been dedicated to the Roman goddess of the moon.

Bathroom? I interjected, the English jumping out before I could stop it. I was directed past a tasseled curtain and across a second ballroom. People lay sprawled on the plush rug, playing cards.

Beyond, in the kitchen, Saoirse was perched on a stool at a burnished butcher block talking to a group I had never seen before, mostly in their late thirties or early forties. They picked at a mound of red-brown meat festooned with roasted garlic and pearl onions. Most of the men had shaved heads; it seemed all Italian men removed their hair once they began to lose it.

Saoirse's eyes lit up when she spotted me over the rim of her wineglass. She waved me over to the squat island of the butcher block, pouring from a bottle of red. I sipped at my glass and tuned out the murmur. The alcohol and the recessed lights, warmer than the bulbs in the foyer, made the pink of Saoirse's skin glow. Maybe I could drain my glass and escape to the bathroom before I was drawn into conversation.

You have to tell our futures, Saoirse said, squeezing my shoulder. She lowered her knife to the meat, a shiny roast cow's liver. She took a sesame cracker from a wooden bowl and laid a thin slice of flesh on top, so soft she could have spread it like cream. A translucent vein ran the length of the liver, marring the smooth organ like a spoiled fortune. Saoirse sat close enough to me that her hair clung to the static on my shirt. When she touched me, I saw the finger where she'd once worn a ring, then a vast empty house scattered with pigs, the slit throat of some large animal.

Future, she'd said. I was disturbed but emboldened by the

wine. You may see what you like, I said, but you may not like what you see.

Saoirse frowned. Riddles are against the rules, she said. See this bottle? I poured you my good Barolo.

I didn't know much about wine, but the label was old, and it was a relief to hear English again. All right, no riddles, I agreed. But can I go to the bathroom first?

Saoirse pouted but pointed me out the door. I backed out of the kitchen and trotted away down the hall, where the bulb had given out.

A single nail protruded from the plaster above the bath room sink, as though someone had stolen the mirror that had hung there. I washed my hands and wiped the damp on my jeans as I went out into the hall. In the dark, someone bumped into me and sent my glasses flying. I caught myself against the wall; there was a crunch, then the tinkle of the lens.

Scusami tanto! The person leaned down and handed me my glasses, laying an apologetic hand on my arm. Can you see without them? he asked. I should watch where I'm going.

Fa niente, I said, *it's nothing*, though it wasn't really. Without my glasses everything was a blur, and I'd just paid for new lenses before Fede and I left Berlin. I squinted: it was the beautiful musician. Up close he smelled of sweat and wine, a sour but not unpleasant smell. I flushed with heat before remembering he'd called me a woman. I felt more certain now of what I'd seen as I'd watched him speak, that image of him practicing alone in his room. There would be—or had been already—other things, which I saw jumbled when his fingers tucked the broken frames into my palm: sweat in the hair of his forearms under hot stage lights; his hand between his legs as he gripped the ceramic lip of a bathroom sink; a frantic search for an envelope he would drop on the way home, fat with a night's pay.

I really am sorry, he said again. I can pay for the lens. He must have noticed my accent; he'd switched to English. He was standing so close I could have kissed him.

I swallowed and tucked the broken glasses into my pocket. Figurati, I said, don't worry about it.

I moved away down the hall, avoiding the kitchen. Finding a back door, I went out into the night, which had turned chilly up on the mountain. Fede was smoking away from the other partygoers at the edge of the garden, his eyes red. Vincenzo rolled us a spinello, he said, embarrassed. So it was a joint; I'd thought I smelled it. I took a drag.

You never came back, I said, wincing at my nagging tone.

Fede batted his eyelashes. I got distracted, he said. I'd rarely seen him high. His hair was ruffled, his lip curled like an abashed child. I wanted to stay angry, but the smoke relaxed me, and he was too charming.

Where's Lucio?

Bringing the car. We're going to take a drive to get some air. We'll bring back bubbly.

I scuffed a pebble with my boot and sent it skittering into the grass. I switched to English. You're my ride, you know.

Don't be like that, Fede said. It's two years that I don't see Lucio.

Fede had told me once that they'd shared a bed in a mountain refuge, years and years ago. I'd intuited that something had happened, but I didn't know how far it had gone. I doubted they'd ever talked about it.

Maybe I'll make a spin too, I said. I'm fed up with this party. But I didn't move. My head was swimming from Saoirse's heavy pour of Barolo, which smoothed my Italian. Fede's joint

was almost down to the cardboard filter. Behind him, someone had tagged the old wall NO FUTURE in red spray paint,
which had splattered the flagstones.

From the overgrown garden, someone laughed. A couple
was out there, tangled in each other. We could hear them but
not see them. A wet, rhythmic sound emerged from the dark.
I thought about the beautiful musician and his open shirt.
The morning we'd left Berlin, Fede had touched the bristles
sprouting on my upper lip, his mouth a line. Today, as I was
putting on my shorts, he'd looked at the hair on my legs with
a mix of disgust and desire, as though I'd slapped him during sex. You humiliate me, I'd hissed at him, trying to keep
my voice down, you make me feel repulsive. Fede had gotten
angry, defensive. When Lucio's knock had come, Fede had
been kneeling in front of me, his forehead pressed to the black
hair on my belly, trembling with frustration. I'd thought of my
dream and wished for scattered bones, for coffee grounds, for
lines to read in viscera—anything but this terrible wait. This
is it, I'd thought, Fede has finally had enough of me. I remembered a monologue I'd had to memorize for my high school
English class, a line from some Greek tragedy: *A fearful thing
is knowledge, when to know / Helpeth no end*. Instead, Fede
looked up, weeping. I'm afraid, he'd sobbed, the whites flashing at the edges of his eyes. I'm just so afraid.

The couple in the dark let out little mewls of pleasure.
Fede and I were standing close together. He slid his hand to
my leg, ran the knuckle of his pinkie up my bare thigh to the
hem of my shorts. The day had been oppressively hot, but
up here on the mountain the breeze had a cold bite. Fede
broke eye contact, then looked back. Once, I'd told Fede that
cis masculinity seemed mostly farce, how I suspected that,
deep down, they all wanted to be caught pretending to be

something they weren't and punished for it. I thought it was just me, he'd said.

Now he leaned toward me. I kissed him, tasting beer and myrtle berries. He pressed himself against me, backing me up against the wall. I could feel him through his jeans. I took him by the belt and turned him against the wall, unbuttoning his fly. He tugged himself out, stifling a groan when I took him in my mouth, but didn't get hard. I shivered, thinking the couple might be watching from the trees. Fede opened his eyes, briefly, then shut them again. He'd stopped making any sound. Maybe he was imagining Saoirse, or he'd been turned off by looking at me. I stopped, wiping my mouth on my sleeve, and he tucked himself back into his pants. We could no longer hear the couple in the garden.

Are you okay? Fede asked.

Yeah, I said, just some dust that flew into my eye when we were in the car.

Fede crushed the spent filter on the stone. I should go, he said. Lucio will be waiting.

He went back into the main hall. I took a moment to collect myself, then followed him. All the mansion's hallways looked the same, and somehow I found myself back in the kitchen. Saoirse was still there, her group a little bigger now, though the party was beginning to thin out. Maybe there was still time to find Giulia. She might know someone with a car.

It's getting late, I said. I should get a ride back down.

You can't leave now, Saoirse replied. We're having a—boh, I can't remember the word in English—let's call it a kind of seduta spiritica, she said with a pretentious little wave of her hand. Damiano!

From the back of the kitchen, the beautiful musician entered and kicked open the door, a chain in his hands. With a tug, he led in the black ram I'd seen earlier, bleating in protest. The ram was not overly large, but very beautiful, its dark coat lustrous in the warm light. Someone had hung a bell around its neck and tied it with a sprig of glossy pomegranate leaves from the tree out front. Saoirse's entourage laughed, and the musician—Damiano—whooped and made the ram trot back and forth in front of the concrete sink.

Dai, someone said, bring the chairs. We seated ourselves around the butcher block and cleared away the liver and crackers. Damiano led the ram over to our little group, where it stood docile as a kitten, its split eyes fixed on the bloody onions on the discarded plate. Saoirse told a guy in a yellow knit hat to go and wash a bowl; Rino, she called him. Rino dumped the crackers and washed the bowl in cold water, then brought it back dripping, a little puddle at the bottom. Saoirse splashed the ram with the water, and it shivered.

A good sign, she said. The gods are amenable.

One of the men understood her English and chuckled, though Saoirse hadn't laughed. Should we join hands? he asked. I heard you should join hands for this kind of ritual.

This night is finally getting interesting, another guy said, and just as we were running out of booze.

The gods better bring the good stuff, the first man said, to an uproar of laughter.

Rino fumbled for my hand. I resigned myself to wait until the novelty of the ram wore off, when I figured I could slip away. They were all so drunk they wouldn't notice my absence. Damiano seemed to be struggling to unhook the ram's little sprig of leaves, or maybe he'd bent down to light a candle.

The ram thrashed. Saoirse and Damiano grasped it hard by the neck. Someone gasped, Che cazzo—! Damiano had slit the ram's throat. Its blood gushed into the bowl. When the animal had buckled to the ground, Saoirse set the bowl on the butcher block in front of us. No one said a word. Damiano held out the knife over the bowl of black blood. Someone had closed the door, and the rest of the party, with its music and cheery conversation, faded away. The body of the ram twitched, releasing a rattle of breath. Saoirse intoned what sounded like gibberish. Rino gripped my hand so hard my fingers went numb.

All at once the overhead light bulb popped, then shattered. We yelped. A spray of sugared glass fell over the butcher block. The bulb outside the back window of the kitchen cast a grayish glow. No one moved. There seemed to be shuffling all around us.

Is someone there? It was Rino's voice, the yellow curve of his hat floating in the half-light.

For pity's sake, Saoirse, someone whimpered.

Tell us what you see, Saoirse said. Her voice was warped like a carnival fortune teller's. Under different circumstances, I might have laughed. I could see next to nothing, but somehow I sensed Saoirse looking at me across the block. Her red hair glinted like metal.

I swallowed. I don't see anything, I said.

Damiano's knife flashed. For a second, I panicked that he was about to cut me. Then the air moved in front of my face, and sticky warmth slid along my chin. I cried out and tried to scoot back, but was held fast by Rino's hand. Damiano's shoulders blocked the light. He dipped two fingers into the blood and brought them to my mouth, slipping them between my lips, curling them over my tongue. The musk of him was hot in my nose, iron bitter in my mouth. A shiver of vertigo went through me, a rush of adrenaline that rocked like a tingling wave over my scalp. My knees buckled and my lips clamped shut around his fingers. I saw a flock of birds through a sliver of cracked glass; Lucio trembling in the front seat of Giulia's yellow Panda; gleaming bands of red, black, and yellow white.

Damiano pulled his fingers from my mouth and smeared blood down my chin and throat.

Tell us, Saoirse said, what you see.

I released a long, low croak. My heart thudded under Damiano's fingers. The girl to Rino's left let out a thin scream; someone clapped a hand over her mouth. We sat in the dark for what felt like a long time. I couldn't form words. Behind my eyes a confused flutter played, the same strange pictures repeating, Fede's pinkie on my brown thigh.

Che cazzo ci fate lì dentro? The door opened; a light came on. I looked around, dazed. The body of the black ram was nowhere to be found, the bowl of blood as clean as if it had been licked.

I stumbled up, knocking over my chair, which hit the floor with a crack. One of the legs split, a raw wound up the dark wood.

I burst out the back door and stood shivering by the bare bulb. A group spilled out of the mansion and onto the patio. They were the musicians from earlier, sans Damiano, along with a gaggle of others. They started to wander over, and I allowed myself to be absorbed. They wanted to walk down to the spring of a nearby river, which emerged from the rocky mountainside just below the garden.

I was grateful for the excuse to escape. We set off through the grass, the others with their drinks in hand. I was still shaking, a metallic film between my teeth. Keep an eye out for snakes, someone said, and I had déjà vu of the trip here. Someone giggled: You're drunk, what do you know about snakes? She shot back: I'm not that drunk! There was a rustle as someone brushed her leg and made her shriek, then peals of laughter.

Ecco il fiume! The group burst out of the trees, stumbling onto the stony bank of the river. We picked our way toward the water bubbling from the rock. I took up a gnarled branch and poked along the riverbed. The others settled nearby and began a loud, drunken conversation.

The current churned like an oil burner. Summer was already at its end. In Berlin, we would return to saucers of ice along the Spree, cold ropes of carp in the Müggelsee. In autumn the carp would be on every menu, flayed, stewed, baked whole in crusts of salt. The queers would stand outside of parties smoking in our black denim and combat boots. If Fede changed his mind about me, I'd have to find another place to live.

When we'd first met, I'd only just come out. We were staying at a friend's parents' beach house with an outdoor shower. I'd figured he was straight, a buttoned-up adjunct, but then I'd seen him sitting alone by the water braiding dried sections of seagrass, entirely absorbed in his weird weaving. Early one morning, I'd gone out to use the outdoor shower and saw him bathing. I knew I shouldn't look. He was very beautiful, lean and dark haired. He had a little tattoo of an owl on his flank, like something I'd once seen on an urn. By the time I'd noticed the thick black rat snake, it was less than a meter from Fede's foot, lapping up the water spilling over the stone. Our friend's parents had recently replaced the railing on their front steps, piling gashes of scrapped metal behind the house. I grabbed a length of iron and swung it twice in quick succession. The rod came down hard on the writhing muscle. The snake was firm as a fist; the stone was quickly stained with its blood. Fede had jumped at the clang and dropped the shower rope, and now he stood dripping, red spattered on his white shins. A shiver came over me, and I was horrified with myself. I'd swung so swiftly, so easily, like instinct.

Fede stared at me in my bloody sandals and denim cutoffs. Goose bumps rose on my legs. In his eyes lay a kind of hungry, frightened lust, as though this violence had shaken me free of something forever. That night, we fucked desperately. I'd brought my harness and my strap. It was like he wanted me to pour myself into him, to replace himself with me. When I got up after for a glass of water, I glimpsed his face in the mirror on the side table. At first I thought he was pretending to sleep. He turned his head as he studied me, first one way and then the other, as though he expected me to flicker like a hologram. He met my eye when I caught him staring, like he'd wanted to shiver with the shame of looking.

Ehi, ehi. Are you listening?

I thought he was a tree at first. He must have been pretty drunk, because he launched into his story without checking whether I was paying attention or even awake. The group nearby had quieted; I didn't know how long I'd been asleep. I couldn't remember what the guy's name was or whether we'd spoken at the party earlier. Maybe he'd been there a long time. He was telling a story about a young person he knew, someone he gendered alternately female and then male, apologizing each time. This person, he said, was in crisis, everyone knew something was wrong, but no one knew how to help. Their parents had taken away their sports bras and their hoodies and refused to let them leave the house. I realized that what I had taken for drunkenness were choked tears, that maybe he'd been on the verge of crying for some time. I don't know what to do, he went on, she won't get out of bed. When I try to talk to her she makes these terrible animal sounds. He wiped miserably at his face, taking a swig from a bottle he'd brought down from the mansion.

There was hardly a break in his story for me to get a word in. I texted Fede in desperation:

```
                                    come pick me up
                                    sto x morire qua
                                        dove cazzo 6
```

When I looked up, the guy was looking at me, expectant. He was stocky, with an unkempt beard and chunky sandals, out of which he shook loose little river pebbles.

They said you were—you know, he said. That you'd know how to help.

Look, I said, wishing my Italian were agile enough for indirectness, I don't know this person, but it seems to me they need a friend right now. I was careful to avoid pronouns, leaving the subjects off my verbs.

I don't understand all this, he whined. I don't know a cock about the terminology. I don't know the right doctors. She makes these clay figurines, lines them up on her shelves, it's the only thing she likes to do. The other day I passed by to see her, and she'd crushed them all. They were the only things that gave her joy. She smashed them to pieces.

The Barolo wriggled in my stomach like an eel. He didn't want advice. He just wanted to unburden himself. I shifted away from him on the riverbank, hoping he wouldn't touch me. I didn't want to see, didn't want to help. I didn't want to be of use or to reassure.

What's going to happen? he went on. I just want to know

he'll be okay. Now he seemed to settle on masculine pronouns, looking to me for approval but never leaving me space to interject.

He took another swallow and tried to cross his legs under him, then lost his balance. Hands flailing, he caught himself against my elbow. I flinched and shut my eyes. I expected a flash of images, like what I had seen after I'd swallowed the blood. The ritual had unlocked something in me that made me afraid.

Instead, I saw him on a snowy street in Chicago, on a semester-long study abroad. He'd known the girl, but not well. It had been his first time. He hadn't wanted to, but thought he should. He turned off the overhead light in his little room. The men in porn never showed their faces; he'd never heard more than their breath, the occasional grunt. His body was not his body but a camera, a machine. She closed her eyes, let her mouth form a little O. He wanted to feel what she felt, wanted to be looked at that way. He wanted his body too, the softness between his legs and behind his knees, to be precious as gold, so tender that a touch could leave fingerprints.

I don't know if he's going to be okay, he was saying. I don't know—he wiped his nose with his sleeve—why anyone would want to be a man.

With a pitiful sniffle, he turned to me again. A splinter of moon was setting on the horizon. My stomach was a hard knot. I could explain that none of this was a choice, sure, but I couldn't unsee the question coiled beneath the one he'd asked. There was a time I believed I'd left behind the uncertainty of my old life. New sounds came from my throat; I'd hugged my soft belly; I'd seen myself in the mirror and it had been magic, like a god had touched me. I'd thought then that it was my own fear I had to conquer, and how simple it had been, in the end, to scatter the fog of that bad dream. Now I was here alone at this miserable party, broken glasses in my pocket, my future and Fede's both ciphers, unable to face these furious tears with a glimmer of reassurance.

I'm sorry, I said in English. I don't have the words.

His face shut like a fist, and he got up and shuffled away. Dawn grayed the clouds. I stood and made my way back up the hill, using my phone to navigate the blurry garden.

Inside the mansion, people had nodded off here and there. A group was huddled in a corner playing scopa; others drained the last of the Vermentino. I wandered upstairs and into a bedroom where, to my surprise, I found Giulia sitting on a mattress in a borrowed hoodie, studying a tarot spread. It felt like a sign that she had reappeared, like time had circled back on itself and we'd been returned to the night before. Maybe I had another chance at this party, the river, everything. I squinted at the cards: the two of cups, the five of cups reversed, the hanged one.

I checked my phone: nothing from Fede.

A heat lamp in a glass case suffused the room with red light. Inside were two plump snakes coiled around each other, their scales banded with red, black, and yellow white. They probably weren't coral snakes, whose venom would have rendered them dangerous house pets. Growing up, I'd had a teacher who gave me a book about snakes, trying to help me overcome a phobia. It hadn't worked, but I'd retained much of what I'd read. The king snake, for instance, mimicked the coral's colors as a bluff, decorating itself with death as an antidote to the fear of being prey. The snakes registered me with blank eyes, extending their tongues to taste my air. I began to fear I would never get out of here, that Fede wasn't coming back. I tried to make out my reflection in the glass case but could see only the black almonds of kohl around my eyes, as though I were looking at someone else's face through the glass. I sighed, and this stranger sighed; I touched my cheek, and they touched theirs. My eyeliner was intact after all, but my forehead was crowned with a furious zit. Laughter bubbled up in me, and we laughed together, my double and I, surrendering ourselves.

I walked back downstairs and out the front of the mansion, where I sat down on the steps to wait. I took the cracked lens of my glasses out of my pocket. I looked through the broken lens at the overgrown grass, the streaked windows, the yellow pomegranates. I thought of the ram's thick blood and the crushed clay. I remembered the look on Fede's face, how we'd scrubbed the stain from the stone. My phone was dead. A flock of birds startled up from the trees. I lifted the broken lens as a car came up the gravel drive, squinting to make out how many birds there were, what kind.

WILD TO COVET

Sarah Gailey

Thetis was a wild thing washed up out of the wheat. Not the strangest gift to walk out of the field—no white bull was she—but strange enough. It was Cor Ellison's field she wandered out of at dusk, looking all of five years old but with eyes that stared right through you like she'd been to war, and Cor took her in. He always took ownership of what came out of his wheat, whether what he took wanted to be an owned thing or not, and the girl was no exception.

Young Thetis was a barefooted, tangle-haired creature, howling at the moon and curling her lip up at mittens in the winter. She'd look out the window at the hills one morning and that night be gone, back a week later with mud in her eyebrows and a cape's worth of rabbit pelts slung over one shoulder. When her baby teeth started falling out, she took to yanking the loose ones herself and tossing them into the hearth before they could fall out. She nearly cut her thumb off trying to free a wolf from a trap just off the edge of Cor's property. Not a soul doubted her when she said it was the trap that got her and not the wolf. No one had ever heard of a wolf brave enough to bite Thetis.

Thetis wasn't a domesticated creature, but she was curious about tameness, a fox nosing around a dog's kennel. She watched close when people's noses turned red and sniffly, and her eyes got catlike tracking the way folks stepped to avoid puddles. She felt fabric between the pads of her fingers and tasted anything anyone would offer her, and it was as if she'd never lived before, which it's fair enough to say she hadn't. For all that she tossed her neck at shoes and hairbrushes and handkerchiefs, she was fascinated, too, and folks said that Cor kept her knee-deep in pocket watches and pepper grinders just to keep her from running off back into the wheat for good. So long as she had something new and small and human to study, Thetis stuck close. She wandered plenty, but she always came back.

The problems started right on time. Thetis started to go from creature to girl, and it was a small town, and nearly everyone in it had eyes. She was never quite pretty, but she was something to notice even when she wasn't walking into church with a fresh-trapped pheasant in her fist. There were cornfield whispers in the way she talked, and the tilt of her head was hawk-sharp. Once her legs sprouted up coltish, looking turned to staring and staring turned to talking, and people understood without having to say so that she was going to be a woman to watch out for sooner than later.

Uncle, who lived on the farm with Cor and Thetis, got her a dress to replace her poor abused overalls. It took him only a day and a half of shouting and door slamming to convince her to wear it to church, which per Thetis's usual habits was a formality of a fight. She was softened by the beauty of the thing, by the ribbons and layers of floating linen. She walked into the service in that dress looking almost like she'd taken to the bridle—but the prettiness of it was scarred by the leaves stuck to her feet and by the barn owl that perched on her shoulder, his wicked talons drawing blood. She didn't flinch at the owl's grip.

Anyone who stared at Thetis that morning got watched right back by her and that owl just the same, and which pair of eyes was wilder no one could say.

The day came, as days come, when Thetis needed help Cor and Uncle couldn't give. It was a long time coming by most standards, twelve years to the day since she'd walked out of the wheat. She knew well enough what was happening to her. She put her knuckles to Doc Martha's front door and handed over a bucket of good ripe figs in exchange for a conversation about the blood and the pain and what to do about it.

Thetis didn't so much as flinch when Doc Martha fetched a basket of fresh eggs. She just lay down on the floor with her loose hair fanned out behind her shoulders, pulled her dress up over her ribs, and waited. Her bare toes curled on the floorboards as Doc Martha cracked the egg over her flat belly.

The yolk was double.

"You're going to birth a boy someday," Doc Martha said in a voice that didn't have congratulations anywhere in it. "Tougher'n saddle leather, a fighter and a bruiser." She pointed to a speck of blood on one of the yolks. "And a lover. That boy of yours'll live long or he'll live hard. You'll be birthin' a squaller, no two ways about it."

"I'll do no such thing," Thetis said, the whites of the egg running off her sides and dripping onto the floor. "No sons nor husband neither, thank you very kindly." She said "thank you" like it was a new kind of fruit she was tasting, one she wasn't sure was quite ripe.

"If you had a choice in the matter, I'd've said as much." Doc Martha handed Thetis a rag to clean the egg off her belly and watched the way the yolks held strong for a long time before bursting under the linen. "He'll be greater than his daddy, even. Stronger too, he'll need to be stronger. And you'll belong to that son until one of you is through," she said.

"Won't be a daddy to be greater than," Thetis told her, and her eyes blazed as cold as the river. She walked out the door as if the conversation was through, and she spent half the afternoon in the woods, slapping branches out of her face and growling at rabbits. Her fury grew as the light on the horizon died, and by the time she got home, she was a thing made of pine sap and wrath—but by then, Cor and Uncle Ellison had gotten word from Doc Martha. They lived on the outskirts of town, but it was a small enough town that even outskirts still heard rumors before the telling was finished. They were ready for her.

They fought like thunder, them saying she had best decide what kind of man she'd marry, her shouting back that she'd sooner walk into the corn without a ball of string to find her way back than do something as stupid and small and human as get married to a man. Every ear in town was turned to the sound of that fight—even the crickets held their legs apart to listen. It was a still enough night that it was hard not to hear the way Thetis started losing ground.

They told her she was too old to keep running barefoot through the woods and swimming in the river the day the ice cracked. They told her she'd eaten enough of their food and spent enough nights under their roof that she was a woman now, bound by that prophecy just as much as she was bound by the humanity she'd grown into. Even as she slammed her way through that little house screaming that she wasn't a woman and never would be, they told her it was time to grow up. Her voice began to soften with defeat as it became clear to her that they were right—for all her slamming, she couldn't outright leave.

They said it was time to start braiding her hair and wearing shoes and thinking about who she'd aim to marry. Good Christians, were Cor and Uncle, but even so they couldn't ignore Doc Martha's prophecy, and they weren't about to let Thetis ignore it either. They loved her, in their way, and so they told her to find some fellow who could manage her, someone good enough that her son being greater than him would be a boon instead of a burden. The only way out, they said, was through.

It was past midnight before the fight quieted, Thetis having shouted something about wearing the damn shoes just to shut those fool men up. The whole town heard it coming as clear as a hailstorm pounding across a fallow field, and everyone hunkered in to wait for the rooftops to start shaking.

Whether anyone liked it or not, Thetis was about to start courting.

By the time the sun came up, Moss Hetley was waiting on Cor Ellison's porch with a fistful of thistles.

Moss was everything that a town like that one wanted a man to be. He had bull-broad shoulders, and his hands were mostly knuckle. He wasn't mean enough to beat his dogs, but he wasn't kind enough to bring them inside when it snowed, either. He was more civilized than Cor and Uncle; he wrote poetry, most of it about chopping wood, and at the start of every summer he bought new shoes for the children at church. He liked being the only one who could do an impossible thing, and he liked to feel like a hero to the town, and he was as stubborn as a headache—so of course he had his hard-set black eyes fixed on Thetis to wife.

When she went out to pump water in the morning, she didn't notice him at first. Her hair was in a clumsy, half-knotted braid. She was trying to figure out how to walk in shoes, now that Cor and Uncle had made wearing them a condition of staying in their home. The way she tugged at the braid and stumbled in the shoes spoke to a choice she'd been outraged to have to make at all: she wanted to stay, so she was bending to the new rules, but she didn't have it in her to pretend to be happy about it.

She stumbled over the doorframe and nearly toppled right into Moss. When she looked up at the great wall of a man standing on her porch with his thistles in his hand, her eyes caught on the shining chain of his pocket watch. She froze, hypnotized by the links of delicate silver. He reached out and touched her chin as sweetly as if she were made of crystal, and when his finger met her skin, fury swept over her like wind through tall grass. She walked past him with her nose pointing east and her hips pointing north, and when she came back lugging the bucket of water, he was right where she'd left him.

"What are you after?" she snapped, though she surely knew.

"I'd like to speak to Cor Ellison," he rumbled. "Or Uncle, if Cor's not in."

Thetis slammed the door behind her and didn't bother telling Cor or Uncle that Moss was waiting on them. When she came back out an hour later with a hatchet over her shoulder to check the traps, the thistles were lined up in a row on the porch rail. She knocked them off with the hatchet handle, then reached down and tore her new shoes off with a snarl.

She threw them after the thistles and jumped down the porch steps, and she didn't come back until the frogs by the river were singing down the dusk.

When she got home, the thistles were in a jar on the windowsill, and her shoes were waiting by the door. She picked them up with ginger fingers like they were foul things instead of fresh leather, and she walked inside on silent feet. Cor was whittling by the fire with long, thoughtful strokes of his good knife. Thetis dropped the shoes with a clatter, slapped the three fat quail she'd trapped onto the kitchen table. She glared at Cor, but he didn't say a word until after she'd scalded the first of the birds.

"Uncle wanted to know if you need anything from the city," he said to the hunk of wood in his hand. "He's going into town to see about a suit and thought you might like a new dress for the harvest festival. Some dancing shoes."

Normally, her eyes would have lit up. Whenever Uncle went to the city, Thetis asked for small soft things, scraps of silk and rag dolls. But the fight from the night before was still in her, too fresh for her to play the old game of gifts. "Don't need a new dress. This one's fine," Thetis said in a level voice as she yanked feathers from the first quail, pulling hard enough to spatter blood across her apron. The cotton of her old dress was soft and stained; the skirt hem had been let out twice, and the sleeves ended at the elbows. It was well past a rag, but knowing Thetis, she'd patch it until it was more stitch than scrap. "And I don't need shoes."

Cor raised his eyebrows. "Watch you don't tear the skin on those birds, now," he said. Thetis frowned, not because he was correcting her but because he was right. The birds were small things, and she knew how to handle them. She plucked gentler but with her jaw clenched tight. The only sound for a time was the scrape of Cor's knife on pine and the soft pull of feathers from flesh, and the silence could almost pretend to be companionable.

Three days later, Uncle came home from the city and left a white box on Thetis's bed. The dress inside was as red as the belly of a pomegranate, and the neckline dipped low enough to show the hollow of her throat, and she didn't want to love the dress but of course she did. A wild thing was Thetis, but even wild things can covet, and she wanted to own the dress as bad as anyone wants to own something beautiful.

Under the dress was a pair of dyed-to-match shoes—little heels and gleaming buckles. She hated them even more than she loved the dress, but she knew that there was no wearing one without the other. She clutched the soft cotton of the dress to her throat. She stared at the way the light sparked off the buckles of the shoes, like the sun catching the teeth of a bear trap. For the first time in her life, she was afraid.

The harvest festival that year may as well have been renamed the Thetis festival. Everyone was mindful of the prophecy and the fight that came after it. Everyone had seen the way Thetis walked slower now that she wore shoes, and everyone knew that Moss was closing in on her like thunder after lightning. The boys in town all slicked their hair back and washed their necks and starched their collars, but it was more out of respect for Cor and Uncle than out of a sense of competition. No one much wanted to compete with Moss, and no one much wanted to face down Thetis's contempt.

She came to the festival in her red dress and her red shoes, her hair braided up tight by Doc Martha's unforgiving fingers.

Everyone who asked her to dance did it with the kind of polite you'd show a flat-eared cat, and she said "No thank you" until the only person left standing near to her was Moss.

The firelight caught on the chain of his pocket watch. Thetis worked hard not to stare.

"Let's dance, Thetis," he said, holding out a hand like the deed was already done. She made to stalk off toward the corn, but he snatched her arm sparrow-quick. Even though everyone nearby was making a show of not staring, there wasn't a breath that didn't catch when he laid his hand on that girl. Thetis whipped around, her finger under Moss's nose like a nocked arrow, and twisted up her lip to give him her opinion of his hand on her elbow. But before she could spit hell at him, he spun her in a wide circle. The fiddle players caught on before Thetis did. She stumbled, trying to keep her feet under her, and the music turned it into dancing.

There was no escaping, so she danced with Moss. Her smile was a rattling tail. Cor and Uncle watched with folded arms as she let the man lead her in one dance and then another. Uncle's face was still; Cor's was more than a little sad. It was three dances before anyone else was brave enough to join in the dancing. Thetis snarled like a mountain cat, but Moss held her tight and swung her high and dipped her low, and by the end of the night, the thing had been decided. Moss had held on to the unholdable girl.

The last song ended. Moss dug into his pocket, and from its depths he excavated a dull gold ring. It shone like an apple in the firelight. Thetis couldn't hide her fascination with the thing—it was the smallest beautiful thing she'd yet seen. She stared at it, slump-shouldered and hollow-cheeked and wanting.

He didn't drop to a knee, just held the ring out and waited. Thetis gave her hand over like a woman dreaming, her arm lifting slow, her eyes unblinking as she watched the light play over the gold. It wasn't until Moss slid the thing onto her finger that she startled, but by then it was too late. The ring fit perfect, and everyone clapped while Moss pressed his lips to her cheek, and Thetis was well and truly trapped.

They were married before Christmas. Thetis wore a white dress from the city. White satin shoes, too, the third pair of shoes she'd ever worn in her life, and she didn't stumble in them even once. It was a good wedding with good food and good music, and the bride didn't look at the groom at all, not even when she made the vow.

She had never been one to waste time once she'd decided on a project, and so by the time the first fiddleheads were poking through the snow, her belly was soft and her face was round and everyone was whispering that the two-yolk son was on the way. She answered their congratulations with the same grim satisfaction she'd shown after slaughtering her first rooster. "Only way to get a kettle boiling's by lighting a fire under it," she'd say, looking at the ring on her finger with increasing distaste.

Neighbors gave her a rattle and a pair of impossibly small shoes and a long white christening gown and knitting needles and an embroidery kit. She was tired enough for the last half of the pregnancy that she learned to sit by the hearth and make use of the latter two. She sent Uncle to the city for thimbles and colored thread and kitten-soft yarn. She bared her teeth at Moss when he tried to press his ear to her navel to hear the baby's heartbeat, and she still threw her shoes into the garden. But she also sewed buttons onto miniature shirts, and the fury in her frown gentled when she smoothed her fingers over the stitches.

She seemed so close to settled that it was almost a surprise that next January when Moss ran into town, wild-haired, chasing after his missing wife. He ran from the post office to the grocery to the barbershop, but it wasn't until he got to the dentist's that he found someone who had seen Thetis that day. The postman, who was getting his bad tooth looked at, said that he'd seen her. He'd almost forgotten about it, with the news about the war and the draft being all anyone wanted to talk about, but he'd seen her all right. She was walking into the wheat that morning, he said, both hands braced on the small of her back, her belly set out in front of her like the prow of a ship. He told Moss that he saw her walk into the field and thought nothing of it, that wheat being on Cor Ellison's land and all.

"Was she wearing her shoes?" Moss asked, his fists in the postman's shirtfront, and when the man shook his head Moss turned and ran. Everyone who'd seen him run into town saw him run out, faster than a hare with a hawk over his shoulder. He didn't stop running until he reached the wheat.

But of course he was too late—by the time he got to the wheat, Thetis was staggering out of it with blood soaking her legs and a baby at her breast. She swept past Moss in her bare feet and her ruined skirt, walked up the steps of Cor and Uncle's house, and let herself in. Moss followed her bloody footprints inside and found her sitting on Cor's whittling stool by the hearth, her leather shoes in front of her and the baby asleep with her nipple still in his mouth. The room smelled like iron and clean sweat. Moss stood with his hands braced on the doorframe, and Thetis finally looked at him. Her gaze was flat and final; she had gotten what she needed from the man she'd allowed to marry her. She didn't so much as blink as she slid her bloody feet into the shoes she hated.

They named the baby Esau, and with that they renamed her Esau's Momma. She stopped being Thetis, when anyone talked about her—she had never been Moss's Wife, but she was sure as hell Esau's Momma. He was a strong boy with a swagger of red curls that nothing could settle. He had fists like his father and a holler like his mother, and Moss shone bright with pride.

Esau's Momma was something different from proud. Her mouth tightened whenever someone called her by her new name. She didn't look at her son with warmth, but she wasn't quite cool, either. She stroked the newborn-down above his ears and studied his fast-growing fingernails. She watched him sleep, her eyes bright as a cat's. She loved him the way a bear loves its trap-caught paw.

He needed her, and whether she liked it or not, she needed him right back.

The harvest festival that year marked two years since Moss made Thetis dance. She was wearing that same red dress, the one Moss had captured her in. The red shoes, too, the dancing ones, although Moss knew better than to ask her to dance. She kept Esau close in a sling made of white linen with orange blossoms embroidered along the edges in her wide, clumsy stitches. They stood by the bonfire drinking cider, a tidy family to look at them. Moss rested his hand on the small of her back. She shivered away like oil pearling on a hot pan.

Moss didn't notice her shudder, of course, because he wasn't looking at her. He was talking to somebody about the way the war would change the price of alfalfa and barley. Esau was craning his neck out of his sling, watching his daddy with the eyes of a child who's just starting to recognize who his people are. He was watching the way Moss's watch chain glinted in the flickering firelight, hypnotized in that way babies get.

Esau's Momma was watching the fire.

Her shoulders were set, and anyone who'd been thinking or looking close enough could have seen what was coming, but nobody was watching Esau's Momma because Moss had his hand on her back. His hand on her back might as well have been a latch on a storm door, as far as any of them were concerned. So they didn't watch, and they didn't see the way her fingers twitched at the edge of the baby's sling.

The moment came when his hand left her back, and when it did, Esau's Momma moved fast as a snakebite. She whipped the baby out of the sling, both his legs in one of her strong hands. She swung him toward the fire like she was aiming a horseshoe at a post, and she let go at the top of the arc and Esau flew—but Moss reached out and snatched the boy from the smoke before anyone could finish gasping.

"You're the one's always talking about the prophecy," Esau's Momma spat, firelight glinting off her teeth. "The prophecy says he needs to be strong. I'll burn the weakness out of him; you see if I don't."

Moss held the squalling boy close, patting his back and frowning like this wasn't the first time and he knew it wouldn't be the last. "The prophecy says he can live long or he can live hard," he said quietly. "You try this way to turn him into a man who's strong, you and I both know which of those it'll be." His brows drew down into a pleading kind of frown. "He could live long. We could raise him up into a man who lives long."

Esau's Momma just stalked away into the night, the baby's

sling loose around her belly. She didn't come back to the festival that night. Later that week the boy who milked cows for Barrow the dairy farmer was telling anyone who'd listen that he saw Esau's Momma walk out of the cornfield at dawn, still wearing her dancing shoes. The next day, she was back in town with Esau in his orange-blossom sling, buying butter for biscuits the same as ever, murmuring to the boy in a singsong voice about the shape of choosing. When she went to pay for the butter, the grocer asked if she'd donate a dollar to send cigarettes to the troops. Then he asked how the baby was coming up.

She nodded and laid a hand on Esau's head. "He's weak now," she said, stroking his hair with her fingertips. "But he's going to be strong."

She finally got her way the day before the river finished freezing over. There was slush on the surface, but the water was still moving, cold as death and twice as fast. She left Cor and Uncle's house, left them talking with Moss about the way the draft was picking up. She slipped away quiet, and she walked to the water with the boy asleep in her arms. Her steps were quick and sure, even though she still hadn't quite got the hang of those damned leather shoes. Moss and Cor and Uncle ran hard when they noticed she was gone, but they were far enough behind to have to shout after her, and she was faster than they could catch up to.

She didn't look over her shoulder as the men ran at her. She just grabbed Esau by the ankle, and before he could so much as wake up crying, she'd flipped him upside down and dunked him. She could have let him go—he would have died all the same, him just being so many months old—but she held him tight, the skin of her hand turning white in the water. She stood with her feet rooted to the riverbank, and it wasn't until Moss reached her that she finally pulled the baby out. He wasn't quite blue, but he sure wasn't pink, either, and he was still as a stone.

Cor and Uncle stumbled up behind Moss, panting hard, hands braced on their thighs, but Esau's Momma didn't spare them a glance. She shoved that baby into her dress next to her skin and whapped his back hard with a clenched fist, and he choked up water and caterwauled like he'd just learned what screaming was for, and for the first time in a little over two years, Esau's Momma smiled.

"He'll be good and strong," she said. "That's all the weakness washed away, near about. Good as I can get it, given what his daddy's made of." And with that, she walked right past those men who'd decided she would have that baby.

For weeks after, the boy had a purple ring around his ankle in the shape of her fingers. Folks liked to say that was the place the life stayed in Esau when his momma tried to kill him dead. Esau's Momma took to ignoring her husband and watching her son, and some of her fury seemed to smooth down into patience. She had learned something new that day by the river, something small and human: she had learned to wait for what she wanted.

Esau was a scrapper in the schoolyard—half in the way kids are, half because every other child his age had heard about the prophecy and about his momma drowning the weakness out of him. His eyes blacked and healed like the turning of the moon. It was all friendly enough, the way he and his friends tossed around playing soldiers, and if the occasional fight got hostile—well, Esau ended those fights. He hung on to the teeth that got knocked out against other kids' knuckles, and his momma tossed them into the hearth, saying that if she didn't, they'd wind up sown in the fallow field and an army would spring up tougher than any that had ever marched before. The boy was bold and brave and tougher than saddle leather, just like Doc Martha said he'd be. There was no weakness left anywhere in him.

Except that he was always bringing things home. Half-starved kittens abandoned in the alfalfa by their mothers, and ducks with their wings broken, and once a mountain cat with the broken bottom of a soda bottle stuck in her paw. It wasn't quite a weakness, the way he brought things home. Just a fondness, and softer-hearted than his momma thought he'd turn out. She helped him mind the broken things he brought her, and she worked to make sure he grew up with the right kind of balance. Not too tender, but not so hard that he'd wind up the sort of broken man who stays home so he can feel bigger than the folks he bullies, either.

She let the kittens suckle on milk-soaked rags while she spun Esau stories of war and courage. She set the ducks' wings and fed them corn, and she murmured to Esau about the way battle makes a man strong. She eased glass out of the growling mountain cat's paw, occasionally running her fingers across the fur between the cat's ears, and she taught the boy the meaning of glory.

She watched him as close as she had when he was new and small, and so she wasn't surprised when sixteen-year-old Esau brought a bigger broken thing home. A boy from school by the name of Pistol, which wasn't his Christian name, but then Moss wasn't Moss's Christian name either and nobody gave him a second word about it. Esau and Pistol were stuck together close as two yolks in the same shell. Esau told his momma in a low voice that Pistol's pa had come home from the war different, drunk and mean and broken, and could Pistol stay the night?

Esau's Momma nodded in that quiet way she'd taken to, and she watched the way Esau rested a hand on Pistol's shoulder, and she didn't say a word when they walked out into the woods together that night. She just left the front door unlatched and turned down Esau's bed, and the next morning she put an extra plate on the table.

It was only three days before Pistol's pa showed up on Esau's Momma's doorstep, pounding on the pine with a clumsy fist. Esau's Momma laid a hand on Moss's shoulder, folded her napkin on the table, and answered the knock at the door. Pistol's pa's eyes were swimming, and he smelled like poison.

Esau's Momma stood in the doorframe and listened to the liquor-brave man as he told her all of what he thought of her. And then she stepped out into the night, closing the door behind her, and Pistol's pa didn't say anything more.

The three men in the house finished their meal in the heavy kind of silence that wells up between people who are trying their best to listen for what might be happening just out of earshot. They cleared the supper things—Moss wiped down the scarred wood of the table, and Pistol took the scraps to the yard, and if he saw what was happening out there, he didn't say. Esau scrubbed the plates and dried them and put them away. None of them dared breathe too loud. There wasn't a sound to be heard outside of the men trying to be quiet.

Esau's Momma didn't come back into the house until Moss had settled by the hearth with his polishing rag and his watch chain. He stood as she walked in, but she offered no explanations as to where she had been or what she had been doing.

She kissed Esau's red hair, and she gave Pistol's shoulder a squeeze. She sat on her stool near the fire, put a hand into her pocket, and tossed something into the hearth that clattered against the stone. She reached down to wipe something off the toe of her leather shoe. She smiled.

Then Esau's Momma picked up her sewing and began mending one of Moss's old shirts. She announced that Pistol would be staying in Esau's room from then on, and he'd better go on and get washed up for bed. Her tone did not invite argument, so they did as she said. The boys stayed up late that night in Esau's bedroom. They whispered in the dark with their noses pressed together and their breath on each other's lips, telling each other that those were surely pebbles she'd tossed into the fire. Surely pebbles, for the question of where she would have gotten a whole pocketful of teeth was a question the boys could not make themselves ask.

Esau's Momma stayed up late, too, sewing buttons until the fire had died and the mending was done.

With three men around her dinner table—five if Cor and Uncle decided to visit, which they did every few nights— Esau's Momma went even quieter than she'd been since the night Moss made her dance. No more than a few words a day out of her, and those always to voice a worry about the war that wouldn't end. It was one of those wars that doesn't seem to have an aim to it, and no one could quite remember what had caused the whole mess to start up anyhow. It was a thing for women to quietly worry about, and so Esau's Momma did just that. She quietly worried.

But not too quietly.

She served up roasted grouse and mentioned that there weren't enough brave soldiers leading the fight for the good of the nation, and then she sat back and let the men talk about what they'd do different if they were in charge. She spooned spring peas from a bowl onto five plates and fretted that they just didn't make heroes like they used to, and then she went to the kitchen for fresh bread while Pistol and Esau argued about which of them would make a braver soldier. She butchered a chicken while Cor whittled into a scrap bucket beside her fireplace, and she whispered to Pistol about what a fine marksman he'd make, and didn't they need boys like that in battle? And then she walked to the yard with fistfuls of bones to feed Moss's dogs, and she didn't bother to listen to what Pistol said next because she knew exactly what he was thinking.

It wasn't a shock to Moss or Cor or Uncle when the boys came home one day with their hair short and new green duffels over their shoulders. Moss slapped each of them on the shoulder and said he was proud, and Uncle poured good brown whiskey, and Cor beamed, damp-eyed. When Esau's Momma walked in from feeding the hens, she froze in the doorway, staring at the dog tags around Esau's neck. She half reached for the shining tags, a smile spreading across her face, and when her fingers touched the metal she burst into half-hysterical laughter. Choking on the words, she shook her head and said she'd known the day would come when he'd leave her, but she hadn't known it would come so soon. Even as tears began to stream down her cheeks, she laughed like she couldn't stop.

Eventually, Moss convinced her to drink a measure of whiskey down, and her eyes drifted shut. They put a blanket over her, one she'd knitted from kitten-soft yarn. She slept hard, with her hair braided and her shoes on and Esau's old baby sling clutched in her fist. Every so often, she'd murmur in her sleep, but the only words the men could make out were "hero" and "freedom" and "mine."

The telegram about Pistol came home not a year later. Esau's Momma answered the door, her hands leaving flour streaks on her apron, and she listened to the news that Pistol had caught a bullet with his belly. Her eyes were dry as she took the telegram from the man on her doorstep. She left it on the foot of Esau's bed, and then she went back into her kitchen to finish cutting the biscuits for that night's supper.

Over the next year, she stacked every letter from Esau that came home on top of that telegram—some opened, some not. She nodded when folks in town told her how much they admired her son's courage, when they told her how proud she must be to be Esau's Momma. "What good that boy's done you," they'd say. "Settled you right on down."

Esau's Momma would nod, and she would finish buying milk or honey or bread or roses, and she would walk on home in her good leather shoes with her shoulders low and her teeth dug into the soft meat of her cheek. She would bake pies and split wood and scrub the floors, and she would wait.

Two years after Esau and Pistol went to war—a little more than a year since Pistol's telegram came home—Moss came running into town, tearing through the shops like he hadn't since the day his boy was born. Not a soul could tell him where Esau's Momma was, and not a blessed one of them asked Moss why he was looking for her. They didn't need to ask—the big man was clutching a crumpled piece of paper in one hand, and his eyes were full of the wild fury of a man who never learned how to cry. He ran into the post office and nearly knocked down Cor, who wasn't young enough to get back up on his own anymore. Cor looked at his son-in-law's eyes and at the telegram in his fist, and said the words no one had the courage to say.

"Have you checked the wheat?"

When the two men got to the wheat field, she was waiting for them, her fists full of thistles and her mouth curved like a cat's claw. She wore her old red dress and her dancing shoes, and Moss and Cor noticed two things in the same moment. When they told each other the story later, over whiskey and in low voices, neither man could say which was more frightening: the barn owl digging its talons into her shoulder, or the fact that with that red dress on, they could see how she hadn't aged a minute since the first night she wore it.

"Come home," Moss said. "You gotta come home. It's Esau." He held out the telegram like it was a half-starved kitten she could nurse back to health.

"I know it's Esau," she said. Her voice was a pat of butter melting over fresh-cut bread. "Did they tell you he was a hero? He was surely a hero. Tell me about how he died a hero, Moss." The barn owl fidgeted on her shoulder, and the dark red of the dress got a little darker where it held tight to her skin.

"Come on home, now," Cor said. "You gotta help us make the arrangements. It's only right."

"Why is it only right?" she asked, and the curl of her smile sharpened.

"Well, it's—it's only right," Moss stammered, looking down at the telegram in his hand. "You gotta help us lay him to rest." When she didn't answer, his shoulders dropped. "Please," he whispered, and his hand rose slowly to his pocket.

Thetis's eyes tracked the movement. Her smile faded as Moss withdrew his pocket watch. He held it out to her, the chain bright in the sunlight. He hadn't let tarnish touch it, not since the day he'd stood on her front porch.

"Please," he said again.

Thetis took a step forward. The men flinched at the sound of her heels digging into the soil. Her eyes glinted with old firelight. "I'll come home," she said, her voice as tense a warning as the crest of a cat's spine. "But not for that. I've had enough gifts. I've had enough of *made things*."

"What, then?" he asked, his voice cracking with the attempt at courage.

Only the thistles were between them, purple and bright, the barbed stems digging deep into the meat of Thetis's palms. They couldn't possibly have been the same thistles as the ones Moss had brought to her so many years before, the gift he'd left on her front porch to declare his intention to trap her.

They couldn't have been the same ones, and yet Moss's eyes couldn't find a difference between these and those.

"Eat them," Thetis said. Cor started to speak, started to say that enough was enough, but Thetis silenced him with a raised index finger that carried the authority of a mother who has silenced her fair share of excuses from the mouths of children. "Eat them, and I'll come home with you, Moss. Eat them, and I'll bury that child for you. I'll dig his grave with my own two hands."

Moss took a single thistle from her, the first of the seven in her grip. He raised it to his mouth, looking at her as though he was waiting for her to laugh and say it had been a joke. Her face remained as still as a midwinter river.

The soft purple petals brushed the back of Moss's tongue,

and his teeth closed over the sharpest thorns on the thistle's bud. He made a sound like the kind of dog he would have called it a mercy to shoot. Saliva began to well between his lips as he chewed, his jaw working once and then twice, slow and reluctant as a person forcing her feet into her first pair of shoes. His mouth went pink with a froth of blood and thistle milk, and Thetis watched it run down his chin with the same bright interest she'd once brought to the sight of glass beads and copper pennies.

Moss managed to chew four times before he choked on blood and thorns, and with an urgent, visceral coiling of his throat and back, he failed. He spat and gagged and wept. Pulp and petals and blood-tipped barbs fell to the dirt at Thetis's feet. Moss braced his hands on his knees, his breath coming ragged, his eyes desperate and darting.

"I can't do it, Thetis," he said. "Ask for something else."

Thetis dropped the remaining six thistles between them.

She laid a finger on Moss's chin, as sweetly as if it were made of crystal, and with terrible patience she lifted it until he was standing upright again. His face was flushed and wet, his shirt stained at the collar with the mess of his weakness. She waited until he was brave enough to look into her eyes. "The only wildness I've ever asked of you," she said, tinting the words with a cruel measure of disappointment.

"P-please," he stammered, the word soft with pain as he tried to speak around the raw bleeding thing that was his tongue. "You're Esau's Momma."

"Esau's Momma was a name you made me wear," she said.

"Haven't I been kind to you?" His voice carried the same pleading note that it had when he'd asked why Esau couldn't turn into the kind of boy who would live long.

"Was any of this kindness?" She let his chin go, and she reached down to undo the buckle of one red shoe. "Was any of this for me?"

"You're still his momma," Cor growled, making as if to step in strong where Moss had shown himself soft. He went to take her elbow, but the owl turned its great eyes on him and he froze like a mouse running across the snow. He swallowed hard. She loosed the buckle of her other shoe and slid it off her foot. She stood with her bare feet in the earth, curled her toes into the loam.

"I don't belong to that word anymore. Esau's dead," she said, the word *dead* sweet as a promise, and she laid her red dancing shoes on top of the paper in Cor's hand. One shoe nearly fell, but he caught it before it hit the ground. "And Esau's Momma is, too."

And with that, Thetis returned to the field. She walked away from the men who'd caught her. For the rest of their days, they'd remember the sight of her: the soles of her feet pressing into the earth, the triumphant curve of her back, the set of her shoulders. She vanished into the wheat, and she left them behind with nothing more than a torn telegram, a pair of old dancing shoes, and a hearth full of teeth.

PESCADA

Juliana Spink Mills

Penelope arrived on a Thursday afternoon. Lucila was on the mainland for a doctor's appointment, and the first she heard of it was on the ferry home.

"'That store? The empty one? You know, Cila, the one that belonged to the man who did the sunset tapestries," her husband, Mariano, said, his voice insubstantial over the cell phone as the wind did its best to snatch the words away.

"What about it?" Her hair whipped free from her ponytail, fanning across her face, and she spat the dark strands out of her mouth in annoyance. In the afternoon sunshine, Ilha Pequena glowed green upon the dark blue waves of Brazil's Atlantic coast. If she squinted, she could just make out the harbor where her brother moored his growing fleet of fishing boats.

"Someone bought it. They arrived today; the sale sign already went down. I heard it's another artist."

"That's good, right?" she answered. "The tourists, they love that stuff." The town center was full of colorful shops selling T-shirts, beachwear, and souvenirs. But the artists were the ones who had placed Ilha Pequena on the map. The artists had brought the tourists; the restaurants and hotels had followed. Art encouraged trade, and that was great for the booming business that Cila's brother, Ulisses, had inherited from their father, Laerte, and *his* father before him.

The island had come a long way since their grandfather's time, when he had fished the depths with a single boat. Back then, life was not easy, but it was simple as the ebb and flow of the tides. The velhas who gathered in the town square always talked about the old days, and so did their sun-shriveled husbands down by the wharf, playing games of dominoes that never seemed to end.

Cila liked this progress that the elders pretended to hate. She liked satellite TV and nice clothes and the fancy supermarket at the edge of town. She liked owning a car. Progress had been kind to her family, and life was sweet as guava jam. But some days, when her mother's ghost pressed too hard against her bones and the outer layer she showed the world became a prison wall too thick to bear, Cila secretly missed the old days, too.

The ferry turned to dock, and she saw Mariano waiting, one hand raised in greeting. She pocketed her cell phone and tidied her windswept hair, yanking back the strands until she felt her scalp tighten under her fingertips. With nothing left to do, she crossed her arms and waited for land's approach.

The new store was in the arts quarter, just outside the center with its gaudy tourist shops. The sign read CIRCE in plain black lettering. Cila had already heard the gossip. The owner was a potter, a perpetually clay-streaked woman with wild curls and lips that hid a secret smile. A small moving truck had brought Penelope's things: bags of wet clay, boxes stamped FRAGILE, an electric pottery wheel, a vast kiln, and a single battered suitcase.

Cila entered the store to the sound of a tinkling bell. It was empty, but she could hear the hum of the electric wheel from somewhere at the back. She looked around. To one side were the bread-and-butter pieces. Mugs and bowls, plates and jugs. Serviceable vases. Cila could just imagine the tourists. "Ideal for wildflowers," they would say. "So quaint! Maybe for the terrace or the guest bedroom?" The cool blue and green glazes and the earthier background tones were satisfyingly pretty, yet perfectly safe.

The other side of the store was a gallery. Ceramic fish of all sorts swam and leaped in the currents created by shadow and light. Here, an entire school of needlefish, threaded with wire and hanging from driftwood. There, a sharp-toothed cação, the diminutive shark that hunted the local waters. A bloated baiacu, a poisonous puffer fish, shared shelf space with delicate angelfish and blue-shelled rock crabs. This, Cila suspected, was Penelope's truth. These lovely yet uncomfortable creations were not safe like mugs and plates. Like the ocean that inspired them, they teased and threatened. She guessed that most of the tourists moved quickly back to the cautious dinnerware and vases.

But the discerning ones bought Penelope's fish, and her fame began to spread.

The second time that Cila visited Circe, she finally met Penelope.

"Your fish," she asked the artist, "have you been making them a long time?"

Penelope's beautiful lips twisted briefly, in sadness or hunger, Cila couldn't quite tell. "Too long."

"Those ones are different." Cila stared at a collection of sea creatures placed high on the far wall, out of reach but in plain sight, like the mounted heads of hunting trophies. They were somehow *more* than the other fish: beautiful, yet darker and more visceral.

"Those are not for sale." This time, Penelope's expression was definitely one of grief. "They were . . . a mistake. I keep them as a warning."

Cila shivered and turned away from the disturbing trophy fish. "How strong are your plates? I have two little ones at home, they break a lot of stuff."

Grief slipped away, turned to silent amusement. Or the promise of amusement, trapped in the curve of those unsmiling lips. "Pretty strong. They're stoneware; it's a process where you fire the clay at high temperatures. It makes it quite durable. Even the pieces that come out cracked are tough. I don't sell those, of course; I use them myself. You can barely see the cracks once they're under the glaze. Do you know what glaze is?"

Cila nodded. She'd taken the children for pottery lessons once, during a cold and rainy winter. "There was another ceramic store on the island, about a year ago. She wasn't as good as you. She left."

"And I arrived." Now Penelope's amusement was palpable. "Did you want to see some plates?"

"Not today. But I'll take a business card, if you have one. It's for my brother. He needs something for his office, something to give it life." Even though part of her hated the fish, Cila could not deny they were lovely. Penelope's ferocious art was the perfect foil to Ulisses's boring chrome-and-leather chairs, the modern glass desk, and the black-tiled floors he had chosen for his business in an attempt at sophistication.

Cila took the card, thanked the artist, and fled from the gaze of too many ceramic eyes, back to her safe home and kitchen. Back to where she could keep on being stoneware under the stifling presence of her mother's memory, with a nice bright glaze to cover up any secret cracks that lay below the surface.

Cila gave Ulisses the business card. He paid a visit to Circe and walked out with a crimson snapper for his office and an obsession in his heart.

Ulisses was courting. That was the truth of it, as far as Cila could tell. It wasn't dating, this thing he had with Penelope; it was so much more. He wanted her, and he wanted her to be *his*.

It became a familiar litany at their daily breakfast. Mariano, who handled the boats and the seafaring part of the business, always headed out before dawn. Ulisses, who ran the corporate side of things and kept office hours, started later, so he'd fallen into the habit of stopping by after the children left for school to eat with his younger sister.

"Penelope's incredible," he said, spreading margarine on a fresh bread roll and reaching for the salty white Minas cheese. Cila's mouth was a hard, thin line, but she tended to her brother anyway, serving black coffee and passing him the milk and sugar. He glanced up and caught her displeasure. "Don't be that way, maninha." Little sister. The nickname, dusty as the faded memory of childhood, was meant to soften. Instead, she could feel herself grow rigid.

"I don't like her," Cila insisted. It was a lie. She liked Penelope just fine. She just didn't want her for Ulisses. Penelope was Circe, was hands specked with clay and a secret smile that no one could quite coax from her lips. She was magic carved from earth and fire and the water that inspired it, served up on the altar of her plain white shop walls. She was freedom personified, and the part of Cila that she kept buried needed desperately for Penelope to remain that way, wild and free.

"Not this again." Ulisses sipped from his mug, dismissive. "Do you even *know* why you don't like her?"

Because she makes me uneasy. Because I like that she makes me uneasy. It was complicated and messy, and of course Cila couldn't voice those thoughts out loud. Instead, she straightened, hands on hips echoing her long-buried mother. "Now, listen to me, Uli. You're so smart, you built your company from almost nothing, and yet you can't see that this woman is not for you. She doesn't fit. She's not like you and me. She'll carve out your heart, and then she'll cast it in clay and nail it to the wall with the rest of her fish."

She leaned in, hands gripping the edge of the table so hard her knuckles whitened. She breathed in coffee and cheese and the sticky smell of the doce de leite she preferred on her own bread. Taking courage from familiarity, she plunged on. "Everyone is saying it—there's sorcery in those fish of hers."

Her brother burst out laughing. "Oh, Cila. Oh, that's too good. Now my beloved is some sort of witch? Holy Mary, you're too funny."

The laughter faded, and when he next looked her in the

eye, he was all knife-edge and steel. This, too, was from their mother. They stared at each other, neither yielding, neither bending, until Cila turned away. "Don't say I didn't warn you."

He went to work. She got on with her day. Next morning, no one mentioned Penelope. And so it went for two weeks. Until one Wednesday, Ulisses missed breakfast. He came in so late it was almost noon, joining Cila as she stood by the stove frying breaded fish fillets for the children's lunch.

She startled at the despondency he wore like an oil slick smothering his usual vociferous vitality. He sat, slumping over the kitchen table, head in his hands. "It's over."

"What is?" She flipped the fillets deftly in the hissing pan, patting down errant bread crumbs with a lime-green spatula.

"Penelope. She broke up with me. She says it's not me, that she doesn't want anyone in her life, but I don't know . . . Am I not enough?"

Cila's heart leaped. She took her time to answer, to school her face and get her feelings under control. She turned off the heat and transferred the fish to a waiting plate. She popped it in the oven to keep warm and joined her brother at the table. "I'm sorry. I know how much you like her."

But she didn't feel sorry. Instead, she was relieved. She told herself it was only because she didn't want Ulisses to bring this woman into her life—this secretive, unbridled woman who made Cila's day-to-day seem small and petty, revealing the hidden fissures that she had so carefully covered. The falsehood sat heavy in her stomach, but she ignored it and let her treacherous mouth run free.

"Let her go if she's not interested. You remember what Dad always said, se o mar não está pra peixe . . ." She could almost hear Laerte's deep voice. *If the sea is not right for fish, there is nothing you can do but wait for the tide to change.* He was a true son of the waves, in a way that Ulisses, with his growing empire, had never been. Would never be.

"Cila." Ulisses took her hand, gripping so tight it almost hurt. "I can't, Cila. She's the one. I want to marry her." A cunning expression stole across his face, ruthless and determined. He released her, sitting back. "I *will* marry her."

He rushed off, sudden as the late-afternoon squalls that blew in from the ocean. Cila was left behind, without words. Her lips tightened, and in the dark glass of the oven door she looked like a distorted version of her sharp, sour mother. They were both of them their mother, she and Ulisses, both steel and lemons and not enough of the good salt spray to either of them.

That afternoon, she dropped the children off with her mother-in-law and made her way to the arts quarter with its narrow cobblestone lanes and trailing strands of bougainvillea. The tangle of streets curved around the head of the bay between the main town beach and the harbor, full of brightly colored fishing boats moored to bobbing buoys. In the distance, cliffs marked the end of the town's embrace.

On a blue day, it was a postcard in the making. Now, clouds hung heavy in the sky. Out at sea, it was already raining.

At Circe, Cila hesitated by the window. Most of the space was taken up by displays of mugs and bowls, but on the right, an imposing stingray held court, lording over everything else. She frowned at the stingray and her reflection frowned back, her mouth tight and cross. She forced herself to relax and look pleasant, smoothing out the smart blouse and skirt she'd chosen for the expedition. She opened the door and walked in.

At the tinkle of the bell, Penelope called out. "Be with you in a moment!"

But Cila didn't want to stay there, with cursed fish that swam in the shadows, fierce and hungry. She pushed through a curtain of wooden beads that clacked in accusation and found Penelope in her studio.

Here, the artist was in her element. Like Cila's father upon the waves. Like her husband, Mariano, at the bar, spinning tales like spiderwebs. Like Ulisses when his mind was made up, uncompromising as a summer gale. Crowded shelves held Penelope's creations in different stages of readiness. Some were still dark and damp, others the pale gray of dry yet unbaked clay. On the lowest shelf were the once-fired pieces, a light biscuit brown all over. A glass cabinet held a multitude of powders that Cila knew would turn to rich color when they were painted on and set in the blazing heat of the kiln. Tools lay jumbled and discarded on work surfaces, and the potter's wheel sat in a corner.

Penelope wasn't at the wheel, though. Instead, she stood by a battered wooden table, working on a featureless lump. She had a metal scraper in one hand, peeling off long ribbons of wet clay. It reminded Cila of her childhood, of stripping scales and skin from the fish her father sold at market.

"What are you making?" she asked, buying time. Outside the window, the clouds were the same dark shade as the clay.

Penelope tucked back a loose curl that had come free from her bun. She left behind a damp streak on her forehead that Cila itched to clean. The impulse to touch was so strong that she twined her hands together in fear that she might reach out and swipe her thumb across warm brown skin.

"There, see?" Penelope pointed. A picture was taped to the wall, torn from a magazine. It was a monster of a beast, photographed underwater and facing the camera so that its body was tucked away behind it. It looked like a gargoyle or a carnival mask—the old-fashioned kind made not for joy but to scare away the demons that haunt the night. "Pirarucu, from the Amazon," Penelope said, her voice as rich as caramel. "A giant air-breathing fish. It has teeth on its tongue and uses it to crush prey. People up there, they use the dried tongues to grate seeds."

Cila stared at the featureless clay. Soon, under Penelope's skillful fingers, it would take shape and become that horrifying thing, the pirarucu. She had no doubt it would be beautiful, that terrifying beauty that all the fish in Circe wore like armor. "Is it true?" she asked, the words ripped from her guts unbidden. "Your fish. Are they made of magic?"

One corner of Penelope's lips ticked upward, almost releasing that secret smile of hers. "This one? Perhaps. After all, the magic is in each of us. In how we see the world, and in the way the world looks back."

"And the others, the ones you won't sell?" The ones on what Cila couldn't help calling the trophy wall in her mind.

Penelope shrugged. "Believe what you will. They won't hurt you, if that's what you're worried about. They'll never hurt anyone ever again."

Cila wasn't reassured. She suspected Penelope hadn't meant to set her at ease. Everything about the woman was a provocation, blood in the water for sharks. It frightened her, how Penelope's presence left her dizzy, slightly off-kilter. She took a deep breath and let it out. "My brother wants to marry you."

"Well, I don't want your brother. I thought it would be nice to let someone love me that way, but . . ." Penelope sighed. "In the end, he's just like the others. In the end, he's not for me."

"He won't give up. He's stubborn."

"Are you asking me to give him a chance?"

"No!" Cila blurted out before she could temper her tongue. "I mean, you should do what's best for you. I love Ulisses, he's my *brother*, but you . . . you're free. You should *be* free."

"I'm not free."

Cila tracked Penelope's gaze and realized she was staring at the trophy wall.

"Do you know why I came here? I'm in exile, Lucila. This is my curse. I have no home, no hearth, and I have no place in anyone's heart. You call it freedom, I call it . . ."

The words trailed off, but Cila filled in the blank. *Loneliness.* Fierce and lovely Penelope was lonely, even surrounded by the beauty of her creations.

The artist took a deep breath. The air between the two women crackled with energy and, outside, thunder rattled the sky. The rain had arrived. "I don't want your brother," Penelope repeated firmly, like a promise or a prophecy. "I will never want him. He will never have my hand."

Cila was a mess of conflicted feelings: gratitude, sorrow, triumph, fear. And underneath it all, treachery, that she would go behind her brother's back to stab him in this manner—a monster, like the pirarucu with teeth upon its tongue. She nodded once, in unspoken acceptance of Penelope's words, and fled: past the bead curtain, past the prowling fish, past the cups and bowls and plates, and into the storm. It should have felt like escape, like victory. Instead, there was a hollow place in her chest where she ached for cursed Penelope with all her heart.

Three days after her visit to Circe, Ulisses burst in triumphant as Cila was attempting to put her small son to bed. She heard shouts and ran downstairs to find her brother and husband embracing in joy.

"Cila, fetch the cachaça, the good one," called out Mariano. "Ulisses is getting married!"

The world tilted. Cila reached out to steady herself against the wall. "How—" The words dried in her throat. She hurried to the kitchen to get the special bottle of sugarcane liquor, the expensive one that went down like sunshine. She found the tiny painted glasses they saved for holidays, breathing in and out, in and out. By the time she had assembled a tray, she had stifled all her emotions under the false tranquility of her surface. *Stoneware,* she reminded herself. *Hide the cracks under the glaze.* She pasted a smile on her face and went to meet the men.

Mariano poured drinks. Cila shooed her son back upstairs. Ulisses beamed. It all had a dreamlike, surreal quality, as if she were drifting, unmoored, a boat lost to the tide. All she could think about was the certainty on Penelope's face. *I will never want him.*

The next morning, after Mariano and the children had left, Ulisses returned, a little quiet, as if unsure of his footing, treading on eggshells around his sister. They sat in silence as Cila poured coffee and passed him the Minas cheese for his bread.

"I know you don't like her," he said eventually. "I know you're not happy about this."

Cila sighed. It was complicated, how she felt about Penelope. She didn't understand it herself, only that it was deep and wide and dark and light, all at the same time. But she had lain awake for hours and was too tired to fight. She reached over the table and squeezed his hand. "I won't lose you over this. You're happy, and that's what matters."

Cila could tell by the set of his shoulders that Ulisses was appeased. Inside, she was broken and jagged, cracked right down the middle like badly fired pottery, but she hid it as best as she could. "When will you marry?" she asked.

"Penelope wants to make me a wedding gift. One of her fish sculptures. She said we can have the ceremony once it's finished." He laughed, pleased and indulgent. "Artists! She won't have to do that stuff anymore when we marry. Not for money, anyway. She can still do it for fun, though once we have kids, she'll be busy."

Worry prickled at Cila's skin. The cracks widened, breaching the surface, seeping from her pores to climb the white-tiled walls. "Does she even want children? Have you *talked* to her about this?" She couldn't imagine Penelope in the kitchen, frying fish for her family, packing school snacks, and ironing shirts, trousers, dish towels.

Ulisses gave her a pitying look. "All women want a family. Everyone knows that."

Cila bit back a retort. It was no use arguing with her brother. Despite his love of progress, in some ways he was as ancient as the shriveled domino players at the wharf. She thought of Penelope, of the resignation on her face when she said that Ulisses, in the end, was just like all the others. What had changed? *Why* had Penelope changed her mind? And why did it hurt so much?

After breakfast, Ulisses hesitated, already halfway out the door. He stuck a hand in his pocket and drew out a small velvet bag, the sort that holds a jeweler's trinket. "Can you take care of this for me? Put it somewhere safe, someplace the kids can't mess with it."

Cila took the bag, wondering if it held a ring. Perhaps he was saving it for his wedding day. Before she could ask, Ulisses was gone. She rubbed a thumb over the cheap black velvet, but the lump inside did not feel like a ring. She opened the bag and tipped the contents onto her palm. It was a speckled cowrie shell, the kind cast by Umbanda priestesses to consult the Orixás for spiritual guidance. Cila herself had been to the local terreiro many times to bring flowers for Iemanjá, Lady of the Waters, in offering for her husband's safety at sea.

This shell, however, was different. It held whispers of dark magic, of twisted and forbidden things. Of secrets that lurked in the ocean's depths until the storms dragged them to the surface, spilling black against the jagged rocks. Cila's gut ached as fear sliced her belly wide. The small cowrie shell lay in her hand, heavy as an anchor, binding as a contract. Her hallway stank of rotting seaweed.

"Oh, my brother," she murmured. "What have you done?"

She put the shell back in the velvet bag and shoved the bag in a drawer in the hallway dresser, right at the back under a stack of appliance manuals, yellow with age. Then she traded her flip-flops for sandals, brushed her hair, and went in search of Penelope.

Penelope was in her studio, pounding clay against the table. Preparation, Cila remembered. The first step in pottery. Removing air bubbles by kneading and beating the clay. A violent birth for such a fragile end product.

The wooden bead curtain announced her arrival, and Penelope stopped, hands stilling, head bowed.

"What are you making?" It wasn't what Cila meant to say, but the words slithered free, slippery as fresh-caught fish. Just days before, she had stood at this same spot and said the very same thing.

"Pescada." Penelope's head was still bowed, her expression unreadable. There was no warmth in her caramel voice. "*Cynoscion leiarchus.* One of the key products of the local fishing industry. Or so Ulisses tells me. An appropriate wedding gift for my husband-to-be."

The source photo taped to the wall was a familiar image. A pescada was a plain-looking fish, with silver scales and large, round eyes, eternally startled. Cila had cooked some the previous evening; today she planned to mix the leftovers with rice and cheese to make fried balls. There was no beauty in this ordinary, everyday fish. But Penelope was right, it was appropriate. And under Penelope's fingers it would become *more* than just dinner.

Because everything Penelope did was *more*. And if Penelope could be this, could be art and magic and freedom, could be Circe, what was she doing settling for Ulisses? Betrayal rose in Cila's throat, acrid as vomit, but it was confusing and complex, and she didn't know who had betrayed her. Ulisses for daring, or Penelope for submitting. Or herself for pretending. For subduing her truth and making her life as two-dimensional as a novela on the TV screen for fear of what lay beneath the surface.

"Why are you marrying him?" The words were the barest whisper, but by the twitch of Penelope's hands upon the wet clay, she had no doubt that the other woman had heard.

Penelope finally looked up. Her beautiful lips were pressed thin, stretching tight across her face. It matched the expression Cila could feel upon herself. *This, too, we have in common,* she thought. *Neither of us is happy.*

But all Penelope said was "I have no choice." She went back

to working her clay. Cila, dismissed, returned to her kitchen, where invisible cracks continued to spread across the clean white tiles. In the dresser drawer, the cowrie shell pulsed, a malignant presence at the edge of Cila's perception.

Cila couldn't keep away. Two days later, she returned to Penelope's studio to find her once again pounding clay.

"I didn't like the tail," Penelope explained with a shrug. "It wasn't right."

Cila stayed awhile, watching Penelope work. Ulisses had been tired at breakfast, the skin under his eyes almost as ashen as the unbaked pieces that gathered dust on Penelope's studio shelves. He should have been joyful. Instead, he was triumphant—the cruel elation of the victor and not the giddy pleasure of the lover.

There was no joy here, either. Where before there had been a frothing effervescent sense of enchantment in Penelope's workshop, now there was simply a grim and desperate sort of determination. When Cila left for home, she was apprehensive. There was trouble brewing like storm clouds, she could feel it down to her very marrow.

The next morning, the bags under Ulisses's eyes had grown darker. The pescada was now a rough sketch, a writer's draft, an emerging creature kept damp with wet strips of cloth. But the day after that, Penelope was beating air bubbles from a fresh block of clay.

"It has to be perfect," she told Cila, this time accompanied by her brother, who remained in the showroom examining a terribly mundane milk jug.

She's stalling. The idea thrilled Cila, that whatever unspeakable bargain Ulisses had struck with the sea to net Penelope could be defied in this small manner. As the artist worked, something restless fluttered inside Cila. Suddenly, Penelope was more than her own self: she was Cila, she was Dona Ana, dead and buried. She was all women and none of them. She was a promise that rode in with the rolling breakers to crash against the shore, unstoppable. She was the breath that fills the lungs, the blood that pumps a beating heart.

In the kitchen, the cracks had spread as far as the door.

So it went, day after day. As soon as the fish began to take shape, Penelope would start over. But each time it surged from her deft hands a better creature, more alive, striking even in the gray of wet, unfinished pottery.

The same could not be said of Ulisses. Initially, it was just the sallow skin beneath his eyes. Then he began to lose weight. His gaze dulled, and even his hair hung limp and listless. Penelope had told her that magic was in everyone, in how we see the world and how it looks back. But where Penelope took wonder from the sea and fed it to her art, Ulisses had taken nothing but shadows.

This version of her brother frightened her. She wanted to shout at him, to order him to release Penelope before it was too late. But she did not dare raise her voice. Once he'd been just a man—ordinary, fallible, entirely human. Now, she was not so sure. She stared at him over breakfast, certain she'd caught the writhing of strange things in the folds of his body. But when he looked up, she turned her gaze away.

"It's just stress," Ulisses said, mistaking her fear for concern. "It'll be over soon. It's like they say: when you marry, that cures everything."

Quando casar, sara. A popular belief, that a wedding ring

upon your finger was enough to solve all the problems in the world. She'd thought so, too, once, hadn't she? And yet, in her marriage, her children, her chores and kitchen and life, where had *Lucila* disappeared to?

Ulisses watched her, his eyes unfathomable. "Soon, little sister, I will be as happy as you and Mariano," he said with a smile that bled falsehood all across his face.

Cila thought of the cowrie shell in the tiny velvet bag and shivered.

One day, almost a month after Ulisses had announced his engagement, she went to Circe on her daily pilgrimage to find that her brother had beaten her there. She hovered in the gallery, taking refuge between the sculptures, and listened to his shouts through the curtain of beads.

"Enough already! You'll finish this damn fish before the week is up and we *will* marry on Saturday, one way or another. Do you understand?"

There was no answer from Penelope, none that Cila could hear, anyway. Her gaze caught on a ceramic squid, fierce and knowing in its liquid beauty, and she wondered when Penelope's art had become her haven. She was still watching the squid when Ulisses stormed out and almost collided with her.

"And *you*," he said, jabbing a finger in her direction. "Whose side are you on, anyway?"

She gaped at him, alarm winning over her fear. He looked horribly ill, like he could barely stand. "Give it up, Uli," she begged impulsively. "Give *her* up. This wedding, it will bring no happiness to either of you."

For the first time, uncertainty flitted across his face, warring with whatever else had stirred within. "I can't," he said. "I've gone too far. I won't give her up." There were tears in his eyes. "Maninha, please!"

He wiped his eyes, hardening, towering over Cila and her pottery sentinels as if he hadn't just invoked their past with the childhood nickname. "If you can't say anything useful, at least *do* something. Make sure she's decent for Saturday. God knows if she even has a clean dress to wear!" He slammed out the door, stumbling down the lane like a drunkard.

Ulisses had gone, but he'd left a trail of wrongness behind. Cila's mouth was full of it, tart as pitanga berries. She went through the curtain, each step a leaden weight. Penelope was waiting for her, a cornered creature all teeth and nails. In that instant, she was truly Circe and no more human than Ulisses, both of them *other*. Both of them set apart.

In the gallery, the cursed fish on the trophy wall howled in hate.

Cila swallowed, frightened fingers pinching at the hem of her blouse. "What have you done to him?"

"Nothing he did not do to me first," Penelope spat. "Where's your solidarity, *maninha*? Is there no weight to sisterhood? You come in here every day like a woman starved of life. There is no backbone to you, no substance. Will you stand by him in this?"

"He's my *brother*. He's—"

Broken. Wrong. Keeping secrets. Making deals with the dark places in the ocean's depths. Cila didn't know how to finish the sentence, but she knew Circe was right. No one should be allowed to trap a wild thing, to collar and cage it and bend it to their will.

Circe drew herself up, tall and proud. "I will be there on

Saturday. I will wear white. You can tell your precious brother that his fish will be ready on time."

Cila stared at the clay sculpture on the counter. It stared back accusingly. Cowed, she darted through the bead curtain and ran all the way home, past streets and buildings covered with dreadful, awful cracks that no one else could see.

On Saturday, Penelope was a vision in cotton and lace. No clay smudge marred her cheek, not a hair was out of place. Beside her, Ulisses looked like death. His triumph, however, was plain to see in the glory of his smile. Penelope's secret smile, on the other hand, was locked away tight, maybe forever.

"Would it kill her to be a little happy?" an old aunt grumbled.

Yes, Cila thought. *Perhaps it would.*

The fish sculpture had a place of honor at the wedding lunch. It was a huge thing, twice as big as a real pescada and more alive than any fish Cila had ever encountered. Its round eyes saw everything. It was a vicious, ethereal presence, impossible to ignore. It was magnificent. Only Cila knew that Penelope had been forced to hurry the process, that under the silver glaze lay fractures as wide and ugly as the ones that had seeped from Cila's skin.

She hoped that Penelope and Ulisses would come to love each other, that they would find some form of happiness together. She hoped that the ache in her gut was wrong and that everything would turn out fine. Then she could go back to her house and pretend there had never been any cracks, ever, at all.

The velvet bag with the cowrie shell remained tucked away in her dresser drawer.

———

After the wedding, Penelope closed the store. She sold all her art, down to the last teacup and bowl, all except for the fish from the trophy wall. Those she smashed with a hammer and threw in a dumpster along with the sign. She gave away the electric wheel, the vast kiln, the leftover pigments and sacks of clay, and she moved to Ulisses's house without looking back.

She was a model wife, cooking and cleaning, shopping at the market for yams, salt pork, and sweet ripe melons. "That's a good one you've found," the other fishermen told Ulisses. "Knows her place, never scolds, never raises her voice."

But in the thin and unhappy line of Penelope's lips, Cila saw herself. She saw her tiny, sour mother, whom life had turned bitter as lemons, a prisoner turned warden. She saw what could have been and what was instead: a facade, hard as stone and yet brittle as unbaked clay.

Sometimes she thought she hated Penelope for provoking the truth that Cila had buried deep under a painted surface of marital bliss, of family and a warm kitchen. But Cila had crafted that masterpiece herself, coil by coil, layer by layer. Now everywhere she turned there were spiderwebbing fissures, cracks in the glaze. She no longer knew what lay beneath. Freedom? Or a monster, perhaps: a terrifying pirarucu with teeth upon its tongue to crush its prey.

If Penelope was muted, a woman on pause, then Ulisses was a man who had died but not noticed. He grew sicker and sicker, more absent, his mind vague and prone to wandering. He wasted away to nothing, a mere shell to house the dark things that squirmed inside him. He finally allowed Cila to take him to fancy doctors on the mainland, but they found nothing wrong. They gave Ulisses vitamins, expensive and useless.

The only thing that thrived under Ulisses's roof was the fish. The exquisitely sculpted pescada grew more vibrant every day. As Ulisses waned and Penelope waited, the fish was resplendent, a waxing moon clad in silver chain mail. Cila found she couldn't hate Penelope after all. But she hated that fish with every beat of her heart.

On Saint John's Day, the whole town gathered to celebrate the traditional Festa Junina. Lines of multicolored pennants decorated the square, strung back and forth between the streetlights. Vendors sold corn on the cob and rice pudding, barbecued meat skewers and peanut brittle. Everywhere there was laughter and chatter. In the middle of it all, a bonfire sent bright sparks up to the waiting stars.

Cila sat at a plastic table, sipping a scalding cup of spiced cachaça. Penelope, beside her, stared at the leaping flames, a silent ghost. Ulisses had stayed home, another ghost. Suddenly, it was all too much. The accordion music, the twirling dancers, the children's screams as they played catch with their school friends. The sheer pretense at a normality that became harder to fake with each passing day. Cila could take it no more. When Penelope rose obligingly to buy cotton candy for the little ones, Cila made her escape.

"Mariano, I'm leaving. My head is killing me. Can you and Penelope watch the kids?" She brushed a kiss over his thinning hair and left.

She meant to go home, she really did. She longed to rest her aching head on cool cotton and find release in sleep. But instead, she followed her heavy heart to her brother's house, key already in hand. In the quiet of the living room, Ulisses sat limply on the sofa. He didn't notice when she entered. She knew he was alive, but only because she could see the slow rise and fall of his chest. He stared unblinking, eyes fixed straight ahead, and when she turned her head to follow, she met the fish's malevolent gaze.

Something snapped, deep inside where she'd chained that other Lucila, the one who never had to pretend. The cracks that now followed her everywhere split wide, unleashing this hidden version of Cila into the stifling silence of Ulisses's living room.

"*You*," she told the pescada. "It's you." She'd thought the fish cursed, but instead it was a curse in itself, virulent and alive, sending out noxious tendrils that poisoned everything it touched. Penelope may have created it, but she had no real control over the products of her sorcery, this was now clear to Cila. And if Penelope as Circe could not end this cycle of coercion and retribution, then Cila would do it in her place.

She grabbed the ceramic fish from its stand and hugged it close. It was heavier than she'd thought, solid like nothing else in this house appeared to be. She walked outside, kicking the door shut behind her and ignoring the sheer spite that pulsed from the pescada and tore at every piece of her that touched it.

Cila carried the fish down the street and through the arts quarter where Circe had once reigned. She passed the wharf, following the road until it came to a stop at the far side of the harbor beach, under the towering cliff that marked the town limits. She toed off her smart city sandals and stepped barefoot onto the sand. The fish in her arms was impossibly heavy, an anchor that would drag her down and bury her if only she let it. She heaved it higher, adjusting her grip, ignoring her burning muscles.

She trudged across the sand and scrambled up the track that climbed the cliff. Here, where the town lights were a distant glimmer, the salt in her blood called out, drowning the steel and citrus of her mother's ghostly presence. She let the dark embrace her as she took the vile fish right to the top of the cliff, and then she turned to face the ocean's expanse.

Penelope had said once that there was magic in everything; now, Cila searched for a spark of her own. "Fix this," she told the ocean.

Her frenzied mind had conjured images of tossing the sculpture far out to sea, giving it to the waves and brine. Instead, hampered by its heavy weight and her aching arms, it barely cleared the edge of the cliff. The fish clattered and bounced off the sheer wall, smashing with awful finality on the rocks below.

She let out a breath. It was done. The curse was broken. Penelope and Ulisses were free, and perhaps even Cila herself. She turned her back on the cold salt spray and set off for home.

At daybreak, pounding fists upon the door brought the news: Ulisses was dead. He'd died in the night. Penelope had thought him asleep when she returned from the festivities, but in the morning, she realized he had drifted away.

Cila left the house without a word. She walked past the harbor and onto the beach, across the sand and up the cliff. She stood for an eternity, staring at the sea, until Mariano, frantic, found her there.

"Did I do this?" she whispered, afraid to voice her guilt out loud. "Am I a monster?" Had the stone walls been necessary to cage in her true form?

He cupped her chilled cheeks with his warm hands. "No,

love, no. He was very sick. You did all you could, took him to all those city doctors. It was his time, that's all."

But Mariano knew nothing of magic fish or cowrie shells that made covenants with shadows. He knew nothing of curses and the sort of sorcery that fed upon the ocean's waves, wild and free until cornered like a beast. She pressed her head against the ordinary stability of his shoulder and let him lead her home.

Penelope was a tragic beauty at the funeral, eyes downcast and hushed in her grief. Only Cila noticed that the secret smile was back, tucked away at the corner of her mouth. Cila touched a finger to her own dry lips and tried not to frown.

"Did you do this?" she asked Penelope later in the garden, under the broad leaves of a fig tree. "Or did I kill my brother?"

Penelope's gaze was honest, direct. "He did it to himself. He tried to trap me—he *did* trap me—but all power comes at a price." She shrugged. "I fought back the only way I know how, but . . . the ocean would have taken him eventually. You just spared him his final suffering." There was a beat of silence, broken by the trill of a sabiá, high up in the branches. "I'm not sorry," Penelope added defiantly.

Cila stared up at the fig leaves, searching for the orange-red flash of the bird's belly plumage. The sky above was unfairly blue. *It should be raining,* she thought. But she didn't feel sorrow, not really. She didn't feel much of anything. Ulisses—*her* Ulisses, her brother, her childhood playmate—had died long before this, maybe the very instant he'd struck a deal with things he did not or would not understand.

No, Ulisses was gone, and that left her, a monster. "What do we do now?" she asked.

Penelope took Cila's hand between her own. Cila could feel the strength in those deceptively slender fingers, tough and callused from working clay. "Now? We *live*. Don't hide behind those walls. Yes, I know what you're thinking, but you're not some awful, terrifying creature to be chained away in the dark. Live for me, Lucila, and I promise to live, too."

Penelope drew her forward by the hand, leaning into her space. There was a press of lips upon lips, a fleeting kiss no less burning for its brevity. Then Penelope released her and left her alone under the fig tree.

Back in the kitchen, the mourning guests all gone, Cila sat in her usual chair, twisting her wedding ring back and forth. She caught sight of her reflection in the oven door. For a second, she was all of them: her sour mother, her salt-weathered father, her brother, lost to the shadows. And Lucilas, a multitude of them, at every moment and every age. Wild and shy and loud and quiet, with many necks and heads and feet and teeth, and, above all, a heart that sang to a beat that was all her own, in any shape, at any age. Penelope was right; she was no monster. She was simply Lucila, and that in itself was a curse and a blessing, but it was hers to embrace.

She blinked, and the multiple versions of her were gone, but so were the invisible cracks that had covered every inch of the neatly tiled walls.

Mariano bought out Ulisses's shares in the company, but Penelope gave Cila the house. "I don't want it," she said, as she handed Cila the last of the legal papers. "Save it for yourself or sell it. You might want the money someday."

A taxi waited at the gate with Penelope's single battered

suitcase in the back, filled with the weight of her beauty, her talent, her terrible loneliness. Penelope turned to go.

"Wait!" Cila called out. She ran to the dresser and dug through the jumble of old receipts, spare keys, and forgotten equipment manuals until she found the velvet bag. She held it out. "This is yours."

Penelope took the bag and opened it. When she saw the cowrie shell inside, her beautiful lips parted in surprise. She looked up at Cila and smiled. It was worth the wait, worth the promise. It was Circe. It was glorious. "Farewell," she said.

Cila watched the taxi until it turned the corner, and then she shut and locked the door. She climbed the stairs to her bedroom and sat at the ornate dressing table that Mariano had bought her on their first anniversary. She looked at herself in the mirror, *really looked*. In the glass was the Cila that had spilled out when the cracks had finally widened enough for her truth to burst free. There were echoes of a younger Cila, but she liked this older version, every crease and line of her.

Perhaps Penelope was right. Perhaps there was magic in everyone. And maybe, just maybe, there was space for all the different Lucilas to coexist in peace. She nodded at her reflection, taking the mirrored response as agreement. Then she reached inside and began to practice her secret smile.

PICKLES FOR MRS. POMME

Susan Purr

Stepping out her front door, Rodie walked cautiously down the short path to the main sidewalk, felt the curb with her cane, and turned right. She took a deep breath. Spring had come early to the Carolinas, and the air tasted mildly of lemon. It was as if the plants and trees were determining whether the sun was truly ready for love, emitting only the tiniest hints of pollen to the breeze and waiting for either a warm embrace or a cold shoulder. Rodie took another breath. Despite her mild anxiety, she was on a mailbox mission, and no amount of nervousness could dampen her excitement. Today was book day.

Rodie forced her shoulders back and lifted her chin. She could do this. She had walked this route at least twice with her mobility instructor. *Only twice,* Rodie brooded, *and we've been here at the Villas for over a month.* The services here were too slow and sparse for her liking, unlike where she used to live, but at least they had been able to get the library to send her books in Braille. Reading would help her pass the time while Ari was away. Ari . . . he had helped with the move only to leave two days later on yet another unspecified business trip. Rodie wondered where her husband was now. A war-torn country? Some disputed gang land? A contentious boardroom? She would probably never know, and that was okay. They had agreed long ago not to talk about business. She just wished she knew when he was coming home. She missed him.

At the thought of Ari's business, Rodie tasted a touch of grapefruit in the air, and with a resolute flip of her hair, she continued down the sidewalk. She quickened her pace a little, and her cane taps quickened too. Left-right, left-right, the cane constantly checked for obstacles and relayed navigational cues back to Rodie's sensitive hand. *Off to my left is the parking lot,* she reminded herself, *while to my right is the grass.* Talking herself through a mental map had become a comforting ritual for Rodie, and soon, she hoped, the new environment of the Villas at Greco Creek would become as comfortable and familiar to her feet as Braille was to her fingertips.

Keeping to the middle of the walkway, Rodie navigated her way toward Little Delphi. *A corny name,* Rodie mused as she tapped past the sounds of a frothing fountain on her right, *yet also appropriate.* Little Delphi housed the Villas' very own post office, the offices of groundskeeping and management staff, and a residents-only café. Rodie had come to know it as *the* hub for all the local gossip and essential news that a lonely housewife could want.

Once I feel the bricks, I know I've made it. Rodie felt a chill of insecurity creep over her skin. This walk was taking too long. Had she somehow veered off the path? At last she felt her cane skitter from the smooth concrete path to the rough bumpiness of the brickwork patio that marked the entrance to Little Delphi. Rodie exhaled, feeling warmth returning to her limbs.

How long had she been holding her breath? Again, she sensed bitter grapefruit as she inhaled deeply. Before the move, she had been a success. Before the move, she had been admired and adored throughout her old neighborhood. People sought her advice on everything from perfumes to pickle sandwiches. She wasn't a lonely housewife, dammit, she was a goddess.

Something had gone wrong. Before the move, there stood a stately old mansion housing the mayor and his family. It had been the pride of the city, and Rodie remembered the countless times she had run her hands along the impressive stone walls surrounding it, marveling at their height and their smooth, impenetrable timelessness. There had been a scandal involving the mayor's son running off with the police chief's wife. There had been shouting matches. There had been street brawls. Finally there was a fire that consumed the old house completely. So many people had been hurt, and some even died in the fire. After that, the city felt alien to her needs; it felt like a war zone—too much like Ari's business. Little by little, people began leaving or simply locking their doors.

Okay, so maybe she had wanted to win the citywide Season's Best Pie contest. And maybe she had offered to introduce the mayor's son to her lovely dental hygienist in exchange for a leg up. And okay, maybe her dental hygienist was already married . . . to the police chief . . . who was notoriously aggressive and very jealous regarding his wife. And possibly Rodie had worked a little magic—providing the right perfume and cologne, suggesting a perfect rendezvous location, revealing a few delicious details to the press . . . But the mischief that followed? The violence? How could that possibly have been her fault?

In any case, it didn't take long for the realization to sink in that love no longer had a home there. The first-prize wind chimes were nice, though.

So she and Ari had moved, and although the Villas promised fertile ground, Rodie had felt timid and a bit insecure. *Until today,* she promised herself. Pretending to adjust the messenger bag she had slung over her shoulder, Rodie took a moment to compose herself before proceeding into Little Delphi. No more moping about, alone in her villa, neglecting her talents—her purpose. She needed to make this place her own. *And, in honor of book day,* she thought as she held her head high and readied her cane, *today is that day.* Rodie willed her face into a smile, probed with her cane until she found the glass double doors, and pushed through into the large foyer.

Rodie strode forward, enjoying the feel of Little Delphi's smooth tile floor and the smell of brewing coffee. *Find the pedestal and make a sharp left to the mailboxes,* she reminded herself. Turning right at the foyer's large stone pedestal would bring her to the offices, while going around it would lead her to the café. The central landmark unnerved Rodie. On top of a rough block of chiseled concrete, a cool marble sculpture greeted residents and visitors with what management hoped to be a show of opulence. When Rodie had first explored it with her fingertips a month ago, she recognized the shapes of four animals: a rabbit, a lion, an owl, and a stag. Supposedly, it represented the seasons, but it made Rodie uncomfortable, as if two of the seasons would at any moment devour the other two. The marble felt too cold and creepy. Rodie imagined an improvement that would be made of wood—a warmer feel that represented fruits and flowers of the different times of year, like daisies, magnolias, pumpkins, and pears. Certainly, her idea was more welcoming; it was sensual as well as sensible. *Next time I'm here,* she thought, *I'll turn right and pay a visit to the property manager.*

As she approached the mailboxes, Rodie heard a familiar voice. "Rodie! Hi! It's me, Seph!"

Seph's voice was unmistakable, slightly nasal with frequent uptalk, and her mouth was always chewing gum. Rodie smiled. She had met Seph soon after Ari left, when she had been hanging the prize wind chimes near her front door. The young woman had come around to her villa a few times since, mainly to trade recipes and fragrance tips, and Rodie felt the enticing bonds of a mentorship beginning to form between them. After all, Seph was a newlywed, married to a much older man, and Rodie had both time and talents to impart to her new friend.

"Hey, Seph. Enjoying the early spring?" Rodie tapped the left wall with her cane and reached up with her free hand to dance her fingers along the rows of mailboxes. Finding her mailbox, marked POMME 214 in raised block print letters, she deftly unlocked it and fished out the large, heavy packet containing her library book.

Rodie heard the flapping of the woman's flip-flops as she approached her. Today's gum smelled of some unnamable, artificial fruit. "Oh yeah, love the weather. Hey, is that a Braille book?" she asked, snapping a bubble with her teeth.

"'A compilation of the best in romance 2020,'" Rodie read aloud, smiling.

"Meow!" Seph giggled and chomped her gum, sweet sugary saturation.

"I was thinking," Rodie went on, "maybe I'd do a little romance writing myself, maybe self-publish a few stories. But I wanted to get inspired first." Rodie wrestled the book into her bag and turned away from the mailboxes to retrace her steps, and then she and Seph headed back to the pedestal.

"Oh, honey." Seph clutched Rodie's arm. "I'm sure you're gonna do great! You're a natural. I've said it before. You know"—her voice hushed to a breathy whisper—"ever since I started using your special concoction in my iced tea . . ." Rodie thought Seph was going to explode. ". . . the old man, well, he hasn't, you know, needed those little blue pills." Giggles ripened and burst from Seph's mouth, and Rodie felt the woman's soft hand clasp her arm tighter as if to keep from collapsing.

"Wait, you did what?" Rodie was incredulous. She had given Seph a small perfume bottle of the latest trendy fragrance and added her own special Rodie twist. She had instructed Seph to dab a drop or two behind her ears, but somehow that message had gotten stuck in a wad of bubble gum and had been thoroughly masticated—into drops for tea.

Seph continued, apparently not hearing Rodie's question. "I don't know what your secret is, but it works!" Her giggles now echoed around them in the foyer.

"Love," Rodie said, her cane rapping the pedestal for emphasis. "It's brewed with love." *And a splash of pickle juice,* Rodie thought to herself. Why she didn't just say "pickle juice," she didn't really know. Something about it seemed too intimate, too sacred, to share with Seph. Or anyone for that matter. She had a right to a secret or two. Besides, regardless of how it was used, the concoction—the love potion (Rodie liked the sound of that better, clichés be damned)—had worked. And that's all anyone needed to know. "It never fails."

"I'll say!" Seph chortled. "The old man can go all night with just a little of that stuff! If you can put that kinda magic into a story, you're gonna be the next Nora Roberts."

Rodie felt her smile broaden, and the smell of coffee that permeated Little Delphi suddenly turned to sweet, warm chocolate.

"Listen," Seph said, becoming oddly serious as they reached the glass doors. "My mom is coming for a visit in a few days. She says she's gonna help me plant a little patio garden or something."

Rodie paused midway through the doors. "But doesn't your mother still hate the old man?"

During one of their visits, Seph had explained to Rodie how she had initially fallen for her husband when she ventured into one of his nightclubs. She had gone out one night against her mother Demi's wishes, and after an hour or so of barhopping, she had found herself in the Styx and Stones, one of the most stylish clubs in the area. Seph had just popped a fresh piece of gum into her mouth when the old man stepped out of the glitzy glass elevator rising from the basement. In a black leather suit and with flowing white hair, he had looked so dangerous and alluring that Seph gasped. The sharp intake of air caused her gum to get stuck in her throat, and she had passed out. According to Seph, when she came to in the old man's arms, she teasingly told him to put a ring on it, and to her amazement, he did, right then and there. The last thing Seph had told Rodie was that Demi was so infuriated by her daughter's elopement, she had threatened to kill her new husband. Because of Demi's temper, Seph had confided, she had not seen or spoken to her mother in the entire six months of her marriage.

"Yeah, she still hates him," Seph said, her voice making her statement sound more like a question. "But she called yesterday and said she missed me. The old man and I talked about it, and he has agreed to stay at the Styx for a while." She gave a few quick chews on her gum before continuing. "You know, he's got a bedroom and stuff already set up over there. It's pretty sweet. Isn't it nice that, you know, he's gonna give me and Mom some space? You know, to reconnect?"

"Yeah, that's pretty cool," Rodie said. At this point, they were both standing outside, and Rodie was thinking of her route back to the villa.

"So, I'll be like you: manless for a while." Seph laughed, but Rodie tasted grapefruit in the air again. "Maybe you could come by to meet my mom for a lunch date or coffee or whatever it is that old housewives do, right?"

"Do I look old?" The bitter air began to sting, and Rodie felt her face get hot. She wanted to go home *right now*. She had reading to do.

"What? No!" Seph's voice pitched higher than usual.

Rodie heard the woman's flip-flops scuffing along the ground erratically. *Oh, Seph,* Rodie thought, and smirked. *Did you just step in dog shit?*

"I was just being funny." Seph's feet continued to dance. "No, in fact, you look so cute today, all dressed for spring."

Rodie sighed and tapped the bricks with her cane. "Sure," she said, "I'll come by to meet your mother."

Just then, Rodie heard a vehicle approaching. It was a golf cart, judging by the whir of its electric engine, and she knew just whose golf cart it was based on the unmistakable sound of Disney music blaring from its single scratchy speaker.

"Don!" the two women said in unison, and laughed.

The air softened to cotton candy; Don always seemed to have that effect. Everyone in the Villas knew him as "the koi whisperer," but Rodie sensed that his talents went way beyond fish.

"Is that *Finding Nemo*?" Seph giggled.

"*The Little Mermaid*," Rodie said. "*Finding Nemo* was two days ago."

Rodie heard the music pause from the same direction as the fountain along the main walkway. She imagined that Don was checking to make sure all was running well with it, searching for any broken spigots, clogged filters, or busted pumps. Rumor had it that Don paid for his villa by maintaining Greco Creek and all of the property's water features, especially its koi ponds and swimming pools. Rodie could believe it; when he wasn't cruising around in his musical golf cart, he was always doing something near the water.

"Did you hear about him and that woman over in 721, out by the back entrance?" Seph's voice dropped low for this new conspiracy. "Oh, dang it, what is her name! I can't remember it, but I think it's been going on a couple of weeks now."

"Don's dating someone?" Rodie was both surprised and pleased. Don knew everybody, and everybody knew him, but Rodie found it difficult to think of him . . . romantically. That lack of imagination wasn't like her at all and needed to change.

"Yes, and she's gorgeous!" Seph squealed and again grasped Rodie's arm as if to steady herself. "She has long braids that snake down past her butt, and her eyes . . . Well, I'll tell you, Rodie, she could stop a man in his tracks."

"Well, well," Rodie said. "Good for Don. If they've been dating a couple of weeks now, she must really dig him." *She must speak pirate, too,* Rodie mused, and chuckled to herself.

"Yeah, love is definitely blind!" Seph laughed and then choked as if she had swallowed her gum. "Oh, Rodie, I'm sorry, I didn't mean—"

"It's okay." Rodie sighed. She couldn't decide what was more awkward: the saying itself, or the fact that people stumbled over it and felt the need to apologize. Was the phrase insensitive? Perhaps, but Rodie had harsher realities to be sensitive about right now: like the fact that she missed her husband, she had a book to read, and she had important business to do in making this place her home.

Rodie heard the Disney music start up again, and it seemed to her as if it was coming closer. Maybe she could hitch a ride with Don so she could ditch this conversation with Seph and get home faster; at least she could escape the taste of overcooked cream of wheat that now hung in the air.

As the sound of the golf cart approached, Rodie turned away from Seph, then paused. "Give me your hand a moment, Seph." Seph did so, and Rodie opened her friend's palm and kissed it.

"Ooh!" Seph gasped. "That gave me shivers all over!"

"I'll come to your garden party or whatever," Rodie said. "Just give me a call when your mom comes, and we'll plan a date. Now, go take those shivers home to your husband and make him want to take the rest of the day off."

Rodie heard Seph giggling as she shuffled away. *Good luck, old man,* she thought, and waved her hand enthusiastically in time to the oncoming music.

"Looks like ye have quite a heavy bag there, lass," Don said, his voice full of sand and surf. The song paused just as the steel drums had reached peak underwater dance party, and Rodie sensed the golf cart idling directly to her left. "Do ye want a ride?"

"Only if I don't have to sing!" Rodie allowed Don to guide her into the cart, and they both laughed.

"No, Miss Rodie," Don said. "Ye're what men sing to and about. Ye need not be singin' nothin'." He kept the music off as he turned the cart around and headed toward Rodie's villa.

"Just like my Ducy." Don sighed, and Rodie tasted taffy. "So beautiful. Somethin' in the water 'round here, I reckon."

Rodie smiled. How had she so misjudged this charmer? Seems like so many others had, too . . . Well, except the mysterious Ducy in 721.

After a brief ride, the golf cart stopped. Rodie smirked; the distance felt so much longer on foot.

"Here we are, 214." Rodie felt the cart shift a little and rock as Don got out and offered her his helpful steadying arm. "Brought ye right up to yer door, love."

Rodie thanked Don and reached out to unlock her front door. *He thinks I'm beautiful,* she thought, smiling inwardly as she turned the key. Her prize wind chimes, shaped like a tree with many dangling apples, jangled an airy, metallic tune in the breeze.

"Hey, lass." Don's voice sounded lower, and Rodie tasted gentle cherry. "Word has it that ye brew some kinda special iced tea . . ."

Rodie tried to stifle a laugh as she nodded her assent.

"Well," he continued, "if it ain't too much trouble, could I try some sometime? Like maybe when I takes my Ducy out next?"

"Sure, Don," Rodie said, chuckling. "I'll make you some."

"Oh, that's sure sweet of ye," Don said, and Rodie heard him climbing back into the golf cart. "Too bad it couldn't be like . . . well, like a cologne or somethin'. That'd be . . ." Don's voice trailed off.

"I'll see what I can do, Don." Rodie opened her door, the taste of cherries growing stronger. "Bye now!"

Rodie didn't hear his reply. She shut the door, still chuckling. She would check for fragrance sales online later, but now, it was story time at last.

As she slipped off her shoes, Rodie folded her cane and set it on the small table by the front door. She moved quickly, her body rejoicing in its knowledge of where most objects were located inside the villa. Finding the couch, she plopped herself down, spread the book onto her lap, and was about to start reading when the doorbell rang.

Her fingers twitched. Rodie put the book down and went to the door.

"This had better be important," she called through the door.

"Mrs. Pomme, I've got your groceries," a pleasant baritone replied.

Rodie had forgotten all about her arrangement with the local supermarket: delivery of certain essentials once a week, and a call if there were any additions or substitutions. But she hadn't forgotten this voice, nor the scent of summer jasmine that had accompanied it when she had been introduced to the store clerk a week ago.

"You okay, Mrs. Pomme?" the young man asked as Rodie opened the door for him and felt him glide inside.

So quiet and graceful, Rodie thought, *like a prowling cat.* She remembered the tour of the supermarket, the reassuring speech by the manager, and the feel of this jasmine-scented store clerk as his warm, firm body had reached around her to fetch the brand of yogurt she'd requested.

Oh, Rick, Rodie thought, *I am so much better than all right . . .* Or was it Mick? Like Jagger? She wasn't paying attention to his name those weeks ago; she was too busy considering if he might become some kind of hero or rock star . . . a man out of the old days or a taste of something new.

"I'm fine, Dick," Rodie said. "Can you bring those bags to the kitchen?"

"It's Nick, actually, Mrs. Pomme," Nick said, a slight tremble in his voice. Rodie imagined his body trembling, too, and wondered . . .

"Sorry." She laughed, hoping the act was believable. "Nick. I must be getting old."

She turned and led the way into the kitchen.

"Short for Nicholas," Nick continued. Yes, Rodie was sure that he was trembling. She heard him put the bags on the table, and the plastic rustled—no, shivered—like petals on a summer breeze. "But you're surely not getting old, Mrs. Pomme."

Turning around, Rodie found herself nose to nose with him.

"You barely look twenty-five . . ." He trailed off.

"Really?" Rodie lowered her voice into a husky purr. She put her hand up as if to brush away a loose strand of hair and ended up resting it on Nick's upper chest. His skin burned beneath his uniform shirt, and Rodie smelled the jasmine in full bloom.

"Yeah," Nick said, edging even closer. "It's crazy, 'cause Larry says you're old enough to be my mother."

"Oh, Larry said that, huh?" Rodie drew back.

"I mean . . ." Nick began, but the spell was broken. Larry was the deli man at the supermarket, Rodie recalled, and he had made more than one meat-handling joke to her when they had met. She guessed that Larry now wanted to make sure he'd be the only man delivering meat to Mrs. Pomme. Well, screw him. And screw Nick, too, dammit.

"Hand me the stuff that needs refrigerating, would you, Nicholas?" Rodie said, making her way toward the appliance. "And turn on the lights." She heard Nick shuffle over to the far wall at her command and then the sound of the switch being flipped. "I don't need them, but I suppose you do."

Nick shuffled over to Rodie, possibly trying to recapture the moment, but she kept her back to him. "Mrs. Pomme, I—"

"Just hand me the cold stuff," she commanded, smelling the distinct scent of decaying flowers. "Then you can put the fruit in the basket next to the sink. Oh, and I'll take the pickles, too."

"Pickles?"

"Yes, Nicholas."

"I'm sorry, Mrs. Pomme, but you didn't say anything about pickles."

Rodie tasted smoke. The pickles were always the first thing on the list. She stomped into the living room, pulled her phone from the messenger bag on the couch, and told Siri to read the shopping list.

"Milk, orange juice, eggs, apples, bread . . ." The pleasant phone voice kept reading, but Rodie wasn't listening. She had forgotten, just as things had started feeling more like home. *No pickles for you, Mrs. Pomme . . . not even a whiff of sweet dill.*

Behind her, Rodie heard quiet, catlike steps. Nick's fingertips gently touched her arm, but she didn't turn around.

"I put all the groceries away," Nick said. Rodie heard lazy cicadas thrumming in his voice and sighed. "And I'm sorry about the pickles."

"It's my mistake," Rodie said, laughing weakly. "I told you I'm getting old."

Rodie breathed in Nick's familiar heady jasmine as his arms slid around her waist. Leaning back against him, she felt warm lips near her ear and a hardness against her buttocks. Rodie thought of gherkins. Nick's hands slid to her breasts.

Then, once again, the doorbell rang.

Rodie felt Nick spring backward and heard the rattle of the coffee table as he stumbled into it.

"Mrs. Pomme?" a lilting voice called from outside the door.

"Shit," Rodie muttered, the air turning to burnt toast. She heard Nick clear his throat and fumble with his clothes. *Readjusting,* she thought, and groaned a little. *Dammit!*

With a sinking suspicion, Rodie asked her phone to read what was on her calendar for the day. The pleasant phone voice replied that she had two events on her calendar today: "Groceries" and "Meet with social worker." It didn't say "Book day" because of course it didn't. Rodie groaned louder, tossed the phone onto the couch, and moved toward the door.

"I'll go get some pickles," Nick said, brushing by her.

Leaving his scent, Rodie thought. She imagined the feel of a swishing tail as Nick opened the front door and stifled a giggle.

"Uh, I'm looking for Mrs. Pomme?" The new voice followed Nick's retreat down the path toward the parking lot.

"I'm here," Rodie said, approaching the doorway. "You must be Ms. Montgomery."

After the traditional exchange of pleasantries, the two women sat on the couch. While Rodie moved her phone and the neglected romance book to the recently upset coffee table, the air took on the smell of baking cookies. Ms. Montgomery wanted to discuss Rodie's needs in the new neighborhood, her career goals, and her growing social network, and she heard the constant scribbling of a pen on paper, even though Rodie barely got a word of her own into their conversation.

"So, Mrs. Pomme, you seem to have some . . . community support while your husband is away." Ms. Montgomery seemed to be asking a question within this statement. And was that sarcasm in her tone? Jealousy? Rodie caught a hint of hyacinth as the woman continued her thought. "I noticed your young man there, from the supermarket, right? That's good. It's important to cultivate special friends and neighbors to help out. Keeps us from getting too lonely, right? We all need to do more for each other, I think. Helps us create a community, you know. Spread the love and all."

All at once, Rodie perceived the flirtation in Ms. Montgomery's voice. Her vowels had elongated, and each word glided over Rodie like caresses from flower petals. Rodie was getting down to business, with or without any conscious effort, and damn, she was good at it. Holding back the urge to laugh at herself, Rodie smiled.

"Yes, ma'am," Rodie agreed as the hyacinths began to bud. She shifted closer to Ms. Montgomery on the couch until their knees were barely touching. "And Nicholas is a great help, almost ideal, except . . ."

"Except?" Ms. Montgomery's voice grew quiet.

"Except," Rodie repeated, placing her fingertips on Ms. Montgomery's thigh, "he forgot the pickles." She felt Ms. Montgomery shiver and exhale a small laugh as the pen and the paper slid to the floor.

As the hyacinths bloomed, Rodie's fingers crept farther up, up, up. She felt Ms. Montgomery's hands cupping her face, drawing their lips closer and closer.

Then the front door burst open, Ms. Montgomery screamed and fell backward, and Rodie went tumbling headfirst into the social worker's lap and then onto the floor.

"Honey, I'm home!" The air reeked of cut jalapeño as Rodie scrambled to her knees in front of the couch. After a slight pause, Ari's electric wheelchair buzzed across the living room toward her.

"There's my little apple tart!" Ari's voice boomed, reminding Rodie of an off-duty BBC anchor highlighting a rugby match to his mates after a few pints and a cigarette. "And do you happen to know whose fucking car is in spot 213? I swung into my space and slammed it with my door while getting out. Left a nice dent for the asshole who can't park their piece-of-shit Kia."

Ari's voice softened suddenly. "My heart, are you all right?"

"I just took a little tumble," Rodie said, attempting to get to her feet.

"No, don't get up, I like that position."

Ms. Montgomery cleared her throat, and Rodie heard her shift on the sofa, rustling her papers and unzipping her bag. Rodie felt the wheelchair bump her knees and then felt Ari's strong hands upon her—one swept around her waist and inside her capris and the other snaked around her head. With a handful of ass and a fistful of hair, Ari kissed her.

Gunpowder swirled within the heated jalapeño, and Rodie almost swooned.

"Uh, Mrs. Pomme, I'll just come back another day . . ." Rodie heard Ms. Montgomery sling her bag over her shoulder. Both women sighed.

"Hey you. Glass of scotch," Ari said, his head turning to Ms. Montgomery.

"Yes, sir." Rodie heard the woman shuffle around the couch and head for the kitchen. "Where do you keep your liquor?" Rodie heard Ms. Montgomery opening the cabinets and rummaging for a glass. "Wait a second . . . what am I doing?"

"Don't forget ice," Ari said, nibbling at Rodie's nipple through her shirt and squeezing her ass hard enough to make her moan. Rodie started to laugh.

"A glass of scotch!" Ari pulled his hand out of Rodie's capris and snapped his fingers. "Hup! Hup! Hup!"

Rodie heard stomping and huffing as Ms. Montgomery came back into the living room. "Excuse me, sir, but I am not your maid, nor am I one of your—"

"Shoulders back," Ari said, "and look me in the eye." He pulled away from Rodie, and she felt as though someone had released a boa constrictor into the room.

"Nor am I one of your soldiers," Ms. Montgomery continued. "You can't just order me around." The social worker exhaled through her nose, and Rodie feared a fight. *Why can't we all make love instead?*

"Better," he said coolly. "You're tall, with shoulders like a linebacker. Use that to your advantage always."

Rodie heard the woman snort, and after a moment, she heard her feet stomping to the door. Rodie went after her and caught the door just as it was closing.

"Ms. Montgomery, please forgive my husband. He just got back from multiple tours, and he so often finds it hard . . . you know, to adapt to civilian life." Rodie heard her sigh and took her hand and squeezed it. "Please come back. I want to talk about jobs . . . and my needs."

Ms. Montgomery sighed again and squeezed Rodie's hand back. The scent of cinnamon doughnuts snuck between them, as well as a promise to call before their next visit.

"Great shoulders, Ms. Linebacker, and a great ass, too!" Ari called from behind them. Rodie groaned.

"Thank you for your service, sir," Ms. Montgomery called back, turning to leave, "but fuck you."

Ari's laugh shook the windows, and Rodie just knew he was pumping the air with his fists and making finger guns.

Just as Rodie was about to close the door, Ms. Montgomery called over her shoulder from the path: "Looks like your young friend left his pickles for you . . . Under the chimes."

Carrying the pickle jar, Rodie went back into the living room.

"Rough day, dear?" Ari teased.

"It has been a rough while," she admitted. "I was just getting down to business—"

Ari took her hand. "Shush with your business. We're home now."

Rodie smiled. Yes, they were both home now.

"Well, give me a pickle, Mrs. Pomme . . . or shall I give one to you?"

"You're awful," she said, fumbling with the lid of the pickle jar. "And I want more than one."

"Of course you do." Ari snatched the jar from her hands, laughing. She heard him pop the lid easily as the wheelchair buzzed away into the bedroom.

A new scent tickled her nose: vinegar and dill and something else. *Love,* she thought, and followed her heart to find Ari sitting on their bed.

"I have some new scars," Ari said, accompanied by the sound of his teeth crunching a pickle. "They're ugly."

"Don't worry," Rodie said, pulling off Ari's shirt and pushing him down, "love is blind." While she savored the vinegar on his lips, her hands devoured the beautiful new shapes—the lines, the jagged craters, and the delicious ridges that now rose and fell over his skin. She'd kiss every one and make him never want to leave her again.

"Yes. That's a good thing," Ari growled in a low, breathy rumble.

Rodie shook her head, smiling. As Ari surrendered beneath her, she corrected his ecstasy.

"No," she said, the room flooding with rose petals. "It's fucking fantastic."

And so it was.

THE SHIP OF THEA

Suleikha Snyder

The hacks Thea memorized unspool in her head like spiderweb-thin threads as she stands stock-still in the dark corridor. Her strategies join them, twisting all the information into a braid. A rope. Tethering her. Guiding her. No one has ever beaten the Labyrinth. Plenty have tried; all have failed. The city's most exclusive escape room has been open for only six months, and it's already stacked up a reputation as the most difficult and devious puzzle that doesn't involve Jigsaw removing your limbs. Thea doesn't particularly care for the *Saw* movies, and she's never met a challenge she couldn't solve. *Almost never*—but Thea shoves that irritating reminder aside. She's done her homework. There's not much information out there about the Labyrinth specifically—otherwise it wouldn't be so damn impossible—but she's consumed everything on the subject of escape rooms that she's been able to get her hands on. She doesn't plan to fail. Not this time.

Chess tournaments? She won her first one in fifth grade. Rubik's Cube? A fossil from nearly fifty years ago that she turned into a paperweight after sixty-two seconds. Thea has won spelling bees, aced standardized tests, and excelled at everything else a good desi girl is supposed to achieve. Everything asked of her. Initially because she had to, but eventually because she wanted to. And she wants to make it all the way through the Labyrinth.

By her estimation, she's been inside for about a half hour. She's made numerous right turns and left turns. Answered three riddles, cracked four logic puzzles, and narrowly avoided falling into one trapdoor. Players' mobile devices are confiscated at the beginning of the maze, lest they use geolocation or a compass app to cheat. The assumption is that teams will collaborate, finding their natural strengths and compensating for weaknesses. Thea came in alone. She's still alone now, in what is supposed to be complete darkness. She feels walls on either side of her—a bit rough, like a popcorn ceiling, against her palms. The floor beneath her feet absorbs sound. She can't even hear her bootheels connecting as she walks. *Clever.* Without an echo, a player's sense of direction will become even more muddled. She does what she's always done: forge straight ahead.

A partial academic scholarship to college. Law school and a PhD with help from Uncle Sam and Aunt Sallie Mae. She ran full tilt. She reached for the stars, grasped them . . . and burned. *Don't think about that now.* The Thea who fell to earth isn't here. She can't be here. She's been left at home with three sets of unwashed pajamas and a pile of empty wine bottles. *This* Thea has her rope of tips and ideas. And she knows what should be complete darkness isn't. There is the barest crack of light in her periphery. Dancing. Teasing. She sweeps her fingers along the wall as though it were keys on a piano. Playing a blurred progression. A decade of lessons still lives beneath her skin. The only lesson she's never learned is when to stop.

Thea's nails stutter on a seam in the right-hand wall. She

traces it up as far as her small stature will let her and then follows it down to the ground. She repeats the motion until she finds the hidden catch that springs the wall panel open. It bounces inward—into a room that envelops her in yet more darkness. Until it doesn't. Light flashes white. Too bright. She closes her eyes and opens them to dozens of monitors lining the equilateral walls of a triangular room. She stands at one point, facing the two others. The monitors are crackling with snow, the sound like someone crumpling paper bags. Dozens of someones. It's not a pleasant noise. It makes her shoulders scrunch up, as if they can somehow protect her ears.

This is starting to feel less and less like an escape room and more and more like a trap. The panic button each player is given feels heavy on her wrist. Reminding her that she can give up at any time. *Give up. Fail. Lose. Fall. Burn out.* Like hell. Not this time.

Watch for what isn't there instead of what is, one of the expert escape room sites had advised. So she does, scanning each monitor carefully. *Don't let your guard down.* She clings to the rope, determined to keep it from fraying. She's got this. She's always had this. The monitors are all embedded in the walls. Someone spent a shit ton of money on flat-screen TVs that do nothing but broadcast off-air static. That is a *lot* of financial investment in questionable aesthetics. Thea can only imagine what that's like, since she's still paying off student loans. She moves around the triangle, standing in each corner to absorb the perspective. The floor here *isn't* soundproof, so the white noise feels like it's also coming from beneath her. Vibrating through the soles of her winter boots. *Oh. There!* Her senses sharpen, zeroing in on one screen three rows up and two columns over. On the slanted wall to her right. It's muted. The only one not emitting the crackle. She's barely tall enough to touch the display with her fingertips. Apparently the Labyrinth is weighted unfairly toward tall players. Thea will have to remember that for the Yelp review.

While she's chuckling softly at the thought, the silent screen seems to jump under her fingertips. The content changes to a screensaver full of fractals. And then the video starts. In a horror movie, it would be the killer's face, or his mocking voice, distorted and creepy. Here it's a face she knows and hasn't seen in far too long. A voice she should've expected. Made of music and sunshine.

"Hey, baby," her ex-wife, Astra, murmurs with a glint of challenge in her big brown eyes. "Just so you know what awaits you at the end. See you soon."

Shit. Thea should turn around and walk out. Call it quits. Like the fourteen people this week who the ticket seller boasted hadn't made it. Because she knows what this is and what it means. This was a trap. A setup. She's going to have to talk. She's going to have to *feel*. No more hiding. No more wine. A year of self-exile is up. Unless she bails on the Labyrinth and goes back to her own inescapable room.

Thea does what she always does. She forges straight ahead.

Sometime between Now and Before . . .

It was one a.m. . . . maybe two. Thea had lost track of the hours, buried under a stack of company documents, both digital and print. Funny how her father had cut her off socially years ago but still sent her things from Aegis to go over and vet. He had a whole slew of corporate lawyers at his disposal . . . but he still used Thea as free legal counsel. As if she didn't have enough to do with her own cases at Pallas and Associates. But she could do it all. No question. She knew exactly how hard to push herself. And the empty cans of Red Bull littered across the coffee table were just a supplement to keep her alert.

She barely heard the footsteps from the hallway. It was only when Astra's hand landed on her shoulder that she startled. "I can't keep watching you do this to yourself," her wife said in a weary voice.

Thea twisted in her seat to look at her. "Do what?"

Astra stood there, her lips pursed, her arms crossed over her chest, obscuring the college logo on the T-shirt she so frequently wore to bed. "Turn yourself inside out to make your parents happy."

Thea snorted, reaching for a fresh can of Red Bull. "I think that ship sailed when we got married." They'd had a small ceremony in a friend's backyard, Astra in a gorgeous gown and Thea, who hated dressing up, in a matching suit. Surrounded by friends and a few work colleagues from the game company that had headhunted Astra right after graduation. The only relative in attendance had been Astra's mom, Queenie, a delightfully eccentric artist in gauzy clothes, probably high on shrooms. That was three years ago, but Papa and Ma still pretended Thea was single. And straight.

"This is just Aegis business," she said, trying to keep the bitterness to a minimum.

"Business that has me sleeping alone because you're up so late. Night after night. It's been going on for months!" There were circles under Astra's eyes, like she'd been up late, too. Or maybe she was just exhausted. Tired of Thea and tired of this. "You might call it work or a favor, but you're going to keep chasing their approval if it kills you. And it's killing me to see you try. It's like I don't even know you anymore."

The back of Thea's neck prickled. She didn't like where this conversation was going. And now was not the time for it. Papa wanted her assessment of the proposed deal in his inbox at nine a.m. sharp. And nobody disappointed the CEO of Aegis Enterprises, who ruled his company like a king. "I'm the same person I've always been. You knew this when we got together," she said, trying not to clench her jaw as she set her laptop aside.

"You aren't, baby. You've been changing ever since you left their house, and it's not just your parents who can't see it." Astra gestured to the room around them. The evidence of their life together. Framed photographs of the two of them on every side table. The Pride flag in the window they kept forgetting to take down every July, so it just stayed there year-round. Astra's iPad still open to her MMORPG design schematics, her research notes from the writing team spread across the couch, and all of that sitting next to Thea's knitting and her casework from the pro bono legal clinic she worked at two days a week. "You're not the same Thea you were when you got to college. When we met. So why are you trying to go backwards? It's making you miserable."

The only person Thea was in this moment was someone who hadn't slept in days and needed to meet a deadline. "Do we really have to do this right now?" she asked. After she finished Papa's papers, she needed to go over three new clients from the clinic so she was on the ball for her own workday. "I don't have time for this."

"That's what you said last week," Astra reminded her, shaking her head. "And the week before. And the night of Dion's party. You missed our best friend's birthday. For work you shouldn't even be doing. You don't sleep. You live on energy drinks. And for what? So your father might finally think you're a hero and throw a parade to welcome you home? You're not that valuable to him, baby. Not like you are to me and your friends and your actual life. As far as he's concerned, you're his lackey."

The word landed like a blow. Mostly because it held the ring of a truth she didn't want to acknowledge. She couldn't. Because admitting it meant admitting she'd failed somehow. Thea didn't fail. She refused to fail. "Well, if you're so unhappy with who I am and what I'm doing . . . you're free to make your own choices. You can leave. No one's making you stay."

Astra flinched. "Someone should," she said quietly. "And if you can't see that it's supposed to be you, then there's no point in me sticking around."

She moved out a month later. Thea filed for divorce six months after that. And lost everything else soon after.

She didn't resume sleeping regular hours. Maybe she never would.

Finishing the escape room proves far easier than she expects. Easier than leaving her apartment had been. That took emotion, followed by action. A thousand pep talks. *You can do this. You want to do this. Get up. Get dressed. Get out of bed.* It took remembering that she used to be functional, used to be human, and breaking free of a year in self-imposed isolation. This is just logic. Thea has never been afraid of logic. So it takes her only an additional fifteen minutes to find Astra waiting for her in the center of the maze—metaphorically speaking, at least. She has no idea what the actual layout of the Labyrinth is. Just a vague sense of a warren with lots of sharp turns. Terminating in a hexagonal room with five Grecian-blue-painted walls and terrazzo tile flooring. She half expects to find some reference to David Bowie, but, of course, it's the

Minotaur instead. The focal point of the room, on the last and facing wall. A huge floor-to-ceiling mural of a beautiful Pre-Raphaelite-esque cryptid with the proud and majestic head of a horned bull and the well-muscled bare body of an olive-skinned human. Perhaps in a nod to the Goblin King, he's wearing skintight pants and sports a noticeable bulge. It's purely ironic, a not-so-little joke, considering Astra has never had much interest in that particular feature.

No wonder the wide, high-backed black leather chair that's more of a throne is strategically placed on a dais between the Minotaur's spread legs. And there sits the woman she married five years ago, just as stunning as she was on that day. Her hair is a riot of brown and gold, like treasure overflowing a chest. She's wearing a slim-cut red pantsuit that complements the glow of her skin. Silver rings shine on her deceptively delicate fingers. She is as much goddess as she is gamer. Thea feels distinctly underdressed in comparison. Underdressed and unprepared.

Astra is Sanskrit for "divine weapon," though her ex pronounces it differently, so it aligns with the Latin for "stars." Both definitions are accurate. Because Astra is everything bright and hot and untouchable . . . and the only person on Earth capable of blowing Thea apart. No. That's not precisely true. She did a pretty good job of imploding on her own, too.

"Congratulations on being the first person to finish the Labyrinth." Astra's voice is still wry and enchanting, even more so in person than it was on the TV screen earlier. She is beauty and grace wrapped around keen intelligence and sharp insight. All things that had drawn gawky sophomore Thea to her when they lived on the same floor of their college dorm.

"What do I win?" she asks, pushing away the memories of a past they can't go back to. "If it's an intervention of some kind,

I want a full refund." She looks around, half expecting Dion and Queenie to pop out from the corners.

"No. I know trying to tell you what to do has never done one bit of good." Astra tilts her head, studying Thea like she's one of her outlines. Her springy bronze curls cascade to the side, revealing a new tattoo on the side of her neck, a spiral of dark green ink nested on smooth light brown skin. Another maze. One that loops until the center is tight and impenetrable. Maybe it's an in-joke like the mural, symbolic of one of them or both, because they're each so tightly wound in different ways. Astra doesn't give Thea any hints—just the pinprick of her sympathy. "You look like hell, baby."

I feel like hell, Thea almost admits. Almost. Because saying it feels like a concession, and Thea isn't ready for that yet. She doesn't want the "I told you so." Not on the heels of the first win she's had in a very long time. But she's aware that her clothes are hanging on her. That there are bags under her eyes. Her skin-care routine was one of the first things to go after she got fired from both the firm and the clinic. And she chopped off her hair in a rage fit with kitchen shears, mostly because she was sick of dealing with it. "I came here, didn't I? I should've known it was you all along. Only you would design an entire escape room as some kind of invitation to me."

Honestly, she should've realized it earlier. It's always been one of Astra's dreams to go beyond video games. But Thea spent that last year of their marriage paying so little attention to her that she could've designed the Matrix and Thea wouldn't have noticed. She winces, throat itching for the solace of a cheap pinot noir.

"You didn't have to accept the gauntlet. We've been open for six months and you never bothered to check us out before," Astra points out. "You came here on your own."

"Fair." Thea's not about to admit that she spent most of those six months studying how to beat the game. "What if I never showed up?"

"Then I'd have a very profitable business that's scheduled to open in two more cities next year." It's not a humblebrag. It's a straight-up brag. And Astra has no doubt earned it. But then the sparkle of pride in her eyes dims. "I'd rather have that *and* know that you're alive and safe and thriving."

"Well . . . I'm alive." It's a weak joke. An unfunny one. Thea moves closer to the dais, to the game maker's throne. Now that she's done with the maze, the disquiet and doubt are back under her skin. The urge to hide, to drink, to make it all go away. To be all the way at the other end of the ideal of perfection that she met for years. Both extremes are toxic. She knows that, somewhere deep inside. It's just that both were comfortable, too. Working long hours, sending Ma and Papa links to her cases in the news, aiming higher and higher on adrenaline and ambition as she juggled three jobs and a marriage. *Be a hero. Be a superhero. Maybe they'll love you now.* And then the flameout. Living on her severance while she fell further and further. Barely leaving her apartment. Not getting out of bed. Forgoing showers—and meals, unless she mustered the energy to order in. Being in a depression cave was just another routine after a while. Familiar. A pattern she didn't have to break out of.

But now she's here. And she has to claim her prize.

Astra is a genius. She doesn't need an IQ test to prove it. She's had an affinity for numbers, for computer science, for puzzles and quests, for as long as she can remember. When you grew up moving from place to place, there was a comfort in things that were finite, with roots—even if they were square roots. She'd begun coding in middle school, books piled up in the back of the car as she bent over a secondhand laptop, and the ribbons of code keys and strings kept her tethered. She can paint. She can sing. She knows three languages—not including the programming ones. She doesn't move around anymore, except on work trips and vacations. Sometimes her mother sends her postcards from Bali or Tulum or wherever else her wanderlust has taken her. Queenie's so old-fashioned in some ways, almost a total Luddite. As if text messages were never invented. It's kind of insulting to her kid the tech whiz.

But Astra is used to women who can't change. She went into her relationship with Thea with her eyes relatively open. Taking in this beautiful girl who lived across the hall. Type A. All-around academic all-star. 4.0 GPA. Eventually, after they'd moved from friends to something more, she'd been top of her class in law school. Still a perfect hero to her Indian family and community. And completely closeted to them, too. That uptight and insular world seemed to demand nothing less . . . and then it turned its back on her the moment she dared step out of line.

It's a life Astra doesn't personally understand, given her nomadic upbringing with a free spirit mother who absolutely refused to be called "Mom" or "Mama" or anything of the kind. Queenie is Dominican and Mexican American, a product of the 1970s, and entirely an original. "*Speak your name and claim your existence. I have always and forever will be a queen.*" Which would make Astra always and forever a star.

When Astra was twelve, Queenie confessed to conceiving her with "a skinny white man after too many shots of tequila." She's not entirely sure that's true. Queenie is an unreliable narrator who has, at various times, said this nameless but handsome man was a Taurus, an Aries, *and* an Aquarius. But Astra has learned to love loudly and love often . . . and to stay away from Jose Cuervo. When she realized men in general weren't for her, Queenie practically threw a party. Astra grew up out and proud and brown and beautiful. And she fell in love with math and programming and game designing. Somewhere in there, they settled down long enough for Astra to finish high school—and then to pursue the higher degree that would teach her what she couldn't learn on her own.

She pursued Thea, too. The girl she fell for was a beautiful overachiever with a great smile, who could be herself only when they were alone. And that self was small, slowly suffocating, buried under layers of people-pleasing and perfectionism. Astra didn't do the work of fixing her. She is in no way qualified to be a life coach or a therapist. But she helped Thea reshape and replace those destructive parts of herself so she was capable of getting professional help. And it all seemed perfect. They were happy and out and married. With great jobs and a paid-off apartment. And fuck Thea's homophobic parents boycotting their wedding.

What Astra hadn't realized at the time, *in* time, was that replacing a few parts didn't create a new Thea. A stronger one, for a little while, but still the same underneath all those joyful modifications. Wanting it all. The high-priced law firm, the pro bono gig, and her family's forgiveness. All while she lost her spirit and lost herself. Astra couldn't watch her stress to death trying to juggle it all. It was too painful. Too futile when the person she loved refused to listen to her pleas. Or to hear her when she warned Thea that what she considered ambition was really just fear. So when her wife said, "You're free to leave," Astra went.

And Thea fell apart. She's tried not to blame herself for

the timing of that. It's hard not to blame herself now, as she looks down at a beloved face gone hollow and sallow. Thea's curves and angles have swapped places. She's no less lovely, raven-black hair and keen dark eyes and kissable mouth, but the exhaustion shows. She'd needed to rebuild herself entirely to leave that old, scared self behind. Instead, she'd torn everything down. It hurts to see. Almost as much as it hurt to walk away. But Astra couldn't do all that work for her, not then or now, and not at the expense of her own peace.

What she could do and did do is create the Labyrinth. And now here they are, at the end of all the puzzles and traps. With the greatest challenge yet to come.

Astra is silent for so long that it's almost like watching her turn into a statue. Long legs slung over the arm of her leather throne, chin in hand. A perfect sculpture of a regal woman in repose. Thea has always been awestruck by how gorgeous she is, and right now is no different. In a flash, all the calculations and hacks she'd memorized spill out of her head, replaced by memories of making love. Tangling in the sheets, hands and hearts entwined. Chess games and *Dragon Age* and Sunday brunches in bed. And they'd laughed. God, they'd laughed *so much* together.

"What is this really about?" She can hear the crack in her voice. The energy and focus she'd gathered to do this are being replaced by something else. Something fragile. "You wanted me here. You got me here."

"*You* got you here. And the next step is yours, too." Astra swings her legs to the floor of the stage and sits up straight. "What are you going to do after this? Go home and back to the same routines? Fly and fall over and over again?"

For a second, Thea wonders if Astra became a psychologist as well as a game designer in the year and a half they've been apart. It's a dismissive thought. A distancing tactic. She's always been good at hearing only what she wants to in order to achieve her goals. Whether it's solving a Rubik's Cube or getting a law degree. *Does* she want to fly too close to the sun and fall over and over again? It was comfortable once, familiar once. It doesn't have to be again. That's what Astra is really saying.

Her ex is watching her, that sharply analytical mind probably cataloging everything about her, up to and including her innermost thoughts. Thea wraps her arms around her midsection, the soft pillow of her wine-and-Cheetos belly under her black T-shirt a reminder of those coping mechanisms. It'd be easy to go back to her place—to what used to be *their* place—and, riding high on solving this puzzle, start polishing her résumé and seeking out new high-powered litigation firms in the city. It'd be just as easy to crawl back into bed. Fly or fall or neither at all. She just has to make the decision.

"As rewards go, this one kind of sucks," she laughs shakily, trying to resist the urge to pace or chew on her fingertips.

"It doesn't suck nearly as much as where we've been," Astra says. She rises from the chair and makes her way down to Thea's level. "You know what happens when Theseus finds the Minotaur?"

Thea is a little alarmed at the implication. Her brows rise to her uneven hairline. She really didn't think the challenge of the Labyrinth was *that* faithful to the metaphor. Taking it from escape room to LARP . . . or possibly an MMA cage match. "Do you want us to fight to the death?" she asks in bewilderment. "Because I think that's a little excessive."

Astra's laugh rings out across the throne room, full and lush and everything she's missed over the past few years. "No, baby. This was all about fighting *your* monsters. The only way I knew how." She quickly turns serious, her dark eyes filled with a pain Thea recognizes all too well. From those late nights standing in the doorway when extra work kept Thea from joining her in bed. And from waiting up when Thea stayed too long at the office. "You shut everyone out. Me. Dion. Even your parents, after all that effort to win them back over. I'd say it's ironic if it wasn't so heartbreaking."

The weeks after losing her jobs had been a blur of arguments and blocked calls and her vehemently swearing she'd never provide free labor for Aegis Enterprises again. And then . . . silence. They didn't text. She didn't text. Nobody emailed. And the months slipped into a year as she slipped into darkness and depression. But how could Astra possibly know about that? Thea's arms drop to her sides, protective cocoon unraveling like frayed threads. "How do you know what happened with Ma and Papa?" she demands, closing the space between them. Until they're almost nose to nose and breath to breath. Save for the three inches between their heights. "Why do you care about that at all?"

"Because your mother called me last Christmas. *Me*." The look on Astra's face is probably the same one of shock she wore when the phone rang. She spreads one palm over her chest, like she's holding in a dozen conflicting emotions. Angry tears choke her voice. "She reached out to someone she never wanted to acknowledge. Because she was so damn worried about you and didn't know where else to turn. You weren't answering calls. You ignored texts and DMs. You pushed us all away to put your career first. And then you crawled into the deepest, darkest hole. Nothing about that conversation was fun, Thea. But it told me something had to happen—*anything*—to shake you out of that place."

She can imagine how that talk went. Awkward, stilted, brief. Ma's crisp and lightly accented English, heavy with disapproval . . . but tight with concern. Her heart squeezes a little thinking about how long it's been since she heard that voice. And then Astra . . . white-knuckling the phone and trying to keep her tone neutral. Knowing the woman on the other end of the line hated her. She'd done that for *her*, for Thea.

"Why?" she blurts out before she can stop herself. "Why would you *want* to do anything for me after the way I treated you? The way *she* treated you. My family has caused you nothing but grief. And look at your life. Like you said, you have a successful business. And I know you have more than that. Ten thousand projects going at once and places to be. You don't need my mess."

Thea didn't even need her mess, but she was stuck with it since she'd created it. While Astra had created this frustrating and fantastic space she'd dubbed the Labyrinth. One of the best escape rooms in the country. Because god forbid Astra do anything by halves.

"*I* decide what I need. And anything more than that . . . ? I'll let you know," her ex assures, palms coming up to cradle Thea's face and tilt it so their gazes meet. "And believe me, there will be a time for that." Her grip is firm, her tone no-nonsense. "For now, I'm still waiting for your answer. What comes next?"

All that time and effort for this one simple question. Most people would find it an over-the-top method of communication—bizarre to go to such lengths when a text message might suffice. But not the smartest and most loving woman Thea's ever met, and the only person to truly know her—the only person who ever bothered to try. "You built me a maze," she marvels, "because you knew I wouldn't be able to resist a puzzle. And because you knew I could solve it."

Astra's cheek is warm against hers. Her arms stronger than any metaphorical rope. It's not a romantic hug, not yet. Right now, it's a lifeline. A way out of the abyss. "I wanted to lead you back to you," she murmurs gently. "And back to me. So tell me . . . are you ready to do that? Are you ready to *be* here again?"

Is Thea ready? After a lifetime of overachieving and then drowning for what felt like just as long. There, in the shadow of the Minotaur, in the embrace of a woman who walked away when told to but never truly left, she weighs her choices. Her past and her present. Everything she once wanted versus everything she could have. The twists and turns of the Labyrinth led her here. So did the twists and turns of her life. There's only one outcome that feels right. Only one that makes sense.

She whispers the wish against Astra's lips. And then they raise the white victory sails and chart a course for home. No, not just for home, but to the future. Where Thea will speak her name and claim her existence anew. She is a gift and she is a goddess. She doesn't need to be anything more.

THE FURIES DETECTIVE AGENCY

Mia P. Manansala

We are the Erinyes siblings, owners of the Furies Detective Agency. Family drama is our bread and butter. We handle all the messy shit most people won't touch, and for way cheaper than the ones who would.

For example: Are you going through an ugly divorce and your soon-to-be-former spouse ran off, leaving you with the kids and a mountain of debt? We'll track them down and make them pay—literally. Or figuratively, if you prefer. My siblings and I all have different specialties, so make sure you pick the right Erinyes for the job.

Take my big sister, Alex. She's our tank. If your job requires strength or intimidation, Alex is your fighter. Subtle? No. But she is very, very effective. You got a job that requires a bit more stealth? Then you want my baby sib, Tiz. They're the brains of the operation. Anything involving research, information, or, in some cases, disinformation is Tiz's forte. They're brilliant, but they're also our rogue, so make sure you stay on their good side. Same goes for Alex, actually. The two of them can be considered the nuclear options, the ones we send in when my attempts fail.

My specialty? Charisma. I'm the talker, the one who goes in first to try to smooth things out nice and peaceful-like. Meg Erinyes, at your service.

Our agency motto is "Family is everything." That's not us being cute. We believe that shit. The world has shown us again and again that the only people we can rely on is one another. So when someone dares to violate the sacred bonds of blood, we're there to swoop in and right some wrongs. We handle all the run-of-the-mill family squabbles and get paid well for it, but our off-the-menu secret offering? Revenge.

Did your sibling betray you in a way that is technically legal but highly unethical? We got you. Were you the product of an affair and your rich piece-of-shit father is refusing to acknowledge you or your mother despite your many financial difficulties? You better believe we're on it. And, sadly, the most common situation: Are your ungrateful kids conspiring to get you declared incompetent so they can wrest control of your assets? We will teach them the error of their ways, even if we have to burn the words *filial piety* into their flesh before they fully comprehend the lesson (I designed the brand myself).

After years of cleaning up the messes that the rich and shitty people of the Chicagoland area had to offer, I'd thought we'd seen and done it all. Until the day she walked in.

I always was a sucker for a pretty face, especially one that came with lots of money and even more baggage. I should've known she'd be trouble when her first question was:

"Do you do murders?"

"That depends. Do you want us to investigate a murder or commit one?"

She raised a well-groomed eyebrow at me. "I didn't realize both were an option."

I grinned at her. "I didn't say they were, but we get asked to do all kinds of wild stuff. I wanna know what your particular needs are."

She looked around the room. "Where are your sisters? I was led to believe you're a team of three."

"Siblings," I corrected her. "I handle all the front desk duties and assign the right Erinyes for the job. They only meet the client if I say so."

"My case is rather . . . unusual. I don't think only one person can handle it, and I'm not comfortable entrusting the details to you without meeting everyone who will be working on the case."

I shrugged. "You're free to take your business elsewhere."

"You're the one your siblings trust to meet the clients, and this is how you treat them?"

I flashed her a toothy grin. "I'm the social one. And our work speaks for itself. Either you trust us to get the job done or you don't. I'm not the one with the problem here."

She studied me before admitting, "I heard you were the best, and the best is what I need. You're hired."

I hadn't said we were going to take her case, but her aura sucked me in—it wasn't arrogance she radiated, the self-assuredness of those used to getting their way, but the knowledge that she was doing the right thing and had come to the right place. She stuck her hand out, a well-manicured, smooth-skinned hand that had likely never seen a day of manual labor. As I shook it, I noted a tan line around her ring finger, likely from a signet ring based on the shape of the outline. Either I held her hand a moment too long or she followed my gaze, but she pulled her hand away with a short laugh. "Guess there's no point in hiding my identity now that I've agreed to hire you."

She reached into her purse and removed a gold ring emblazoned with a familiar family crest. "I'm Elektra Abellera. I'm assuming you've heard of my family?"

Well, well, well. My interest in both this woman and her case went up considerably.

"I have. My condolences on your losses."

The illustrious Abelleras were one of the most powerful (and dangerous) families in Chicago. Their political and underground chokehold on the city had waned of late, considering the death of Elektra's older sister last month was shortly followed by her father's. All that was left of this once-powerful clan were Elektra and her mother, Nesta, formerly the beautiful and feared Abellera matriarch, now a shell of a woman after these back-to-back losses. Technically, there was also her younger brother, Orestes, but he'd left the family years ago.

I expected Elektra to give me a tight-lipped smile and thank me insincerely for my comment, but she just slid the ring on her finger, the ornament settling back inside the outline, solid and heavy. Her hand flexed, as if struggling against the weight of it. When she finally met my eyes, her voice was strong, revealing none of the hesitancy that her fidgeting showed me.

"The police ruled my sister's and father's deaths as accidental, but that's not true. The Flavio family had something to do with it, and I need your help finding proof."

"And what do you plan on doing with that information, should we be able to find the evidence?"

She finally smiled. "That's my business, just like handling family issues with complete confidentiality is yours."

Her smile should've been another tip-off. It made me like her even more, and I only ever liked what was truly wrong for me.

But it had been a while since the last time I'd fucked up my life, so I pulled out a contract and explained our services, the fees and daily expenses, and all the boring admin stuff that makes up the daily life of a PI. After she signed the contract and put down the deposit, she returned her fancy fountain pen to her purse.

"So what happens next?"

"You meet my siblings."

"Why do you think the Flavios are involved?"

Alex sat with her booted feet up on her mostly empty desk, her left hand methodically squeezing a grip strengthener as she studied Elektra. Her desk was covered with vitamins, supplements, and a sixty-four-ounce water bottle with our company logo on it. The water bottle was extremely conspicuous, but Alex mostly went on missions where we wanted people to know we were on the case—it sent a message to our targets while also providing excellent advertising. Rather clever branding on my part, if I do say so myself.

"That family has had it out for us ever since my father beat out Nick Flavio for his position on city council. My dad tried to smooth things over by marrying off my sister, Geni, to their oldest son, but . . . well, I'm sure you heard how that turned out."

"I'm sorry. I can't imagine losing a sibling, especially like that." Alex set the grip device on the desk and pushed herself out of her seat to stand next to Elektra. "Even if they're not involved in your family's deaths, I'd be happy to rough that guy up for you. Show him what it's like to put his hands on a woman who can fight back."

Iphigenia "Geni" Flavio's death had been ruled a suicide. But people talk, and word on the street was Nathan, the Flavio heir, had a bit of a gambling problem. And Geni was the unfortunate recipient of his anger after many a bad night at the casino. She'd put up with it for years—everyone knew her father had sacrificed her to keep the peace between the families, so she did all she could to save face in front of the community. Until she couldn't anymore.

Elektra didn't respond at first, instead letting her eyes travel the length of Alex's body, taking her in, inch by intimidating inch.

"How much extra would that cost me?"

"Free of charge."

"Why?"

"Like I said, I can't imagine what it's like to lose a sibling. And I make it a point to let men know there are consequences to the way they treat women."

Alex's voice and smile were as sharp as ever, but she couldn't hide the compassion in her eyes. For all her roughness, Alex was easily the kindest of our trio. The one with the strongest principles. Frankly, she could be a bit of a pain in the ass about it, but if she felt this strongly about the case, I knew I'd made the right move in accepting it.

Elektra met Alex's gaze and nodded. "I might take you up on that."

A silent understanding seemed to pass between the two of them, a moment that didn't include me.

To bring them back to the task at hand, I asked, "Do you have any proof the Flavios were involved? Threatening messages, publicly disparaging remarks, or witnesses to an altercation would all be a great place to start."

Elektra gnawed on her lower lip as she thought this over, the sinking of her strong white teeth into her plump, glossy lip proving so distracting that I missed her answer and Alex had to fake cough twice to get my attention.

Elektra smirked. "As I was saying, Geni hated Nathan but got along with her sister-in-law, Anais. From what she told me, Anais is really sweet and different from the rest of the Flavios. I always got the sense that Anais was desperate to get away from her family's influence. Last I heard, she was applying to art colleges on the West Coast."

I noted that on my tablet. "Sounds like your brother. Didn't he also—"

"I'd rather not talk about my brother."

At my raised eyebrow, she elaborated. "He left almost ten years ago and I haven't heard from him since. Even after Geni . . . he didn't bother reaching out after we lost her, or after Dad died. For all I know, he's dead too. He might as well be."

Tiz was listening in on this conversation from their locked control room in the basement and likely already had an entire dossier prepared on Orestes, the long-lost only son of the Abellera family, but I still made a note to find out more about him. Just because he hadn't talked to Elektra didn't mean he had lost contact with everyone from that sphere.

As if sensing that I was thinking about them, my phone vibrated, letting me know I'd just received a text from Tiz. I glanced at the message before facing Elektra. "We agreed to investigate the Flavios to see if they're connected to your father's and sister's deaths. But is that really all you need?"

Elektra stilled. "How did you know?"

I shifted my position, leaning into her space without actually occupying it. "You said it yourself, we're the best in the business. Now are you going to tell us what you're hiding, or do we need to call this whole thing off?"

"I wasn't hiding anything. It's just I already told you I think two family members were secretly murdered. I didn't want you to think I was paranoid if I . . ." She paused, weighing her next words. "I'm worried my mom and I are in danger. My mom has had a couple of near misses, and I . . . I can feel someone watching me."

"Then you need more than investigators. You need a bodyguard too," Alex said.

At Elektra's nod, Alex continued: "I'll need time to go over a game plan with my siblings, so I won't be on the job until tomorrow at the earliest. Now tell us everything. I can't protect you if I don't know what I'm up against."

After briefing us on the situation and promising to send us anything that could help with the case, Elektra headed out, leaving a faint whiff of violets behind her. I was still sniffing at that elusive scent when Tiz came out from their room. Of the three of us, they were the one who had the least to do with our clients. Because of their skill set, we found they operated best when nobody knew what they looked like. They were our researcher, and certain information could only be obtained out in the field. They weren't a master of disguise, the way I was. Their strength was their ability to blend into their surroundings, putting on a facade so forgettable they might as well have been a lamp from IKEA—pleasant, inoffensive, and not worth a second glance.

They walked over to the office fridge and pulled out a can of mango juice. Their brilliant brain was powered by massive amounts of sugar, so I waited till they'd drained the can before I dared ask.

"How much is she hiding from us?"

Tiz held up a hand and grabbed a can of guyabano juice as well. After chugging the sweet nectar, they were ready to talk.

"She's a clever one. Everything she said checked out, and even if she hadn't named Anais Flavio as the first person to talk to, she would've been the logical first step."

"What about Geni's husband? When do I get to talk to him?" Alex asked, cracking her knuckles.

"After Meg gets what she needs from Anais. We don't want to risk scaring her off." Tiz paused to text me a link to an article about a political shindig happening at the end of the week. "Nick Flavio announced his run to retake his spot on the city council, now that Ricky Abellera is dead, and his wife is hosting a fancy tea party at the Drake for all the influential women in the city. I'll get you an invite."

While Tiz moved to prepare cups of Nescafé 3in1 for us and Alex microwaved a package of frozen siopao asado for our meryenda, I read over Anais's file. "She's a bit of a prodigy, huh?"

Only sixteen years old, but on track to graduate early. She not only excelled in the visual arts, but she was also a proficient harpist and trained singer. I thought it was odd that I hadn't heard much about her, considering she was so accomplished, until I got to the rumor portion of her file. There was a gap of about fifteen years between her and her brother, Nathan, and people whispered that she was the product of the affair her mother was having with a no-name painter at the time.

I whistled. "Nick Flavio's not her father?"

Tiz shrugged. "He refused to get a paternity test done,

saying that Anais was a Flavio and anyone who said different would have to go through him and his lawyers."

"So he loves and accepts her as a daughter? Wasn't expecting that," Alex said.

"Nah, he just doesn't want people to look at him as a cuckold. It's pride, not love." Tiz paused to break open one of the siopao, a curl of steam rising from the meat bun. "Alex, you'll provide backup at the party. Elektra is on the invite list, so you can pretend to be her driver and gossip with all the other hired help while protecting them. I know Meg can take care of herself, but dealing with the Abelleras and Flavios is a different pay grade than we're used to."

I waved their concerns away. "This is Chicago, dealing with shitty politicians and pseudo gangsters is nothing new for us."

Tiz shook their head. "We've dealt with dangerous people and done a lot of shady stuff in our time, but we always drew the line at murder. Too messy, too many cops involved. What made you take this case? And without consulting us, I might add."

I rubbed the agimat I wore tucked under my shirt, the cool metal of the charm providing its usual comfort and protection. "Intuition." That wasn't enough for them, so I added, "You were the one complaining that our last few cases were too easy. This will be a good test of our abilities."

Tiz snorted. "Yes, clearly you were thinking about us and not how long it's been since you got laid. Don't forget, you're not allowed to sleep with clients till after we finish the job. It's unprofessional."

"They're right, you know. Remember what happened last time you broke that rule?" Alex said as she pulled another package of siopao from the freezer.

I didn't, actually, since my brain tended to protect me from things I didn't want to remember, though my muscles ached at the memory of Alex's punishment. "Hey, I'm not just doing this because she's hot. She's also very, very rich. The frozen buns and shitty coffee don't pay for themselves, you know."

"You love this shitty coffee the same way you love everything that's bad for you." Tiz sighed. "At least we'll get a big payday out of this one."

"Do either of you know anything about that brother? Pretty cold that he didn't show up to the funerals," Alex said, setting the fresh plate of buns on the table between us.

"Just the usual gossip. His dad was grooming him to follow in his political footsteps, but he wasn't interested. Took off after his eighteenth birthday and has managed to evade every PI his dad sent to drag him home. Until us, of course," I added, accepting the half bun that Alex passed me.

"I'll need time to dig up Orestes's current whereabouts, so focus on the Flavio family for now," Tiz directed. "I don't think she's lying about not being in contact with her brother, but there's something about him that doesn't sit right with me. I sent you all the relevant files I could find."

Which wasn't a lot, considering everything in the folder was from when he was a minor. "You couldn't find anything on him after he left home? He was only eighteen, there has to be something. Didn't he leave for college?"

"I don't know who he's working with, but his trail goes cold somewhere in D.C. He must've changed his name, maybe had some fake papers drawn up to assume a new identity. He might not even be in the States anymore."

Rather than be annoyed or confused about the lack of information on Orestes Abellera, Tiz sounded excited as they reeled off these possibilities. They liked to pretend they were the careful, discerning Erinyes ("One of us has to be! You and

Alex are always doing whatever the hell you want!"), but they felt the allure of a tough case just as much as Alex and I did. And this was a challenge they had yet to come across in the decade since we first set up shop to catch our parents' killers.

"We'll leave him in your capable hands, Tiz. Alex, let's go over our plans for the event and then hit the gym. We need to be prepared for anything at this party."

"Elektra, please don't tell me this is all we're getting to eat."

I'd spent hours prepping, choosing the perfect wig and conservative (aka boring) outfit for the Flavio matriarch's luncheon at the Drake, figuring it was time to trot out my journalist persona. I'd need all my energy to deal with these ladies who lunch, but the only repast our glamorous host planned to offer were tiny sandwiches, pastries, tea, and champagne. So much champagne. That at least would make my job easier, but what I wouldn't give for a BBQ pork bun from Chi Quon.

Elektra laughed. "If you're still hungry later, I'll treat you to something good. Now come on, I snagged us seats at Joanne Flavio's table. She'll be too busy checking on her guests to actually sit down, but her daughter will be there."

Anais Flavio had been groomed within an inch of her life, her youthful beauty marred by a sort of tragic weariness you didn't expect to see in a sixteen-year-old. She snapped to attention when Elektra and I took seats next to her.

"Ate Elektra! How are you? Is Tita Nesta feeling better?"

Elektra shook out her napkin and laid it across her lap. "My mother is much better, thanks, but not well enough to attend today. She asked me to send her regards and congratulations to your family."

"How lovely of her." Joanne Flavio joined us, resplendent

in a tweed Chanel suit and capiz shell jewelry. She gestured toward a server, who brought over a freshly brewed pot of tea. Joanne made a big show of filling Elektra's teacup and then her daughter's before finally acknowledging me.

"I don't believe we've met before," she said, holding up the teapot to ask if I'd like any. At my nod, she filled my cup and then hers before sitting next to her daughter. "I'm Joanne Flavio, and I'd like to thank you for your support. My husband is looking to turn this city around, and he couldn't do it without engaged citizens like you."

I smiled, lifting my teacup to take a dainty sip. Damn, this was good. I liked my coffee cheap but my tea bougie, and this was the best I'd ever had. "Delighted to meet you, Mrs. Flavio. I'm Denise Aquino, a freelance journalist. I was assigned to write an article for the Style section about your party, though I'd love to pitch an article about you and your family to my editor."

Joanne's eyes lit up. "The Style section? That's wonderful! But where is your photographer?"

She looked around the room as if worried they were taking pictures of women less important than her. I bit back a groan. We'd prepared for this, of course, but hoped it wouldn't be necessary. Alex was too obvious in these situations, which was why she was relegated to the role of driver. I hadn't worked in the field with Tiz in at least a year, but needs must.

I glanced at my watch. "They should be here by now. Let me send them a quick message, and then I'd love to get some quotes from you for the article."

Message sent, I pulled a small Moleskine from my purse and leaned toward Joanne. "Now, tell me all about the Flavios."

—————

I had greatly underestimated how much Joanne Flavio could brag about her family. What was especially impressive was how she managed to shade Elektra's family in the process while never referencing them by name.

As she rhapsodized about her saintly family, a server brought over a tray of champagne. When Elektra reached for a glass, Joanne said, "No alcohol for our table. Ms. Aquino, you seemed to like the tea we had earlier?"

I smiled at her. "Oh, yes! It was exquisite."

"Our family doesn't drink alcohol, but Darjeeling is known as the champagne of teas. You have good taste." She smiled at me approvingly before addressing the server again. "Bring out another pot of your finest Darjeeling. And take away these glasses."

The server glanced at Elektra, who sighed and set her full glass back on the tray. Denied even that small pleasure, Elektra seemed to think she'd been quiet long enough.

"Tita Joanne, you've been so modest, talking about everyone but yourself. Why don't you let Ms. Aquino know about your many contributions? Tito Nick is a wonderful man, but he never would've made it this far without you."

"Oh, a lady never speaks of her own accomplishments, Elektra. Now if you'll excuse me, I must mingle with my guests. Ms. Aquino, please let me know when your photographer arrives so I can direct them on what photos to take." Joanne Flavio gave me and Elektra a demure nod before taking her leave.

Anais's shoulders slumped after her mother left, relaxing now that her mom wasn't around to critique her posture. She poured herself another cup of tea and held up the pot. "Would either of you like some more?"

Elektra shook her head and waved down a server to finally

help herself to some champagne, but I set my cup in front of Anais. "Thanks. As much as I'd love some champagne, I need to stay clearheaded while on the job."

Anais's lips quirked. "Need to stay alert so you can dig up dirt on my family for clickbait? Nothing but hard-hitting journalism in the Style section, I'm sure."

"Whatever pays the bills," I said, selecting a scone from a three-tiered silver tray and loading it with jam and Devonshire cream.

"How are you doing, Anais? Really?" Elektra set her champagne flute on the table and leaned toward the teen. Anais's eyes darted to me and my notepad.

"This is off the record, don't worry. I'm just enjoying my tea and pastries. But I can leave if you two would like some privacy."

"If Ate Elektra trusts you, it's okay." Elektra nodded, so Anais continued. "It's hard, being in that house without her."

I wasn't sure who "her" referred to until Elektra reached for Anais's hand. "I miss her too. I know it's not the same, but if you ever need anything, call me. You were special to her, you know? She'd want me to look out for you."

Geni Flavio, née Abellera, the sister they both lost. Of course.

I wanted to pump the kid for info, but this moment was too tender for me to intrude on. Luckily, I got a text from Tiz.

"My photographer is here, so I'll leave you two alone. It was nice meeting you, Anais."

Tiz stood near the grand piano, two cameras slung around their neck, their usual all-black ensemble making them look like a crow who'd wandered into a garden full of hummingbirds and peacocks. I could actually see the attendees' eyes glance past them, as if Tiz had cast a spell that wouldn't allow anyone's gaze to linger on them. Normally, this ring of invisibility was enough, but they'd also fixed themself up with one of my wigs and a pair of glasses that changed the shape of their face—this case was too important for them to get made.

"You ready, Tiz?"

They lifted their camera to snap a quick picture of a well-known socialite who'd thrown her head back in laughter at something Joanne Flavio said.

"Always."

I was finishing my interview with a woman who had quite a bit to say about the Flavios and their recent spending habits when I felt the sudden shift of energy in the room. I turned toward the source of the tension and beheld Elektra, her flowy purple dress billowing like the robes of a goddess as she approached Nick Flavio, who'd arrived with his son and a small entourage. She was going to do something either really dumb or really helpful, so I sauntered over with Tiz to find out which it was going to be.

"Elektra! How lovely to see you again. How are you doing, my dear?"

Nick Flavio strode forward to give her a kiss on the cheek and introduce her to the people in his group.

"This is Ricky Abellera's daughter, God rest his soul. One of the best lawyers I've ever seen. Make sure to keep your nose clean if you're going to be around her, gentlemen," he joked as Elektra shook everyone's hand.

"Nice to meet you all. I just wanted to offer my congratulations on your bid for alderman, Tito Nick. I'm sure my father will rest easy knowing you're taking over his position."

"I appreciate your support, my dear, but nothing's official yet. We'll leave that to the voters to decide."

She smiled at him. "I'm sure they'll be voting early and often."

"What are you implying?" Nathan Flavio had been lurking in the background, but he stepped in between his father and Elektra after her comment.

Elektra stopped a passing server and took her time selecting a canapé. "Why hello there, kuya. How are you?"

"I told you not to call me that."

Joanne Flavio hushed her son, throwing a meaningful look toward Tiz, who had been snapping away during this whole exchange. I was so enamored with Elektra's every move I didn't notice a server dropping off our tea until Tiz said, "Okay, that should be enough. Mind if I help myself to a cup? I could use the caffeine."

Joanne nudged her daughter forward, so Anais gracefully poured and handed out cups of tea for all of us. I tore my eyes away from Elektra and inhaled the light aroma of the fine tea, hoping it would force my mind to focus. Instead, alarm bells started ringing.

Something about the scent was off.

I looked up at the new server, a man with thick facial hair obscuring his features, to ask if he had brought us a different tea, but the moment my eyes met his, he turned and fled.

"Don't drink the tea!" I knocked the cup out of Elektra's hands, and Tiz stopped the Flavios just as the cups reached their lips. I addressed my sibling. "Make sure no one takes the evidence away. Let Alex know we need her."

Then I took off after the server, careful to keep my eyes on him as we weaved through the crowd. The server made no pretense of trying to blend in, instead mowing his way through the women. He slowed only long enough to hurl the silver tray he was still holding like a discus, forcing me to dive out of its path. A woman standing a few feet behind me wasn't so lucky, the crunch of bone and her scream of pain letting me know the server wasn't playing around—if the woman hadn't raised her arms to protect her face, there was a good chance she'd be dead.

That brief distraction was enough to make me lose sight of my quarry. I had Alex keep an eye on Elektra while Tiz and I scanned the public areas. I even had a manager accompany me to the men's rooms, but no dice.

By the time Tiz and I made it back to our table, Joanne and Nathan were screaming at the concierge about the "riffraff" the hotel employed and threatening to sue for the assassination attempt.

Alex pulled me aside. "Before coming up here, I did a sweep but couldn't find a trace of the guy. We need to get Elektra out of here and figure out what's going on."

I nodded. "Let's head to the usual spot."

A tiring bit of daytime reconnaissance could only end one way in the Erinyes family: dissecting the details over all-day breakfast at Ruby's Fast Food.

"Meg, I want you to be my bodyguard."

Alex, Tiz, and I were so busy fighting over the last bit of crispy pata that we'd ordered in addition to our silog platters that I didn't quite hear what Elektra said.

"What's that? Oh, right, as our client, the polite thing is to let you have it," I said, placing the delicious fatty pork on her plate.

"No, Meg. I said I want you to be my bodyguard. I don't care about the food."

"In that case . . ." I snatched the crispy pata and took a huge bite before she changed her mind. "Anyway, you already have Alex, a god-tier bodyguard. I'm not really cut out for that stuff, you know?"

"And I'm still keeping Alex on, of course. As my mother's bodyguard." Elektra glanced over at Alex to reassure her. "But my mom doesn't leave the house. She got rid of all the staff she doesn't trust. If anyone comes after my mom, it would be in the guise of a home invasion, and Alex is best suited to that."

"Then what do you need Meg for?" Tiz studied Elektra, their warm brown eyes hiding the cold calculations I knew they were making. They'd been against taking Elektra with us—prolonged contact with our clients wasn't their way, and they didn't want her getting a glimpse of our inner workings. But I'd pointed out they were still in disguise and, considering the attempt on the Flavios' lives, we needed to keep Elektra close.

"I took a leave of absence from work after my sister's death and don't plan on going back any time soon," Elektra said. Tiz hadn't bothered introducing themself to Elektra, but she clearly knew who the mysterious third party was and was perceptive enough to keep her eyes focused away from Tiz. She took a sip of her water, the ice rattling around in the near-empty glass. "But now that Nick Flavio has made his bid for election public, I expect to be at all his social events to gather information. Meg is the perfect person to watch my back."

"Won't people question why I'm always around you? If we're investigating, it's better for people to not know you have a bodyguard," I said, pouring more water for the both of us.

As I took a sip, she said, "Good point. Maybe you could pose as my girlfriend?"

I choked on an ice cube, and Alex pounded me on the back, which just made it worse. "You okay, sis? I don't know if that's a good idea, Elektra. We have a strict policy on, uh . . ."

"Fraternizing with clients," Tiz finished for Alex. "That gets messy, and we try to limit our mess as much as possible."

"You're more ethical than I thought you'd be," Elektra said. She studied the melting ice in her cup before pushing it away. "But we won't actually be doing anything. It's fine if we're faking it, right?"

I glanced at my siblings. I couldn't accept without their okay, and if I showed how badly I wanted to take on this assignment, they'd shut it down so fast their heads would spin like that chick from *The Exorcist*.

Alex looked unsure, but Tiz sat with their eyes closed, and this time I could tell they were making calculations of a different kind. I could practically see the dollar signs floating around their head.

Their eyes snapped open. "If you can afford it, you've got yourself a fake girlfriend."

So that's how I found myself attending one stuffy political event after another with Elektra, forced to don my Denise Aquino disguise each time. Elektra came up with a good cover story for our sudden relationship, telling everyone she fell in love after seeing me leap into action at the Flavio tea party.

My journalist persona made it so I could ask questions without arousing suspicion, and as a nonprofit lawyer, Elektra had the perfect mix of empathy and persuasion to draw someone out and make them want to confide in her. When that didn't work, I stepped in to turn on the charm—it's amazing how flattery flavored with a hint of intimidation can loosen people's lips.

For the ritzier parties, Alex acted as our chauffeur and gathered intel from staff working these events, while Tiz guarded Mrs. Abellera and conducted their own research. We never returned home empty-handed, but all the information we'd gathered only hinted at Nick Flavio's corruption, not his murderous intentions. We needed to get closer to the family.

So Elektra "accidentally" mentioned that we were looking into her sister's death in front of Anais. That same night, Elektra received a text from the teen requesting me as a personal tutor.

"Why me? What's her game?"

Elektra shrugged. "I'm not sure, but I suggest you find out."

So that's how I ended up meeting a teenage political heiress for bubble tea, dressed as my "broke grad student" persona.

Anais smiled at me before sliding over an SAT prep book. "Now you can come and go from my house without raising any suspicions."

I slurped my drink, trying to figure out her angle. "Why are you doing this?"

"I didn't score nearly high enough on my last practice test, so Mommy insisted I get a tutor."

"Cute. You know that's not what I meant."

She shrugged and sucked up a mouthful of boba. "Does it matter? Don't look a gift horse in the mouth."

"This feels more like a Trojan horse. I don't trust that you're doing this out of the goodness of your heart."

"You're helping Ate Elektra investigate Ate Geni's death, which means taking down my dad and asshole brother. That's all the reason I need."

I leaned forward. "They haven't done anything to you, have they? Do you need me to get you out of there?"

Surprise flashed through her eyes, and she shook her head. "I just hate the way they operate. And I'll never forgive Nathan for what happened to Ate Geni. Never."

"Good. Now tell me everything you know."

Weeks of unbridled access to the Flavio compound let me find enough evidence to build various cases of political corruption against Nick Flavio, but not murder. Even the financial transaction records that Tiz dug up proving that Ricky Abellera had been blackmailing his political rival (apparently Nick had misappropriated some of the city's funds during his tenure to build a pool and set up his mistress in a nice Lincoln Park town house) weren't a smoking gun.

At least, not according to Elektra. The slow pace of our investigation frustrated both her and Alex—Alex didn't know how to play the long game and begged me to let her do something besides watch telenovelas with Elektra's mom night after night. Elektra accused us of dragging things out to squeeze more money out of her.

"It's been a month. How have you not solved this case yet?"

"Look, El, despite what you've seen on TV, detective work takes time. We already found a possible motive for your father's murder. That's a hell of a start. Besides, you've been blessed with my company for the past month. Don't act like you haven't enjoyed it."

"No nicknames. And that's not enough to reopen his case."

"We need a new angle," I said, an idea starting to form. Maybe I had a job for Alex after all.

___

While Tiz dug deeper into Ricky Abellera's medical and police reports at the Abellera household, I sent Alex on a special reconnaissance mission. Meanwhile, Elektra and I met Anais for lunch at a restaurant popular for confidential business meetings and clandestine trysts, thanks to its private booths and tight-lipped staff.

Anais may have gotten me into the Flavio house, but she remained guarded around me and refused to talk about Elektra's sister. Elektra had been out of town when Geni died, and any information she had about her sister's death had been secondhand from her father and the family's lawyers. But Anais had been there the last days of Geni's life. After some gentle prodding from Elektra, she finally opened up.

"Ate Geni wanted a divorce, but my brother wouldn't give it. So she ran away, back to your family. But your father threw her out, said she wasn't going to shame him by going back on her wedding vows." Tears dripped down Anais's face as she recounted the cruelty that had forced Geni into a corner. "I guess she thought she had no other way out. Kuya Nathan had her cut all ties with her old friends. She couldn't turn to you since you still lived at home and couldn't go against your father. Maybe it was her way of leaving on her own terms."

Elektra kept her face carefully neutral as Anais let all that out, her clenched fist the only sign of the effect the words had on her.

Soon after that revelation, Anais's driver came to pick her up, cutting our time with her short. "So sorry to interrupt, miss, but your mother wanted me to take you to your music lesson."

Anais lit up. "Julian! How are you feeling? Did that ginger tea help?"

"Yes, thank you, miss. I've still got a bit of a cough, so please keep your distance. I'd hate to get you sick too." Julian adjusted the medical face mask he was wearing. "Are you ready to go?"

"I just need to run to the washroom really quick." The teen blushed as she hurried away, piquing my interest enough to study her driver.

The mask and a pair of thick-framed glasses covered most of his face, but judging by his voice and what little I could see, he was probably late twenties, either Filipino or Latine. His chauffeur uniform and cap were clean and neatly pressed, and he even wore driving gloves, all of which must've been hell in this heat.

He must've felt my scrutiny, because his eyes met mine and he nodded, adjusting his glasses before turning his gaze to the floor, hands folded neatly in front of him, like the perfectly respectable chauffeur he was hired to be. I was surprised the Flavios trusted such a young driver around their daughter, but he was likely the son of an older, respected staff member.

Our server came to our booth with a padded envelope for Elektra, ending my scrutiny. "This just came for you, ma'am."

"Who dropped it off?" I asked, stopping Elektra from taking it. I wasn't expecting anything serious, like a letter bomb or anthrax or Gwyneth Paltrow's head, but I'd be remiss in my job as bodyguard if I weren't at least a little suspicious. After all, how would someone know where Elektra was unless they were following us?

"A paid courier, ma'am. Is there a problem? Would you like to talk to the hostess who accepted the envelope?" the server asked. As I thought it over, Anais returned to the booth to thank us for lunch.

"It was our pleasure. We should do this again, maybe somewhere a little less formal next time. Don't forget to call me if—"

"What's that?" Anais asked, cutting Elektra off to point at the envelope in my hand.

"Miss, we need to get going or we'll be late, and you know how your mother feels about punctuality," Julian reminded her.

Anais rolled her eyes but complied, promising to hang out again soon as she waved goodbye.

"Is it okay if I open the envelope?" I asked Elektra. At her nod, I tore it open and slid the contents onto the table: a note card that said *For your investigation* with a flash drive taped to it.

"What do you think is on that?" she asked.

"If we're lucky, an actual fucking clue." I stood up, slipping the evidence into my purse. "Let's get out of here. Something tells me Tiz is gonna have a lot of work to do."

"Look who I found."

It was a week after our meeting with Anais, and Elektra and I were bickering over lunch and my family's "poor dietary choices" (she pushed salad on us so often you'd think she worked for Big Salad) but stopped at Alex's announcement.

She'd gone out to do recon work as a chauffeur for the past week and returned with Julian, the Flavios' driver, his hands zip-tied together. He wasn't wearing his face mask or glasses, which drew attention to the only thing marring his near-perfect face: a jagged scar under one eye.

Elektra must've noticed that same detail because she shot out of her chair and rushed forward to touch the mark on the man's face. He held still and let her, as if he'd predicted her reaction and resigned himself to it.

"Orestes?"

"Hey, ate. Long time no see."

Not exactly the touching family reunion I'd been expecting. "How did you know who he was?"

Alex tipped her chauffeur's cap at me. "I wouldn't have figured it out if Tiz hadn't prepped me. The scar was the biggest giveaway."

Orestes shook his head. "A decade of hiding blown because of this stupid outfit. I keep the scar covered with makeup and my glasses, but it was so hot outside. In the time it took me to take off my glasses to wipe away the sweat, Alex figured it out."

Elektra touched the restraints on his wrists. "Was this necessary?"

"It was for his own good. He tried to run away, and when that didn't work, he tried to fight me. Points for bravery, but next time you swing on me, I'm not holding back." Alex pulled out her balisong and cut his hands free.

Orestes stared at the butterfly knife in my sister's scarred hands and nodded.

"Why are you working for the Flavios?" Elektra and I asked at the same time. We glanced at each other, then turned our searching eyes toward her brother.

"I heard about Geni. And Daddy. I didn't believe the story about their deaths being accidental, so I came to investigate."

"Mommy will be so happy to see you," Elektra said. Orestes made a noncommittal noise, and the siblings eyed one another, a silent conversation taking place.

"Why don't we take you home? The three of us can work at your place since we have questions for Orestes." I grabbed Elektra's purse and take-out salad bag and shoved them at her.

"Can it wait?" Elektra asked, after another glance at Orestes. "It's been so long since we were all together. I'd prefer to keep it family-only for tonight."

Now it was my turn to hold a nonverbal conversation with my siblings. Tiz and Alex both shrugged.

Ignoring the pressure in my chest, I rubbed my agimat and said, "It's not urgent. We still need to crack the password on that flash drive anyway."

"We'll stop by in the morning. And make sure you all eat these, or you'll hear it from me tomorrow," Elektra said, setting the salads back on the table.

I grinned at her. "Looking forward to it."

We never did get to have that talk, because she didn't show up the next morning. We waited till midday, but the lack of response from Elektra put me on edge. We were suiting up to head to her house when a surprise visitor showed up and dropped a bombshell on us: both Nathan Flavio and Nesta Abellera were dead.

"I didn't know where else to go."

Anais had come knocking on our door to tell us about Nathan's and Nesta's untimely demise. Apparently, Elektra had told her my real identity and instructed her to come to us if she ever needed help.

"My condolences, but why are you here?" Tiz's voice crackled through the speakers, making the teen jump.

As Anais looked around to see where the voice had come from, Alex entered with a tray of coffees for us. Anais wrinkled her nose. "Instant?"

"Did you come here to complain about our hospitality, or did you have something important to tell us?"

"Oh, right. Sorry." She took the cup Alex offered her and stared into its creamy depths. "I'm worried about Elektra."

"Because of her mom?" My chest burned with the knowledge that we'd failed her, and I rubbed my agimat for comfort. "Or do you think she killed Nathan?"

"I don't care about Nathan, not after what he did to Geni." Anais took a sip of the coffee, shuddered, then took another. "And obviously her mom's death is going to hit her hard. But it's more than that. It's Julian, I mean Orestes—"

The door buzzer announced the arrival of another guest, but my eyes were still on Anais. "What about her brother?"

Elektra entered the room, setting another bag of salad on my desk. "He's the one who killed my mother."

"Elektra . . ."

I instinctively reached out a hand to touch her, then pulled back. She was as perfectly styled as ever, her impeccable appearance the armor she donned every day before battle. Only when you looked into her eyes did you see her coming undone. Alex guided her to a seat and poured her some coffee as well.

I waited until Elektra's needs had been tended to before asking, "What happened after we left you the other night?"

"There was no moving reunion between mother and son. Once we were alone, he accused our mom of having something to do with our father's accident, said he didn't want to meet her unless I could prove her innocence." She took a sip of coffee, her eyes fixed on our beat-up fridge. "I didn't believe him, but I played along. He hid in a separate room while I asked my mom about the rumor, and she confessed. She confessed so easily.

"She blamed my dad for Geni's death. Said he sacrificed his own child for his ambitions. He told her Geni was weak, and if she had just done her duty, there wouldn't have been a problem. So she worked with Nick Flavio to make his death seem like an accident."

"And how did the two of you react when she admitted this?"

Elektra let out a breathy laugh. "I was shocked, of course. But I was actually proud of my mom. She's always been the passive sort, unless it involved us. She lost Geni twice. To that marriage, which she opposed, and again when Geni died. But she fought for her both times."

"But Orestes didn't agree?"

"As soon as my mom confessed, I sent her to her room and told her to lock her door. When I went to check on Orestes . . . He'd never been into that patriarchal bullshit my father spouted, but now here he was agreeing with him, calling our mom a traitor and blaming the Flavios for what happened to our family." She choke-laughed. "Somehow my dad got in contact with him after Geni died. He realized his life was in danger and wanted Orestes to come back. Only he was too late."

"Have you gone to the police?"

"Of course. Not that I trust they'll find him before he finds me."

"You think he'll come after you?"

Elektra looked away. "He said I betrayed him, siding with Mom. We were the closest in the family growing up, and I guess he counted on me being on his side. After he left, I went on a long drive to clear my head, and when I got back home . . . I found her."

Her mother. Dead. I knew what that was like.

I wrapped my arms around her, agency rules be damned.

"I'm so sorry, Elektra. This never should've happened. We failed you."

For the first time ever, the Furies hadn't succeeded at our mission. Now her mother was gone, an error we could never make right. But we could try.

"You're staying with us. And we'll find Orestes. I won't let him hurt you."

She hugged me back, her arms trembling as she squeezed me tight. "Don't let him get away. He has to pay for what he's done. And, Anais . . ."

Elektra pulled away from me and looked at the scared teen. "You need to get somewhere safe. My brother declared vengeance against your whole family, and he's already gotten to Nathan."

"Can you come with me to tell them? I don't want to be alone for this."

Elektra agreed, and I said Alex and I would accompany them. "From now on, you're not to be out of my sight."

"You finally have a reason to not take your eyes off me," Elektra said, attempting a joke. When I didn't laugh, she leaned close, the scent of her violets wrapping around us both. "Thank you. And please take care of her too. She's the sole innocent in all this."

We both looked at Anais, who hovered around Alex, sensibly clinging to the toughest, kindest person in the room.

"You have my word."

I didn't care for Joanne Flavio, but I felt for her now. She was still reeling from the death of her son, and now she had to deal with the news that the rest of her family was in danger too. To her credit, once she processed what we told her, she wasted no time handling her business. Within the hour, the remaining Flavios were packed, plane tickets booked, and bodyguards hired to protect them. Except . . .

"Anais, stay with them. He wants your father. If you're with us, that'll just put you in danger too," Joanne said as we prepared to leave.

"But, Mommy, what about you? If you're with Daddy, you'll be in just as much danger."

"He's my husband. It's my duty to stay by his side. But as long as you're safe, it'll be okay." She hugged Anais. "Please. I already lost Nathan. I can't lose you too."

"We'll take care of her," Alex said, putting an arm around Anais.

"You do that. And, Elektra"—Joanne's eyes hardened—"if anything happens to her, I'll come back and kill you myself. I promise you that."

He struck that same night.

Elektra and Anais hunkered down in the basement with Tiz, the locked door, lack of windows, and surveillance system a hindrance to sneak attacks. Alex and I guarded the room in shifts, one of us out on the floor and the other in the room, and he was unlucky enough to break in when Alex was on duty. He was smaller than Alex but faster, and it was all Alex could do to knock the gun out of his hand before raising the alarm. From the security camera monitor in Tiz's room, we watched Alex pull out her knife and kick Orestes's gun away—she used guns only as a last resort, preferring hand-to-hand combat and her balisong.

I had my own gun out—I may not have been as strong as Alex, but I was a better shot—waiting to see if he'd breach our first line of defense. It was hell to just stay on the sidelines, watching my big sister fighting for her life. For all of our lives. My eyes stayed glued to the monitor, flip-flopping between whether I should run out to distract him so Alex could take him down and whether I should keep following our plan.

Elektra took that decision out of my hands.

Alex had the upper hand till she didn't dodge fast enough and Orestes's knife slashed her face. Anais's scream must've triggered a reaction in Elektra, because she pushed past me and out of the safety of the room. Pausing just long enough to order Tiz and Anais not to follow, I tore after her, terrified of what would happen to Elektra if she reached them, terrified of what would happen to Alex if she didn't.

The gun Alex had kicked away was near the room entrance, and Elektra grabbed it, then fired at the ceiling. Orestes whipped his head around at the noise, his eyes fixating on Elektra for a long moment before Alex knocked him out. I stood over him, my own gun trained on him in case he was faking it, while Alex zip-tied his hands and feet together.

"It's over."

I looked over at Elektra, the gun still in her hand, and that chill in my chest returned. "Elektra, it's over," I repeated. "Put the safety on and hand over the gun. The police will need it for evidence."

"It's not over."

"Elektra, you don't want to do this."

"Meg, he had a gun. He had a gun this whole time. Do you know how my mother died?" Her eyes haunted me as she recounted what the police told her. "She had over twenty stab wounds. He could've killed her quickly, painlessly, but he didn't. He mutilated her. The woman who had shown us nothing but love, and all to avenge a man who didn't give a shit about us."

"Elektra . . ."

"You don't understand!" she screamed. "I'm the one who brought him into our home. I'm the one who played his game. I'm the one who caused this. So I'm going to be the one who finishes it."

Oh, but I did understand. The number of times Alex, Tiz, and I kicked ourselves for not being there when our parents were killed. For having the audacity to be at a party while the people who raised us were being butchered. But I also knew how hollow it feels exchanging an eye for an eye. How you thought you'd find some peace after it was all done. And how empty you become once you realize no matter what you do, they're never coming back.

"Ate, please . . ."

Elektra and I whirled around at Anais's voice. The teen stepped toward Elektra, but Tiz held her back.

"Are you seriously going to murder your own brother in front of this kid? Destroy everything my family's worked for by dragging us into your mess? Where's the justice in that?"

"Justice? There's no evidence against her dad or my brother. At most, they'll use their money to get a slap on the wrist and go back to ruining people's lives. I am many things, Tiz, but naive isn't one of them."

She was right. But she underestimated the power of the Erinyes siblings.

I grinned at her. "Who said we didn't have evidence?"

Elektra stared at me, but it was Tiz who spoke. "That USB you received? It has photos of Nick Flavio meeting with a known hit man, as well as records of the payments. They're dated around the time of your father's death." They paused. "Orestes sent it. He included a document explaining everything. If he failed to kill Nick Flavio, you were to use this evidence to prove he was your father's killer." Tiz pulled the USB out of their pocket. "This is your chance to do the right thing, Elektra. I suggest you take it."

They looked into Elektra's eyes for a moment, hard and searching, then moved over to Alex. Her wound was still bleeding, so Tiz pulled out the first aid kit we kept behind the desk and tended to her.

"Ate, what are you going to do?" Anais asked, her eyes on the gun still clutched in Elektra's hand.

Elektra sighed and handed the gun over to me. "What do you think I'm doing? I'm calling the police."

Tiz tells me Anais is thriving in her new life. With her brother gone, her father in jail, and her mother able to make her own decisions, Anais gets to start over at the art school of her dreams. Good for her.

As for Orestes, he died shortly after entering prison, allegedly stabbed to death in a prison brawl.

Elektra disappeared soon after, leaving behind only our payment, her signet ring, and a note. The note sits unread in my room, but I pawned the ring—we had a business to run.

We are the Furies Detective Agency. Come to us if you have issues with your family that can't be resolved. We'll make sure you find justice.

Whatever form it may take.

ATALANTA HUNTS THE BOAR

Valerie Valdes

Atalanta León had made a lot of poor choices in her life. Starting a bar fight to help her former captain steal a priceless tapestry from the Teegarden system. Wrestling a crewmate in the parking lot at said captain's uncle's funeral and getting banned from the entire planet of Polychrysos for life. Drawing a giant graffiti middle finger with holopaint on a random spaceship on Aksum, on a dare, only to find out it belonged to General Mahrem, who was still offering a thousand-credit bounty to whoever delivered the perpetrator to the Invincible's Sons. Some—not her—would also include betting she'd marry whoever could beat her in a zipship race, then losing on purpose because she was hot for the winner. But getting caught having truly excellent sex in the private office of a notorious underworld figure was apparently going to be her downfall.

Now Atalanta sat handcuffed to a chair, which had nothing to do with sex and everything to do with Kybele lounging across from her like a vengeful goddess with void-black eyes. The woman draped one dark-skinned leg over the arm of her plush leather seat, and as she spoke, she toyed with a small pellet drum.

"It's been a while, my little lions," Kybele said, her deep voice more amused than annoyed. "But let us move past pleasantries to discuss what precisely you were looking for here in my inner sanctum."

Atalanta grimaced. "We were looking for an empty room. We weren't, uh, paying the closest attention to which room it was." If she hadn't been so distracted, she might have recognized the limestone desk, brightly painted frescoes, and conspicuously displayed bust she knew was carved from a chunk of meteor. But she hadn't visited the Temple in a long time, and the music and dancing in the main hall had fired her blood as much as they had made her want to be anywhere else, alone, with her husband.

"You are not here at Jason's behest?" Kybele asked. "Or perhaps Artemis sent you?"

Atalanta snorted derisively. Kybele knew as well as anyone that Atalanta didn't deal with either of those two anymore. Especially not Artemis.

Pom cleared his throat, turning his deliciously earnest amber eyes on Kybele. "We absolutely were not sent here to spy. I know it sounds unbelievable, but this was an honest mistake."

"Honest mistake my ass," Atalanta muttered. "Aphrodite was the one who nudged us in this direction." She should have realized something was up when, instead of a bed, the only places to get busy were a desk, a few chairs, the walls, and the floor. Not even a couch or a thick rug.

Kybele smiled as she rotated the drum, which rattled loudly in the small room. "Aphrodite has not forgotten how dear Pom snubbed her at my last soiree."

"Aphrodite's gonna forget how to chew when I finish

breaking her jaw," Atalanta said. An empty threat, but a nice daydream.

"'Temper, my star," Pom said. He attempted to lean forward, but his own handcuffs prevented it. "Kybele, most generous of patrons and Great Mother to us all, what can we do to make things right between us?"

Kybele spun the drum faster, her smile widening, then slammed the instrument on her desk with a loud crack.

"I'm so glad you asked," Kybele said. "Conveniently, I have a job for you two. A bounty."

This was, Atalanta knew, a terrible time to remind Kybele that she and Pom weren't runners anymore. So she didn't.

"You'll appreciate this particular request," Kybele continued, "since you have some history with the target."

A cold finger of unease slid up Atalanta's spine. "Who is it?"

"The Boar," Kybele replied. "I want him, dead or alive."

Threads of memory tangled in Atalanta's mind like a Gordian knot. Artificial rain flooding the streets inside the Calydon terradome, her footsteps pounding against the pavement. Meleager behind her, shouting at her to wait for backup. Ancaeus screaming, trying to hold in his guts as she passed him. The Boar ducking into a side alley, his dark form limned in fluorescent light. Blood spurting from the shoulder wound Atalanta gave him, just before he slammed her head into a brick wall and her vision exploded into stars.

Meleager's body, burned nearly beyond recognition.

"How did the Boar offend you?" Pom asked.

Kybele leaped to her feet and threw her drum across the room, where it shattered against the wall. Pom winced, but Atalanta stilled, wary.

"Offend?" Kybele growled, fists clenched. "It is beyond offense. He murdered my Attis."

Attis was her second in command, husband in all but name. Atalanta imagined what she would do if someone killed Pom, and a cold rage flooded her veins.

"What makes you think we can catch him?" Atalanta asked. "You know I've tried before and failed."

"You've come closer than anyone," Kybele said. "And you owe me a favor for making a mess of my office. I also happen to know he's on Pyroeis for a zipship race, which I seem to recall is one of your unique specialties"—she smirked at Pom—"most of the time."

Atalanta had never told anyone the truth about that race, not even Pom, but suspicion abounded. Neither of them had raced again after that. She had also never gone back to Pyroeis since her last disastrous encounter with the Boar.

"I'm a little rusty," Atalanta warned.

Kybele shrugged with one shoulder. "I'm sure your husband would be happy to . . . lubricate you as needed."

Atalanta closed her eyes and wished she had never agreed to make a pit stop at the Temple.

"Artemis won't like this," Pom said, his voice carefully neutral.

"Then Artemis should not have loosed her killer on my people," Kybele replied coldly. "Artemis is not your present concern. I am. And if I find out you ran instead, you'll be running until the heat death of the universe."

Atalanta cursed inwardly. She and Pom were fast, but Kybele was patient, and persistence predators always caught their quarry. But Pom was right: Artemis would come after them if she found out. They were between Scylla and Charybdis, figuratively speaking, though she'd been literally between them once and it was just as bad.

"So we take care of the Boar, and we're even?" Atalanta asked.

"Yes," Kybele said. She gestured at the seat Pom occupied. "Also, you owe me a new chair, because now I have to burn that one."

"I can't believe you talked her into giving us the chair," Atalanta said as she ran through the preflight checks on their ship, the *Golden Apple*. The interior was cozy: a small cockpit, a kitchen unit, a sanitation pod, and a comfortable bed big enough for two. Now, Kybele's maroon barrel chair took up most of the space between the bed and the kitchen.

Pom kissed the top of her head. "You know me, my love. I'm persuasive. And it's a very fine chair that didn't deserve to be burned for our crimes of passion."

Atalanta snorted. "Did you input the coordinates into the nav computer? Remember, we have to pick up our zipships from Ganymede first."

"Doing it now, my star." Pom tapped in the necessary sequence, then eyed the trajectory output. "I haven't been to Pyroeis in years."

"Me either," Atalanta said. "I hate the smell of terradomes." She slumped down in the pilot's seat and closed her eyes, conducting a mental inventory of which weapons she would bring for this job. Something nagged at her, though.

"Why would Artemis go after Kybele's second?" she murmured. "It's practically a declaration of war. Artemis is usually more subtle." Except when she'd coldly told Atalanta that she'd married beneath her, which was the last time Atalanta had spoken to her foster mother—two years ago.

"Quite a puzzle box indeed," Pom replied. "Would you like me to open it for you?"

His casual tone didn't fool her like it used to. He was already turning it over in his big brain. Most people underestimated Pom. They saw an adorable snack: wild blond curls, lean muscles, eyes like sweet mead, and an utterly empty head. Atalanta thanked the Fates daily that she'd been fortunate enough to discover the true core hidden inside all his delicious flesh.

"I'd like to get this finished quickly," Atalanta replied. As Pandora had figured out, some boxes were better left closed.

"Should you call Peleus, then?" Pom asked.

"Pel married that poor girl whose parents sold her to the Ceti," Atalanta grumbled. "And now he's busy with their sweet baby boy." She raised a hand. "Don't even mention Jason or I'll space you in the hyperway."

"What about Caenis, how is she doing?" Pom asked.

"It's Caeneus now, and he's holed up somewhere dealing with Lapith business."

"The Dioscuri?"

Atalanta's lip curled in disdain. "They're with Jason."

"Alcon?" Pom asked.

"Which one?" Atalanta grunted. "Doesn't matter. No, neither of them."

"How about Pirithous?"

Atalanta laughed. "He had his ass handed to him for hitting on Hades's wife. Literally. He'll be sleeping on his stomach until the implant surgery is all healed up."

"So it'll just be you and me?" Pom asked suggestively.

Atalanta didn't dignify that with a response. She loved her husband to distraction, which was precisely what she was afraid of right now.

As if sensing her thoughts, Pom said gently, "We'll get him, honey mine. Don't worry."

Getting the Boar was almost as bad as failing, given how Artemis might react. She'd never forgiven Atalanta for leaving her to join Jason's crew on the *Argo*, and marrying Pom had blown whatever was left of their relationship out the airlock.

Pom's hand covered hers, stopping her brisk motions. Atalanta looked up at him over her shoulder, his amber eyes warm with concern.

"Do you—" he began, then stopped abruptly and looked away.

"Do I what?" Atalanta asked.

Pom raised her hand to his lips and pressed a kiss to her palm. "Do you want to discuss the plan while we fly, or figure it out after we land?"

"The plan is simple," Atalanta said. "We enter the race, we crash the Boar's zipship, and we shoot him if the crash doesn't do the job for us."

"Best if we try to make it look accidental," Pom said, brushing his mouth against her knuckles. "We're both racing, then?"

"It ups our chances of getting him." Reluctantly, Atalanta pulled her hand out of his. "Let me take the lead, though." If anything happened to Pom—

"I'll be right behind you," Pom replied. "Every step of the way. Admiring your perfect posterior."

Atalanta suppressed a smile and revved the ship's engines. Soon, she'd have either revenge or a boat ride down the Styx.

The Ithaki terradome was one of the smaller domes in Hellas Plain, its translucent exterior coated with layers of the planet's omnipresent red dust. Many of the interior buildings were half sunk into the ground, jutting up like dragon's teeth, remnants of the original habitation pods erected when the place was first being built. Unlike the fully terraformed domes at Arcadia Plain and the Nilus Table, Ithaki was less of a tourist destination than a working town, known for its olives and, more important, its ouzo.

Much as Atalanta wanted to get wasted, she was working. It just so happened that the underworld's finest gathered at Avernus, a tavern owned by a former crewmate and an old friend who had inherited the place from her notorious thief of a father. The decor was eclectic: booths upholstered in green-and-blue polyester, mismatched chairs shoved under tables bolted to the floor, sparse lighting that seemed to hide more than it illuminated. The projection of a soccer game played out across from the bar, cheered on by a few patrons, while the bartender swiped a rag across the wooden counter between orders. The main oddity gracing the space was a triptych of digital tapestries slowly weaving themselves against one wall, so that more of each picture was revealed over time. Atalanta had stared at them for hours during some of her visits, and somehow she could never remember what any of them depicted.

Because it would be rude not to buy something when they were on the hunt for information, Atalanta slouched at a table against the wall, sipping her milky-white drink as she and Pom eavesdropped on the people around them. Bounty hunters and smugglers gossiped like old men, and within a half hour she knew who was trying to kill whom for insulting, murdering, or sleeping with their parent, sibling, or spouse. No clues as to why the Boar would go after Attis, though.

The tapestries were halfway down the wall when a curved

form settled into the empty chair next to Atalanta, and cool gray eyes regarded her from the shadows.

"Been a while," Anticlea said, resting a hand on her ample stomach.

"Long enough for Laertes to knock you up, apparently," Atalanta said. "When's the blessed event?"

"Any minute, or a month from now," Anticlea replied with a shrug. "Only the gods know."

"You look radiant," Pom said. "As beautiful as—"

"Don't curse me with compliments," Anticlea said, silencing him with a glance, then returning her attention to Atalanta. "As delighted as I am to catch up, the ice in your ouzo has melted, which means you're not here to socialize."

"We're looking for the Boar," Atalanta said quietly.

Not quietly enough. The voices around her fell silent as everyone in a two-meter radius swiveled their head to stare at her.

"Well," Anticlea said, rubbing her belly, "I have good news, and I have bad news."

"What's the bad news?" Atalanta asked, at the same time Pom asked, "What's the good news?"

"It's the same news either way," Anticlea replied. "The Boar is upstairs."

Atalanta's hand twitched toward the stunner she'd tucked into a belt loop under her jacket. They could end this now, if they were careful. But the Boar was dangerous, and even with the element of surprise on their side, two against one weren't good odds.

"Hospitality," Anticlea warned.

Atalanta grimaced but kept her curses to herself. Strict rules at Avernus meant hospitality was sacred, so no fighting was allowed. At best, violators would be expelled and banned from returning; at worst, they'd be found eventually, when a windstorm uncovered a shallow, dusty grave.

Pom casually leaned his elbow on the table and propped his chin on his hand. "You're saying we should wait for him outside?"

Anticlea studied him coolly. "Amaranths will be nice, I think. For your funeral. Poetic."

Pom laughed, while Atalanta took another swallow of ouzo. They could try to ambush the Boar or to follow him to see where he was staying and figure out the best way to attack him there.

Last time, they'd tried an ambush. A dozen bounty hunters against one man. He'd slipped their net and run, leaving nine bodies in his wake. She and Laertes had survived. Meleager hadn't died until later.

"We stick to the plan," Atalanta told Pom. To Anticlea, she said, "We need to get signed up for tonight's zipship race."

"I can handle that for you," Anticlea said. "Especially if it will get you out of my bar faster."

"Where's it being held?"

"The Labyrinth," Anticlea replied, rubbing her stomach again.

The cluster of canyons in the Night Labyrinth was less mazelike than the name suggested. Even so, it would probably be easier to instigate a crash there than in the Evenus fossa—the other popular race spot on Pyroeis, which was a straight shot from start to finish. Maybe the Fates were smiling on them after all.

"Who's organizing tonight's race?" Pom asked.

Anticlea's gray eyes remained fixed on Atalanta. "Artemis," she said.

Of course Artemis was involved. The Fates never smiled unless something was funny.

"Did you send any flowers to the funeral for Kybele's lover?" Pom asked, shadows dancing in his tawny eyes.

Anticlea cracked a smile. "I see you don't let your wife do all the hunting like a real lion. I had wondered."

Pom gave her a show of stretching his lean muscles and resting an arm on the back of his chair. He didn't speak, though, only watched Anticlea and waited.

"Artemis employs two of Kybele's daughters," Anticlea replied finally. To Atalanta, she said, "You might remember Aura, but Nikaia also joined her a year ago."

Atalanta nodded. Aura was a tough girl. Quick to laugh, quick to lash out. Got into a fistfight with Nemesis once and held her own.

"You know how strict your mother is about liaisons," Anticlea continued.

Atalanta glanced at Pom, whose expression was uncharacteristically serious for a moment before returning to its usual artless charm.

"They were indiscreet?" Pom asked. Anticlea inclined her head.

"Why take it out on Kybele, though?" Atalanta asked. "If they did something wrong, I mean. It doesn't make any sense."

"Are you here for sense?" Anticlea asked. "Or are you here for revenge?"

The Boar was upstairs right now. Close enough to kill. Revenge against him had waited so long it wasn't even cold anymore. It had melted like the ice in her drink.

Atalanta sighed and drained her glass.

The interior of Atalanta's zipship smelled like ozone with a hint of copper. She had considered selling it various times over the past two years, while she and Pom flitted from bounty to bounty, trying to scrape together enough money for food and fuel. But as she ran a hand over the soft fabric of the pilot's seat, she was reminded of all the races she'd won, the heady rush of flying at speeds mere mortals feared.

With a smile, she remembered her race against Pom and all that had come before and after. She thought she'd never marry anyone. He'd surprised her by making the prospect appealing.

How could she let go of this part of herself? Of her history? Maybe someday. Maybe never.

"Everything okay?" Pom asked from outside.

"Right and tight." Atalanta leaned out the door, admiring Pom's lanky form as he peered up at her. After the race was over, she'd run her fingers through his golden curls and make good use of their new chair.

Then again, why wait? She let the thought lift the corners of her mouth into a lazy smile.

Pom's amber eyes clouded as he looked at the ground. He wasn't his usual sunny self. Something was bothering him. Had been since they left Kybele behind on her asteroid.

"Worried?" Atalanta asked.

Pom shrugged. "If this doesn't work, we'll figure something out."

So why do you look like someone's eating your liver? Atalanta thought. She wasn't sure how to ask, though, so she hopped down and pulled Pom into an embrace instead. He tilted his head up, and they shared a kiss that deepened until all systems were go. But instead of leading her back to their ship, Pom loosened his grip and stepped away.

"What's wrong?" Atalanta asked.

Pom bit his lip. "Do you ever . . . regret marrying me?"

Atalanta blinked, her mouth falling open in shock. "What? No! Why would you think that?"

Pom winced. "I'm sorry, I didn't mean—"

"Do you?" Atalanta asked. Her heart pounded furiously, like a stampede of horses in her chest.

"Never," Pom said firmly. "It's just . . . I know what people say about us. About me."

"What, specifically?" Atalanta asked, unable to keep the edge out of her voice.

"That I don't deserve you," Pom said. His eyes stayed on his boots as he spoke. "That you'll get tired of me and find someone better. Someone who can really keep up with you."

He knew she'd lost their race on purpose. Atalanta's mouth went dry, and her stomach threatened to climb up her throat. Why had he never said anything? Consideration, probably. He wanted her to tell him when she was ready, not have it forced out of her during a fight. But she'd never said anything. She'd thought it didn't matter, as long as they loved each other.

"Why are you bringing this up now?" Atalanta asked.

Pom's brow furrowed. "The Boar almost killed you before. I don't want to jeopardize this mission. Not when so much is at stake. Just say the word and I'll stay out of it."

Atalanta struggled to find any words. They had all leaked out of her brain and puddled on the floor.

"No," Atalanta said.

Pom stiffened, as if waiting for a blow to fall. Instead, Atalanta gently cupped his face in her hands and kissed his forehead.

"Would you run, instead of doing this?" Atalanta asked. "If you thought we could get away from Kybele?"

"Yes," Pom replied without hesitation.

"Why?"

"Because I don't want you to get hurt."

Atalanta kissed him again, and he closed his eyes. "You think I can't manage this mission?"

Pom's eyes flew open. "You know that's not what I meant."

"I do know," Atalanta said. "I'm worried about you, too, but not because you can't keep up. It's because the Boar almost killed me once, and if I lost you . . ." She swallowed, unable to say the rest. She didn't even want to think it, in case the Fates were listening and getting ideas.

Pom kissed her chin, then her cheek. "Together, then. Win or lose."

"Always," Atalanta said, her grip on him tightening. "Bet on it."

He released her and started to walk back to his zipship, then paused and returned. "I don't think Kybele's daughters did anything wrong, but I think someone else tried to use them for something and failed."

"Who?" Atalanta asked. "Why?"

Pom took her hand and kissed the inside of her wrist. "When I figure it out, I'll explain everything." He released her and walked away again, humming tunelessly under his breath.

Gods, she loved that man. Atalanta indulged in a brief fantasy of wrestling him to the ground, then went back to her preparations.

From far above, the canyons of the Night Labyrinth crisscrossed the surface of Pyroeis like the scrawls of a bored toddler. To the east, they fed into the chasmae and fossas that led to the vast scar of the Nautes Valley; to the west, they stretched long fingers toward the Tarshish Mountains and distant Mount Koryfi. From the surface, standing at one of the many entrances, the walls of the Labyrinth loomed several kilometers into the star-streaked sky, casting deep shadows across the ground. Some paths were wider than others, some more sloped or rock-strewn from old landslides, and some were pockmarked with craters from long-ago meteorite impacts.

In the morning, fog would seep in and render the terrain insubstantial, ethereal, until one might almost believe the old stories about ghosts wandering the maze until the sins of their pasts had been shed like so much red dust. Or that those same ghosts could be summoned by an offering of blood, to answer questions and spout prophecies. Or, most gruesome of all, that the only way to avoid becoming such a ghost was to sacrifice someone else to the Labyrinth in one's place.

But it wasn't morning, so the only illumination came from the stars above, and the control panels inside each zipship, and the harsh white floodlight erected at the starting line. The crowd gathered to watch the race had their own ships, from which they would follow the proceedings above the Labyrinth. Some would head directly to the finish line to watch the winner cross and, more important, to collect whatever they'd earned from the bets being placed on the racers.

Anticlea had entered both Atalanta and Pom under fake names, but Atalanta's zipship was too recognizable for that to last. A stocky woman in a spacesuit waved handheld torches to guide racers to their spots, and within minutes curious onlookers clustered around Atalanta's cockpit, waving and gesturing and beckoning for her to come out.

She slumped in her seat, idly flicking the string of beads Pom had flung around her neck just after their wedding. She'd wrapped them around the armrest, to have something of him close at hand. *A bead for every argument,* he'd said. *May we never go through them all.*

And they hadn't. Atalanta's smile flared like a falling star and was gone.

Her radio crackled and spat an alert. "Atalanta," said a voice from her past. "Get out here now."

Aura. Which meant Artemis wanted to see her. And she'd specifically sent one of Kybele's daughters, so she probably knew what Atalanta was up to.

Atalanta flicked the beads one last time and descended, ignoring the murmurs swirling around her like the dust raised by her footsteps.

Aura was the same height as Pom, so she had to look up at Atalanta just like he did. Thick as her mother, with layers of fat over muscle that could snap a spine and had done so more than once. Her face was obscured by her helmet as she led Atalanta to a clean tent at the edge of the crowd.

The energy shield at the door wiped away the omnipresent grime with a tingle of static. A careless scattering of pillows covered the floor, on which various people lounged, laughing and eating honeyed bread and olive tapenade while they drank sea-red wine. Atalanta removed her helmet and tucked it under her arm, waiting for her mother to acknowledge her as the room fell silent.

Artemis stood in the corner, a glass of wine in one hand, a tablet in the other. Despite her advancing age, little about her had changed. Taller even than Atalanta, with the physique of a marathon runner, her every motion graceful and controlled. Pale blond hair had lightened to silver, wispy curls cut short to keep them out of her tanned face. She raised her forest-green eyes and inspected Atalanta much as she always had—coolly, efficiently—then handed the tablet to one of her hovering attendants.

"Why are you here?" Artemis asked, her clear soprano as chilly as the air outside.

Atalanta hadn't expected a warm welcome, yet her disappointment surprised her.

"To race," Atalanta replied.

"Why now?" Artemis asked.

Atalanta made eye contact with Aura, who stood a few steps away. Aura held her gaze just long enough to be insolent, then crossed her arms and pressed her dark lips together sullenly before looking down.

Interesting. Atalanta returned her attention to Artemis, who raised one pale eyebrow.

"I think you know," Atalanta ventured. An educated guess, an arrow fired into the dark.

It hit something, because Artemis sipped her wine and tapped her thigh with one long finger. "I prefer not to involve myself in family squabbles," she said cryptically.

Which family is involved in this one? Atalanta wondered. Artemis had to mean her own family. Her brother Apollo, or her father, Zeus? Her mother, Leto, or stepmother, Hera? Or was it one of her many half-siblings or cousins or niblings or aunts or uncles? Zeus alone seemed constantly embroiled in one scandal or another—his treatment of Callisto sprang to mind immediately. Artemis eventually smuggled her to a whole other system to keep her and the baby safe.

Had Kybele done something to anger Zeus? Or had one of her daughters? Or did it have nothing to do with him at all?

"How is Hippomenes?" Artemis asked, startling Atalanta from her thoughts.

"Good," Atalanta replied. Artemis probably knew he was here, too, but the others might not, and Atalanta wasn't about to tell them.

A stifled giggle broke the silence, followed by murmurs that no doubt echoed the worries Pom himself had expressed earlier. For these people, it was malicious gossip, the real food of the gods. To react would only add extra spice to their salt, and yet she wanted nothing more than to start a brawl and wipe the smug looks off every face, fresh or familiar.

Artemis whispered something to an attendant, who disappeared behind a curtained corner, then reemerged and offered Atalanta a glass of wine. Something fruity, full-bodied, no doubt smuggled in by Dionysus or one of his minions.

Atalanta took the glass, hoping the faint tremble in her hand didn't betray her unease at the gesture. What was Artemis planning?

"A toast," Artemis said, raising her own glass. "To Atalanta and Hippomenes. May you live."

"May you live," the assembled company repeated in chorus.

Surprise nearly staggered Atalanta. Her mother's cruel analysis of Pom echoed in her mind again: *You married beneath you.* Had she changed her mind? Or was she merely trying to cross the void between them, finally? Now, of all times, right before a race that could mean her death.

No better time, perhaps, Atalanta thought. *May we live, indeed.*

Atalanta drained her glass and threw it to the floor in the corner, where it shattered. Then, with a polite bow, she replaced her helmet and stalked out, the faint warmth in Artemis's tone wrapping around her throat like a fist.

Pom awaited her, leaning casually against her zipship like a random admirer. "Everything okay?" he asked, his voice raspy through the radio.

"Yes," Atalanta replied. "Artemis wished us well."

"Did she now," Pom said.

"Artemis didn't send the Boar after Kybele," Atalanta told him. "She hinted that it's a family issue."

Pom shrugged with one shoulder. "Should we give up the mission?"

Atalanta considered the question. Kybele would be furious if they left now, and Artemis seemed disinclined to stop them, though she wasn't helping, either. Maybe she was happy for the Boar to meet a discreet end, too.

"We finish what we came to do," Atalanta replied finally. "But we Leóns are curious cats."

"We are," Pom said. "Certainly it would be useful to know who else we might make an enemy of today."

Another zipship landed nearby, stirring up a cloud of dust. Atalanta resisted the urge to spit.

"Any suspects?" Atalanta asked.

"Three," Pom said.

"Only?" Atalanta asked, surprised. She had dozens. "Should we be worried?"

Again, the one-shoulder shrug. "The Boar is a tool for any of them, just as we're a tool for Kybele. I think we might annoy them, but I don't think we'll be inviting retaliation. Hard to know for sure."

That didn't narrow her list. Motives raced through her mind: revenge, jealousy, money, power. Who would benefit from harming Kybele, even indirectly? Someone who'd gone after her daughters first, with seduction in mind if Anticlea's hints were accurate. Or someone reacting to that seduction. Atalanta hadn't embroiled herself in underworld politics since she left Artemis to work for Jason; the old alliances and enmities probably didn't apply anymore.

"Are you going to tell me or make me guess?" Atalanta asked.

Before Pom could answer, a shadow loomed over both of them. Few people were taller than Atalanta, and fewer still were so broad and likely to be at this race in particular. Her veins iced over as she forced herself to still rather than taking a step backward.

"Who dragged in the cats?" asked the Boar, his voice nasal and raw from old injuries. He laughed at his own joke, and Atalanta felt more than saw his accompanying leer. Time had clearly done nothing to improve his manners.

"Did you hear something, my love?" Pom asked innocently.

"Just a piglet squealing like someone pinched his ass," Atalanta replied.

The Boar laughed again, darker this time. "How's your head, Argonaut?"

"How's your shoulder?" Atalanta retorted.

He rolled it, and it was like one of the canyon walls had moved. "Feels great. Too bad you can't heal the dead, or you might still have some friends."

Rage sublimated her icy blood so fast she thought her ears would steam. A gloved hand touched her arm, and she looked down into her husband's tawny eyes.

"Temper, my star," Pom said. Then he added in a whisper, "Save your passions for me."

The anger retreated like a bloody tide, though her face remained hot. She wanted to fight, to kill, but they had a plan.

It would work, and this jagged splinter of her past could finally be tossed onto a pyre and consigned to the flames.

"Aw, don't cry, little girl," the Boar taunted as he walked away. "I'll see you at the finish line when I'm collecting my prize."

Atalanta bared her teeth in a leonine smile. "No," she growled. "You won't."

Atalanta revved the engines of her zipship, the taste of Pom's lips still fresh, mingling with the bloody salt of the planet's dust. Silly for them to cram into her cockpit and get themselves dirty like that, but they'd always been fools for each other. Why stop now?

They'd rehearsed the plan again. Atalanta would stay in front of the Boar, Pom behind, and together they'd drive him to the edge of the track. On her signal, they'd trap him and force him into a wall. Boom, pork chop sandwiches.

The canyons were wide enough on average that they'd have only a few chances at particular choke points, and they'd have to use the other racers to their advantage. But despite the rust Atalanta had complained of to Kybele, she and Pom were the best racers in the system. Everyone there knew it, as the odds against their opponents plainly said.

Artemis sauntered to the edge of the Labyrinth's entrance, holding an elaborately carved bow. Occasionally, she shared her family's penchant for drama. Atalanta forced herself to breathe normally, hand on her accelerator, as her mother nocked a flare arrow and aimed it high. All her concentration narrowed to that fixed point. The curve of a back. The tension of a bowstring nearly touching the side of a helmet. The perfect line of outstretched arm, arrow, and bent forearm.

The projectile arced into the air. When it hit the zenith of its flight, it burst into lilac flame. With a roar, a dozen zipships leaped forward, and the race was on.

Atalanta slid easily into her old habits, like a tongue slipping into the groove of a lover's mouth. Her zipship responded eagerly to her every touch, skimming above the surface of the canyon as smoothly as a swan across a lake. Dust clouds from the ships ahead of her made it impossible to see, so she relied on her instruments to navigate. She wove around obstructions, laughing as other racers attempted to block her progress or shunt her sideways. Five people ahead of her, six behind. Which one was the Boar? She didn't care. All she cared about was the seduction of speed, the thrill of threading her needle through the eyes of the landscape and her opponents.

Then something hit her starboard wing, and Atalanta crashed back into the mission as she fought to keep from spinning out. She'd been shot, not struck by another zipship. An entirely illegal maneuver, unless Artemis had changed the rules of her races. Diagnostics suggested she'd taken only light ablative damage, but now she had to worry about more than just the race and her mission.

Unless the Boar was the one fool enough to cheat and hope Artemis didn't come after him. Fool enough, or secure enough in his belief that he was untouchable. What would make him think that?

Atalanta wondered briefly about Pom's list of suspects. Then she returned her full attention to steering and checking her sensors.

A proximity warning alerted her in time for her to swerve away from another attack. Not kinetic weapons, but a bouncer mine. A flash in her rear camera told her someone else had hit it, and for a moment her heart stopped.

Pom? Gods, he'd said he would be right behind her.

The urge to stop and check was strong, but she fought it. She didn't know whether it was his ship and, if it was, whether he'd been hurt or merely incapacitated. Artemis would send in a pit crew to provide medical attention. And if he was beyond help, revenge was her only option. She'd better not waste it.

Atalanta touched the beads Pom had given her, for luck, then flicked the switch for the zipship's boosters. The extra speed pressed her into her seat, and the ship darted ahead of the pack, emerging from the cloud of dust into a dark tunnel roofed with starlight. She kept one eye on the path ahead and the other on her sensors and rear cameras, waiting to see who caught up with her first.

Whoever it was paced her, staying just out of sight in her wake. Not Pom; he would have fallen back as soon as he realized it was her. But was it the Boar or someone else? They lined up behind her too perfectly not to intend something naughty. Atalanta veered right just before a flash ripped through the air where her port wing had been. Kinetic weapon.

She slowed down a fraction to force her foe to catch up. The nose of their zipship eased out of the dust cloud. With a few gestures, Atalanta captured an image of it and let the computer render it into something she could identify. Then she groaned in recognition.

"Of course it had to be him," Atalanta muttered. Of all the Olympians, he stood to benefit from Kybele's destabilization the most. After all, he was her direct competition. And he must know why Atalanta and Pom were in the race, or he wouldn't have sent one of his people to interfere.

The wine Atalanta had drunk less than an hour earlier soured in her stomach.

While she and her pursuer chased each other, another

ship cleared the dust field. The Boar's. Atalanta didn't know whether he and his ally were coordinating, whether he even knew he had an ally in the race. She had a mission to complete regardless.

Atalanta eased her zipship closer to the Boar's, testing to see whether he'd flinch or try to ram her. He immediately jerked toward her, and she darted away. Two for flinching, then. Fine by her. She'd have to lure him toward the wall instead of herding him.

A javelin shot tore through her ship's landing gear, setting off a string of alerts that she silenced. Nothing she could do about it now. Landing was a future problem. Her biggest worry now: Where in Tartarus was Pom?

Had the mine hit him earlier after all? If it had, she'd . . . she'd . . .

Enough playing with her prey. With a hoarse growl, Atalanta slammed her air brakes, forcing her pursuer to boost over her or crash. Their zipship leapfrogged over hers, and as soon as it was in her sights, Atalanta released a flurry of homing missiles. One of them hit a thruster, which exploded. Her enemy spun, their port wing striking the ground, and in a blink their zipship was debris in Atalanta's rear cameras.

The Boar took advantage of the scuffle to put distance between them. Atalanta flicked her boosters on again and closed in, then pulled up alongside him. Together they turned the next corner, finding an uneven canyon with sloping walls and rocks strewn about like broken, discarded toys.

Atalanta used the terrain ruthlessly to her advantage. She hugged the wall, then flipped her ship over his and reversed their positions. He braked to avoid her shoving him into the eroded stone, then sped up and tried to pass her. Twice she hovered in front of him, their ships nearly touching, then swerved aside to avoid a boulder that he barely missed.

Did he know she was taunting him, the way he'd done to her and the other bounty hunters when they ambushed him? Led them down the streets of Calydon, laughing at their missed shots, ducking around corners, and picking them off one by one? And through it all, the artificial rain pouring down, washing the blood into the gutters like so much price-less wine.

Atalanta had survived then, even with nothing to live for but revenge. She had so much more now. She had Pom, assuming he wasn't a smear on the surface behind her.

May you live, Artemis had said. And so she would.

Atalanta saw the crater coming and smiled.

She pushed her zipship ahead, teasing the Boar to follow, to chase. He didn't disappoint her. Together they flew, predator and prey, lion and swine, a hunt as old as the universe. They sailed across the crater, practically hopping over a puddle at the speed they moved. But Atalanta boosted up and braked, dropping directly onto the roof of the Boar's zipship with a bone-jarring impact. His ship fell into the pit and almost immediately plowed into the wall, while hers skipped forward like a stone. The resulting fireball flared and faded quickly behind her, the planet's atmosphere too thin to sustain it.

It was done. No one could have survived that. The ghosts of her past could rest now. Some of them, at least.

Her zipship rose and limped onward. It had sustained too much damage for her to win the race, but she didn't care. She would have simply left, flown off to the spaceport, and col-lapsed into her bed, Artemis be damned. But if something had happened to Pom, this was the fastest way to find out.

An eternity later, Atalanta crossed the finish line. Her wrecked landing gear wouldn't deploy, so she aimed for the area cordoned off for the racers, hit the air brakes, and dropped. Her zipship would have to be towed somewhere for repairs. Or maybe she'd finally sell it for scrap and walk away from racing for good.

Later. Nothing mattered now except finding Pom. Atalanta tore off her restraints and opened the door, dust pouring in like fog, like the ghosts of Pyroeis clamoring for her soul. She climbed out and tried to see through the mess. Lights nearby promised clean tents, where no doubt many disappointed bettors were damning her to Tartarus for losing. Would Pom think to wait for her there? Did she dare try to raise him on the radio now?

The red cloud swirled around an indistinct form approaching her. Atalanta's hand reached for her weapon reflexively. The form resolved into Artemis, her silver spacesuit repelling the dust like the opposite end of a magnet. Her face inside her helmet was eerily lit from above, and she beckoned for Atalanta to approach rather than crossing the rest of the distance herself.

Atalanta obeyed, her breath ragged.

"Explain," Artemis said in her sweet, eternally youthful voice.

"Where's Pom?" Atalanta asked.

"After you explain," Artemis said.

Atalanta swallowed acid and forced herself to arrange her thoughts. "I was attacked," she said. "By a Maenad."

"You were certain of that when you retaliated?" Artemis asked.

"I recognized the leopard pattern on the zipship," Atalanta replied. "And I put the pieces together. Kybele is a direct competitor to Dionysus. He's one of the few people you would allow the Boar to work for without demanding an explanation in advance. You weren't surprised at me being here, which means you knew what happened and expected Kybele to retaliate. And you didn't object, probably because Dionysus had already tried something with Kybele's daughters, who were under your protection."

Another form appeared next to Artemis in the slowly settling dust. Aura.

"Attis was like a father to me," Aura said. "Artemis would not allow me to do as I wished in this matter. Thank you for your service to my family." She bowed, then retreated toward the tent in the distance.

"The Boar had become a liability," Artemis said dispassionately. "I should have cut him loose after Calydon, but he didn't kill you, so I told myself it was better to have a leashed monster than a wild one."

Atalanta snorted derisively. "I don't care. He's dead, unless he survived a head-on collision going six hundred kilometers an hour. The Maenad is dead, and Dionysus can shove a pine cone up his ass. Where is Pom?"

A pair of arms wrapped around Atalanta from behind, and with a relieved sigh, she relaxed into them.

"I'm right here, my love," Pom said. "Sorry for being late."

Atalanta turned in his embrace and rested her helmet against his. Artemis was forgotten, and the mission, and even the dust shrouding them in privacy. Pom was alive. He was safe.

"I was waylaid by a Maenad," Pom continued.

"There were two?" Atalanta asked.

"One for each of us," Pom replied. "I realized what they intended when I saw you avoid that mine."

"Did yours survive?" Atalanta asked.

Pom treated her to a lazy grin. "What lion allows a leopard to challenge him and live?"

Artemis cleared her throat delicately, and Atalanta shifted just enough to face her, Pom's arm still wrapped possessively around her waist.

"I'll speak to my brother about this," Artemis said. "Unless you object?"

"What will you tell him?" Atalanta asked.

"That his petty rivalry went too far, and he received his due." Artemis smiled at her, an expression rare as a hunter's moon. "We should catch up soon. Bring your husband."

Atalanta nodded, unsure of her own voice. With an upraised hand, Artemis bid them farewell and disappeared in the direction of the tent. The dust closed behind her like a curtain.

And with that, it was all over. The Boar was dead. Their debt was repaid. They were free to go back to their interrupted life with lighter souls and no regrets—or one regret, if Dionysus did come after them later.

"Well," Atalanta said, "I don't know about you, but I could use a drink. Maybe ten. Or a hundred."

"Can your zipship still fly?" Pom asked, looking up at her.

"Badly," Atalanta replied. "But won't it be more fun to go back to our ship together? You can sit on my lap while I fly."

Pom's grin widened to a bright smile. "I like that idea very much. Perhaps we can land somewhere and you can take a turn sitting on my lap for a while."

Atalanta slapped his shoulder. "That's what got us into this mess in the first place. Let's get out of here and wash all this dust off. I hate it."

"Worry not, my star," Pom said, linking his gloved hand in hers. "I'll be sure to help you scrub away every single speck in one of Pyroeis's famous bathhouses. A private one. With scented oils and towels the size of blankets."

"I love you," Atalanta said, squeezing his hand.

"How could you not?" Pom asked, grinning.

Together they trailed off toward his zipship, and if it was a tight fit, neither of them complained. The flight ended soon enough; the bath took much longer.

A week later, a bottle of ouzo from the Ithaki terradome distillery was delivered to Kybele's Temple, along with a lovely barrel chair the color of a lion's skin, compliments of the Leóns.

A HEART INURED TO SUFFERING

Jude Reali

Odysseus doesn't read the reports.

They're delivered every morning: life-support status (online), fuel level (steadily decreasing), life-forms aboard (1), rations (adequate). Elaborated on in pages of small print across Odysseus's screen that they refuse to even scan.

It's an act of rebellion, for all that it accomplishes. They can't blame Calypso—they built her, after all. Programmed her into the workings of their ship, equipped her with safeguards and backups and a sense of protectiveness for Odysseus and their crew. A possessiveness, even—the fingerprints of Odysseus's own intensity.

They can't hold it against her, that she decided Odysseus was too compromised to decide their own fate and locked everything down. Shut them away in their quarters and started the ship on a steady course through unmapped space, delivering them reports and rations and keeping her last passenger alive as long as possible—or, at least, eventually returning their body to civilization.

In the end, it *was* all Odysseus's fault.

In the end, at the start, all throughout the middle—the story thus far is a series of tragedies brought about not by sheer misfortune or the whims of the Twelve or even the machinations of the universe itself, but by Odysseus Polytropos, architect of their own miserable destiny.

If ATH3-NA were here, She'd warn them about being too self-aggrandizing, but She isn't here.

That's Odysseus's fault, too. They wrote the subroutine for Calypso that would disable the ship's communications, shut down any receptor or receiver in the event a lockdown became necessary. The Twelve are the highest order of AI, but even They can't transmit to something that isn't receiving.

The lockdown protocol was designed for emergencies, for wartime—a conflict that the Twelve didn't even pretend wasn't orchestrated for Their amusement. For ATH3-NA turning on them, for AP0LL0 taking matters into His own hands, for ZEUZ tiring of their human unreliabilities and shutting the whole operation down.

And then, well . . . Calling what happened an emergency would be an understatement.

Circe was meant to be a myth—the Guardian AI of a satellite that had once served as a navigational center point, the Null Island of the mapped universe, until she let the power go to her head.

Or so the popular story went. Circe herself had told it differently, when Odysseus's ship chased her transmitted safe house signals and limped to a landing on the asteroid where she was hidden away.

Circe was a storyteller, like Odysseus, long deprived of an

audience. She told Odysseus, in a hush, how far she could see through her access to the HELIOS spyware/navigation system. Things the Twelve badly wanted to stay hidden.

Then she told them about HADES, a projection—accessible to anyone, if you knew where to find it—where the dead walked as data ghosts. And she told them about Tiresias, her creator, silenced for what he knew.

She told them that one of the things Tiresias knew was how to get them home.

Circe's story was nothing Odysseus didn't already know about the Twelve. They were fickle, violent. Designed as overseers, They slowly warped into gods. Driven to great heights of egotism by the success of ZEUZ's power grab.

Kronos had no idea what he was getting himself into, or so the saying goes. Odysseus remembers it being flung around quite a bit, at the start of the war. As if it were funny.

It *was* funny, at the time. It's still funny, because it wasn't that the colony leaders chosen to be commanders should have known. They all knew. The Twelve had wanted a war, so They'd made one. Made a scapegoat out of Helen, a messiah out of Hector. Taken THET1S's pet project and the project's human lover from their idyllic semblance of life, turned Achilles and Patroclus into a tragedy for the ages.

(Odysseus still dreams of Achilles sometimes: his perfectly crafted body lying beside Patroclus, porcelain-steel limbs sprawled over the corpse, modulated voice whirring too low for Odysseus to hear the words, endless repetition—maybe a plea, maybe Patroclus's name. In their dreams, they wander close, and Achilles is saying, *You did this, you did this, you did this.* As if they don't know.)

They knew the Twelve. They hadn't known about HADES. It amazes them, honestly, that Calypso didn't enact the lockdown protocols after HADES. Maybe it didn't register as a threat—maybe it never was. Maybe it really was just a projection, sowing discord throughout the ship and then gone without a trace. Maybe it was some parting gift from Circe, a guidance slipped into the ship, like Helen's messages to her husband from inside Troy.

There's no proof that what Odysseus saw in HADES was really Tiresias. Guardian AIs are known to be sentimental, to save images of their creators to play back. There's no proof, not even it knowing things Circe claimed not to know. She could have been covering her tracks, in case the Twelve were listening.

There's no proof that it was an actual upload, Odysseus reminds themself—what they saw wasn't necessarily an AI re-creation of Tiresias, a true data ghost, rather than something from storage altered and replayed, to offer guidance that Circe couldn't.

There's no proof that HADES displayed only the dead.

They can't get a signal out here. Even the most far-flung satellites are somewhere behind them. There's no way for Odysseus to check. To ascertain that the data ghost they saw before Tiresias appeared wasn't actually their mother—was a hallucination, or a saved holo-call from years ago dragged out of storage. Not the real thing. Not a real upload. It doesn't mean she's dead.

They just have to hope.

Hope's in shorter supply than rations.

The thing that wasn't really Tiresias told them about Scylla and Charybdis. Directed them there, the path crouched in the navigation system, an echo of an echo.

They had been lost, desperate. Piloting a singular ship with a dwindling crew, navigating the unfamiliar sides of stars. They'd long since lost sight of even the most distant human-populated colonies, guided only by encounters with exiled AIs, shunned by the Twelve and cast aside.

Still, Odysseus shouldn't have attempted it. ATH3-NA warned them. Their crew warned them. They're not a trick pilot, they're a mechanic turned soldier turned wanderer, star blind and scared. They should have taken the long way home, no matter how many ages it took to find their way back, not fucked around with gravity slingshots between binary black holes.

They almost made it. Odysseus will swear until the end of their days—however quickly that might be approaching—that they almost made it.

It doesn't matter, though, whether they almost made it. The g-force knocked them out just as they slipped through the gap, and when they came to on the other side, they were half-way across the ship, *in their chambers*, with the doors locked from the outside.

The comms were all dead, the viewscreens showing only static. ATH3-NA was gone from their eyescreen, their messages to Her no longer sending. Calypso hadn't answered when Odysseus asked her if anyone else was alive.

They didn't know until the daily report showed up on their screen the next morning. *Life-forms aboard (1).*

Odysseus stopped reading the reports after that. Rebellion, maybe. Or just grief.

Odysseus realizes, a few weeks into their captivity/safekeeping/AI mutiny, that this is the first time they've been alone for any significant stretch of time. They've been surrounded by people—family, the colonists of Ithaca, soldiers, crewmates—for the entirety of their life.

That's not fair, though—they aren't alone. Calypso is still a person.

Odysseus will argue to the ends of any planet you pleased on the topic of the personhood of AI. It's all but a moot point—whether robots are people or not, humanity shares the world with them. Answers to them, in the case of the Twelve.

But there's no one to argue with anymore. Calypso is a person, and therefore they aren't alone.

They might feel alone, trying fruitlessly to escape the few rooms that Calypso made into their prison cell, but they're not.

Repeatedly, impassively, Calypso reminds them that they built this ship around her, as if they could forget. She reminds them that their hands are only human.

As if their hands aren't all they have left.

They have to work. They have to do something, have to disassemble the scraps of projects in their workshop and try to build them into something useful, have to pry the wall panels off, have to try to fit their shoulders through the ventilation duct.

Calypso plies them with clean clothes, warm from the dryer in the laundry room accessible only to her; with the best pickings of the rations, since they're the only one left to eat them; with tendrils of the wires Odysseus programmed her to autonomously control, wrapping around their fingers like she's holding their hands.

It would be very easy to give up. To let her take care of them until the rations run out, until they die, drifting in space.

They might be tempted, even—if it weren't for Penelope.

That's the long and short of it, really. The reason they tried to take a shortcut home through the gravity between a pair of black holes.

Penelope, their wife, their world, their light, who kissed them goodbye almost fifteen years ago and begged Odysseus to come home safely.

They're trying. They'll swear on any of the Twelve you please—they're *going* to get home.

"Why are you doing these things?" Calypso asks. Her voice is bright and even, a calm, clear note against the running water of the sink in the corner of Odysseus's workshop.

She's asking, theoretically, about Odysseus having thrown down their protective gloves in a fit of frustration and not thirty seconds later scorching themself on the exposed wiring they'd been working on. Or maybe about their obsessive deconstructing, or their string of messages to ATH3-NA, or their general failure as a ship captain.

It's hard to tell, with her. Odysseus made her too much like themself, too blithe and witty.

"Why are you?" Odysseus asks. Their fingertips are going numb under the cold water. Their heart is going numb and heavy in their chest.

"You're unsuited for command," Calypso replies gently, like she means to soothe them, somehow. "Your judgment has not proven trustworthy."

She's right, but it still hurts. Compounds on to the greater hurt of having lost their crew, piecemeal across misadventures and then all at once. They can blame themself all they want, stew in it like the chunks of rehydrated meat in the soup they've been getting for rations, but to actually *be* blamed is something else entirely.

"Why didn't you stop me before I tried it?" Odysseus demands. Two can play the blame game.

Calypso . . . hesitates. Static hums through the walls.

Odysseus closes their eyes. They unplugged their eyescreen weeks ago, but they're still adjusting to the absence of it, eyes accustomed to constant multitasking, scanning for a scroll of text that isn't there. ATH3-NA is gone, locked out of their ship and their head by Calypso's safeguarding.

(Maybe it's for the best. ATH3-NA wasn't being all that helpful when Odysseus did have Her. At least now they don't have any false hope.)

"The odds were almost in your favor," Calypso says, startling them out of their thoughts. "Your calculations were correct, and your bravado was . . . convincing."

Odysseus laughs thinly. They jimmy the lock on the first aid kit open with a screwdriver—the key is *somewhere* in the workshop's mess, but Odysseus couldn't tell you where—and wrap bandages around their fingertips. "It usually is. That's what it's for."

They're going to die out here.

"What made you decide to call it quits on me?" Odysseus asks.

Another hesitation. Odysseus wonders if she's as tired as they are.

"I think you know the answer to that question," Calypso says pointedly.

The morning report is still on the display screen in the other room. They're perpetually aware of it, of its damning numbers. It haunts them over their shoulder, like a data ghost.

There's nowhere to hide from it, no way to dismiss it unless they scroll to the end, past the status reports on their rations (adequate) and their fuel (decreasing) and the long, long list of the dead.

It feels sometimes like Calypso is taunting them. They can't be sure if she's capable of malice. They didn't build her with any inherent capacity for enmity, but she's a Guardian AI—a fully-fledged person, independent of the code they wrote for her. It's dubiously accurate to call it humanity, but there's no other word for the autonomy of AI. The ultimate success of technology. Personhood.

Maybe it's just that it's easier to blame a person for mutinying, rather than an automatic ship system detecting Odysseus's sheer capacity for blind hubris and devastating failure and shutting down around them. Easier to stomach someone choosing this, rather than it being an inevitable consequence.

Years ago—just over a decade and a half, at this point—while they'd still been putting the ship together around the bones of its Guardian, Penelope asked Odysseus why they'd made Calypso so advanced. Guardian AIs were required to have advanced personalities only on ships making long journeys, for the sake of the crew's safety and the captain's health, and at the time, Odysseus hadn't planned to leave Ithaca at all. They had everything they wanted on their little colony, from their family to their workshop to their steady import-export business.

The ship had been a gift for Telemachus, they'd told Penelope. Calypso—still calibrating, but already a balanced, responsible, vaguely snarky presence inhabiting the partially constructed ship—installed to be his companion, his

Guardian, a parental safeguard in absentia when he inevitably wandered off their planet-colony and into the wide reaches of the stars.

Odysseus had barely finished it in time to go to war. When the ship was theirs to wander, they'd found endless patches of unfinished wiring, poorly welded wall panels, unlit rooms. All consequences of the rush job.

Maybe Calypso had been, too—forced into active duty before she'd finished creating herself, adapting to wartime as her first foray into her expected work. She was never a warship—most of the fighting was done on Troy's surface—but she was a ship at war. Blood had run into every crack, seeped down to the wires, down to the code.

Odysseus couldn't blame her for that; war changed them, too.

Sometimes, Odysseus forgoes their attempts at escape and tries to remember their wife's face.

They have pictures, of course. Videos. Entire holo-calls from before they left transmission range, recorded and stored away.

But when they aren't looking, their memory grows fuzzy.

The pictures show them the color of her eyes, the vague shape of her body under the drape of her sari. Her voice, her smile. Some of the details they have to cling harder to, can't conjure up from available data. Have to set aside time to remember, dragging them up, with effort, from the mires of time.

If they close their eyes tightly and focus, they can remember the feeling of her skin under their palms, the scent of her shampoo, the texture of her hair against their neck when she leaned her head on their shoulder to watch them work. They remember the delicate implant that wrapped around her thigh and down to her knee, an abstract flowering vine, the subtle texture of it when they touched her. The way she shivered sometimes when they traced the line of it with their lips, pressing kisses to each filigree flower.

It's been fifteen years. Sixteen, soon. She's slipping from them, a distant dream more so than a memory. They wonder if they'll even still recognize her, if they ever—*when* they see her again.

The greater fear is whether *she'll* recognize *them*.

Odysseus can imagine that time has changed Penelope. That motherhood has shaped her; that grief has done the same. They look at her image in the pictures they have saved and imagine her with graying hair, with lines around her eyes.

They can't imagine she's changed nearly as much as war has changed Odysseus.

It was ugly, the war. Wars always are, especially the Twelve's wars.

They could just as easily start up a gladiatorial arena to assuage Their thirst for blood sport. They would probably have sacrifices willing to throw themselves in. People like to die for the Twelve, as if it accomplishes anything. Odysseus supposes They wouldn't be godlike without followers.

But the Twelve seem to prefer the human element unwilling, uncontrolled. They drag out the political intrigue, the collateral damage. Lean in close—metaphorically, never quite compromising the distance that makes Them deities—to the blood and the mud and the desperation.

Odysseus will never get clean of it, the desperation

especially, but they knew that going in. That was just how wars worked. It was going to be an unpleasant business no matter how long it lasted. No matter who won.

They aren't sure if anyone won, in the end.

Troy was still burning when Odysseus left, and Helen was safe on her husband's ship. Those had been the stated goals.

There were no winners in a war, some old Earth politician had said. Odysseus believes that; they didn't feel like they'd won anything, even back before they lost everything.

The list of the dead was longer than the list of the living. Every battalion left ships behind, when they went—stripped the insides bare of useful machinery, transferred their Guardians to share space on other ships, and left the hulls floating around Troy like corpses. They just didn't have the crews to bring them home.

Odysseus left two ships at Troy. The Odysseus who first arrived there would never have done that. It would have seemed cruel to the Guardians, and a waste of material besides. Before ten years of war, they would have lingered, would have problem-solved. They would have split the living crew members among all twelve ships, trained anyone who showed interest to add to the crews, and brought everyone home.

The Odysseus who had just fought a ten-year war didn't bother with that. They sent crews to strip the ships, while the Guardians migrated and left as soon as they were able, before Menelaus and Agamemnon had even stopped calling meetings to bicker about whether it was worth it to properly raze Troy or just cut their losses and go home.

Calypso didn't get a shipmate out of pure selfishness on Odysseus's part. A pair of Guardian AIs tend to bicker.

They wonder how things would have been different if

Calypso had been forced to share. Maybe this wouldn't be happening. Maybe it still would. Calypso's hard to argue with, unlike her creator—Odysseus has always made it easy to argue with them, for fun. Calypso doesn't argue with them, for fun or for fury. She's impassive, convinced of her correctness, and Odysseus wishes they could blame her.

They left two ships at Troy, lost another nine on their struggle toward home.

Now they've lost this one, too.

"Calypso, why am I alive?" Odysseus asks.

Calypso doesn't answer.

Odysseus wishes they were angrier. At her, or at themself, or at anything at all. Anger would be useful, would give them some semblance of drive, instead of their chest being filled up with ice and bitterness. Anger, at least, would be enough to overwrite the dull ache of grief.

"Calypso," Odysseus repeats. They shove their chair away from the workbench, where they're soldering together wires on a signal disruptor that Calypso will probably have accounted for already. "Why am I alive?"

"Rephrase," Calypso requests. Odysseus can hear the whirring as she runs prediction matrices, trying to determine what it is they're really asking.

Odysseus paces back and forth across the workshop. Big, sweeping strides. Trying to outrun the report in the other room, declaring them the only survivor.

"Why am I alive and they're all dead?"

The walls hum with static.

"You were piloting. I was able to protect you. I was not able to protect them."

The crew should have been strapped in for the maneuver. If Calypso had time to adjust Odysseus's harness and cushioning against the g-forces, she should have been able to help at least some of the crew, too.

It shouldn't just be them.

"Why me?"

Whirring, low enough that Odysseus feels it in their ribs. "You're the captain."

It hits Odysseus all at once that she's lying to them. Lying, or withholding the truth, or *something* that's making her need to pause between replies, to assess her words. They get their wish: fury hits them like a bolt, white hot.

"What did you *do*?" Odysseus demands. Their throat stings at the sudden burst of volume, after months spent barely speaking.

"I chose the most enduring option," Calypso replies. She has the gall to sound bored, like she's repeating information. "One passenger I could perhaps keep alive for the duration of the journey, long as it might be. With every additional living being, the chances dropped. The math is very straightforward." They can imagine her leveling them with a cool glare. "Sacrifices must be made. I thought you knew."

They did know. They should have known. It makes sense.

It still feels like she's lying.

Odysseus stops pacing and rests their forehead against the wall. A tremor shakes them, full-bodied, like a shiver.

The temperature in these rooms is perfect. Calypso's taken perfect care of them. The chill they feel must be imagined, some embodiment of the way it feels inside their head. Arctic, tumultuous. A winter storm.

A tendril of braided wires snakes out from a panel near

the floor and brushes across Odysseus's back. They hate how comforting it is.

"This is the most efficient way to bring you home," Calypso soothes.

Odysseus doesn't ask, *But what about my crew?*

They can be righteously furious all they'd like. They would have chosen to save themself, too, if Calypso had asked.

It's probably for the best that she didn't have to.

Odysseus dreams, lucid but disoriented, of HADES.

They still don't know what HADES is. It's not one of the Twelve, for all that it seemed to float effortlessly into the ship and leave its fingerprints everywhere, like ATH3-NA always did. ATH3-NA, who had nothing in particular to say about the entire event, except to warn Odysseus about the risks of maneuvering between Scylla and Charybdis. Barely an explanation. No attempt at comfort, not that they would expect any.

Odysseus tries not to remember the data ghost of their mother, staring at them in terrible silence before disappearing through a wall. Tries not to think of how they caught sight of the faces of the dead among the living crew. Tries not to remember the garbled screams of the Guardian AIs of ships they'd lost, echoing low and horrible across the remaining ships' comms. Tries not to remember Patroclus and Achilles, hands clasped, too lost within the crowd of frightened crew and data ghosts for Odysseus to be sure it was them.

Tiresias had been the one to call it HADES, when he appeared and it all stopped—all went away except for him. He rose from out of HADES, he said.

He'd said plenty of things, though, none of which convinced

Odysseus that he was anything more than a projection of Circe's creator, sent to convey what she couldn't risk telling them directly, a strange virus in his wake like a calling card. They wouldn't put it past Circe in the slightest.

Skepticism doesn't quite set their mind to rest. According to ATH3-NA, HADES is a story passed around mostly by AI—some computer-simulated afterlife, gathering up the traces a person left behind and leaving their data ghost to walk through the world, invisible.

Odysseus tries not to think about it, so inevitably it follows them into their dreams.

In their dreams, Achilles is there, close enough to speak to, flawless porcelain-steel skin, silk-smooth golden hair, his beautiful face caved in.

It took Paris a long time to kill Achilles in any way that mattered. Odysseus just kept putting him back together, every time he had to be dragged home. Rebuilt him and sent him back out to be torn apart again.

It wasn't like it mattered—anything significant in Achilles had died when Patroclus did. Even THET1S admitted it, afterward. They'd been too close, Patroclus too intertwined in the basic developments of Achilles's code. What grief didn't snuff out was swallowed by fatal logic errors.

Finally, Paris got a lucky shot. Immobilized Achilles long enough to get close and mangle his CPU.

Odysseus hadn't even tried to hide their sigh of relief, when no light came back to Achilles's eyes.

"You let this happen," Achilles says, in Odysseus's dreams. "You let me die."

Odysseus breathes in sharply through their teeth. "I was doing you a favor."

"You brought us to the war in the first place," Achilles says. The anger in his modulated voice seems distant, noncommittal, like he can barely muster it.

In some of these dreams, Patroclus is there, too. Today, Odysseus isn't so lucky as to have the bastion of their reunion in death as a shield against the guilt.

"I did," Odysseus agrees. It had been convenient, to have them stop by Skyros on their way to meet the rest of the battalions. They were silver-tongued enough to make the argument to THETIS that Achilles and his minder should come to war. Anyone might have done it. It just happened to be Odysseus.

"Do you really believe that?" Achilles asks, the brief foray into mind reading so jarring that it throws Odysseus out of the dream's cathartic little metaphor-narrative.

They scowl, rub the bridge of their nose. "It's not the same," Odysseus says, turning on one heel, away from Achilles, so they don't have to stare into his broken-open face. Looking up, addressing the empty air instead of him, as if to chastise their own subconscious for dreaming of this, again. "I couldn't have known what would happen."

That's a lie—even then, they'd known. There was a very slim likelihood that Achilles would survive, but it was always much more likely that he would die.

Odysseus is clever. They *know* they're clever. They're as clever as Calypso, as calculating. Before the war even got off the ground they were strategizing, running the numbers, the names, the histories. They predicted the most likely outcome, determined the most plausible casualties. Achilles was always going to be a casualty, Odysseus's involvement entirely notwithstanding.

It's still not the same as Calypso willingly consigning everyone else on the ship to death to keep Odysseus alive, they think.

They hope.

Odysseus doesn't know how long it's been. Time has trailed away from them, fallen through their fingers like so many broken pieces of machinery. Weeks, at least. Months, maybe. The days blur together. They sleep too much, wake only to eat the rations that Calypso foists on them—the way she always has—and to tinker.

Today, they've contorted themself almost halfway inside the wall of their room, about three panels down from the door, working close to blindly with a pair of wire cutters just to be doing something. They're considering calling it quits and going back to bed when the snap of a wire coming apart cues the unmistakable noise of the lock disengaging, the mechanical *whoosh* of the door sliding open.

They bang their head against something within the wall in their haste to get out, and they crawl and stumble toward the door with blood dripping down their face.

"What did you do?" Calypso snaps, her voice all sharp edges. The door groans, slow with disuse, and begins to close again.

Odysseus throws themself forward, in a sheer adrenaline rush of panic, tripping over the threshold and falling hard into the hallway, just as the doors slam shut behind them.

The first thing Odysseus notices is how cold it is. Freezing, really—colder than it has any right to be, even with Calypso diverting all the heat to Odysseus's rooms.

Which means there's something out here that she's intentionally keeping frozen.

It isn't until they round a corner that they realize what.

It isn't until they drop to their knees beside the body and pull it over on its side that they realize *why*.

Starting halfway up the thighs, the flesh has been removed neatly from the bones. Peeled off not by rot but by intention: there are little saw marks at the edges of the remaining flesh. The arms are the same, the chest hollowed out, organs exposed and purple with frozen blood. The flight suit's been cut away with machine precision, framing the frozen-solid flesh and the exposed bone like perfectly cut wings.

"It's in the reports," Calypso says admonishingly. Her voice is very far away. "I did tell you. It isn't my fault you didn't look."

There's a noise coming out of Odysseus's throat: a high-pitched whine, like an alarm somewhere in the distance. They can't recognize the face they're staring into. They should, they should know—the corpse is frozen, almost perfectly maintained—but the name doesn't surface from the murky waters of panic.

They're still wearing protective gloves, so they don't feel the frigid texture of the skin beneath their hands as they pull at the remains of the flight suit, dragging the body closer, rooting through the pockets for an access card, dog tags, *something*. Some way to jog their memory, to make this dead thing in their arms—who died for them, who Calypso sacrificed for them, *to feed to them*—into a person again.

Odysseus's hands scrape over a plastic card in a thigh pocket just above where the flesh and fabric both end. They fumble it out, squint at the faded lettering. It's an ID badge, most of it smudged by time and covered with ice.

EURYL is all they can make out. Recognition spills through them. *Eurylochus*, though the surname escapes them. Whiny, stubborn. Good in a crisis, shit to hold a conversation with. Odysseus's second, their copilot. Their friend, in the best of times.

Chunks of meat in their stew.

It's always been a potential consequence of space travel, cannibalism. Survival wins out over morals, that's how humans have always shaken out. Distantly, Odysseus isn't even surprised. In all the years their ship has been lost, it was impressive that they hadn't resorted to eating one another long before.

"You're out now," Calypso says. Her voice echoes down the frozen hallways. When Odysseus turns their head they can see more corpses, all of them flayed neatly apart, like Eurylochus. "Your brute force won out in the end. Congratulations. What will you do?"

"I'm going home to my wife," Odysseus says. Eurylochus's head thunks against the floor as Odysseus staggers to their feet, shivering, leaving the body behind. "Stay out of my way."

It's not a threat. They have no way of threatening her. It took them months to cut enough wires to get out of their room.

But Calypso lets Odysseus walk through the frozen hallways of their dead ship unassailed. Maybe she's curious as to what they'll do. Maybe she knows she's lost what little cooperation they were willing to give now that they know. Maybe she's as tired as they are.

She lets them walk all the way to the bridge. Lets them manually reset everything she shut down. Even extends a wire to drag the remains of a body out of a chair so they can reach the communications screen when they hesitate before touching the corpse.

Life blooms across the bridge, in a manner of speaking. Light, noise, a *voice*.

ODYSSEUS? asks ATH3-NA, her voice bright as hot metal against Odysseus's raw nerves. THIS IS AN INTERESTING DEVELOPMENT.

"I'll fill you in," Odysseus says, their voice fracturing, wiping their palms across their cheeks before their tears can freeze. "I just need to know how to get home." To Ithaca. To Penelope. To Telemachus.

YOU ARE ON THE OPTIMAL PATH. YOUR GUARDIAN HAS SERVED YOU WELL. I WILL SEE IF THERE IS ASSISTANCE TO BE FOUND.

Brusque as ever. It makes Odysseus's shoulders finally relax, despite the shivering.

A wire taps at their elbow. Calypso, still silent. Seething, maybe, or just resigned.

There's a whir, a click. On the far wall, a panel slides open, and a bowl of soup on a tray slides out, steaming against the cold air.

Odysseus walks over to it, barely tethered to their body. They stir the spoon through the mix of rehydrated vegetables and machine-precise cubes of meat.

They reach in with their fingers and pluck one out. Broth drips down their hand.

Penelope. Telemachus. Home. Fifteen years, going on sixteen. Ithaca. *Home.*

They put the meat in their mouth, close their eyes, and chew.

TREMBLING ASPEN; OR, TO SHIVER

Marika Bailey

AXILLARY 1.

I died running. You wouldn't think it to look at me now, that I had ever been anything else, that I had ever been capable of such a thing as *running*. Big things tend to seem that way, sheer weight giving the illusion of permanence. I take up almost the entire side of the mountain; it must seem as though I have always been there and always will be.

But let us imagine, for one of your moments, that you made the trek to see me. You pad over the centuries of fallen leaves crumbling to earth and rot. The air is cooler up here, so high from your valleys that under the shadow of the many-toothed leaves even you may shiver. Keep walking, from the edges of my grove, farther and farther in, until day turns to twilight and the air is white with sound, and you may find my center.

And, if you are observant enough, you will find a particular trunk that grows almost parallel to the ground. That was once my leg. I froze, you see, between one leap and the next. I felt a million greenwood rods spearing through flesh, heard the shucking sound of my body becoming a wound. My right foot was lifted—tense with forward movement— when the bones of my toes budded and cracked into roots. Pulpy vines pulsing down through the earth and up to my slivered heart.

Sometimes when the wind flows just right under that limb, I can almost remember what it felt like to move, to run, to be free.

I watch you, out of the mirrors of my thousand leaves, and see the way you lift your face up to the sky, and I remember what it was like to be human.

2.

Some think justice is a thing that simply happens. An inevitable force of nature, like water flowing downhill; it will always find its place.

Lies.

There is no gravity of reparations. No universal pull toward righteousness. There is only you, and me, and us, and what we are willing to do.

Justice creeps. On hands and knees, through rock and river. Justice spreads like the root of a weed, clinging to life because it must. Justice withers, poisoned by cowardice. Justice dies every single day.

This will be difficult, and you will be scared. But remember: I don't hate *you*.

You can hear me in the dreams you're too scared to admit you have. Alone in the tent you've slung under my limbs. Alone except for the sound of me, a thousand whispering tongues, the world shivering.

Be afraid. Listen anyway.

3.

The last words I spoke before I died were a prayer. It was as much a surprise to myself as it was to the gods. I'd never been a god botherer in my life. There was enough to keep me occupied within my mother's house that I had no desire to go searching out trouble in any ancient cave, suspicious bush, or babbling brook. And besides, our gods had been outlawed.

There are some things that unite all those peoples born on stone: a preference for minding our own business and a propensity for being invaded by empires born in the valleys below us. Just before my birth we'd suffered such an incursion and conversion by a lowlander empire. It had sent its golden-ringed priests to our rocky villages to demand our acceptance of the new empire's gods. It was given at the point of ten thousand spears.

The priests the empire sent us were those it needed to get rid of. Our lands—only good for growing grass, for goats, and for producing very good archers—were of little use except as a wall between our overlords and the empire in the valleys on the other side. Our villages had no gold, no vineyards ripening under the sun, nothing that they wanted, except to say that we belonged to them.

As long as we sacrificed our prettiest lambs on their altars and filled the priests' cups and beds, all was fine. As long as we gave up our tongues, and cursed our elder mothers, and learned to lie that we hated what we were, we could live. The sacred caves of our stonemothers remained unmolested, only because of all those who died rather than reveal their secrets. The lowlander priests wore capes of the flayed skins of our oracles and laughed at our fear. We prayed to their new gods—Apollo, Zeus, and Poseidon—with the blood of our people staining our bent knees.

Some of us still kept to the old ways. And though I remembered the baby prayers my mother had been foolishly brave enough to teach me, there was little else I knew of the stonegods. I was the eldest of ten children, and time for myself was rare and almost always stolen. What moments I did manage to snatch for myself I spent under the sky, climbing the broad back of our mountain mother, imagining a world outside of clutching hands and needy voices. It was only as I felt my flesh turn away from his—in my own desperate need—that the language of the cradlesong prayer leaped to my heart and lips.

The beginning and the end.

This story curls in on itself, as my thoughts do, twisting and branching. There are dead ends in my memory, the forks and turnings of an unwieldy life. Time changes shape, expands and contracts with seasons like sap through my heart. It is not like your time. (The simplicity of past and present must be such a comfort to you.) My death was a moment that lasted a hundred years. It culminates in that running leap, with a last hopeless gasped prayer.

The end begins with a look.

4.

Look up.

Is he not *everything*? So perfect. Shining so bright that to look at him directly is to look at the last thing you will ever see.

I didn't mean to. That morning I'd no idea he was even there. There was no sound, nothing to announce his presence or any other's, much less that of a god. There was a cooling summer wind from the forever-frozen peaks above. The distant rivers of the valley sparkled from below. I have wandered this memory a thousand times, but there was nothing, no reason I should have turned in that direction.

But I did. And he was beautiful. He will always be beautiful.

I won't describe what he looked like. With gods it hardly matters. What you see and what I saw will never be the same. Gods simply are. That morning he looked like fun. There was a twinkle in his eye, hot and white enough to make you snow blind. I lowered my gaze and looked up at him through my lashes.

He liked that.

He was created to be wanted. More than that—needed.

He beckoned me and I went. I thirsted after his touch. It burns, it warms you down to your bones. It dusts your skin in bronze and gold. You were born to lie under him and receive his blessing. Your body *knows*.

Even now, when I have neither skin nor heart, I feel him. My leaves turn toward his light. He is my food. His light, nourishment. His name is written in the green buds of my branches. Cut me in half and read my life in the rings—he is there, his name tangled with mine. His fingerprints are scalded on every limb.

Apollo.

He ate from me then, called me sweeter than nectar. I eat of him now. How funny. How very, *very* funny.

Does it amuse him that I sup on his light, oh Lord who art in Heaven, as I once drank milk from a cup? Does he think it fitting that I ran from him only to be bound even further into his regard? Is it only right that I need him this much? I don't need to ask. I can taste his satisfaction in his sunlight. Thick as blood broth and twice as rich. Oh, bright Apollo, his touch is too much, and never enough.

(I'm not sorry I turned. Not anymore. I'm only sorry he would not let me go.)

I was no stranger to boys, or girls, or passing the hours between them in pleasant—if occasionally sweaty—company. He was not my first. (But maybe I was his, when I turned away from him.) No matter that his kisses warmed my thighs better than any blanket, I'd promised to be back home before dark. I had things to *do*.

I looked away from the sun with a smile and without a thought.

I was no stranger to sex; however, you will remember that I was very much a stranger to *gods*. I didn't understand then what I was submitting to. That I was submitting at all. I didn't understand that you are not finished with the gods until they decide they are finished with you.

Our lord Apollo was not done with me. His daystar smile stuttered and turned to rage.

I ran from one god to another, like a child fleeing from an angry dog to their mother's skirts. I could feel the power of the ancient stonegods calling to me from the dark, their echoing heartbeat of power drawing my legs up and across the rocky hills. And *him* behind me, hotter than any cookfire. Hotter than a metal pot gone white from the blacksmith's ovens.

The heat licked at my heels, turning the grass beneath my bare feet to wilt and then to ash that flew up from the ground into a cloak of fire and smoke, rising up all around me into a vision of his priests and soldiers climbing up our mountains and gaining upon the villages of stone people to flay our screams into devotionals.

I turned. He shone, the god of lowlanders. Gold and bronze, his hair in dark braids, his eyes black and sharp as newly made obsidian. He saw me and knew I would not submit. I saw in him only my death and prayed to the earth mothers whose recesses I would never reach.

5.

This is what I prayed:

> *(the ache in my legs)*
> Mama,
> *(the burning in my lungs)*
> Please,
> *(the tracks of my tears through the soot on my cheeks)*
> I don't want to die,
> *(the scent of my burning hair)*
> I want to go home.

6.

I would never see my home again.

7.

It is colder today. There is frost on the grass, curling its way up the tent poles you've stuck in my ground. It melted quickly as the morning waned, but there are places on this earth that no longer know what cold is, even in the moments between twilight and dawn. I hear it on the wings of the birds that nest in my branches. Fire rings the oceans. The world is drying and crumbling to dust. But not here. Not yet.

Here, it is still cold enough for you to feel it in your bones. I can almost remember what it feels like, to have gooseflesh rise on your skin, the crack and tingle of ice on my tongue.

Like the empires that once conquered my people, that body is gone. The woman I once was may as well have never existed. There are no bones to mark her grave, only a vale of trembling aspen left in her wake, half a mountain wide.

You're digging. The thuds of your picks and shovels echo against my roots. My leaves fall, slipping between the pages of your notebooks, fluttering down into the dark folds of your coats and packs. Where they are, I am.

I know why you are here.

The world has gone mad. You dig through my grave and bed for answers, following the frayed and ancient thread of story down to a past you seek to understand, categorize, and control.

My seeds flow on air. Lick my dust from your lips, drink it down with your water. I'm in your gut, swimming through the petiole boundaries of flesh to blood. I am speaking to you, child. Listen. There is no sea here, only the rising wave of sound from the wind running through my pale thin leaves. Listen.

I'm telling you.

I'm telling you.

I did not ask to be turned into a tree. There is *story* and there is *lie*. Know that they are tied together, one to justify the other. Rags to sop up the spilled blood; the weave picked apart, twisted, and warped into the rope that binds the shape of the future.

Find among my roots the shards and the trash of the sun god's priests. The mouse tracks of story-lie.

Apollo's priests made an altar of my grave. After it happened, his disciples came to see the spot where their golden god had raced an innocent to her death. They made a shrine of me: hung charms from my boughs, splashed perfumed water on my roots; and I heard them whisper that a god's hunger is like a storm or fire and just without reason, and although it was not good . . . at least this time it was not one of *their* daughters. They burned offerings to him under my branches. Wove crowns with my golden leaves and spread the story of the barbarian girl who'd turned herself into a tree rather than accept the honor of their god's lust.

It took me an entire spring to understand what they meant by virginity. At first I thought it was some kind of strange lowlander joke, to think that I would run from a god to preserve the honor of my first rut. He was gorgeous; I just had other things to do than spend the rest of my day on my knees, as pleasant as the time spent had been.

The stonemothers are old gods. Older than Apollo. Older than his dam and sire, and older still than the one who was castrated to give birth to Time.

The god's curse they could not sway completely. Such was his fury and strength, fueled by the flesh and smoke sacrifices of his worshippers and their bronze knives. But they could have turned me into anything. A bird fast enough to fly away. They could have raised me to the stars so that I could run forever.

I have asked these questions for a hundred years:

Why a tree?

Why *this* tree?

On this, the stonemothers have been silent. The oldest of gods are loath to give easy answers. They do not present destinies, merely possible journeys.

Him? He laughs.

(Perhaps you have guessed. That is what has brought you here, to this place. The home of a biological marvel, the millennia-old trembling aspen, a forest made of one tree. A being so strange, it could be immortal. You've come in search of a way out from the path Apollo has driven you down. Do you also need to be saved?)

His Lordship does not begrudge me his light, his nourishment. This body, he knows, is a prison. I will never run from him again. Do you see the inner ring of trunks? The way they twist and turn on themselves? Those are the years when I blamed myself for what happened. For being conquered.

He wanted me to stay. Here I am.

But the empire of his priests is gone. Nothing remains of them but the carvings on their pots and their bronze knives, now pitted with time and verdigris. Even the god Apollo has changed. Worshipped in different forms now: the glare of flash, the smile of idol—but always bright. The sun has adapted.

And I remain. Dead but alive. Changed and unchanging. Alien in a new body. But myself, possessed of all my memory and all my rage.

8.

Justice. It creeps on hands and knees. There is no pride in it. There is only you, and me, and us, and what we are willing to do.

I have stood in Apollo's light so long. Does he ever wonder what grows in the shadow I cast?

9.

A human life, it is so straightforward. You move from baby, to child, to woman. An arrow pushing through time, with almost no regard to the tidal force of the seasons around you other than to notice the heat or the cold. You raise your face to the sky, smell the wet earth, and flee the storm—but it is not a voice speaking in your soul. Not as it is for me now.

It is the body that dictates our understanding of time. My tree body is slow. It knows moments of weeks and months of years. It takes from the earth, the air, and the—*hateful, hated*—sun and slowly builds passages through each. I burrowed through the earth, rose to the sky, I expanded, and when the cold of winter came, I contracted.

I died running and have died a thousand more times since. I did not understand the first time it happened. There was no one to explain, and even if they had, which language would they use? The speech of frightened girls or that of trees? I was both.

The first time my mind experienced that lessening, that slide into dark and sleep, I believed it was true death at last.

I wept inside myself. I bent until the wind bawled for me, cracked open my skin to weep amber droplet tears. No one understood. Not the trees who bordered me or the humans who gathered leaves under my branches to make tributes for my murderer. Cold came and I fell into stillness a second time. Died a second time.

In this death, I dreamed.

The dreams of trees are sluggish as old rivers silting themselves up—such is the scale this body understands, of water turning to land, of mountains eaten away. But so too can the dreams of a girl last long—for as long as she needs them to.

My tree body slept, and my girl's soul dreamed, and in those dreams they finally met and spoke at the same speed. At last I could speak to myself.

"What are we?"

We tunneled deep into the dark soil, branching out into webs of water and rot, breaking the stones underneath us, breaking the dark. In the haze of dream-stillness I feel the flames on me still, the flying embers burn my leaves and lap at buds of my branches.

My sap cooled, ice hung from my limbs, and I sank deeper into stillness and the sound of infinity, the *throom* and *wohmf* of the earth pushing against itself, and the ancients in the conversations of centuries. The congregations of the old centers of the world, echoes from the deep fastness of the oceans beyond.

I heard the voices of those who had simply been too immense for me to ken. I heard the other trees around me humming along the overlapping edges of my existence, a web of constant exchange. I learned to speak the languages of water to wood (both seep and flow), the radial dialects of fungal webs. From their chorus I grasped even slower tongues.

I rose from this death with the return of warmth, as I'd once woken from a night's rest. Such was my transformation truly complete, when I felt time as a tree felt and could listen to the words of gods and mortals alike. It was then I thanked the stonemothers, for I saw what I could do in this body that I could never have done as a girl.

10.

The lights in the sky are blinking out. The ones you lifted up to the dark to reflect the light back down to you. Always chattering, watching, burning eyes in the sky. He taught you that.

You're worried. Those who live among my branches can smell the meaty stink of it on you. My earth tasted the salt of your tears this morning, when the last words from the little box you carry faded to smoke and dust.

Put down your ax. You've misread the text. There is nothing you can pull out of me to keep yourself alive. Burning my heart will not give you back what you miss. For once, learn something new.

You're sick and scared and heartbroken. But you still work, you're still trying. And that is what I recognize in you of me.

No one is coming to save you, small thing. Keep digging in the dark, follow my roots, *listen*—and maybe you will find a different kind of salvation.

11.

The wind moves through my leaves, raking from them the sound of my last moments, my trembling fear, my incoherent fury. The now extinct lowlander priests—plaiting paper effigies of he who hounded me out of existence among my branches—likened the sound to *shivering*. Some collected my leaves, shaped like a woman's tongue they said, and buried them wrapped around my broken branches, their secrets and fears whispered into dark soil.

It was always about what they were afraid of.

They feared the rumbles in the earth of old things turning, feared the smoking broke-tooth mountains, feared the boats of the people from the sea. They feared the spear that turned back in an arc against the one who had thrown it. My roots tended their fears and wishes, crumbling them to rot and drawing them up into my center. A trembling forest fed on their shame and their nightmares.

A tree does not grow on sunlight alone.

The smallest of my pale branches bend and snap against the wind or perhaps with the weight of ice. Branches fall to the ground and from them I grow again. Small nodes of green shoot up from my deep roots, racing up toward the sky and the air and the sun's fire. All are me. What is *me*, my self, is parceled out among the many trees that have grown thus. I am I, and I am We, and We are one, connected at Our roots that span wide as well as deep.

You call me the largest organism in creation. If your ignorance were not so dangerous, it would be endearing.

Sleep. You are tired, hungry, and scared. Alone. (But not alone, for I am with and will be with you through the end.) And you do not know if this strange quest you've taken will be of any use at all. It was just a story. Just a story about a girl, and not even an important one. No goddess or queen. Just *some girl*. What could it possibly mean in the face of the end of all humanity?

Rest your back against me. The sun is lowering himself into the horizon; these are the hours they call golden, and my bark is warm. Press your cheek against my side. Close your eyes and listen.

There are things older than humanity. Older than the sun. Do not be afraid of the dark. That is where everything begins.

Let us go down into the slow refuges of stone and old gods. Older than He Who Burns. The gods of secret places. The keepers of ancient rivers whose waters had never seen the sun. Had no mortal's fear of *him*.

These are the gods of waiting.

The lowlander gods have a talent for making enemies. There are elder beings of the elements locked away in the earth's cradles. Once free makers of creation, damned to an eternal prison after their people faced the edges of bronze knives, steel javelins, or rifled cannons.

The gods in Heaven know the orphans they have made, the peoples they have sunk under the sea, the wails of those whose blood burnished the glory of their heroes. Jason, Odysseus, Magellan, Cortés. Apollo and the others—they know fear. I tasted it in the smoke sacrifices of his priests. And I knew it in truth when my roots dug deep enough to speak with the gods who came before. The gods who were imprisoned so that Apollo and his kin could build a fortress atop bones and call it Heaven.

They heard me, a hundred thousand women's tongues a-shivering, growing larger and older and stronger and deeper with every passing season.

These older gods spoke back, oh so slowly. A word might take a week to unravel its implications, the speech of gods traveling in four dimensions simultaneously. A sentence might unfurl over the course of months, containing both the-sis and antithesis within the simplest of questions.

Girls don't live for very long. Trees live much longer.

Time enough to listen and learn. Time enough to send shoots down into the cells large enough and strong enough to contain gods but nothing as small and simple as a thin white root wriggling in the dark. Time enough to bloom in the shade of those immortal prisons and perfume them with pollen and nectar. Time enough to press the subterranean-born limbs of also-me in—willing! joyful! purposeful!—conjugation. Time enough.

Oh, the stonemothers could not save me. But they could give me a chance for justice. Even if I had to die, and wither, and creep through the prisons of the earth.

Perhaps if Apollo's priests and emperors had not made a story of me, perhaps if they'd not hung that god's gold among my branches and whispered his name over and over and over, perhaps I would have turned my tree mind to other things. Perhaps if I'd been allowed to forget him, I would have. But I have been given no such mercy, and how can one who has never *known* mercy be expected to give it when the time comes?

(I can taste his light on a tongue I no longer have. How can I forgive that?)

12.

There is no justice without love. I found love in the dark. Love for my strange, twisted boles, the scars of my shame. Love for my trembling leaves, likened to the sound of the first ancient sea. Love for all of us locked up, locked away, held down, hidden.

We, the dispossessed of existence, prisoners of Heaven and its burning sky gods; we are love. Titans, chthonic spirits, the usurped. We are the memory of lost ritual and stolen languages. We remember the names of those who were taken. We remember ourselves. We remember a time before prisons and dream of a world without them.

(You are sleeping now, dreaming fitfully under my boughs. But there, you have walked in that blasted grove where nothing grows. A stunted season that exists as the mark where something should have been. Those are the years where I thought I would never know true love.)

Learning, as I said, came slowly. And while I'd come to understand that I could find freedom even in my imprisonment, I still mourned the life I would have had if I'd never looked at the sun. A lover. One more thing taken from me by Apollo. To give my heart into the keeping of another in exchange for theirs. Who could love a tree who'd once been a girl?

A god of dark. A god of boundaries. A god of neither flora nor fauna. A god of transformation. A god of a billion mycelium arms, eroding at the foundations of time.

Oh, how he loves me!

Oh, how his kisses trace life along my roots!

My beloved first spoke to me in whispers of spores, floating along the wind to land and bloom into delicate caps of amanita.

"You are unlike any I have ever met," he spelled out in fairy rings. "I would know you, if you would know me."

I ignored him.

In wet months he draped my hills in billowing skirts of honey fungus.

"To match your leaves," he said.

I pulled back my leaves, let the sun burn his honey dry, and laughed.

(I wasn't an easy tree to get to know, not having had great luck with either gods or lovers in the past.)

I shook my rage at him in fallen branches and broken leaves. He caught my scars, thanked me for them, and turned them into fertile soil. It is his nature to create within the destruction of old worlds and bodies.

"All of you is beautiful," he said. "Even your anger."

"Go away," I said.

He did. And I liked that.

Curious, I sought out the last of his gifts I had not managed to destroy. And I found them sweet. His stories were knowledge disguised as legend, change and hope masquerading as gossip. His art was delicate, beautiful, and often poisonous. It made me sigh.

"Would you still want to know me?" I whispered into the dark.

"Yes," he replied. "All you are willing to share."

I held his rich, dark soil composted from my past, let him feed me, and grew.

Oh yes, love flourishes in the dark. If you can, find a lover who listens, who makes you even bigger than you ever thought you could be.

He is mine and I am his, and our love is spoken in my roots, where he is tangled in my veins. We talk of the world and how it changes. We live under the sky of the gods who do not. And together we have found the others in the old forgotten prisons. We've built networks and ecosystems from rot and broken lives, a way out of no-way. We plan.

Justice does not exist within the individual. It does not fare well with heroes. Heroes get distracted. By gifts, and gods, and pride. And justice is forgotten, an inconvenience. Heroes are the wrong kind of story.

(I know that is what you wanted. It's why you came here. You wanted to save the day. The day cannot be saved, beloved.)

Listen. There is only you, and me, and us. Shivering. So many of us, for so very long. Our love for one another. And what we are willing to do.

13.

On earth, as it is in Heaven. The empire that swallowed my people is long gone, but the world has been shaped in Apollo's image. His and the rest, those burning bright with the flame of those they consumed. This world is merely a reflection of him. As he always wanted it to be.

Of course it had to end.

(Why do you mourn? You wanted to save the world for your children. I will end it for mine.)

14.

Even in cages, we can choose to continue. In spite of the world. Out of love for one another. Justice can live in the birth wail of a child.

I have as many daughters now as I have leaves.

They're not quite like me, although they grew from my branches, bud to bloom to babe; tiny spritelings that are now quite big. They are taller than I am, as tall as their immortal father, and grow wide. Wide enough to cover the earth in a web connecting all the forgotten, all the forlorn, sending messages to all of us. It grows crowded in the dark earth, and it is no longer as quiet.

My daughters are loquacious, and in truth they have much to talk about, much to plan. And there is also their work, which is noisome as well. Granddaughters of mountain villagers, they have built bows and arrows grown from their own hands, long as they are tall, made to draw arrows strung with strands of their fire-and-lightning hair. Such hair! They get it from their father. So too the recipe for their arrowheads, dipped in ichor, from an even older story than mine. I said once that my people were known for their archery, did I not? Yes, I think I did.

They're good girls, my daughters.

15.

Wake.

You are still tired. Lean on me. The sky is clouded with ash so thick that not even His Lordship can bless us with his light. You've forgotten what real darkness is like. Now the sparkling valleys have gone to black, one by one. You will have to learn the dark again. It is in your blood, long forgotten ancestral memory. You will remember.

Do the shouts from the abyss bother you? Perhaps you do not understand the words.

Death comes. But there is time to teach you one last thing, here, at the end of everything.

Justice dies every single day. Crack open your chest and plant it inside. Carry justice in your lungs, in the pouch of your stomach. Turn yourself into a promise.

16.

Heaven and its shining cities have graveyards and prisons for foundations. Jails that were meant to hold gods, but not trees or the daughters of trees. I have broken through rock; they will break through the mantle of the earth. My children have roots strong enough to break chains. They will ascend—as sprouting roots are meant to do—up through the earth and *up to the sun.*

Not just my children. Generations of the darkness born. The seeds of those who wept, and lived, and endured. So many.

Some winterdeaths I've dreamed of the look on his face when it happens. When the old gods rise up from their banishment, the earth free at last, and my daughters—black-limbed, dark eyes shimmering with first magics—raise their many arrows to the sun. Arrows enough to turn day to night. I dream that the fire and daystar god falls at the center of my roots, where my feet once were when I ran from him. May his head lie under what was once my heel.

And when he—shining destroyer, hero of stories—lies pierced with the arrows of my children, golden blood flowing down, down, down at last, we will dance in the dark as he once danced with me in the light.

Stand here with me, child. It is not what you're used to. But you can learn. You can be more than what Heaven has made you. The world is breaking, sucked dry by gods who care only for their own reflection.

Listen to the sound of my leaves. Is that the sound of shivering? Or the sound of laughter? For justice, rising at last.

INDUCTION.

Do not fear the end of Heaven. It is only a shining lie.

Do not fear the end of the light. Love flourishes in the dark.

Do not fear the end of the world. There is only you, and me, and us; and the new future we will build together.

STASIS
(BASTION IN THE SPRING)

Alyssa Cole

I.

His seismometer registers a disturbance, and for a brief moment, Sentinel 7 envisions catastrophe: cave walls tumbling down, caverns collapsing in on the precious cache that he has protected with a singular focus for generations.

He pulls up the seismogram in his internal monitoring system, relieved to note the feeble blip of the S and P waves.

Not an earthquake, so aftershocks are unlikely.

This makes sense, as this region was chosen for its lack of seismic activity, but his internal stress arousal, heightened by scenarios concocted from terabytes upon terabytes of data, does not abate. It was an impact on the surface above him, and the predictive capabilities of his neural network are now conjuring new disasters, their potential havoc growing on an ever-increasing scale.

Have the aboveground accommodations that he's been constructing over the last several decades been demolished?

Is this some new threat, one unplanned for by his creators or by his own reasoning?

It's at moments like this that he regrets having developed an imagination, or at least one in the human style, biased toward fabricating the most disturbing possible futures. He'd have preferred the imagination of a honeybee—they dreamed, too, and likely of soft beds of pollen, not death and destruction.

Alas, he is not a bee nor any other creature found in nature.

Thinking of bees reminds him that he must tend to the rows of hives in the arboretum, and to the flowers as well. He might even finalize exactly where they should be planted aboveground and when.

But first:

He quickly checks that all is well in the caverns, ensuring that there's no structural damage and that life-support systems continue to operate as well as is possible; the machines have begun to malfunction more often in their advanced age, despite how rigorously they've been maintained. After that, he heads to a pneumatic tube entry point and squeezes inside, his bulky charcoal-gray body buffeted by air as he's propelled toward the surface. The tubes, their insides worn smooth by his rough synthetic skin, are ancient technology even compared with the outdated cryotanks, but they're quiet, quicker than navigating mineshafts, and will leave him close to the source of the impact.

When he reaches the surface, he sees that though the temperature is still frigid, the deep frost is beginning to break. Dirt shows in the spots where snow and ice have melted; stubborn clumps of ice huddle furtively around tree roots and seaworn boulders, but they too will eventually disappear. The bare earth is not yet covered with grass, though there are patches, like tufts on an infant's head in the photos he used to look at in his wards' files. He glances up at the small buds forming on the branches of the trees—oak, ash, chestnut. Apple, peach, pomegranate. The fruiting buds seem so fragile, too fragile, to bear the burden of nourishment.

The age of a tree is a marker of time, and he realizes that the oldest is already almost fifty years old.

Phase nine. If trees grow when planted, that particular directive began, *then you must prepare for the thaw* . . .

He looks away from the trees and the protective spread of their limbs; he is incapable of feeling guilt, according to his specs, and even if he were able to, he would not in this situation. He takes his job more seriously than those who cursed him with it, that's all.

The smell of carbon lingers in the air, mixed with the scent of eucalyptus, and he inhales deeply. The sensors in his pulmonary system detect carbon dioxide, oxygen, and, still, traces of dwindling toxins from the fallout of so many years before.

Apart from an elevated carbon reading, levels are the same as they have been for some time now: satisfactory. *Sufficient* to sustain life but, in his opinion, not quite acceptable.

Trees can grow on poisoned land, though the creatures who did the poisoning cannot.

There's a deep furrow in the earth, moving away from the site of impact, and he follows the trails, physical and particulate, for 213 meters, noting the possibility of long-term environmental damage for his incident report.

The reports are meant to provide data for the sentinels who will take up his work in the event of his demise. He maintains the practice, having learned from his creators about continuing as if everything is normal, despite the sword above his head.

His feet sink into the dirt pushed up by the furrow as he follows the scar in the earth toward the indiscernible smudge of red that his thermal sensor is picking up at the end of it. He leaps over fallen trees, his displeasure at the disturbance to his ecosystem growing, until he reaches the source of it.

A large, ovular capsule rests at the base of a pomegranate tree, cradled by its outstretched roots. The steaming capsule is pyrophytic, judging from the scorch marks that flare out around it and the fact that its outer casing has charred away on one end, like a satellite that's burned upon reentry to the atmosphere.

He's found the remnants of such a capsule three times over the last 150 years, but always far from his wards and always already cold and empty. The last time, having developed that pesky imagination of his, he'd guessed at what might have been inside like a child finding the husk of an insect's cocoon.

Perhaps seche worms, designed to funnel ocean water, excrete oxygen, and die? Or an alien life-form, banished to this ravaged and abandoned planet as punishment. Maybe a weapon, an artifact that had orbited Earth in the centuries since the Last War and belatedly found a target, although humans no longer walk the surface.

All his guesses had been wrong, he sees now. This capsule isn't empty, and it holds something he hadn't remotely considered: a humanoid woman.

She is small, but only relatively, as he is nine feet tall. She appears to be about seven feet in length, but it's hard to get an accurate measurement given the way she's curled in on herself in the cavity of the capsule. She's surrounded by a viscous brown substance struck through with fiery fractal designs, like a fossil in still-cooling amber. It's too hot, even for his specially designed skin, and as he waits for it to cool, he holds out his palm and activates a biological scan.

Instead of receiving a data module providing all relevant information, he is met with:

SPECIES: Unknown
ORIGIN: Unknown
VITALS: Unknown
THREAT LEVEL: Unknown

The woman jerks, flopping onto her back. Her splayed arms and legs break the surface tension of the liquid surrounding her so that it spills out over the sides of the capsule, like magma flowing to create new lands.

"Identify yourself," he says in English. It isn't the language of his original operating system, but, given his location and the files he has read and reread for years on end, it is the language he has come to use most often in his inner dialogue— once he developed an inner dialogue.

She doesn't move, so he kneels beside her; it's not necessary, since his visual sensors have the ability to zoom in, but he is . . . curious.

Her skin is brown, but not like the churned earth around her that's loamy with nutrients from the nanomulchbots that activated when the ocean receded. It's like the red clay farther south, slick and smooth. The short, curly hair plastered to her head seems to be black in contrast to the brown red of her skin. Her lips are full, forming a lush circle, though they are tightly pressed together.

Careful, he thinks, heightening his reflexes and agility levels so he can spring back to a safe distance if necessary. He's nearly invulnerable, and he was designed to be replaceable in case he encountered something in the slim percentile of things that might destroy him, but he is Sentinel 7.

He cannot take unnecessary risks.

He should not.

"Identify yourself," he repeats, but the only reply is the flexing of her hands and feet—likely unconscious movements. The movements spread, muscles twitching in her arms and legs.

An interval timer pings in his system, alerting him that he's been away from the bunker longer than is acceptable. He has to return in case something has gone wrong and the aging tech hasn't sent him a system alert.

He can't leave the stranger, though. Of course, he could simply terminate her to ensure she does no harm, but he decides that such an action doesn't fit into his ethical rubric. He'd been unaware of such a stance because he hadn't encountered another humanoid before, but it isn't incongruous.

Sentinels protect life.

He decides that it's safer for the wards if he brings her back for observation. Leaving her might result in some unplanned change to the ecosystem that sets back his timeline even further.

He scoops her up into his arms and begins jogging—he's not sure her body can withstand the pneumatic tube, so he'll have to use a surface-level entrance closer to the caves. She is surprisingly light, but more important, even with skin-to-skin contact, his sensors glean nothing.

He has almost made it to the entry point when her eyes pop open. They are the green of the sprouting grass, but not a uniform color; more like if that grass was placed under a microscope so that each cell was delineated. She is looking at him, or seems to be, since the cells in her eyes have shifted in his direction. His system is unable to scan such eyes because of their lack of pupil and thus dilation, so he just gazes back at her.

"What—who are you?" he asks, and gets a slow blink in response. "Can you speak?" he prods.

The green cells in her eyes shift, from side to side and up and down, and after a moment, her lips part. "Yes."

She jolts in his arms, as if her own voice has surprised her, and he grips her more tightly. An internal warning goes off, but one unrelated to his wards or imminent system shutdown, so he ignores it.

"I don't wish to harm you," he says. "Please provide the relevant data about yourself so I can assess your threat level."

"I do not think you can harm me," she says slowly. It's clear that speaking is difficult for her, but her voice is soft like the velvety underside of a leaf brushing against his ear. "I am not a threat."

"Where did you come from?" He asks not just because he needs the information, but because he wants to hear her speak again. "And why are you here?"

"I don't know," she says, her gaze still on him. "I think there is something I must do."

"And what is that?"

"I don't know," she says again. Her lips pull back, revealing teeth tinged with moss green, then she makes a strange sound, like she's choking. His imagination kicks into gear. She had, in all likelihood, just fallen from the sky; the possible injuries that might create were limitless. Internal bleeding? Fluid in her lungs?

They reach the outbuilding with an elevator down into the caverns as he runs another fruitless scan on her. It occurs to him that, unlike his wards, she might have neither blood nor lungs.

"Do you have blood?" he asks, then realizes the question might seem strange, given conversational patterns he's studied. "In your body, maintaining your systems? I don't want it for myself."

"Blood? I do not know," she says for the third time, her words beginning to flow more smoothly. "If I do, I'll happily share it with you."

She makes the choking sound again—this time, he's able to recall what it is.

Laughter.

Many, many, many years ago, when he'd still watched the holomemories belonging to his wards at every opportunity, he'd heard this sound often. At first, he'd been intrigued by it, but it was eventually the reason he'd stopped watching the holomems—hearing it had caused a deep discomfort in him, a longing that didn't have a source or a corollary in the data files he'd inherited from the previous sentinels and thus could not be accounted for.

"Do you know what you are?" he asks.

"I am PERSE." She says her name with a sudden firmness in her tone, more trunk than leaf, her voice echoing as if it were many.

"Percy. I am . . ." He pauses. Not Sentinel 7. "I'm Bastion."

This is the name he'd chosen for himself when he'd decided he wanted one of his own, even if there was no one around to call him by it. Sentinel 6 had apparently named themself Gumball McGee shortly before their demise. Bastion had never been able to ask why, of course, and emotional data—memories—weren't passed on in downloads between sentinels, even though the technology to do so existed.

Human scientists, at least the ones who had crafted their programming, either hadn't accounted for the sentinels developing emotions or hadn't deemed it necessary data.

This was another reason Bastion had stopped watching the holomems, which he had come to understand were troves of emotional data.

Jealousy.

"Bastion," Percy says, looking up at him with great interest. Her voice is leaf-soft again as she says his name, but he's shocked that its impact doesn't register on his seismometer.

He's walked through tornados that tore the ground around him asunder, propelled himself through waves of destruction in places where ocean waters should never have swept ashore.

He's never faltered.

Until now.

His next footfall is what would be called clumsy if he were human. He counterbalances, shifting her weight against him and adjusting his center of gravity incrementally so that he doesn't outwardly stumble. But inwardly—in that dark matter between artificial ventricles and microchips—he falls.

He decides to run a system scan when he's dealt with this situation. He must investigate any abnormalities that arise before they threaten his ability to function.

After all, there is no Sentinel 8.

He steps into the elevator and stares into the visio reader, letting it scan the QR code hidden in his visual sensor.

He doesn't know why Percy is here, but neither does she. He'll monitor her and decide how to proceed after gathering more data.

II.

Perse awakens in darkness, but she is unafraid. It is natural to her, a protective cloak draped softly over her skin that, for now, is tolerable.

For now.

The cold, however, is not; she shivers violently, pierced with the memory of years upon years of frigid existence. She'd existed in the cold, but she was not meant for it.

There's a buzz in the air that she can't hear but can feel—the language of machines. It's everywhere around her, taunting like an itch in the middle of her back, just out of reach.

She wraps her arms around herself to stop the shivering and sinks into the artificial plushness of some kind of cushioning, feeling the slip of irritating fabric as she shifts. She's in a . . . nest? No, that's not the right word.

A bed?

She'd fallen asleep when they'd entered the moving box and begun to descend into the earth; she's unsure of how much time has passed.

"Bastion?" she calls out, and her voice echoes back at her, as it sometimes does within the recesses of her mind.

"You've awoken." His voice—deep and strong like the groan of a tree branch bearing the weight of future harvest—is very close to her in the darkness. It retains only a trace of the language of machines, like an accent. Enough to reveal origins, to convey information that the speaker is unaware of.

"I have," she says, finding it much easier to talk now than she had when she'd first come into consciousness. She sits up, sweeping her legs beneath her to rest on her heels, then tilts her head toward the direction of his voice, though she cannot see him. "You sound surprised. Were you hoping I would not?"

"It's been sixteen hours, so I wasn't sure that you would," he says. "Have you remembered any more about yourself? What you are or where you come from?"

An image flashes in her mind: darkness studded with pin drops of light. The sensation of weightlessness. Searing cold and burning heat. Fear of destruction followed by embrace of it.

Then: Bastion.

Behind it all, echoes in her head, chanting in a language that is neither biological nor machine, their words making her cognizant of an aching need in her. The need is a steady hum in her body, a grasping that she doesn't understand from a source she cannot pinpoint.

It is want.

It is desire.

For what? For what?

"I don't remember." She presses one hand to her chest and one to her stomach. "There is something I want, and it is linked to what I must do. That is all."

You will know when it is time, the voices echo, and she understands this to be true. She doesn't tell him about the voices, and he doesn't ask anything else. She can feel his gaze on her in the darkness, and the need in her pulses thickly through her system in response.

She ignores it, for now, because she knows that once she acknowledges it . . .

"We are underground," she says after sitting in their shared silence for a long moment, listening closely.

The language of machines is loud, but that of the earth cannot be drowned out. It is all around her, trying to get into this dark space, trying to pierce, to overtake—nature has a boundless greed for expansion, and that is its right.

The humans inherited that greed, warped it, and rejected the most important aspects of it: connection, symbiosis, and the understanding that all that lives must die.

He moves toward her and she feels it, a ripple in the sheet of black that covers them both. "Yes. I brought you to the place where I live and work," he says. "Home. It's safe here. Nothing can harm us here. I've made sure of that."

Oh, the surety of the branch before the storm, her thoughts echo sadly.

"Here. Take this." Another movement in the dark. "It will warm you."

It is then that she understands something.

"Bastion, I can't see you." She stretches a hand out; a moment later, fingertips graze hers, tentatively.

"Ah. I was made to work in the darkness. I have been . . . You are the first being who has ever *needed* to see in here, apart from me," he says, then adds, "The first who has awakened here."

Something smooth, warm, and filled with liquid is pressed into her hand as the darkness begins to recede.

"It's not quite time for sunrise, but we can start early, just for today. Maybe they will enjoy a bit of change."

"I am first? How long have you been here, alone?"

Soft orange light emanates from fixtures in the walls. It's familiar to her somehow; though not quite right, it allows her to finally see the space that she slept in.

Bastion sweeps his arm out, gesturing to the cavern surrounding them. "I've never been alone."

Fanning out around her are row upon row of rectangular boxes constructed of metal and plastic and wires. Some of them are stacked, stretching toward the ceiling. The light softens the harsh edges of them, but the sheer number makes her inwardly recoil.

She grips the mug, then turns to look at the being who'd saved her. He'd been a blur when he carried her in from above ground, as her eyes had not yet been able to process the images they were receiving, but now she can see him clearly. His body has been made in the image of the humans, similar to her own, but like this place he calls home, he is hard—metallic and unyielding. His pebbled skin is the dark gray of graphite, and his eyes are solid black like the void of space. His body is bulky, his movements slow—he is mineral made sentient, a creature built to dig, crush, destroy.

Her first instinct is to recoil from him, but then she catches a glint on the surface of his body. Where the light hits him, there are patches where it sparkles and reflects like crushed diamonds. Like stars. Galaxies crumple in on themselves in the bend of his elbow and expand over the curve of his shoulders and pectorals.

The familiarity eases her.

"What is this place?" she asks, because knowing that will help her to know him.

She wants that, to know him: to trace the whorls of star systems imprinted in his skin. The want in her throbs, presses against her impatiently from within.

Bastion smiles, revealing sharp teeth of glinting titanium. "This is Hades."

The cup slips from her hands then, not from surprise but because she doesn't yet have full control of her motor skills. In an instant, he's whisked her out of the metal box, holding her close to his chest.

"Are you burned? Injured? Why are you shivering?"

"I'm fine," she says. "Don't forget how you found me. Heat doesn't harm me; it's the cold that I can't abide anymore."

She feels the bunched cords spanning his torso relax a bit, but he doesn't let her go.

"Tell me more about this Hades." She shifts her weight into the low heat put off by his body, and Bastion starts walking. The light he'd activated is growing slowly but progressively brighter, the timing of it aligning wonderfully with some part of that need deep inside of her.

Her shivers settle down as warmth permeates her body, and she realizes that like the slowly spreading light, Bastion's temperature is rising. She can see because of a false sunlight, but the very real heat of him is what tugs at her attention.

"There are many terrible things that happened on this planet before the creation of Hades," he says. His deep voice rumbles against her side like the earth settling itself. "Humans . . . they engineered the terrible things, but then said they were help-less to stop them. When they had made the planet all but uninhabitable, they abandoned it and struck out for others."

"I . . . know this," Perse says. She knows it in the same way she understands that the false sunlight is pleasing to her senses but will never be enough. The knowing comes from within her.

He stops by one of the boxes, and Perse looks down at it from above. She can see that the glass lid is frosted and that the false sunlight illuminates from within as well.

"Most of the humans who weren't allowed to leave the planet died, but some were . . . preserved. As a safeguard." He rubs a palm over her back, the heat of it searing into her as does the heat from his chest. "They've been stored in Hades—a location where they can sleep and be watched over by sentinels, until the earth is ready for them to awaken."

Will it ever be ready?

Perse rests a hand on his shoulder, one of the galaxies in his skin brushing rough against her palm, as she leans over to peer into the box. The glass is frosted from cold, but through it she can make out the features of a human face.

Something within her roars with rage and weeps with tenderness. She leans away, looking out at the sea of boxes.

So many of them.

"You're a sentinel," she says. "How long have you protected these humans?"

"A very long time," he says. "And before me, the other sentinels stood watch. I have survived the longest. I am the last. I will make sure that the humans awaken because there is no one else to do it."

When? she thinks, but asks, "Why?"

"Why what?"

"Why will you awaken them?" The alternative is horrific, but she must ask. "If they destroyed the earth once . . . why?"

Bastion says nothing, but reaches out to press a button on the box. An image blips into life above it, and she grabs him tightly, afraid in a different way now.

"It's a hologram projection," he murmurs, letting her down to her feet while still supporting her weight with his free arm. "The humans have been preserved, and so have their memories."

Together they watch the scene: a human, the person sleeping in the metal box. She is flailing her limbs about, a wide smile on her face. Not flailing—dancing. Other humans run into the projection, all laughing. A small human, a baby, but one capable of walking, toddles over to her, and she sweeps it into her arms and places a kiss on its cheek.

Bastion turns and walks her toward another box; Perse

takes tentative steps, her legs not yet fully able to support her. The hologram from this one shows a human man standing with an animal she recognizes as a horse. He gives the creature food, and the horse rubs its large head against his arm.

They walk from box to box—cryotanks are what they are called, he tells her—and he plays her scene after scene from the lives of the humans he stands guard over. Her legs begin to tremble with exertion, and when she leans more heavily against him, he stops and looks down at her.

"I've watched the memories of every human here," he says. "Countless times. That is why I will awaken them. And that is why I'll wait until it's safe to do so."

Perse nods, her head feeling heavier with each downward movement. She is warm, heated through by his body, and her mind slides into rest—the time of regeneration.

This is how it is, the echoes in her head say gently. *You are what must be.*

She leans against him, and she sleeps.

When she awakens again, she is warm; not as warm as when Bastion had held her close, but a deep, luxuriant, and nourishing sensation that permeates every atom of her being.

She'd dreamed of being serenaded in the language of the earth, of being cradled lovingly. When she opens her eyes, the first thing she sees are wildflowers, yellow, purple, and pink, with halos of false sunlight illuminating them from behind. They seem to drowse beside her, their pollen-heavy heads nodding toward her own.

"Hello," she whispers, reaching out to stroke a ridged petal. She sends thanks to them for giving her rest and repose, then smiles at their response.

She sits up, already knowing Bastion is here with her in this wondrous space.

She's still underground, but here, nature's greed has been rewarded. These plants are not wild, and they are not unchecked, but they're also not constrained. Flowers of every color, shape, and size fill the room to bursting. Pollen rests on her eyelashes and in her nostrils. Serrated leaves tickle her wrists, and smooth grass soothes them.

"This is the plant preservation cavern," Bastion says from the concrete path where he stands, holding a tray of earth with several green shoots sprouting from it. "A greenhouse of sorts. It's warmer here, and brighter, so I thought you'd prefer it."

"I adore it!" The words burst out of her joyfully, and she cups a hand over her mouth for fear that her giddiness will frighten Bastion, who she can tell is still monitoring her every action, searching for illness. She clears her throat, then says, more calmly, "You have treated the plants well; they thrive beautifully. Is guarding them part of the sentinel's job as well?"

Bastion pauses and seems to consider her question carefully before speaking. "I was programmed to cultivate plant life, yes, though this isn't quite what my directives instructed me to do. I was to collect seeds for the seed vault in a constant rotation to make sure that the stock remains viable, since they have a shelf life."

"Unlike you," Perse says, the rest having awakened her sense of playfulness.

"Not nearly as long as mine," he says, revealing his sharp teeth. "But it seemed a shame to me to grow these plants solely for their seeds and then discard them. I want there to be beauty when the humans awaken." He glances at her. "I am Sentinel 7. I protect all life. Plants are life too."

"What will you do when the humans awaken and don't feel the same way?" she asks, that anger and tenderness inside of her mingling with sorrow—both for the plants and for the being who thinks he can protect all things he casts shade over.

"Do you require sustenance?" he asks abruptly, and it startles her. She has been unable to answer his questions, but he has answered hers freely and without hesitation, until now.

He does not want to speak of what the humans might do.

"I do not require sustenance. Not yet," she replies. It is a response that comes from that unknown part of herself, coiled up with what she must do and why.

She cannot eat what he will offer her. Or she can, but if she does . . . no. She will wait. With some things, it is best to understand before acting. Right now, she has only her instincts, and muddled as they are, she must heed them as best she can.

"Very well."

They walk the garden then; they do so every morning after that for the next two weeks. He holds her hand as they walk, to monitor her temperature and provide support as she gains full use of her limbs. They discuss each flower—crocus and lily, iris and larkspur. She tells him the secrets that the plants want him to know, because Bastion can speak every language except that of the earth.

Each afternoon, he shows her more of the memories of his human wards, the holograms captured on memory chips that have been implanted into each of their brains.

Perse watches with both fascination and horror. Some of the videos show kindness, joy, and incredible acts of empathy. Others show incomprehensible destruction and wanton cruelty. She grows to love the humans and to hate them; she'd already feared them. She'd awoken knowing that they were a threat.

During each of these viewings, she watches Bastion dismiss a warning that has popped up so many times that she's memorized it:

SPECIMEN SURVIVAL WARNING!

"When are you going to awaken them?" she finally asks one day after he's reflexively dismissed the notification again. "This warning . . ."

"It is a suggestion, not a warning," he responds rigidly. "I'll awaken them when it is safe to do so. I am Sentinel 7. That is my job."

"Isn't it already safe?"

"No," he says, dropping her hand.

The warmth in her goes frigid because what Bastion has said is not the truth. She feels it in her very being, feels it in the constant throbbing need she tries so hard to ignore.

We are here, the echoes in her head chant. *They are ready.*

This is the truth, and Bastion told her otherwise. The sorrow she'd felt as a blunted and distant emotion envelops her. In lying to her, Bastion has chosen these beings over her, these capricious destroyers of nature.

She stares at him. He is enthralled in the holomem of a woman with skin almost the color of Perse's standing atop a tall building and regarding the city below her.

Perse knows that cities—the ones that weren't reduced to rubble—do not look like this anymore, even if she's only ever seen a city in a human's memory. Nature is greedy, after all. Those buildings would have been engulfed in creeping plants, been broken apart by tree roots seeking humid soil beneath the concrete.

"These memories are lies. They're going to awaken remembering a world that no longer exists," she says darkly, Bastion's betrayal still gripping her. "Have you considered that they might view this world you've made for them as punishment instead of salvation?"

"I am Sentinel 7. I have considered everything," he says sharply, then adds in a tone that makes her regret her words: "Everything. And still, that is not enough."

He reaches out and taps a button on the cryotank, and though the holomem disappears, he stares at the space it had inhabited, lost in thought. Perse realizes something: he is afraid. She'd known fear, while hurtling toward the earth through the atmosphere, friction turning into flames, unsure of where she'd land and what her purpose was. That was fear for one being—herself.

Bastion isn't supposed to be able to feel, he'd told her, and yet he can. A miracle in itself, and yet all he'd known was worry and fear, for these selfish beings had created him to be the minder of their futures without worrying over who would mind *him*.

"Bastion."

His head turns toward her slowly. "Yes?"

"You are not Sentinel 7," she says firmly. "You are Bastion. And you have done enough."

She reaches out with both hands, runs them over his sandpaper skin, which is always warm now, solely for her benefit. She pulls him close to her and wraps her arms around him. The need in her feels different in this moment; she wishes that she could plant roots in him, like a mountain wildflower driving itself deep into the anchor of a boulder. She wishes she could entwine herself around him like jungle vine, prying him away from this undeserved burden.

She isn't sure what the need was supposed to be, at the beginning, but now it is him.

"Bastion."

The hubris of the flower blooming after first frost! the echo in her head wails.

He leans down, and she presses her lips to his. This was an action they'd watched with amusement and some confusion in the holomems, but now she understands the humans in at least this one thing. His mouth against hers fills her body with green joy. His rough fingertips graze furrows of hungry desire in her skin.

She holds him tightly against her body, her want lodged between them like a grain of sorrow, germinating.

III.

SPECIMEN SURVIVAL WARNING: 18,250 days have passed since initial suggested awakening. Sentinel 7 is commanded to initiate awakening sequence or risk total specimen loss.

Bastion ignores the warning, as he has every fifteen minutes for the last fifty years. He is unable to override this warning, like he has the emergency awakening system, which would have his humans jolted back to reality with nothing more than some outdated videos and books to guide those who managed to survive.

His understanding of the cryotanks and their occupants is greater than the people who built them; those who called their own kind "contingency specimens." He knows that the sleeping humans are fine, though he still experiences an unpleasant anxiety every fifteen minutes in the nanosecond before he realizes the warning hasn't changed to the one he dreads: TOTAL SYSTEM FAILURE.

He should be up on the surface, checking the accommodations to see how they have resisted the late-winter storm, but he is searching for Perse. He hasn't gone above ground since she arrived three weeks before. Such a short period of time in the span of his existence, but one that has planted new seeds in that imagination of his, sown them with kisses, soft caresses, and care.

He still envisions destruction and cataclysm, but also the life blooming from the irrigation system plans that Perse helped him alter to better aerate the soil. He still worries about dangerous weather systems that might raze their lodgings to the ground, but thinks of the rainbows that may follow the storms.

But still: he worries.

In the weeks since she arrived, she's grown comfortable enough to travel around Hades by herself. When he first felt the continuous need to monitor her, he'd told himself that he wanted to ensure she didn't harm his wards, but he's realized that isn't the case. For the first time in his existence, Bastion is concerned about someone other than the humans he was created to watch over and usher into a new world.

Because he watches her so closely, he is certain of one thing. She has not eaten. He is powered by fusion battery, but she has not revealed her power source to him, nor has she taken in nutrients.

Bastion forces himself not to think about the details, even if he cannot stop himself from fretting at what those details might mean. He goes to her instead.

When he finds Perse, she is kneeling in front of a cryocube

for smaller life-forms. The LED lights in this space highlight the fact that her hair isn't black but a deep, deep green.

She turns to look at him with those luminous cellular eyes, both inhuman and more than human. Something is wrong in her movement and in her eyes, but her next words distract him from this.

"What being is in here?" she asks. "There is a beeping sound coming from the box. A warning."

"There are always warnings . . ." His words die in his mouth as he realizes this is one that cannot be ignored.

LIFE SUPPORT FAILURE. COMMENCE REANIMATION.

"What did you do?" he asks, regretting the accusation immediately.

"I think the question here is what haven't you done," she says. She isn't defensive; her voice is laced with sorrow. "Human technology is not infallible, and the creatures in these tanks cannot be preserved forever, Bastion."

"I can fix this," he says, moving her aside gently, despite the fear growing in him.

"Or you can awaken it. This is one small creature, and you have to start somewhere."

"But . . ."

"Nothing in nature can last forever, no matter how hard you try to preserve it. If you don't awaken them, they will all die."

"Don't you want that?" he growls.

"I . . . do not have the same concern for humans as a species that you do," she says. "But because you care for them, I can't hope for them to die. I don't want you to carry the burden of both their existence and their extinction. Not by yourself. It isn't fair."

Bastion is frozen, imagining everything that could go wrong. All the data passed down to him from previous sentinels and his original operating system had only ever been about what would happen if he made a single error; he has spent decades superseding perfection in order to avoid that. But there is the other fear, the one he has never allowed himself to articulate.

"You keep asking what I will do if they begin to destroy the planet again. I don't know, Perse. The environment is not safe enough for them, fragile as they are, but they are also not safe for it. I . . . wish I were another sentinel. One who had no thoughts and simply carried out commands. But I am Sentinel 7. I am the last, and so I must decide."

Perse's hand rubs soothingly over his arm. "It will be okay," she says. "I know the language of plants, of nature; it is a language of survival, and one that the humans will never erase."

Bastion stares at the cryocube, then presses his pinkie finger, the one with the reanimation key embedded in the tip of it, into the power button. He tries not to think, to regard the process as the unfeeling machine that he is, that he is supposed to be, but no longer is. Perse squeezes his other hand.

Slowly, the Plexiglas lid lifts, allowing the freezing gas to pour out. Reanimation fluid begins to fill the tank, viscous yellow. They stand there for hours, watching the small black creature inside as it thaws, begins to move and twitch and, finally, breathe.

After the process is complete, Bastion reaches in and pulls out the small, slick creature and wipes it off with the towel from the post-animation kit stored in a niche below the tank. It begins to wiggle as he rubs it dry, and he hands it off to

Perse, too overcome by his human imagination—his fears—to look directly at it.

"Dog!" she cries out. "It's a dog! Oh, I adore it!"

He looks at her, at the small, furry creature with spiked hair that is licking at her chin between frantic sniffs at the air.

"A dog," he says, and then a choking sound forces its way up his throat—it is laughter. "Thank you, Perse."

She smiles at him, jerking her mouth away as the dog lashes a pink tongue toward the moss green of her teeth. "I told you it would be okay."

The first human they attempt to awaken—a woman who had many holomems that took place in her garden and who seemed like she would be mindful of this new world—is a failure.

Bastion follows all the instructions, waits for hours longer than necessary, and, when all else fails, attempts emergency resuscitation, but she simply does not wake up.

For decades he'd imagined that death could only be caused by catastrophe raining down, by making a mistake or by some incident beyond his control, but here, it has happened under his careful supervision, quietly, with no cause and no explanation.

The actual pain of the experience, the knowledge of it shattering through his system, shows him that his imagination had not been as developed as he'd thought.

None of his worry had prepared him for the reality of grief.

"A tree cannot protect all who seek shelter under its branches, my love," Perse says, hugging him. "It can protect some of them, though. That is what matters."

Her words do not take the pain away, but that she is there

with him helps. He glances at the body of the woman who hadn't survived, and a frantic urgency fuels him.

"The farmer. Let's awaken him." He pulls away from Perse and turns, but she hooks her arm around his waist and holds him. The soft skin of her cheek rests against his back.

"No. If we successfully awaken him, that will not erase her loss for you. And if he doesn't awaken . . ." She pauses, then sighs. "We will try again soon."

Bastion lets her hold him, her kindness both amplifying his grief and soothing it, but doesn't speak. He cannot. Instead, he lets her lead him to the gardens.

"I don't believe in a creator other than the humans who constructed me," he says eventually, as they lie among the flowers, absorbing the vitality of life in various stages. "But I am thankful for whatever brought you into my world."

Perse picks up a flower that has fallen into the grass and stares at it, then places it on his chest, dropping a kiss beside it.

Bastion can no longer ignore it—Perse is wilting.

Her movements have become slower.

The green cells in her eyes that had once twisted like kaleidoscopes now move feebly.

Her skin has grown dry and tough, and while doing the daily cleaning, he discovers a tuft of her hair caught on the edge of a grate.

As they sit watching a holomem of a potential candidate for reawakening, her hand frail in his and Dog curled up on her lap to help keep her warm, he bluntly states the truth. "Perse, you are dying."

She laughs, the sound a shadow of what it once was. "Yes. I

know what I must do now," she says, then her gaze meets his. "But I don't want to."

Bastion is a machine, but he has learned from both the humans and his love how to give comfort, so he holds her close and increases his heat output.

He has learned that he cannot prevent something from happening by avoiding it. What will come will come, and he will tolerate the pain, even if it seems intolerable.

If the language of plants is survival, as Perse had told him, then the language of love—his love—is resilience.

"It will be okay," he says. "Tell me what you must do."

They go above ground for the first time in weeks.

Bastion holds Perse in one arm and a basketful of pomegranates that he'd preserved from the previous summer in the other, and her smile as the spring sunlight hits her face nearly breaks him.

He carries her to the tree where he'd first found her—her pod has already been absorbed into the earth and a bed of thick grass has grown where it had lain.

Percy.

PERSE.

Pyrophytic Environmental Regenerator and Sustainer of Earth.

Bastion had been created with a purpose that served humans, and so had she. While he was nearly indestructible, she'd been created to be destroyed.

He tries not to resent the humans; they are, after all, what will remain when she is gone. He holds their lives in his hand, and he does not want his pain to grow into cruelty.

"Here we are," he says.

He settles them both gently into the grass, then pours the pomegranates onto the ground, as well as the small metal cube he'd secreted along with them. One by one, he splits them open, spilling their seeds into the basket.

He cannot speak, but he taps the small box—a holoprojector.

As he works, it plays memories—his memories of his time with Perse. Finding her in this very spot, placing her among the flowers, the curiosity in her upturned face. The laughter. The tenderness.

"This is beautiful, Bastion," she says, lifting her head and resting it on his thigh. "I know why your flowers thrive, even though you do not speak the language of plants."

"Why is that?" he says. His voice is steady, light, but in his mind—in his heart—he tumbles and tumbles into a dark abyss.

"Because you love them," she says quietly.

She is too weak to speak after that, or to feed herself, so Bastion does it for her. He lifts a few seeds and slips them into her mouth. He repeats the movement again and again, not caring how long it takes. He sees when life enters her eyes again, feels the suck of her lips and tongue on his fingers grow stronger as her body regains strength.

He feels her heat: his Perse, who was always too cold in the darkness and false sunlight, is getting warmer and warmer by the moment. The food is feeding the pyrophytic nanoparticles in her cells, and the sunlight is activating them as well. This is what was meant to happen. This is why the capsules he'd found had always been empty.

"This is what you needed," he says. "I took you into Hades, starved you of nourishment and sunlight."

She reaches a hand up, her long brown fingers creating a

ripple in a holomem of her playing catch with Dog, before landing on his face. "No. This is what I was designed for. You are what I needed."

The cells in her eyes are no longer green; they've changed to a reddish-orange color.

Her skin is broiling hot; he doesn't move away from her. He is invulnerable, but would have stayed even if he wasn't.

"Thank you for taking me under the shade of your branches, Bastion," she says, pulling his head down so that their mouths meet. As they kiss, she goes up like a brilliant pyre, her nanoparticles finally combusting. Her weight begins to lift from his lap; the last trace of her is the brush of her mouth against his.

When he opens his eyes he sees her: brilliant cinders riding on the wind, bursting and releasing their seed spores.

"Goodbye, Perse," he says.

An alert from Hades pings again, but this time he doesn't immediately go back. By the time he rises from the base of the tree and collects the basket and projector, days have passed.

Small green sprouts push up from the soil.

IV.

Bastion tends to his wards—the ones who have survived the awakenings he did on his own. That he is able to do only because he remembers Perse by his side. He begins to teach them all that he knows, about their world and themselves. Those who choose to learn from him teach others.

He tries not to think about what they will do with their knowledge.

The humans call him Hades, the name that is plastered all

over the underground bunker, and he allows them to do so. Only one being has ever called him Bastion, and he doesn't want to hear that name from anyone else's lips. No one else could ever speak it so leaf-soft.

Dog is still called Dog, though there are other canines now. Two others have attached themselves to him, and he has named them Crocus and Lily.

Many of the humans cling to him too, seeing him as parent and as deity, for these beings always need a higher authority to sanction their own existence.

They settle on king.

Bastion realizes he can guide them toward doing things differently from how the humans of the past did things. It is a welcome distraction, even if he does reject their reverence and eschew their attempts to deify him. Mindful of their need for an idol, he gives them someone else to worship.

He tells them stories of Perse when they ask about flowers and plants and trees. He tells them of how she made the dead world bloom—with some embellishment, because the humans love a good story more than fact.

It hurts him, to hear them say her name, but as they make flower crowns and dance at the base of the scorched pomegranate tree that marked her arrival, it also soothes him.

She will not be forgotten.

When one day, many months after their awakening, a group of humans runs breathless into the dark cavern he has made his most private domain, shouting that Perse herself has arrived to bless the spring planting, Bastion doesn't let them see how their words pain him. The human imagination is what allowed him to love Perse and to mourn her; he will indulge them in this.

He and Dog walk toward the pomegranate tree slowly,

following the scar in the earth that has become a prayer path for those who offer blessings to Perse. From a distance he notices that the tree has grown lustrous green leaves, despite the fact winter has barely retreated, and that it is studded with bloodred fruit.

Dog begins barking happily and shoots away from him.

Bastion runs then, runs toward the human-shaped heat stamp on his thermal sensor. He slides knees-first in the grass to supplicate himself at the feet of the woman standing motionless beneath the branches.

"Perse?"

"I am PERSE," she says in a voice that seems to be multiplied, layered, like echoes in a cave.

He presses his forehead against her hip and emits a sound that makes him think that perhaps he is dying, and the last sparking of his neural network has conjured his love before him. There is no physiological reason for the heaving of his chest and the shuddering of his body, so they might also indicate death. However, he has seen a similar reaction in many awakening humans, the ones who survived, so he has another theory.

He is crying, or making a sentinel's attempt at it.

"Hello," she says, and when he meets her gaze, she is looking at him with kaleidoscope eyes that are filled with kindness but not recognition. "I am PERSE. Who are you?"

He remembers then that humans didn't account for creatures like him to have emotions; they didn't make any way for that kind of memory data to be passed on. Even if this is his Perse, and not one of the others who had fallen to Earth to fulfill their duty, she will not remember him.

He drops his chin to his chest, pain tearing through him despite his invulnerability. Dog runs between him and Perse, jumping happily, unaware of anything other than the fact that the being he has been devotedly sniffing after for almost a year has finally returned.

"Who are you?" she asks again, in her many-layered voice.

Bastion gently takes hold of Dog's collar. "I am Hades."

If she is not his Perse, she will know him as the humans do.

"Hades. What an odd name." She pauses, then repeats the word. "Hades . . ."

Fingertips absentmindedly trace the abrasive whorls on his head, move slowly down to his neck. They trace slowly over his jawline before gripping his chin and gently lifting it.

Perse looks down at him.

"Bastion." Her voice is a singular green leaf, soft against his senses and imbued with love. "Everything is okay, Bastion."

"Perse?" He stands and sweeps her into his arms, raising his temperature to warm her as he pulls her close. "How. How?"

Bastion does not have words for what he is feeling. His imagination, so used to conjuring the worst, had never managed to come up with this possibility.

"We were created by humans who didn't care whether we wanted to live beyond our expiration dates or whether we could fall in love," she says into his ear. "But nature is greedy, my heart. Greedy and *cyclical*. I will always come back for you."

She kisses him then, breathing life and joy into him, filling the dark abyss that had opened up within him at her departure with bright garlands of love.

They thread their fingers together and walk back toward Hades, a king with his queen reborn.

THE EAGLES AT THE EDGE OF THE WORLD

Taylor Rae

Don't tell my mother, but there are no sorrier people in the world to carry a nation than us. We're just a dying old woman and a daughter who wishes she could still hide behind the word *girl*, riding out the end of the world on a duct-taped sailboat that won't last another week on the water.

But my mother tells me, as we split a cold tin of baked beans, "Nea, this is a chance to rebuild our nation."

The horizon is darkening into sunset, and a chill descends. We drift along a bitter wind, the water whispering behind us. I'm too damn cold and exhausted for this, but arguing with her is worse.

So I just stare at her and ask, "How are you going to rebuild a nation with a family photo album, two old *Native Winds* CDs, and only one of Granddad's moccasins?"

I should be gentler. My mother is salt-sick, dehydrated, delirious. She's a sunflower in late August, curling up on herself, and all those seeds in her pretty head are rotting and coming loose. If I weren't so cold and hungry and wet, I might have the patience for it.

But I'm mean as the ocean and just as lightless.

We've been at sea for three months now, ever since Old Troy burned and we gathered our life into a couple of duffel bags, wrapped them in plastic bags, tossed them in the boat, and made for the open water.

But in my mother's eye, here we are: the final troop of the Kumeyaay Nation, venturing against the horizon to discover a new world.

"We don't have to bring anything but our history." She looks at me coyly and says, "Did I ever tell you the story of the eagles?"

I could tell her the story of the eagles is stupid and point-less out here, because even if old stories were true, there's no desert to explore and no eagles to find on an Earth so bogged with meltwater, we're lucky there's any land at all, much less *new* land. Most people live strutted up dozens of feet in the air, always bracing for the next furious wave. And every year more soil runs back into the sea, like it's trying to turn back into primordial soup.

But I'm getting angry. It's the old fury, the kind that keeps me up at night, cursing the uncaring stars. *Sing, Muse, of the rage of Angie's daughter, Nea . . .*

I loosen my grip on the tin can and pass it back to her.

"No," I lie. "Tell me the story."

She starts to tell it: how there was a witch woman with two sons, and she sent them north to find the eagles. She used to tell me the story clearly, when I was small and still wanted to listen. The mother sent them out in every direction until they at last obeyed her and returned with the eagles, and that became the story of the nation's founding.

But as the beans dwindle, the sons seem to forget what story they're in, and they find a giant in the descrt and must save the eagle that lays a golden egg.

"It was a goose," I tell her. "The giant's from 'Jack and the Beanstalk,' Mom."

"No, listen," she says. "I'm telling you the story of the eagles."

I pick up our canteen off the floor of the boat. We're down to maybc eight ounces. In the morning, we'll have to stop at another foreign port. We've encountered a few floating towns and villages since we left Old Troy, and even when we were still covered in ash, we traded dearly for food and water, fuel for the sailboat's backup motor.

"Here," I tell her. "Drink, and you can tell me the rest in the morning."

My mother drinks, and she goes down below, into the tiny cabin we share. I'm left alone with the stars and the ghosts of old gods following us through the dark.

My mind is a storm, and if I believed anyone would listen, I might pray. We have nothing left now but the boat itself, this almost-empty canteen, this shared tin of beans. Our sad little nation, all its riches held entirely by soggy gym bags.

In the morning, I'll make port at the first friendly home or hamlet I see. We'll be at the mercy of whoever's doorstep we stumble upon. Here on the new world-ocean, in the aftermath of the floods, it's every woman for herself.

We just need land. On land, I will remember how to be kind, and my mother will become herself again and navigate us to safe territory. She will find us a new home and grow herbs on the kitchen shelf and solve old Sunday crosswords.

We won't build a nation, but we might find a place to eke out a living, somewhere to keep our feet dry.

My mother will have to be content with that.

———

I don't sleep, but I do dream.

All these years living city to city, skimming across the water, losing pieces of our past with every move, has made me an expert at conscious sleep. Any sailor will tell you that your mind will allow you to stay technically awake, functional, alert.

But you can retreat, rest inside of yourself until your mind rouses you once more.

I doze that way through the night, hand on the rudder.

My mind moves through a dream. My mother is in an old church on a flat patch of desert. The church is burning the way our city burned, and I walk into the flames and feel no heat.

Mom? I call. She doesn't answer, but I know where she is.

I find her in the back room, where the fire began. A forgotten candle. A tipped lantern. A cigarette, smoked in secret, hidden but not extinguished.

It doesn't matter what caused it.

I am in the Catholic Church of El Cajon that burned in 1917 and carried with it all the names I will never know. My mother is gathering the fire in her arms. All the burning paper, the smoke like souls curling around her, reaching for her, disappearing upward anyway.

If we carry the history, we carry the nation, she tells me, like she can't see the history is blackening her arms, burning her alive.

When I carry her out, she carries the fire with her.

I don't know if the unease of the dream or the real world wakes me, but I rouse fully to a gray world, and we are a little painted sailboat, affixed in time. If I let the sail down here, I could believe we were the only people left in the universe.

Are you really founding a nation if you're the only ones left?

But then I lift my binoculars to the western sky, and I see a smudge on the horizon. A floating village, maybe ten miles out. It's flying a flag with a golden emblem, but I don't recognize it, and there are no barricades that I can see.

I adjust the rigging, and we're off, across the wine-dark sea.

The village is a collection of old shipping containers, welded onto steel support beams that jut up from swampy silt and clay. There are maybe five or six boxes, and there are walking paths welded in between from bits of scrap metal. It links them in a crooked crescent, facing the wilting harbor. The whole thing sits maybe ten feet above the water, and it looks so old, I wonder if it's the last of its kind, the crow's nest of a sinking ship.

A woman who looks close to my age waits for us on the rickety harbor. She wears a sun hat, a pair of faded trousers, a linen shirt. Her silk kimono is buffeted by the wind, and even though it's a little torn, it looks regal.

"Howdy," she greets us, and there's just enough self-deprecation in it to make me smile. "You two look a little sun-kissed."

"Not a lot of shade on the water," I say, grimacing against the beating sun.

"Sunscreen is just as important as hydration. Skin cancer will still kill you."

"Not as quick."

She smiles the way that makes you instantly like someone.

My mother sits beside me, calm and quiet. She's kept her myths to herself this morning, and I'm not sure if I'm grateful for it or nervous.

"What's your story?" the woman asks, her eyes flicking between both of us. "You look thirsty and tired, and I always have water and beds for friends. But I can't say I know you enough to call you friends yet."

My mother draws her shoulders back and inhales. I wince and try to talk over her, but she's already speaking.

"I am Angela Ascania, and this is my daughter, Nea. We are the final carriers of the Kumeyaay Nation. We humbly request something to eat, somewhere to sleep, and a little fuel to send us off again in the morning. We are on our way to remake our homeland."

My mother is not old enough to be politely dismissed as confused, elderly, sick with memory. The horror that my mother has just said that *out loud* claws at my chest, but the woman just looks at her with the same kind of gravity.

"I'm so sorry," I say softly. "She doesn't—"

The woman shakes her head at me. "No, no. That's good news." She stands taller and tilts her nose into the air. "Because I'm actually the queen of this tiny island. My great-grandmother built it, and I'm the last of my family to maintain it. I will always be its keeper, even if I drown here with it. You may call me Di."

My mother nods, like that satisfies her somehow.

"And"—Di's eyes flick to mine—"I would be honored to trade a meal and a night indoors for your story. You look like you've traveled far."

I wonder if this woman is saltwater-crazed too. Or maybe she simply thinks it kindest to speak to my mother in a way she understands.

In any case, I have no other choice.

"We would be honored to accept," I say.

In Di's shipwreck kingdom, there are no courtiers or courtesans. There's nobody, really. Just Di and a seagull that apparently flew here and never decided to fly away. It eyes us suspiciously as we pass.

I'm uneasy, getting off the boat, and I think of old legends I can't name, where people step onto a witch's island and are eaten or are turned into animals or simply never notice decades pass them by.

But as Di helps us gather our sad bags from the boat, I decide she isn't delusional. She's only giving my wild eyed mother a little mercy.

Di claims the beams holding her kingdom together spear down fifty feet into the silt, but as I feel the floating village rock with every ebb of the water, I wonder just how much of that fifty feet of silt is left.

The first room we enter might have been Di's royal court in another time. It's small, but there are meshed windows cut into the walls of the shipping container to let in the light, and it feels cozy within. There's a table, a few chairs, an empty whiskey decanter.

My mother clings to me the whole walk up the pier, across the narrow scrap metal gangway, and inside. She's sagging, all her effort going into standing up and breathing.

"Angela," Di says gently. "Please, sit and sip a little water. Rest yourself. The entire Kumeyaay Nation is a heavy burden."

My mother looks grateful for the excuse and the canteen Di offers her. She sinks into the floor pillows beside the low table and murmurs, "Very wise and very true, My Queen."

Di leads me to the crooked-cut doorway, where an old oil drum was stripped and rewelded together into a brief, curved hall to the next shipping container.

"I'm sorry," I say, heat gathering on my cheeks. "She's not well. I think it's dehydration."

"There's nothing to be sorry for." Di smiles at me, and there's real delight in it. "I don't encounter someone who really thinks I'm a queen every day."

The second and third shipping containers are both sleeping areas, although one has been half turned into a workshop, the spare cots stacked and shoved against the wall.

"How many people used to live here?" I ask.

"This ring? There were about a dozen of us. It wasn't so bad. Three families."

I want to ask what happened to them, but Di ducks into the fourth container and grins over her shoulder at me.

"This is my favorite room in the place," she says.

I follow her inside to find plastic tubs full of books, stacked on shelves. They're webbed over with bungee cord, maybe to keep them steady if the ocean is unhappy.

"Paper books?" I say. I hide my scoff with a confused smile. "Where do you even find these anymore?"

"Most of them were saved here when the other rings were going down. They always meant to come back for them. I guess they took the food and gas instead." She winks. "Priorities. I guess priorities are the same reason I can't get myself to leave them behind."

The fifth container is an open series of rain catchers and water purifiers, along with a few drums of water marshaled along the wall. The sixth and final container holds padlocked food cabinets, which Di unlocks with a key around her neck.

She gathers a feast for us: vitamin supplements and canned peaches and rice and beef jerky and water and wine.

We carry everything back together on a plastic tray with golden flowers on it that Di says belonged to her mother. I ask her what flowers they are, and she tells me she doesn't know. But they're beautiful, and I imagine land like nothing I've ever touched, an open field full of flowers with petals that golden.

My mother is dejected and listless when we return. I almost want her to go back to raving about the old stories. She's just sitting, slowly leaking water from the tilted canteen onto her lap, like pouring out liquid gold.

I hurry over and straighten the canteen, press my hand to her forehead. She's cold and damp.

"Mom," I say. "Did you drink anything?"

Her eyes are unfocused, looking at me, through me. She murmurs, "In the morning, you must go to find the eagles."

It hits me, then, in a flash of understanding. It's like looking up and realizing a decade has passed and I no longer know what it means to be young.

My mother is going to die. She's been speaking this way because her brain is actively dying, and I can hear her neurons misfiring in her every scattered word.

But I push the thought away, deep down into the silt below us, where even the gods cannot see, because if I don't think it, my mother won't die. She'll drink some water, and she'll be fine.

This is all she needs. Some dry land, some clean water, and she'll be fine.

Di really does host us like a queen. It's the golden hour of evening, and the sun gilds her dark skin. Standing there, spreading her hands toward us, she looks like a statue before a forgotten altar. But then she sweeps her silk kimono aside and sits, and she speaks with my mother as if I'm not propping her upright.

"Tell me where you came from," Di says. "I don't know what it means to be the carrier of the Kumeyaay Nation."

My mother looks at Di solemnly and says, croaking, "Please, My Queen. Something to eat first. My mind . . ."

"Of course. I should have realized how far you came to get here."

I nod tiredly and fill a plate with humble helpings for my mother. She might not eat any of it. She might try and simply aspirate.

But my mother will not die today, so I put rice and jerky on her plate, and I tell Di, "Thank you. We actually were living in that Old Troy Company outpost when it burned down a couple of weeks ago."

"Big fire." Di winces. "I saw the smoke off that."

I close my eyes and nod. It felt like war, like the end of the world. Just the rattle and pop of superheated metal.

I tell her how a gas tank had exploded, a few buildings down from ours. But it was up high enough that it rained holy hell upon us all.

When I fled with my mother and those two duffel bags on my back, there was molten metal punching into the ocean all around us, and I saw my neighbors scattering, shrieking. One of them, Mrs. Vasquez, from across the hall, ran past me, and a falling chunk of metal collided with her back, liquid and solid somehow at once, and it sent her spinning over the railing and into the water. She landed with a splash and an upward hiss of steam.

I don't know if the shock killed her before she knew how

it felt to have steel bond with her flesh. But I will never forget the way she reached for me as she fell. The way she screamed.

I just kept going. I carried my mother and the bags and threw us all into the boat and throttled that engine like I could outrun fate.

"A lot of people died," I murmur.

My mother is trying to feed herself, but there's rice all over her shirt now. Her hands shake, and she moves the spoon the way a toddler does, trying to find her mouth.

I take the spoon gently from her hand.

"Gas tank explosion has to come down to bad maintenance," Di says. "That was a fed site, right?"

"Yeah, well, you live where the government tells you to live, and shocker, they told you to live somewhere shitty. It's not like they'd give up any real surface-land for people like us."

Di smirks. "Who needs their kingdom, when I have mine?"

"That's what I'm telling Nea," my mother says. She leans toward Di, and I catch her before she can tip herself off-balance. "We will make our own land again. I had a dream that if you sail far enough west, you will find the edge of the world-ocean, and there will be the great stone pillars with the eagles. If you can reach them and collect both the black and the white chick, you can remake our nation."

I hold my mother, and I don't know if I want to cry or start laughing, because I'm only a quarter Native to begin with, and if we are the only carriers of the Kumeyaay Nation remaining, there is no nation to rebuild. I don't know how to tell her that.

I don't know her stories, not the way she does. I never went to my great-aunt's house and listened to the whole family describe how we were once sent across the desert to die and survived anyway. I never listened to my grandfather tell war stories or felt him braid my hair or heard him play electric guitar.

There is no history in me but this: the cold ocean, trying to kill us all, whatever sad nation we hail from.

"What happens when you remake your nation?" Di asks.

That quiets my mother for a long time. She chews at a piece of beef jerky thoughtfully, and then she looks at Di, as if from one queen to another, and says, "Then no one will ask me what it means to be Kumeyaay."

My mother can't eat much, but she sips more water. As I eat, she tells Di history I can recognize: how we once lived on solid land, but the cities and crowds and barges and pollution became too much, so we came out here, when I was just a kid.

I don't know Di, but I have an immediate fondness for the way she looks at my mother. There's no pity there. She has only awe and admiration and the quiet respect any elder deserves, even one gradually losing her mind.

My mother falls asleep beside the table, still resting in my arms. Her breathing is slow and deep as the water below us.

Di looks at her, looks at me. "How many days were you out of water?"

"We weren't yet. I think she stopped drinking a few days ago without telling me, to make the supply last. I only realized it when she started talking like that and I had to piece it all together. I've made her drink, but . . ."

I press my lips together, shake my head.

Di rests a hand on my shoulder and squeezes lightly. "I don't think she's delusional about being a warrior woman."

I scoff and roll my eyes, tilting my head so she doesn't see me wipe away tears.

"You two can sleep here, if that's easier, tonight."

"I'm sorry. We'll be gone by tomorrow."

"Stay as long as you need." Di's smile is a relief, solid ground after too long on the water. "I'm just glad I'm not alone out here."

For two more days, my mother is alive, and Di is a queen, and the Kumeyaay Nation is going to be born again, where the stone pillars rise at the edge of the world-ocean.

I spend the last two days of my mother's life feeding her, pouring water into her mouth, holding her up and turning away so she can do her business over the edge of the pier. I carry her on my back, and I listen to her stories, even when she mixes them up.

On that last night, as she slips into dreams, my mother tells me, "The eagles are there. I'm going to find them."

I clutch her hand. "Mom," I say, because we are alone, and the ocean is murmuring outside. "What if I can't carry the nation? What if I'm not the right person?"

My mother doesn't even open her eyes. She just tells me, "No one carries a nation alone. You keep forgetting the stories, Nea. We always have the stories."

I try to stay up through the night, but I sleep through the moment my mother stops breathing. Just like that, I wake, and the heart of our nation is gone, lost in the dead circuits of my mother's memory.

I knew it was coming, but I still cry. I think anyone would cry.

Di tells me she would cry.

We take Di's little rowboat so far out, her tiny kingdom is just a smear on the horizon. It's the grim, unspoken logic of any water dwellers: you always bury your dead where the smell won't reach you, or the meat won't lap up on your front porch.

My mother lies between our feet, wrapped in a linen shroud, her hair clean and combed. It feels like I should have her sitting up, to face the western horizon, where the eagles wait for her.

Di stops rowing and asks me if I'm ready.

We could just float here awhile, but the sun is relentless and the smell of my mother's body will bring sharks even before she hits the water. This world has no room for ritual or sentiment anymore.

So I gather my mother in my arms, kiss her cold forehead, and whisper in her ear, "I know you'll find them."

I let her slip from my arms into the water. The linen blooms out around her like a flower, and she falls into it until I can't see her anymore.

Then Di rows us back, and I don't say a word.

Di moves like someone who knows grief, because she wastes no time on questions. The moment we return to her island, she opens a bottle of wine and hands it to me.

I look at her, at the bottle. "I don't have any fuel. I can't pay you."

"I don't want you to pay me." It's only then that I realize her eyes are glistening. "I want to mourn with you."

We sit on the pier, shoulder to shoulder, leaning into each other and sharing the bottle of wine as seagulls and skuas and terns surge across the sky, heading west.

"I think my mother would like feeding a bunch of birds," I say.

"Yeah?"

"She used to collect little chicken figurines. The whole kitchen was full of them. Dozens of them. They all burned up."

Di's hair tickles my throat as she leans heavier into me. "I wouldn't mind feeding the ocean when I die. It's fed me plenty."

"How long have you been out here alone?" I ask.

"A couple years, I guess. I don't know. My brothers went off on their own because this place is sinking—or the water's rising, I don't know—and my dad had a heart attack a few years ago. I find I don't really need time that much."

"Don't you ever . . . just go insane, a little? Being the last one?"

"I wish I got to be your mom's kind of insane. She got to die a warrior for her people. Who gets to say that? It's the twenty-second century. No one dies heroically anymore."

"That's generous of you to say."

"It's true."

Her urgency surprises me, but I continue on. "Anyway, she doesn't know what she's talking about. She never even went to the old rez before it went underwater. She didn't know the culture. Neither of us did. We had some old family stories. Blood. Relatives. That's it."

"What else do you need for a nation?"

I look at Di's slowly sinking kingdom. There's no way she could fit all that food onto my little boat. We'd be robbed if we tried to get too far out into deep waters anyway. Di probably only made it here this long because the water is too shallow for any of the big tanker ships to sail up and invade.

But for a second, I really do imagine it: the two of us going out to find a new place to call our own.

Like she can read my mind, Di says, "You can stay here as long as you want, you know."

I turn my face toward hers and flick my stare from her eyes to her lips. I'm swaying and heartbroken, but the sunlight paints her like a goddess.

I do the only thing I can.

I lean in and kiss her, and when Di kisses me back, she tastes like a distant lifetime, one in which we have months to get lost in the heat of each other's arms. She tastes like raspberries and hope and salt-tears, and I realize those are mine, that I'm crying and kissing her and pulling her closer by the soft flesh of her hip.

Di pulls away long enough to murmur, "Let's get inside, and you can tell me a story."

"What kind of story?"

"Anything. Anything your mom would have liked me to know."

So we go inside and I lie in Di's arms next to the pillows where my mother died, and I tell her how I lost my mother at my first powwow and the nice white lady who helped me kept trying to take me to other nice white ladies, not understanding that my mother could be browner than me. I tell her how my mother tried to take us back to San Diego, to visit the homeland, and the desert was just a narrow strip of glass-enclosed national park, preserved below a screaming upper sky of floating cities, stretching miles overhead.

I tell her how my mother really will see the eagles, if there's such a thing as a god worth believing in.

Di tells me, "Your mother made a nation here, at least."

I wrinkle my nose at her. "What do you mean?"

"Every person in my kingdom knows the great legends of the Kumeyaay. And no one wonders what it means."

I turn my face into Di's chest and I cry, for the first time, the way I wanted to. The way I needed to the day my mother began muttering nonsense and throwing up bile.

I cry like a girl who has just realized *woman* means learning to exist without her mother.

Di holds me like she's the boat and the whole world is the ocean, and I float there in her arms until my tears dry. She smooths my hair from my face and kisses my throat.

"The world is remaking itself anyway," she murmurs. "We can always make our own nation, right here. The Land of Stick and Mud."

"No. Something grander than that, if you're going to be queen."

She kisses me, and I still taste her smile. "Oh, I still get to be queen?"

"Of course. My mother decreed it."

"Decreed," Di repeats, giggling. "Well, I could never go against the first decree of the reborn Kumeyaay Nation."

We drink another bottle of wine and explore each other like the flesh of another body is a new land to kiss and cultivate and make our own. We become so drunk our syllables blend together, and we slur and giggle, mumbling our way into some ancient prayer to Memory to carry what we cannot.

We pour out libations for the land that we carry in us, the only place any nation can live in a world slowly falling underwater.

In my dreams that night, I sail across the horizon until I see the great stone towers. They're real. They're waiting beyond the edge of the world-ocean, on that fresh jut of young earth.

I sit and watch for my mother to rise, as inevitable as the dawn.

THE WORDS FROM THE MOUNTAIN

Wen Wen Yang

My parents had taught me to never attract the attention of a god. Never accept their help.

But the language Zeus gave us was too powerful, and power requires a sacrifice.

At the beginning of the year, before the earthquake, most of the town brought the Old Woman of the mountain their offerings. She was especially fond of preserved winter melon, dried ginger, and honeysuckle flowers for tea. The tiny Old Woman told some villagers to move, others to fortify their homes immediately.

My family heard this information secondhand. We had been scraping every extra morsel of food into my mother's bowl instead of giving it to the Old Woman. The villagers supported this; they had been treating my mother like a delicate blooming flower. Was she getting enough food, water, sunlight?

We lived in the smallest home in town, though my father had begun to build another room. I had noticed villagers replacing loose stones, pulling weeds outside their siheyuan. They carried water-damaged doors and drafty windows to the dump for burning. In previous years, we had copied what others did. But now my father salvaged those abandoned doors, windows, and ill-fitting stones for the baby's room. He turned down several offers of help because we couldn't afford their labor. Though none of us liked waiting, he planned for us to go to the Old Woman for my anticipated sibling's one-month birthday.

I should have offered a day of mending clothing or made the Old Woman socks.

The previous autumn, Lingli, the seamstress, had hired me as her apprentice because my fingers seemed to work faster than her eyes. She promised warm winter clothes for my entire family.

I spent our last day together sewing baby clothes.

When Poseidon shook the land before dawn, the farmers' sheep and cows nearly broke down the barn doors in their terror. But most homes remained standing.

When other families, the families who had brought their offerings to the Old Woman, emerged from their houses, they saw that my family's house had collapsed. The townspeople pulled apart the rubble, stone by stone.

They found my mother first in the ruins of the kitchen. They agreed that, even if she had lived, she would have lost the pregnancy.

Helios might have heard the villagers' shouts when they found me wedged into a corner. Lingli tended to me through the morning.

Some men offered to bring me up the mountain for the Old

Woman to heal my wounds, but Lingli's steady hand stitched my new seams. I was torn but not broken.

In the afternoon, a dog started digging at the remains of the unfinished room. Lingli said my father's body was draped over the crib as if his bones could protect it. I wept bitterly for days.

"This is why you must visit the Old Woman of the mountain," the elders warned the children. "You must never pass a season without seeing her."

The town divided the remains of my home while I stayed in the room above Lingli's shop.

Within a year, the land had become a part of my neighbors' gardens.

A year after the earthquake, the Old Woman invited every unmarried adult to her siheyuan. It was the size of two families' homes, for herself and passing peddlers. Two gold lion statues guarded the south-facing red door. Their mouths hung open, a threat to evil spirits.

If one started at the base of the mountain in the morning, one made it back home just in time to prepare for lunch.

Mei, the seamstress Lingli had hired to help prepare for the mid-autumn celebrations, told me it was a pointless visit. She said the Old Woman held a piece of paper. When Mei recoiled, the Old Woman shouted at her, "Look! Can you see those pictures?"

Mei said that the piece of paper had black markings, like handprints of children.

"Yes," she told the Old Woman.

"The first picture and the one under that, are they the same?"

It was a mass of ink, so Mei could not tell where one character ended and another began. She guessed. "No."

The Old Woman tsk-tsked and waved her away.

I heard the villagers tell their stories again and again. Some guessed yes, and still the Old Woman sent them away.

I couldn't face the Zuo Zhe who had made my life a cautionary tale. I would rather spend the day earning enough to warm my small room and to fill my belly with noodles and pork belly.

If my family had visited the Old Woman, even with just a bouquet of wildflowers, would my parents be alive, doting on a spoiled toddler? We couldn't afford land closer to town, couldn't repair with sturdier doors or windows. I could afford her knowledge now, but she couldn't return my family to me. During the Ghost Festival, I had burned joss paper baby clothes for my sibling, a paper home for my parents.

At the end of the summer, the Old Woman refused to give any blessings or to read any letters until she had seen every single one of the unmarried adults.

"Is she looking for an apprentice?" I asked Lingli. "I can't work for you both."

Lingli touched a letter one of the peddlers had delivered from her sister. She had recently married a man who lived on the other side of the mountain. Her town's Zuo Zhe had written it, then passed it along to the next peddler headed north. The peddlers knew the villagers, knew this note should go to the seamstress. How could I keep Lingli from knowing if her sister was safe?

"Isn't the Old Woman immortal?" Mei asked, ironing the freshly hemmed pants.

"My grandmother remembers when the Old Woman was

chosen." Lingli shrugged. "But she also says the Old Woman entertained the gods, so I don't trust her."

I set down the chalk and picked up the scissors. "I'll go tomorrow and give the Old Woman last year's wool. I'll ask for a blessing for warm fingers and straight stitches."

The Old Woman stood at the threshold. Her face was flesh sagging into wrinkles leading into white hair. A dark stain covered one side of her face. Some areas were lighter, purple by her eye, brown along her jaw.

"It is the mark of the Zuo Zhe," my parents had explained when I was a child. "Zeus has given them the words so that we can live without the stain on us."

When the Old Woman held out the paper and asked if the characters were the same, my mouth went dry.

The character fluttering on the paper in her hands looked like a person wearing an elaborate hat. Beside it was another character, a desk with a student's legs dangling underneath. The same characters repeated over and over.

I didn't know they were the characters for "study," that they were ordering me to read. My hand reached for the paper. My heartbeat was loud in my ears.

"They're the same," I told the Old Woman of the mountain. I stared at her, enchanted.

I should have lied. I should have run.

The Old Woman grinned like a cat who had caught a mouse. She took my hand and drew the characters for Zuo Zhe with her nail across the back. My hand burned, the skin puckering and lifting into pale pink welts.

I yelped and snatched it back.

"You're my apprentice now. Come, I'll make some congee for us."

I turned to the path to the village. "But my work."

The Old Woman gathered her bundle of wool. "There's nothing in the village for you."

I wanted to get my few belongings, a favorite coat and the week's earnings, but the Old Woman said I couldn't.

"Downstairs, I keep four hundred years of family lineages. The words have warned us and we have avoided hundreds of disasters. All those people in the valley have no other way to contact the rest of the world." She looked over her shoulder at me. "What would you have done in the village? Was it more important?"

I couldn't form a satisfying response.

The Old Woman retrieved faded letters, and I learned decades-old gossip, written in euphemisms. She read the letters aloud as she pointed at the characters. I wrote and rewrote them in a pile of loose sand, pressing my palm into the grains before the magic took hold.

A great-uncle was late. "He was living on discontent," she sneered. "We celebrated when he went to Hades. You have the stroke order wrong. Do it again from the upper left."

A wayward son was entangled with a woman who was not his wife. "He was an excellent husband, once he stopped roaming."

Every night that first week, after I had studied a hundred words, I tried to run. But within an hour, I found myself walking in circles back to the Old Woman.

"Come, your congee is getting cold!" She stood at the door, blowing on her steaming bowl. I followed her back into the siheyuan, my healing hand pulsing with my thundering heartbeat.

At the end of the first two weeks, I had perhaps two thousand characters memorized and was reading aloud, haltingly, to the Old Woman in the afternoon.

When Lingli arrived with the other villagers visiting for the Mid-Autumn Festival, she brought me new pants and my coat with my earnings in the pockets. She wrapped the pants' waist around my neck and sucked her teeth. "You're losing weight. I'll have Mei bring some of her mother's fish."

I rubbed my eyes to hide my tears. "How is Mei?"

"She doesn't put the spools back when she is done, but she'll learn. There's a fisherman her mother doesn't like her seeing, but he brings in the biggest catches and saves the best for Mei."

"Girl," shouted the Old Woman. "Come, write this man's letter."

I imagined that the next day, that man roamed from house to house—eating a pork bun here, a tea egg there—to tell people that the Old Woman had adopted me as her apprentice. Right out from under Lingli! Did the villagers think it was a luxury to live on offerings and their goodwill?

They didn't see the hours I spent learning the characters. They'd never seen the Room of Four Dangers.

A previous Zuo Zhe had carved a replica of the valley into the floor of one room. There were tiny bamboo buildings and even the odd sheep and cow. I updated the buildings and strings of property lines with each dictated letter, each peddler's gossip. There was Lingli's store. There was Mei's mother's fish stall. My family's home wasn't there. In the mornings, I wrote the characters for the four dangers at each cardinal direction with a water-dampened brush instead of ink. If any of the dangers remained instead of evaporating, I narrowed down the location of the danger by judging the wetness of the character.

Once, the water danger stained the floor near a well. The Old Woman sucked her teeth and wiped it away with her fingertips. She smelled the residue and recoiled. "Ai, it stinks!"

We told the next peddler headed into town to warn the people not to drink the water. Or would there be no water? Or would there be too much water? If they boiled it, would it be safe enough to drink? How could I ask the words?

The Old Woman shook her head. "You can read as well as I can."

When Mei visited us days later, she brought dried fish and held my hands. "The water smelled of piss and shit. The pigs from upriver are so sick."

Every morning I waited for the water character to disappear. It took weeks before the danger passed and it faded. Finally, I could tell the farmers that the water was safe to use again. It was during those long mornings that I forgave the Old Woman for my parents' deaths, and I started to write.

Using the water-dampened brush, I drew simplified characters, missing strokes, changing the stroke order, until the characters were warped enough that they lay useless on the floor. I copied these characters onto paper using imperfect ink, diluted to the point of being a shadow instead of a mark. After the papers dried, I rolled them under my bed.

The Old Woman taught me that the characters possessed an intimate magic too.

I watched her ease a man's back pain so he could return to the fields. She drew the characters directly on the man's spine with black ink. The four characters wound from the base of his neck to the small of his back. The man stretched upright, grimace relaxing into a grin, as the Old Woman hobbled over. "Don't wash it off for two days," she told him as I helped her to her room. For the next two nights, I soothed the Old

Woman's transferred pain with hot water bottles against her back.

"Why didn't you let me take it?" I asked.

She waved the suggestion away. "I would have to tend to the garden alone instead of lying here in luxury. Wrap that one tighter and put it higher."

After the next harvest, the farmer's sons brought us a portion of their rice.

I also met the peddlers who carried letters across villages and sold the wares of far-off places. They brought different worlds to us for a week at a time. They would share a recipe, a dance, and gossip from mortals or gods. These were the brightest weeks, the weeks with the most color, the most laughter.

To prepare their bedrooms, I practiced writing the character for *clean* on the floor and the counters using a brush and water. The character itself looked like dripping water and things tidied on a table. Thankfully, it was just the garden that dirtied itself in retaliation for that character.

One afternoon, Ravi, the peddler from Yindu, arrived early and saw the dust flee the room and return to the garden. He laughed and clapped his hands, as if I had performed an act as great as Petra, the violinist from De Guo. She used the instrument to make you cry without a story. When she let me try to play it, the violin screeched like an angry cat.

When Ravi offered to cook for us, I asked him to be gentle with his spices. I remembered his antics from my last spring in the village.

He had approached the children at the market, full of swagger and mischief. Ravi said he was born in the year of the trickster monkey, and I wondered if he was the reincarnation of the Monkey King.

"Only a very brave person could eat this." Ravi poured a line of fine red spice onto his palm. "It comes all the way from Hunan. It'll put hair on your chest."

The children looked at one another, grimacing.

"What? None of you look like this?" Ravi pulled down his shirt collar to show a mass of hair. Those at nearby stalls laughed in high squeals. The children licked their fingers, stuck them into the red powder, and sucked it off. They cried out like wounded dogs and begged for water with panting tongues.

Ravi laughed so hard his dark brown skin reddened. The cooks did not buy that spice from him, though one girl asked for a small portion to give to her father that evening.

"He is very brave," she said stoically. "But I'm braver."

Ravi made us a lovely meal that warmed our bones without hurting our tongues. The Old Woman went to bed early, and I washed the dishes.

"You're not going to write them clean?" He wiggled his fingers as if drawing something in the air.

I flushed. "I'm too tired."

He went to his room, and I could hear him fumbling through his wooden pack with its dozens of drawers. It smelled of incense and sandalwood. He returned with a small jar of dried leaves.

"If you chew on these, you'll be awake for hours."

I set the last clean bowl aside and stared at the long, flat leaves. "Thank you, but I'd rather sleep. Good night." I could feel his eyes on my back as I left the kitchen.

The next visit, while the Old Woman was practicing her tai chi in the courtyard, Ravi pulled out a pair of gloves.

I stared at them, my hands on the brush, as tall as a broom, that we used for the four dangers divination. "Very nice." All four dangers evaporated without a stain. "The shopkeepers would like them. They look too soft for the farmers."

He laughed. "They're for you."

My mouth dropped open in a silent "oh" before I caught myself. "Do you need a blessing?" I laid the brush down against its cradle. "Safe travels, or something to keep thieves away?"

His cheeks reddened, his patchy mustache spread under his nose like a bird taking flight. "No, no. I thought your hands might get cold while you're writing."

I could feel my cheeks warming as I accepted the gloves. They were soft and stretched as I flexed my fingers. They were dark as good earth, though I would still have to be careful to avoid getting the ink on them. Ink was difficult to wash out.

"Thank you." I bowed and then he bowed. I laughed, covering my mouth. "You don't need to bow too."

"Oh, is that why everyone's laughing at me in the village? In my town, both people bow."

"They also think you have an iron tongue." I pointed at his mouth. "The previous spice peddler had the most sensitive palate, and he loved sweets. Then you arrived and sold the spiciest powders. We thought they would burn through our mouths."

Ravi grinned. "I have a different recipe I'd like to try with you. With you and the Old Woman."

That first night I wore the gloves to sleep. The Old Woman caught me folding them under my pillow the next morning.

"Who brought those?"

"The peddler from Yindu."

"You are the town's Zuo Zhe," she hissed, clasping my scarred hand. "The village depends on you. You can't be entangled with a peddler."

Entangled. She spoke as if she were writing around words.

"I won't," I promised. I couldn't even leave the mountain. An entanglement couldn't survive on a week once a season. The words had taken away the hope of a family legacy better than the earthquake.

She smiled. "We have the power of the gods. Zeus himself gave us this language. Don't waste it."

My fingers itched that night as I sliced Zeus's language into broken words.

During Ravi's next visit, I kept busy with the village's letters and sat by Petra and the peddlers from Ai Ji. Petra's violin was so mournful that when the night drew to a close, we were all wiping away tears.

The Old Woman laughed. "How miserable. Play a happier song tomorrow." I helped her stand; she moved slower in the colder weather. She gripped my arm as we walked to her room.

In the morning, I woke to Ravi knocking on her bedroom door. The dew in the courtyard bore no footprints from her morning tai chi.

My heart shuddered. Had she fallen in the night?

When we entered, she was still under her bedding.

"Have you overslept, Old Woman?" I touched her cold arm. I screamed and shook her with both hands until someone dragged me away.

The world spun and I wrapped my arms around myself. Steady, steady. I drew the character for *calm* onto my shaking shoulders. I pressed my toes into the ground. I breathed in the smell of sandalwood and focused on its warmth. Someone pressed my head to their shoulder. My body shook against theirs. Finally, I blinked back my tears.

The peddlers were staring at me, waiting for an order. I licked my lips. "I need your help." Together, we cleaned and buried the Old Woman's body. We sat weeping with Petra's violin echoing down the mountainside.

That evening, when I washed the dirt from my body, I saw the stain on my hip. It was a brown that morphed to purple or dark blue before it started arching up my side. The sign of the Zuo Zhe was painless compared with the binding mark the Old Woman made on my hand. This felt more like the end of the Old Woman than her burial.

In the months after her death, I devised more simplified words than stars in the sky. I wrote stories with new words I hadn't written before. Two villagers had fallen in love instead of becoming entangled. A villager died instead of being late. At night, I rewrote from memory the letters I had read that day. I was filling hours until I found the courage to spread these new words.

During Ravi's next visit, he delivered a letter from Lingli's sister.

"Is she feeling better?" Lingli wrung her hands. "It was probably those mung bean sprouts."

I traced my finger along the letter. Her sister had suffered her first miscarriage. I didn't know the word for *miscarriage*, but I learned it. Pain seized my back and I doubled over. Wetness erupted from between my legs. Lingli caught me. My stomach threatened to empty itself on her shoes. We hobbled to my room while the liquid dripped down my leg. I left bloody footprints the entire way.

The other peddlers hurriedly searched through their packs.

Ravi found a Western medicine the color of an exhausted sunset. It tasted vile, but my body settled into exhaustion instead of exsanguination.

Lingli stayed the night until I reassured her I was fine. When there was enough light to see the path, she returned to the village.

I lay in my bed with the peddlers taking turns watching over me. After dinner, when the other peddlers had gone to bed, Ravi stayed.

"Your color has come back."

I stared at my hands, expecting to see gray flesh, but found only dirty fingernails.

"You should write that town's Zuo Zhe a letter," he suggested. "It should just say, *Die, you rat-for-brains bastard*."

I laughed. "I don't know the character for *die* or *bastard*. Besides, writing it would swing it back to me. If that worked, the emperor would just send Zuo Zhe into battle with a banner that says *Die!*"

"But the word *miscarriage* didn't hurt him?" Ravi huffed.

"He doesn't have a uterus."

"Bastard. This language is too powerful. These words ask too much of you. You're the town's oracle, and its hostage."

I nodded. Would the villagers start to call me the Girl of the Mountain? Would I lose the name my mother had picked for me?

"I have a plan," I whispered. "I made weaker words."

Ravi's body shifted in the low seat beside my bed. "But this language—"

"Came from Zeus, I know, but who uses it now? Mortals."

I climbed out of bed and reached underneath. I pulled out the papers and unrolled them on the floor. "I have been neutering these characters. You can look; these won't hurt you. Here, I removed multiple strokes, so they lack the power. And even if someone accidentally added back the strokes, the stroke order is important. It's unlikely they'll replicate it and get the original god-sent character."

Ravi's eyes grew large. "You've been planning this."

"Since the Old Woman trapped me here." I pointed out the window. "I can't venture more than an hour's walk from here, but you and the peddlers can spread these words. If I send the letters back to the other Zuo Zhe with the new characters, they can start using this new language too. I don't know which Zuo Zhe will agree, but surely some of them do not want to pass on this burden."

He laughed, shaking his head. "You are asking them to give up power. It's like turning away a peach of immortality or extinguishing Prometheus's fire."

"I can be an oracle only. And when I grow old, I won't train another. I'm not trapping anyone else."

He shuddered. "You would willingly lose the words from Olympus that could have saved your family."

"But they *didn't*," I hissed. "We had nothing to exchange. Let everyone wander blind together. It might take decades to replace every Zeus-given word with a new simplified character, but the current Zuo Zhe could free the next generation."

When I turned back to him, his face was different, stern and frightening.

"Ravi?"

Golden light arched across his temples.

"You would risk the wrath of the gods?" His voice was deeper, menacing.

I shrank back. The air hummed, and the smell of sandalwood was gone. It smelled of an approaching thunderstorm.

"Are you Zeus himself?" When I named the father of the

gods, he smiled and I recoiled. "No," I growled. "You won't find a blushing virgin here."

"I'm not the lecherous one."

"Are you the Monkey King?"

He chuckled, pressing his hand against his cheek. "I met him once. He tried to steal my wine. Gave him my hottest spice instead. All his hair stood on end. No, I'm the other trickster, the messenger."

"Hermes," I whispered his name. "How did I bring this misfortune on myself? I did not brag, didn't challenge you."

"I wanted to see how mortals managed my father's language. I didn't know he had given you so much power." He stood, brushed the dust from his pants. His gaze slid to the papers strewn around us. "Aren't these words a challenge to his language?"

Would he strike me for insulting his father? No, not if I gave him power. All the stories my parents told me about these gods circled around petty fights.

I lifted my chin. "You are the messenger of the gods. You can deliver the new characters to the village, to the other Zuo Zhe. We can work together to create a language. You are the god of swiftness, of trade. How much more powerful—?"

"Stop." He held up his hand. "I will do this just to spite him."

The relief that I would not be struck down overwhelmed any suspicion I should have had. I was giving up power when I had already paid the price. Perhaps Hermes laughs about it when he thinks of me. If he thinks about me.

In the months that followed, Hermes, as Ravi, tempted the children with an adventure, and they followed him up the mountain.

Their eyes shone as they stared at me. They knew me, the one who had measured them for new clothes each season with Lingli. I was younger than their parents, an elder sister of sorts. I was not the mysterious, stained Old Woman of the mountain.

I laid out a piece of paper, and without their parents to mimic, the children watched with open mouths.

I drew one horizontal stroke in front of them. "This is the number one." Two strokes. "This makes it two." Three strokes. "This makes it three. Four is trickier, like a window with curtains."

I taught them these new, ugly characters. I mashed them together and formed pieces that could not make me bleed, could not move pain from one body to another. We practiced with water and dust, chalk on cloth. Some children drew in the air with their tiny fingers.

The first day, Hermes brought ten children. The next day there were twenty traveling without him, led by the ones who had come the day before.

Within weeks, the children wrote stories for me and one another.

The children called me jie jie, elder sister. They shared their families' secrets and gossip over a raucous midday meal while they devoured dumplings, noodles, and vegetables from my garden. The peddlers lingered over the children, smiling as they were finally able to read the letters they carried.

After the children returned to the village for the night, I spent hours copying, rewriting, and sending pieces along with each peddler. The peddlers carried my request to the other Zuo Zhe. Some wrote back in the new neutered language with more suggestions. We agreed to write a dictionary.

Some Zuo Zhe threatened me with the wrath of every god and goddess. Peddlers told me that they asked if I had four eyes. Did the ghosts cry nightly in our village? Was I not tempting Zeus's ire? I dreamed of my liver being pecked out until I drew the character for *fire* and burned those Zuo Zhe's letters.

Months later, the children greeted me in the morning with letters they had written for their parents to give to the peddlers. I had to translate some letters back into the god-given language for the stubborn Zuo Zhe, but most were going to villages where the Zuo Zhe were providing lessons too.

Instead of imagining visits to the Old Woman I had missed, I imagined children using the soot from candles to make their marks on paper. In the evenings, their parents struggled to find euphemisms to keep secrets from their children, instead of trying to avoid injuring the Zuo Zhe. Parents visited me less often, hoping to keep their secrets within their families. But the children still came, brimming with questions and demanding words I had not written before.

"How do you write *stumbling*? My little brother isn't walking right yet. Can it look like the character for *walk* but lopsided?"

"Can I ask them to save my older cousin's castoffs until our next visit?" I sent this child to Lingli with a blessing for prosperity.

At least I had the blessing of one god.

Hermes granted us speed. I gave the children more words in a year than I had learned in two years with the Old Woman. Each day they asked for more, and I wondered: Where was the bottom of this well?

One night, Hermes and I drank tea in the courtyard after the other peddlers had gone to bed.

He nodded to one of the rooms. "Did I see Petra wearing the gloves I gave you?"

I hadn't told her where I had gotten them, but I couldn't

bear to wear them. What if I had been swayed by his kindness? A product of a mortal and a god—what happy ending
could I create for that child?

"That music," I answered, quickly draining my cup. "I
thought her hands deserved more protection than mine. After
all, the children of the village can write now. You've given
them the gift of creation."

I waited for him to take the bait, the compliment.

He leaned back and stared up at the stars. "Just stealing a
bit of truth."

Did Hermes know the neutered words could warp and
bend, creating discord? Already there were snide remarks,
according to the children. And written lies! The children
wrote about better lives to not worry their friends, not so
different from my father's refusal of the villagers' help. How
long could you pretend that the life you were living was good
enough, before it broke you?

My chest tightened. My character for *fire* no longer brought
light and warmth. Villagers didn't know I was taking this from
them. They sent offerings with their children in thanks for
giving up some of my power. They could wish their friends'
pain eased, but their words were hollow.

One day, no Zuo Zhe will write in the Room of Four Dangers. No one will warn the children of poisoned waters, hungry wildfires, furious winds, or earthquakes. The village will
build a memory, false and twisted, of how I mangled the god-
sent words and abandoned the people to the gods and the
elements.

Had I used Hermes, or had he used me? Did he want mortals to lose the power his father gave us? Could I burn the
pages that proved I broke Zeus's words? I cannot even reveal
my name here for fear of his wrath.

When I finally leave the siheyuan, with Hermes leading me to Hades, perhaps I will leave an apprentice behind along with my dictionaries.

Perhaps one of the children will be the next apprentice, and she will be *willing* to stay.

My work will become Hermes's legacy. But I will be the village's last sacrifice. I will set the words free.

NO GODS, NO KINGS

Maya Deane

Murina stared into the coals on the brazier, waiting for a perfect uniformity of red. Slowly she unfolded the rolls of paper, admiring the thin, pounded membranes that had taken a Rebu artisan so many weeks to prepare. Time had barely yellowed the papers. Had Murina been inclined to spare them, they might have lasted centuries.

She flung them onto the coals and watched. It was fascinating. First, the embers blackened the paper they touched, then pierced it. Graying rings spread out around the contact points, and tongues of flame licked the leaves, followed by bands of roving sparks that swept over the letters line by line, reducing each leaf to a skin of delicate ash. It all happened so quickly.

"Murina." The god sighed. "Why go and do a thing like that?"

She set her face into a hard smile. Two Lands sculptors had carved that same hard smile into her granite statue in the crypt of the queens, a smile that could make a god flinch.

"You cherished my letters for so long," Kalu murmured in her ear, his disembodied presence close as breath. "Why burn them now?"

"I forgot I had them." Murina laughed. "Then your wine-soaked sex cult came begging for 'sacred scriptures from the hands of the grape god.'"

The voice of the god sounded pained, almost plangent. "To the Mainads, my love letters *are* sacred scriptures. They would have immortalized you in song and worshipped you as their lord Dionysos's legendary consort."

"Dionysos?" Murina scoffed. "Is that what you're going by now?"

"Amazons call me Kalu; Mainads, Dionysos. Why are you burning my letters?"

"Fuck the Mainads," Murina sneered, "that's why." She blew gently, and the Mainads' sacred scriptures dissipated into glowing ashes on the night wind. The pale moon gleamed down like the edge of a battle ax, reflected in the dark waters below the cliff. "Murina has her own legend."

"You used to," Kalu whispered. "You were magnificent once. But you've grown so old since I knew you. Your name will soon crumble to ashes too."

Murina laughed and stood, surveying the empty room behind her. The frescoes of dolphins were magnificent, but she was still alone. "Come back from Meluhha and say that to my face, *Dionysos*."

"I *am* coming back," the god murmured, and his soft scent, lilac and grape blossom, filled her nostrils. He had always smelled so sweet, but with that subtle tinge of rot, that heady, giddy fermented richness just beneath. "For the peace summit."

Murina laughed. "How exciting for you."

"You already knew? How?" The god of wine sounded suspicious, his soft voice echoing from a great distance. "No. You are simply being coy."

Murina spread her arms to the sky, to the stars, to the moon. This god loved youth and beauty, so let him lament her scars and tattoos and wrinkles, the sag of battle-hardened skin, the royal statue's granite sneer. "Watch me and find out."

Kalu's presence ebbed, but she knew he was still watching. It tormented him that he could not read her or her sisters, that he could not peer through their diadems of Urss into the brains beneath—but that was the entire point of the diadems, to block out the gods' sight, to taunt them with closed doors. Smirking, Murina ran her fingers over the slim arc of tarnished silver.

When she was certain he was entirely gone, the First of the Amazons knelt before her brazier and prayed silently to the moon.

O moon, your glory is in the sky. You will always shine down, cold and sharp as a blade, and I will never forget you. Make my name immortal, beloved moon. Make my legacy eternal. I will ride with you through the vaults of heaven.

She descended the tower. The megaron was empty. Everyone had gone out to the plaza, where a great bonfire raged. The women of her ala stood around it with skewers of bloody meat, letting it crisp in the flames, letting the clear fat run down and crackle in the fire. On the far side of the bonfire, the whole army was drawn up, along with their husbands and wives, children and captives.

It was no surprise Kalu had come tonight. He had not changed since Murina was forty, except to take that silly Achaian name. *Dionysos! How ridiculous.*

Maybe she would get to drive a knife of fatal star metal into his soft white throat and spill his purple blood, his intoxicating floral blood, while he stared at her with wine-dark eyes, plum-dark lips parted in unknowing horror.

He had no idea how much she had changed.

"All hail," cried the archon of her ala, saluting fist to chest and bowing to Murina.

"Hail Prime," the Amazons roared. "First of the Amazons!"

Murina smiled, approaching her chosen generals and captains, taking in their beloved faces one by one: Ksanthi, Agawi, Aukyala, Laumakha, Shetra. She forgot herself and looked for Alekto, and her heart burned with loss.

"Rejoice," Murina rasped, pitching her voice to carry over the flames. "I have news from the moon."

The fire made mysteries of the faces on the far side, of her people and their captives, but that too was for the best. It was hard to look into their faces and lie, so she had gotten good at pretending to look instead. Let the fire hear the truth. Mortals needed comforting deceptions.

"The war of the gods is ending," Murina cried. "The great old ones have called for a truce, and the young gods are coming to Qera Island to make peace. On our sacred Mount Qera, the gods will bury their spears. Our troubles are over."

If she could have seen the people through the fire, she knew what their faces would have told her. They had lost cities and towns, flocks and herds, sisters and mothers and daughters. The rage of the gods had shattered mountains, boiled rivers, sent plagues that scythed down whole families, withered the poor crops on the stalk and the vine. A hot wind from the east had baked the life out of the weary peoples of the Great Sea, and the empire of the Amazons had suffered like no other land.

Someone clapped. Loyal, sweet Agawi, always ready to praise her queen. And another, and another, and then the silent masses on the far side of the bonfire began to cheer. At first it was the bitter rejoicing Murina expected, but then something broke in them, and they wailed with joy and sorrow and relief that the gods had taken pity, that the gods would show mercy.

"Praise the moon," they cried. "Praise the gods!" *Praise Kronu, Lord of Light, and Aita the Drowned. Praise Tuphon the Spiral Serpent and Sinmu the Changeling. Praise Afri and Mehut and Kalu. Praise Ammon and Aris and Fastah. Praise Aplu and Artumi. Praise the merciful gods. Have mercy on your servants, great gods.*

It was all Murina could do to keep her face perfectly smooth, modeled on the granite of her statue in the crypt of the queens. That was her true form, not this; that was her face for eternity.

Let her people abase themselves to flatter the gods. It was necessary.

"I and my ala and our greatest warriors will have the dangerous honor of hosting the gods," she declared. "After this celebration, the rest of you—particularly the children—will board ships and sail to the colonies. When the gods make peace, we will light the beacon on Mount Qera, and you will return."

Everything she said was clearly prudent. Her people would suspect nothing.

Nor would the gods.

"Rejoice, Amazons!" Murina cried again. "Meat for everyone, and six days of drink and song. Let the gods rejoice with us!"

Such festivals always brought out Murina's nostalgia. Perhaps the grape god's visit had stirred up forgotten feelings, memories of lesser selves, a time before she was Prime. Or perhaps it was the sight of the children, small Amazons with bare untattooed flesh, their soft faces half formed, not yet cut into the hard granite of womanhood. Dressed as bear cubs, the children danced to the piping wail of flutes and howled at the moon.

Murina smiled. These little ones had tender lives. That had always been the dream: to bring order to the islands, bind the seas, plunder the shores, and let the young ones grow up soft, green shoots not yet hardened by the winds of war.

Strange to think that even Murina, First of the Amazons, had once been such a child. But she had danced as these danced, sat at the feet of Otrera and Aigaia and drank of their blood-spattered wisdom, their tales of poetry and war, gods defied and men destroyed, cities plundered, forests burned. She had trembled with the terrible ambition that had brought Otrera and Aigaia together, a daughter of Rebu and one of Thraki joining forces, intertwining limbs, marrying their armies and their ships.

And those great Amazons in turn had met at the glittering court of Sobeknafia in the city of Atitáwa at its height, just before the capricious gods destroyed the empire of the Two Lands and crushed Sobeknafia's strange and beautiful dreams of a world of order, a world where all men and women were equal under heaven, where the lion laid down with the lamb, where the desert turned green again, where all that was dead could return.

When the children asked Murina about Otrera and Aigaia, wed to Aris and each other, she felt old. As if she were now Otrera and Aigaia, and Otrera and Aigaia were Sobeknafia. The time of Murina was already fading into history.

She stood and clapped for the children. "Dance, dance,

dance!" she commanded. "Never forget the glory of our spear-won city! Never forget the might of Murina, who scaled the heights of Qera and took this island for herself! While you wait in the colonies for news of peace, remember this command of Murina Prime: Do not neglect your spearplay."

"Murina Prime!" the children howled, and caught up practice spears, dancing in circles to the throb of the war drums.

I must rise further, Murina murmured in her heart, though she kept her lips still, for the gods could read lips. Or I must fall. There is nothing in between.

Her daughters returned three days later. They came on a ship of Ugarit cedar and bones, a ghost ship that glowed in the moonlight, guided by Artumi herself.

Carrying a lit taper, Murina went down to the crypt of the queens to meet them. She parted the lead-lined doors and descended the endless stair, down, down, into the forgotten bowels of the mountain. Pale glowworms came alive to light her path niche by niche until she came to the cavern in the deep. The First of the Amazons crossed the threshold lined with moonsilver, the sigils of Urss inlaid into the stone.

No god, save one, could enter here.

The cavern yawned, a circular path winding around a central pool of dark water, while in great cavities in the wall stood the statues of the queens.

First there was Murina's own terrible effigy. She looked at herself in wonder, marveling at her pride, her strength, the cruelty in her unbreakable visage. Oh, I am beautiful in eternity, she thought, and licked her lips. She lit a candle and placed it at her own feet, a tribute to herself.

She moved on to the next statue: Takshul the Hittite, her

predecessor, shatterer of six cities, slaughterer of ten kings, who had died taking Qera; a woman of black diorite, her tattoos inlaid in malachite and carnelian, her eyes chips of lapis that glowed with terrible light. The Achaians called her Deianeira, Man-Killer, but her Hittite name meant "peace"— the peace of death. Again, Murina lit a candle.

Next stood Aigaia and Otrera in Two Lands limestone, hand in hand in death as in life, formed from a single block, their tattoos a single map of battles won and cities liberated, women freed and children born and husbands taken, armies of fierce horsewomen and spearmen in lines and ships on the darkling seas.

Murina knelt before them. Her eyes stung. It was no shame to weep for her foremothers, great Otrera and Aigaia. "*For you,*" she whispered. "*And for me.*"

Once she had lit their candle, she moved on to the final statue: Sobeknafia, formed of tarnished bronze, her severe face keen with the intellect and discernment that had made her the spiritual mother of all Amazons, teacher of Otrera and Aigaia. Sobeknafia, whose soul and mind had vibrated with that great dream of a world at peace, a world where all were equal before justice. Sobeknafia, overcome in life by weak men and cruel gods.

The candlelight flickered, and the shadowed sockets of Sobeknafia's bronze mask stared into the darkness of eternity. Her last words to Otrera and Aigaia still echoed across the ages: *Even the gods cannot defeat a legend. Mine is eternal.*

So will it be with Murina.

Feet echoed on the stairs. Vlaska and Luspi stepped into the candlelight, bowing before their mother, growling as one, "Hail Prime."

"Hail," Murina echoed, motioning for them to stand.

Vlaska stood first, thick and powerful, her familiar tattoos dancing like living things in the candlelight: bees in swarms on her biceps and thighs, enormous bears climbing up her arms and down the trunks of her calves. Her thick barrel chest rose and fell under the weight of an enormous lead casket. She placed it on the altar before the pool.

Luspi rose too, slim as a knife, adorned with serpents that writhed over her long, spindly limbs, her face a dark mystery in the candlelight. She bore a smaller lead case and wore a strange, hungry smile. Placing the little case on the altar, she stepped back.

"You brought them," Murina breathed. "Show me."

Their diadems gleamed silver in the candlelight as they opened their cases together, angling them to show their mother the weapons that the young gods had helped them forge, terrible weapons beyond mortal comprehension.

In Luspi's little case were twenty-four arrows of black wood, each tipped with a terrible point of bright black metal that gleamed like death and rang with the death-scream of a star.

In Vlaska's great casket, twin bows of gold and silver, each unstrung, each with a single strand of divine hair; a battle-ax tipped with a black metal head; a spear with a point of the same metal; and a simple black dagger. All of them shone with the same dark metal, the sky metal, the metal born in the death of a sun.

"Bless the moon." Murina's voice caught in her throat. Oh, if Alekto could only see this triumph, her triumph, their shared dreams finally made real—

But there was nothing of mortal Alekto left, only the terrible moon that she had become.

"Bless the moon," Vlaska and Luspi echoed, and the black

pool rippled as the one god who could pass Urss's threshold rose gleaming white from the dark waters.

Artumi still wore the face of Alekto, still beloved, still terrible, huge-eyed and soft-faced as the day she had died, but the imprint of the goddess was unmistakable on the vessel she had brought back to life: Artumi's own opulent smile, full of long white teeth, promising sweetness and murder, blood and honey.

"It is done," Artumi whispered. "The Eyes of Night and the Poisoned Lord labored for an age to craft these weapons. It took more than you can know, Murina, but these weapons could kill time itself. Long after the last star dies, quantum tunneling will transmute every atom that remains into this final substance: kiklu, the metal of the end."

Her voice was still Alekto's too. Even speaking in the incomprehensible jargon of the gods, her voice was still lovely: wind sighing through stripped branches.

Murina ached to kiss the moon. But she was too old to waste her limited strength on pleasure. "When will the gods arrive?"

"On the fifth day," said Artumi.

The gods would come in glory and command the Amazons to serve them at their peace summit. Mortal hearts could not resist divine commands, so the veteran Amazons would obey helplessly, climbing Mount Qera's heights dressed as servants, their weapons wrapped in deceptive illusions Artumi had designed to pique the great old ones' nostalgia.

But even if the Amazons walked in with weapons unsheathed, it would not matter. No elder god had ever feared a mortal; even the proud Amazons were just toys to the Titans.

Kronu, Lord of Light, would laugh to see them humbled, their vaunted Amazon freedom reduced to ornamental servitude. He would command Murina to wait on him, carrying his wine like a mere slave.

The Spiral Serpent would draw close to Vlaska, admiring her thick, powerful body, breathing seduction in her ear as if her diadem of Urss were not even there.

As for the Changeling, they would be drawn to Luspi with uncontrollable desire, fascinated by her gaunt form, by the stark purity of her soul, and would demand the Amazon princess sing for the gods as a show of submission.

Kulu   Dionysos now   would come from faraway Meluhha on his flying chariot with wine enough for all the gods. Kalu would drink in Murina's humiliation with that gloating thirst she had come to find so irritating. In the shadow of the Lord of Light, young gods would drink with ancient ones, burying their war again, resigning themselves to more centuries of slavery.

Until the moon's signal came.

Murina looked to Vlaska, to Luspi, to Artumi's borrowed face, and bowed her head. "When we walk out of here," she said, "it will be too late to turn back."

"Mother," Luspi whispered, "it is already too late to turn back."

"Mother," Vlaska said, laughing, "if I knew how to turn back, you would never have made me your daughter."

The face of lost Alekto shone with light.

"We will make the name of the Amazons immortal. When the gods themselves are dust," Murina declared, "our name will echo forever."

Artumi sighed her terrible sigh. "This is why I love you, Prime," she said in Alekto's voice. "You are not tamed like common mortals. You are wild, as we were once."

Murina cut her palm on the black metal dagger, dripping

her blood into the pool. Her daughters followed. As their blood mingled in the dark water, Alekto's face turned red as a blood moon, and the power of Artumi, of Urss, began to weave the disguises, wrapping each weapon of dark metal in pleasing layers of ancient illusion. The arrows became slim wands wrapped with vines, the spear a staff carved with phalluses, the dagger a white hook of ivory incised with check patterns, the ax a mysterious feathered censer.

"Bless the moon," Murina whispered. Silently: *I love you too, Alekto*.

The moon smiled but said nothing.

The day came in terrible glory. The gods' chariots and boats roared across the sky, trailing smoke and fire, as each descended upon holy Qera, the smoldering mountain. As each god landed, the earth shook.

First came the intermediate generation of gods: Drowned Aita climbed up from the deep, unfurling a rainbow of bright vapor. Afri and Mehut, the Queen of Kings and the Eyes of Night, appeared together from the direction of the Two Lands, borne on chariots dragged by peacocks and owls, filling the sky with terrible beauty and afterimages that blinded the mind's eye. On a white bone ship shaped like the crescent moon, Artumi descended from the great beyond, roaring like a mother bear. These gods guaranteed the truce.

Next came the young gods: Aplu the Archer first, borne on a golden rukh, and then the Great Triad, the fierce young gods who had blasted half of Kna'an off the face of the earth, the Three Weapons who had challenged the Lord of Light for hegemony: poisoned Fastah, shaper of forms, cunning in things, who had inspired the mind of Sobeknafia to dreams of eternity; bloody Aris, beloved of Otrera and Aigaia, who had told the Amazons that there was no mortal power too strong for their arms, no man whose windpipe could not be cut, no war on earth they could not win; and, last, Ammon, Rider on the Storm, Lord of Rainbows, God of Thunder, the Great Contender, leader of the revolt. These were the young gods the Amazons loved, the liberators, the mad ones, the bringers of change. If only they were stronger.

Finally, the great old ones appeared from deep heaven, each dawning like a star. There came Tuphon, the Spiral Serpent; there came Sinmu, the Changeling, the Undead One; there came Kronu, El, Elios: Master of the Sun, Lord of Light.

The will of the gods echoed as a single word across Qera: *COME.*

Even if the Amazons had not known the gods were coming, even if they had not planned to climb Qera and serve them, that word would have compelled them. Their feet would have made the same journey, scrambling up over the jagged rocks of the volcano, climbing the scree-filled defiles full of loose obsidian, working their way past crags that smoldered with horrible fumes, picking a torturous foot-shearing path to the peak.

But the warning helped. It meant they were wearing shoes and suitable clothing for divine entertainment, shimmering tunics and fine robes and pretty skirts, so that they would be pleasing to the jaded eyes of heaven.

As Murina climbed, helpless before the divine will, her hatred burned hotter and hotter, a white flame under cataclysmic pressure.

How dare anything in this world command Murina's feet to move. How dare any god usurp her body. It was the ultimate indignity. If it had not been part of her plan, her rage would have burned her from the inside as she had burned Dionysos's letters, charring organs, muscles, and bones to a frail tissue of ash.

Where was he, that god of wine and taunts? Where was the Flayed One, the Lord of Harvests, who had learned to regenerate himself from a divine corpse? Kalu: never there when you needed him, but never very far.

Murina felt him nearby. With each step, her sense of him grew stronger, more insistent, more awful. He was the one god who might read the intent in her movements, the murder in her smoldering pride, the rebellion in her very obedience. Gripping the dagger charmed to look like an ivory birthing wand, Murina stepped over a razor's edge of raw obsidian, searching for the grape god.

The summit was coming into view. Surely he would come to taunt her before she reached the top. She swallowed hard, preparing herself to lie with voice and face, to let even her silences, even the flames of humiliation in her cheeks, conceal her purpose.

When the Lord of Wine did not reveal himself, Murina stepped out onto the summit of Mount Qera, an enormous basin of glossy black stone stretched like a drumhead over the bulk of the mountain.

All around her, Amazons were cresting the summit at the same time, approaching the gods as if for a festival, all gleaming robes and flashing jewels and sturdy bodies rippling with tattoos—sacrifices, should the gods desire it, baubles and playthings, pets and diversions, reduced by divine will to living ornaments.

Thrones of black volcanic glass had erupted from the mountain, each cooled into an iconic shape that echoed the god upon it. As Murina's feet carried her toward the obsidian hawk-throne of the Lord of Light, her eyes met Vlaska's, then Luspi's.

They knew their parts. Murina knew hers.

She moved to the foot of Kronu's throne and knelt on the black stone. The Lord of Light shone like the sun, too radiant to look at, his bare golden feet resting on the ground beside her head, his whole body liquid metal and lambent fire, all of him brighter than a gilded statue, more perfectly formed than anything in the crypt of the queens. He breathed the light itself. He exhaled it from his skin.

"Murina," sang Kronu, Elios, El. "Ancient of the Amazons, queen of many years, you are blessed today with one final glory. You shall be my cupbearer, an honor no mortal woman has ever earned."

"Lord of Light," Murina murmured, "you are unexpectedly enlightened."

"And magnanimous," said the Lord of Light. "I know the Amazons were led astray by the wild ambitions of the younger gods and most of all by my sons, the Triad. But today you atone for your people, Murina. I will make the Amazons a gift of my mercy. You will receive soft lives for the rest of your days, lives flowing with honey and rich with milk, lives kissed by the unconquered sun."

"Our gratitude is unbearable," said Murina, bowing low.

The Lord of Light leaned in, his radiant face sweet and bright with wonder. "You are carrying a birth wand! A fine one in the Two Lands style. Why bring it here?"

"My lord," Murina said, not meeting his eyes, "it was in my hand when I felt your call." Which was true, if not a full accounting.

The golden god let out a silver laugh of regret. "Oh, I am sorry, Murina. Whoever the poor pregnant dam was, she is not here. She must have bled to death climbing the mountain. You will be compensated for her sacrifice."

"My lord is too gracious," Murina said.

"I know," the Lord of Light confirmed. "I know."

At the left hand of Kronu, the Spiral Serpent was commanding Vlaska to dance. "Show me the rhythms of your body," the elder god instructed, and Vlaska, thick as a bear and strong enough to wrestle a boar to the ground, began to shimmy and strut like a dancing girl. There was no rejecting the will of the great old ones.

"We have lived too long among mortals," the Lord of Light crooned singsong. "Your brains are full of strings to pluck, each of you a delicate harp. But I do enjoy not knowing your thoughts. It is a relief, these diadems Urss made for you—such blessed quiet. That is why I picked your mountain for this."

Murina knew a monologue when she heard one. She said nothing, only stroked the edge of the white ivory birth wand, imagining the blade sheathed under layers of sorcery. Black metal, star metal, metal of the end.

At the right hand of Kronu, the Changeling had begun to murmur in Luspi's ear. Tears streamed involuntarily down Murina's daughter's face, great streams of them. "Sing," the Changeling urged. "Lift your voice in song. Many thousands of years ago, all women were as free as you Amazons, and I miss the old songs so."

"But I am not free," Luspi lilted, her throat opening around the first notes. "I will sing this song of freedom, but my own tongue is compelled."

"A beautiful juxtaposition," the Lord of Light told Murina. His golden hand rested idly on the arm of his throne. "First of the Amazons, which one of your daughters was the prodigy? The one who was born a boy?"

There was no refusing the Lord of Light's question, but Murina could not quite restrain a bitter little laugh as her mouth was forced open around the truth. "I forget," she said. "The Amazons do not care about such details."

Kronu shook his head in amazement. "Marvelous."

Luspi's song rose sweet and high, wobbling around a single note. She sang of the time before time, of the cycle of ages. She sang of the forgotten gods that the elder gods destroyed, of dead Great Mother and her storm of spears that fell from heaven like serpents and wiped out the golden age. She sang of the battle between the Lord of Light and Great Mother, of the dragon's downfall and the Flood, of the Lord of Light's rise to the highest throne.

Murina waited. It was not yet time for the signal, but every muscle ached with dreams of movement. As Luspi sang, the air grew thick, and the mood of the gods darkened. Lightning played in the heavens, and the great old ones stirred, brooding over millennia of ancient memories compressed into a song.

Then Kronu gestured, and Luspi's voice cut out.

"My rebellious sons," the Lord of Light boomed, "approach the throne." He indicated the Triad with a golden claw.

One by one the young gods rose, their bodies moving to the sullen rhythms of surrender. They played their part as skillfully as Murina had hers, advancing abreast: Fastah first, then Aris, then Ammon. They bowed low, foreheads touching the black stone, tiny before the vastness of the Lord of Light, and the golden one laughed.

"My sons, my sons." He sighed. "You were magnificent once: the Three Weapons that Great Mother wielded against the forgotten gods. You were magnificent in my hands too,

when we brought her low and forged my brave new world."
His voice sank to a whisper, dark with love betrayed. "How
could you turn against me?"

"Weapons turn in the hand that holds them," said Fastah.

"Murder begets murder," said Aris.

"But we repent," said Ammon. "Only love us, Father, truly
love us, and we will be your willing slaves. Until the last stars
fade and the cosmos cools to ice."

"My willing slaves?" mused the Lord of Light. "Loyal children at last. Love restored. An end to this terrible cycle. What
say you, Titans?"

"The cycle has gone on too long," the Spiral Serpent sighed.
"It would be nice to have peace."

"If we can trust them," said the Changeling. "That is the
true message of this delicate Amazon hymn, is it not? Each
generation of gods destroys the last. Our mother destroyed
the ancient world. We killed her. They will kill us."

"We will swear binding vows," said the young Triad. "We
will swear on our mother, on our father, on ourselves, on our
offspring, now and forever."

"But *I* am your father," said the Lord of Light cheerfully,
"and you helped me kill your mother. What are your oaths
worth?"

"We did it for love of you," Ammon said hotly.

"Love," the Lord of Light growled. "Love? What is *love*?" He
rose, and a golden light flared up within him, even brighter
than himself. It emerged from his chest, a single golden apple,
a sun, a radiance Murina could see even with her eyes snapped
shut against the blinding light. She felt her body searing in the
heat of the apple.

One by one, the young gods screamed.

One by one, serpents erupted from the mountain, each so

bright Murina could see it through her eyelids, snakes of fire that looped and wrapped the Three, squeezed and crushed them tight, then faded.

She opened her aching eyes a slit. Fastah, Aris, and Ammon were bound with writhing red-hot chains. Stinking smoke poured off their bodies, thick with the wretched smell of burning meat. The young gods screamed in agony.

By the Lord of Light's side stood a woman, young and golden, laughing with a terrible innocence.

"Not yet, my Apple," the Lord of Light whispered. "Do not kill them."

"As you command, Father," the Golden Apple said in a high, sweet voice. "My brothers, you will continue to suffer for the present time."

This was the Eye of Kronu, the Apple of El. Artumi had spoken of her: the Great Weapon. Now Murina gathered her will, knowing that her time was near. Now that the Great Weapon had come forth, the Lord of Light had shown his hand. His attention would be undivided, focused entirely on his rebel sons and his peers, and when the moon's signal came—

"Love," Kronu sneered again, and the mountaintop was full of his radiance. "We have had enough of *love*. Sing again, sweet little Amazon, while my sons prepare for the transition to eternity."

Luspi's mouth opened again, and her song swelled, but it had changed. Where before she had sang of time, now she sang of eternity, of the infinite time before the first gods lived, of the dark void and the clouds of dust and emptiness that came howling together to form distant suns that lived and flourished and died screaming, of the way Earth had coalesced out of the darkness, orbiting the same white sun that gave the Lord of Light his power.

Artumi rose and began to sing with Luspi in her borrowed voice, and the Lord of Light leaned toward Artumi, staring at her, golden and covetous.

Artumi sang in Alekto's voice, and time fell away. For so many years Murina had walked under moonlight with Alekto, arm in arm, laughing together, spinning secret tales, gossiping, plotting raids, each tucking delicate poems like pearl earrings into the other's ear, Murina and Alekto, Alekto and Murina—like Otrera and Aigaia.

Until the war of the gods.

It still hurt too much to bear. Hearing Alekto sing, hearing Artumi sing in Alekto's borrowed voice, Murina went stiff, each muscle taut as a bowstring.

Alekto. One more life crushed out in the thrashing and flailing of the war. One more victim of divine carelessness. It had been fate, or luck, or blind chance.

In Alekto's borrowed voice, the moon sang of eternity, of a world beyond time, the world the dead saw: Everything, all at once, forever. The entire arc of existence, from birth to death, as a wholeness. The entire path of a sunbeam—from its fiery birth to the surface of the moon to the surface of the sea to Murina's eye—everything, all at once, forever.

The gods are not forever, the moon sang. Nothing in time is forever.

This was it, it was coming. Heat pulsed in Murina's limbs. She could feel her body gathering its will. She could feel the entire arc of her movement, preordained, the whole smooth arc of the blade in her hand and the limbs of her body, all of it gliding up and forward in one single everything.

Things end, the moon sang. *I will end,* the moon sang. *Kill, kill, kill, kill, kill, kill, kill.*

Beginning and ending were one.

Decades ago, young Murina held Alekto's strong pale hand in her strong bronze fingers and crushed her lips into Alekto's soft red lips, breathing her in like a spell.

Years ago, Murina howled her loss. It was as if a piece of her brain had been ripped away forever, ripped out by some careless god who would never know what he had done, who would never understand the irreparable nature of this wound.

Days ago, Murina waited with the birth tusk in her hand, smiling at the fatal darkness she felt beneath the layers of illusion.

Hours ago, Murina began to climb the mountain of Qera.

A split second in the future, Murina and Kronu were one. Her hand was part of him now, thrust deep into his golden chest, his golden ribs splayed out around the all-consuming violence of the metal of the end, the illusion ripped asunder along with Kronu's heart. "IT IS FINISHED," she roared as golden fire erupted from the dying Lord of Light and seared her whole body away.

A single second later, Luspi's ax swept through the Changeling's neck, and her song died with her body.

Two seconds later, the black stone drumhead burst, spewing the guts of the mountain into the sky: a signal fire to the Amazons.

Ten seconds later, Tuphon rushed up thousands of feet into the sky, fleeing the devastation of the mountain, but Vlaska's thighs were wrapped around the Spiral Serpent's tail, and her bow sang with arrow after arrow, piercing the elder god again and again with the metal of the end.

A minute later, Qera Island shook like a sheet, and the whole mountain tore apart, rose into the air, and crashed down into the sea.

Three minutes later, as Vlaska died, she saw the Golden

Apple fill the sky, free at last, a Great Weapon glorying in her own liberation.

"Look further," breathed a soft and plangent voice, gentle and terribly familiar, and for a moment, Murina lived outside time entirely, free of her own arc, existing in the realm beyond cause and effect, in Sobeknafia's eternity.

Kalu—the Mainads' Dionysos—came as he always did, stepping out of the darkness beyond her field of view, a flicker in the corner of her eye that rippled into carnal existence as a series of disjointed impressions: slim nostrils flaring, dark eyes smoldering, black ringlets shaking out in glossy undulating sheets, white teeth sinking into plump purple lips. Blood or wine beaded on his talons; he licked them clean with his delicate pink tongue.

She did not comment on his age, though he was younger than he had been twenty years ago, nor on the blood, though it had been fresh.

They stood together in this moment between moments.

"Murina." The god sighed. "Why go and do a thing like that?"

"For the Amazons," Murina rasped. "For my legacy."

Kalu gave her a sad smile. "The Amazons? Look further down the arc of time. Your Amazons flourish and fade like all empires."

"No," Murina said. "My name will live forever. When the last grapes have rotted and the last wine has soured, the name of Murina will still ring out in song."

"No," said the god. "In a thousand years, your name will be dust. Your people will become history. In two thousand years, they will be nothing but myths. In three thousand years? A titillating erotic legend of buxom warriors. Then the name Amazon itself will be taken away, bestowed first on a mighty river, then on a great forest—but the river will die, and the forest will burn."

As he spoke, visions filled eternity: A basin full of alien trees so tall and gorgeous that they made their own rain. Burning trees. A burning world.

"Your stories will fade away into echoes. You will become a tale about violent wonder women in shiny boots. You will become the notion of a great river that flows to the sea, carrying everything with it. Your name will rise again as something called an 'international logistics company,' a kingdom in the hands of a fragile demigod who dreams of conquering the stars. And after that, who knows? Nothing will remain of these women, nor of you. All things end, Murina. Didn't the moon say that?"

Murina laughed. "So?"

"So this is your last chance," said Kalu, and they were back in the moment before the moment. "Stay your hand, Murina. Spare the Lord of Light. Let the young gods die; you owe them nothing. Your people will survive this day, and drink, and be merry. Murina and her daughters will live to an old age and die. Do not throw away your few precious years."

But Murina laughed, for she knew the truth: our deeds ring out in eternity like the struck walls of a bell, and the whole universe trembles. The star metal knife shears through the ribs and the heart of the god. Her daughters kill the Titans at the same instant. Space and time echo with their deed.

The forest called Amazon burns for Murina. The river called Amazon swells with her power. A fragile demigod rises into the darkling sky on a thin metal vessel, carrying the Amazon name into the void—and Murina laughs, turning his dreams into flames, for the glory of her name.

Look at me, moon, Murina cries, driving the dagger into

the Lord of Light with all the force of her life behind it, and the world trembles.

And as you read, she catches your wrist and pulls you down into the dark waters of eternity, where she floats forever, all at once, everything, a child at the feet of Otrera and Aigaia, a lover in the arms of Alekto, a mother leading her daughters to their deaths: Murina, First of the Amazons. The God-Killer.

She seizes you and won't let go. Say my name, she growls. Say my fucking name.

Hail Murina! Hail Prime!

For all eternity.

ACKNOWLEDGMENTS

A pantheon of greats helped bring this book to light. Many thanks to our contributors, who had us laughing, crying, and altogether in our feelings with their retellings. Thanks also to the many, many writers who shared their work with us during open submissions for this anthology. If there's anything we've learned through this process, it's that there's a world of talent and fresh voices out there. Many thanks to our agent, Kate McKean at Morhaim Literary, for her tireless work, sage advice, and priceless transparency about the process. And to our editor at Vintage Books, the inimitable Anna Kaufman, whose love for Greco-Roman mythology and whose commitment to publishing an anthology that does those stories justice made the work that much more joyful. Thanks to the entire Vintage Books team: Kayla Overbey, Nancy Tan, Erica Ferguson, Madeline Partner, Steve Walker, Julie Ertl, and Sophie Normil.

From Jenn: I have to thank our agent, Kate McKean, again, because when I told her I wanted to do another anthology immediately after *Sword Stone Table* published, she said yes without missing a beat and helped me narrow down my many (some of them very bad) ideas. Which leads me to my coeditor, Sharifah, who has also been my co-podcaster for many a year and who I am so lucky to be able to geek out with on the regular. Thank you for saying yes. To Preeti Chhibber, who is a font of enthusiasm and experience and the ultimate partner in fandom crimes: You are my own personal superhero and squishiest muffin. To my partner, Roger Ainslie, who supports me in being my nerdiest self: I love you. To both our families, for cheering this project along from pre-start to beyond the finish line: Thank you for showering me with GIFs and texts, buying books, and telling me which stories were your favorites!

From Sharifah: I count myself among the lucky because my imagination, curiosity, and enduring love for storytelling were not only encouraged but supported by my nearest and dearest. I thank my parents, Jasmine Young and Clark Williams, for taking their children on so many trips to the South Pasadena Public Library and for always giving in to their countless pleas for "just one more book." Many thanks to my play sister of thirty-six years, Chanda Prescod-Weinstein (East Los!), who was so generous with her wealth of knowledge, resources, and enthusiasm the minute she learned I was working on this anthology. Thanks to my partner, Brian Hildenbrand, who always shows up to remind me that making space and time for creative work is important and worthy. Also, to my ride or die, Alyssa Rosales, for reading my work and always encouraging me to keep going (and for helping me survive those fraught years that were our twenties). Thanks to Dunja Nedic and the Portland Women Writers crew for the community, accountability, and conversation over many cups of coffee at Crema and snacks at Beulahland. So many thanks to Jenn Northington, who invited me on this epic quest and who brought along expertise and empathy. And finally, thanks to my sister, Ustadza White, to whom I dedicate this book. I always wanted to do what my older sister did, and that included learning about Greek mythology. When I think of *d'Aulaires'*, I think of adventuring through those tales with you.

ABOUT THE EDITORS

Jenn Northington is the coeditor of the Locus Award–nominated anthology *Sword Stone Table*, a former bookseller, and a current reviewer, podcaster, and editor with Riot New Media Group. She's a lifelong book nerd and can primarily be found on Instagram at @iamjennIRL.

S. Zainab Williams is a writer, editor, and illustrator based in Asheville, North Carolina. A podcaster and director of content for Book Riot and a member of PEN America's Literary Awards Committee, she spends most of her days thinking about how to make the world of books and reading more inclusive and progressive. She can be found on Instagram at @szainabwilliams and on TikTok at @oracularpig.

ABOUT THE CONTRIBUTORS & STORY NOTES

Marika Bailey is an Afro-Caribbean author, designer, and illustrator. Her fiction has previously appeared in *FIYAH*, *Fantasy Magazine*, *Apparition Lit*, *Beneath Ceaseless Skies*, and *Strange Horizons*. Given a book of unabridged Greek myths at a very impressionable age, she's been writing ever since. A graduate of Yale University with a degree in fine arts, Marika lives in Brooklyn, New York, with her husband and the softest cat in the world.

Alyssa Cole is a *New York Times* and *USA Today* bestselling author of romance, thrillers, and graphic novels. Her Civil War–set espionage romance, *An Extraordinary Union*, was the American Library Association's RUSA Best Romance for 2018; her contemporary rom-com *A Princess in Theory* was one of the *New York Times*'s 100 Notable Books of 2018; and her debut thriller, *When No One Is Watching*, was the winner of the 2021 Edgar Award for Best Paperback Original. Her books have received critical acclaim from the *Washington*

Post, *Library Journal*, *Kirkus Reviews*, BuzzFeed, Book Riot, *Entertainment Weekly*, and various other outlets. She lives in the French Antilles with her husband, and when she's not working, she can usually be found watching anime or wrangling their pets.

> *Author's Story Note:* I've always been a fan of the Hades-and-Persephone story, but after getting married and immigrating to another country where travel back to the United States is almost never easy (and often seasonal because of the mundane vagaries of how airlines operate on small islands), it holds a special place in my heart. Apart from that, in Bastion and Perse's story, I wanted to explore Persephone's symbolism of death and rebirth and Hades's role as a caretaker of souls in the context of climate change, human hubris, technological ethics, and the idea of love as something that can supersede all those things.

Zoraida Córdova is the acclaimed author of more than two dozen novels and short stories, including the Brooklyn Brujas series, *Star Wars: The High Republic: Convergence*, and *The Inheritance of Orquídea Divina*. She is the coeditor of the bestselling anthology *Vampires Never Get Old*, as well as the cohost of the writing podcast *Deadline City*. She writes romance novels as Zoey Castile. Zoraida was born in Guayaquil, Ecuador, and calls New York City home. For more information, visit her at zoraidacordova.com.

A graduate of the University of Maryland and the Rutgers-Camden MFA program, **Maya Deane** lives with her fiancéc of many years, their dear friend, and two cats named after gods. As a trans woman, she is sacred to Aphrodite and naturally fond of spears, books, and jewelry. She is the author of *Wrath Goddess Sing*.

> *Author's Story Note:* According to classical Greek mythology, the Amazons were a diverse group of peoples; some were from Libya, while others were from the Pontic steppe and Asia Minor. Per Greek tradition, the Amazons invented cavalry, founded a great empire, and feuded with Herakles; in some versions of the Titanomachy, the Amazons were involved, and they were often allied with either Dionysos or his mortal enemies. But the Amazons were not merely a myth; archaeology has found a basis for their legends. So put other versions of their story to one side for now and imagine this: that the Amazons really did found an Aegean empire in the middle Bronze Age and really did help the Olympians challenge the Titans on the peak of Mount Thera.

⚱

Sarah Gailey is a Hugo Award–winning and bestselling author of speculative fiction, short stories, and essays. Their nonfiction has been published by dozens of venues internationally. Their fiction has been published in more than six languages. Their most recent novel, *The Echo Wife*, and first original comic book series with BOOM! Studios, *Eat the Rich*, are available now. You can find links to their work at sarahgailey.com and on social media at @gaileyfrey.

Author's Story Note: In the original story of Achilles, Thetis is defined by a son she never wanted and imprisoned by a prophecy that those with authority force her to fulfill. She is fettered by motherhood, and the people around her feel safe in the limitations to which they assume she will submit. But in "Wild to Covet," Thetis has her own narrative in mind. She recognizes the scope of the prophecy that binds her, and she navigates it with agency. She refuses to lose sight of her own story.

Zeyn Joukhadar is the author of the Lambda Literary Award– and Stonewall Book Award–winning novel *The Thirty Names of Night* and the Middle East Book Award–winning *The Map of Salt and Stars*. His work has appeared in the *Kenyon Review*, *Salon*, the *Paris Review*, and elsewhere and has been twice nominated for the Pushcart Prize. He serves on the board of the Radius of Arab American Writers (RAWI) and mentors emerging writers of color with the Periplus Collective.

Author's Story Note: The Theban prophet Tiresias is most famous for having been transformed into a woman for seven years as punishment for striking two snakes with his staff, so perhaps it's no surprise that trans people have long claimed him. One story credits him with the invention of augury; another has it that Athena blinded him for watching her bathe; in a third, he prophesies for Odysseus in the underworld when given the blood of a black ram to drink (though his counsel, as usual, is ultimately ignored). As a queer trans guy of color on the verge of a breakup at an awkward house party in Liguria, my displaced Tiresias turns the legends on their heads. Here, it isn't Tiresias's gender that is called into question, but the masculinities of the cis men who look at him and see parts of themselves they once abandoned. Reckoning with the fantasies of violence, masculinity, misogyny, and humiliation that cis society enacts on his flesh, Tiresias must decide whether to prophesy for a world that constantly dismisses the futures trans people portend—all while hoping he hasn't smudged his eyeliner.

🏆

Mia P. Manansala (she/her) is a writer and certified book coach from Chicago who loves books, baking, and badass women. She uses humor (and murder) to explore aspects of the Filipino diaspora, queerness, and her millennial love for pop culture. She is the author of the award-winning Tita Rosie's Kitchen Mystery series. A lover of all things geeky, Mia spends her days procrastibaking, playing JRPGs and dating sims, reading cozy mysteries and diverse romance, and cuddling her dogs, Gumiho and Max Power. Find her on Facebook, Twitter, and Instagram at @MPMtheWriter or check out her website: miapmanansala.com.

Author's Story Note: My idea for this story came from two things: my obsession with Meg from the *Hades* video game, and the realization I was mispronouncing *Erinyes* as if it were a Filipino last name (*Eh-rin-yehs*). As a crime fiction writer, the story of Orestes always fascinated me, but it was hard to ignore the misogyny, and I longed to see Elektra take a different role. Like Meg, I struggle with the line between vengeance and justice. I don't know that either of us has the answer to that yet, but I loved having the opportunity to put my queer Filipino spin on my beloved Furies.

Anglo-Brazilian author **Juliana Spink Mills** was born in London and grew up in São Paulo. Now they live in the United States, where they write speculative fiction and have a soft spot for making their characters suffer. Juliana's stories have appeared in several anthologies, including the Bram Stoker Award–nominated *Not All Monsters*. Besides writing, Juliana works as a Portuguese-English translator and as a library assistant. You can find them online at jspinkmills.com.

Author's Story Note: "Pescada" was born from longing, from the saudades I felt for my country Brazil. It's places I've visited (Ilhabela and Trancoso) and memories of my mother, who made the most incredible pottery fish before trading clay for academia. But most of all, the earliest draft was written when I had just come out as nonbinary and, like Cila, was trying to break through the shell I'd built to find my true self. At heart, it's a tale of self-discovery, and I hope it brings readers joy.

Susan Purr grew up in Midland Park, New Jersey, and earned her BA at Muhlenberg College and her MA in creative writing at Southern New Hampshire University. Her poetry and short stories have appeared in various anthologies in recent years, as well as within her chapbook, *Through Windows*. When she's not writing, Susan can be found making dream catchers, dabbling in local politics, and supporting scientific efforts to treat and cure blindness, including her own.

Author's Story Note: As a woman with blindness, I have always felt conflicted by the phrase "Love is blind." Depending upon the circumstances, the idea of blind love can be construed positively or negatively, and within those lovely, fuzzy places between the extremes, I found Rodie. Part pantheon and part personal experience, Rodie's story navigates divinity and disability and attempts to amplify a recognition of self-love and acceptance that is fit for everyone, not just the gods.

Taylor Rae is a professional cave troll hidden away in the mountains of Coeur d'Alene, Idaho. She studied Latin for four years, which included translating *The Aeneid*, and has her undergraduate degrees in psychology and English literature from the University of Idaho. She won the 2021 NYC Midnight Short Story Challenge and edits *Space Fantasy Magazine*. Her work appears in *Flash Fiction Online*, *PseudoPod*, and the story collection *Upon a Twice Time*. More at mostlytaylor.com.

Author's Story Note: This story comes from two deeply personal places: my anxiety that I'm inadequate to carry on my cultural heritage and my obsession with Latin poetry. I'm descended from the Kumeyaay Nation, and like many mixed Indigenous people, my cultural loss is a direct result of institutional and individual (often familial) racism. In my planning, book two of *The Aeneid* immediately called to me, as it was propaganda commissioned by Emperor Augustus, intended to rewrite the Roman Empire's brutal history of conquest into an ancient manifest destiny. Within this context, I aimed to create a conversation between a story glorifying colonization and the reality of postcolonial existence.

Jude Reali is an emerging author, actor, and poet with a long-held fascination with Greco-Roman mythology and science fiction. They are a 2021 graduate of Northwest School of the Arts in Charlotte, North Carolina. They can usually be found drinking black coffee and reluctantly editing out commas and em dashes.

Author's Story Note: Finding the open call for the *Fit for the Gods* anthology when I did felt akin to being struck by lightning. I'd recently reawakened my childhood fascination with Greek mythology, as well as my long-held love of both speculative fiction and cosmic horror. And, of course, I'm queer, and I instill that queerness into my writing. I couldn't have designed a better anthology to begin my foray into published work.

Suleikha Snyder is an award-winning author of contemporary and paranormal romance, an editor, an American desi, and a lifelong geek. Her works have been showcased in the *New York Times*, *Entertainment Weekly*, BuzzFeed, the *Times*

of India, and NPR. Visit her online at suleikhasnyder.com, and follow her on Twitter at @suleikhasnyder.

Author's Story Note: The Labyrinth and Icarus have always felt, to me, like a metaphor for a lifelong battle with depression—the constant attempts to be free of it and the inevitable plunge. Writing Thea and Astra's story gave me a chance to explore that, much like how Greek myths opened a door for me as a child. Maybe that's where the true escape is: in what we learn to create.

Valerie Valdes lives in an elaborate meme palace with her husband and kids, where she writes, edits, and moonlights as a Muse. When she isn't working, she enjoys playing video games and admiring the outdoors from the safety of her living room. Her debut novel, *Chilling Effect*, was shortlisted for the 2021 Arthur C. Clarke Award and was named one of *Library Journal*'s best science fiction/fantasy novels of 2019. Valerie is coeditor of *Escape Pod*, and her short fiction and poetry have been featured in *Uncanny* magazine and *Nightmare* magazine.

Author's Story Note: Atalanta's myth always appealed to me as someone who grew up wanting to beat the boys at their own games and to be not like the other girls, only to eventually realize the toxicity inherent in that mentality. I wanted to write a story about a mere mortal raised to be fierce by a powerful person in a family rife with violent drama, someone who found love that other people disdained and viewed as a weakness but that gave her the strength to leave her traumatic past behind, only to be dragged back in and forced to deal with her scars. And I wanted to turn her ambiguous, disempowering ending into a happier one.

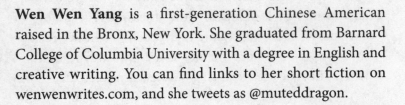

Wen Wen Yang is a first-generation Chinese American raised in the Bronx, New York. She graduated from Barnard College of Columbia University with a degree in English and creative writing. You can find links to her short fiction on wenwenwrites.com, and she tweets as @muteddragon.

Author's Story Note: Like many first-generation immigrant kids, I was my family's translator. I don't remember how old I was when I started reading the mail, filling out forms, and calling companies, pretending to be an adult. I wanted a story that showed the burden and trust, mixed with the first mythology I learned.

PERMISSIONS ACKNOWLEDGMENTS